WET WORK

WET WORK

Christopher Buckley

This edition published in Great Britain in 2003 by
ALLISON & BUSBY Limited
Bon Marche Centre
241-251 Ferndale Road
Brixton, London SW9 8BJ
http://www.allisonandbusby.com

First published in the USA, 1990
Copyright © 1990 by CHRISTOPHER BUCKLEY

A catalogue record for this book is available from the British Library

ISBN 0 7490 0661 7

Printed and bound in Spain
by Liberdúplex, sl. Barcelona

*For Reggie Stoops (1925-1988) and Margo Waite Stoops,
with love always*

Author's note

This is a work of fiction. Any resemblance to characters living or dead is coincidental.

Certain works of art and technology appear under their real names; their authors and originators should not, of course, be held to account for my subversions.

Every normal man must be tempted at times to spit on his hands, hoist the black flag, and begin slitting throats.

H. L. MENCKEN

Prologue

He had done only two deathbeds up to now, and both of them coma cases. Father Toomey reserved to himself the conscious; he got the brain-dead, the vegetal and the Do Not Resuscitate. "Dues," said Father Toomey one night, tossing back his third vodka martini. "It was the same when I was just out of seminary. They think because you're new you'll make a mistake and send them to Hell on a technicality."

There wasn't much challenge in ministering to people who just lay there with tubes going in and out. What drama he'd experienced had been decidedly unpleasant. He'd just finished with the anointing when the hairdresser showed up. The family had provided for a weekly shampoo, set and rinse. The hairdresser pointed to the smear of holy oil on the old lady's forehead and said, "Okay if that gets wet?" Six years of seminary to dicker over forehead rights with a hairstylist to the dying?

But now this. Now this had promise.

He was in an Italian sports car with a name like exotic pasta, being catapulted through the dark countryside by a man with a melted face who'd shown up on the rectory doorstep at three in the morning asking for Father Toomey. When he saw the face he'd gasped, but the man only smiled as if to say, That happens all the time. He was a friendly man, in a gangsterish sort of way, with two heavy gold rings. It was entirely possible, he mused, that he was on the way to the deathbed of a Mafia don. The elements were all there.

"Hope we don't hit a deer, huh?"

Strange conversational gambit, he thought. The man tapped a black box on the dash. "This thing here, it sends out like a kind of Morse code to deer—we can't hear it, but they can—that tells them there's this maniac doing eighty on a road posted forty–five and they should stick to the sidewalk. You like venison? I never had it till I came down here, now I eat it all the time."

"Can you tell me something about your employer?" the young priest ventured.

"Charles Becker."

The priest gathered the name was supposed to ring a bell. "Yes?" The driver seemed amused. He downshifted and the car screamed up a hill, bare-trunked sugar maples flashing by like fence pickets. "He's a businessman."

"I see." There was a long silence. "What kind of businessman?"

"*Good* businessman." He nodded.

Mafia. The priest felt his heart rate increasing.

"Real estate, mining, agricultural fertilizers, aircraft, cod—you know Captain Pete's fish sticks?"

"Sure."

"Those are his fish sticks."

"Is that right? I ate a lot of those fish sticks, growing up."

"There you go. You made him rich. What else? Oil, gas, timber—he owns a good deal of Oregon, I believe it is, or Washington State. You remember when Mount St. Helens blew up, that volcano? Well, a lot of that ash landed on his land. He turned around and sold it for agricultural fertilizer. This is a smart man, Padre." Padre? "Livestock. Weather satellites. One of the movie companies, he owns a good of piece of that. Defense, his company used to do some defense work for the government."

The priest recoiled. *Defense*? What ironic grace had brought

14

him to the deathbed of an arms dealer, he who'd been arrested for demonstrating outside the El Salvadoran embassy in Washington. He saw napalm lighting up the jungle, cluster bombs free-falling from the bellies of B-52s, tanks crushing human beings, ballistic missiles hurtling toward what the "defense" industry liked to call "population centers," saw the sky—the very heavens—polluted with laser weapons. He saw children starving, people dying of AIDS, the homeless shivering on steam grates, battered wives, crack babies abandoned in hospitals, he saw—they were going through a gate, a large gate that seemed to open without human agency. He turned and saw them, two men with—of course—holsters. Remember, he told himself through pursed lips, that Christ went to the home of Matthew, the tax collector. But a defense contractor?

"Halfway."

"What?" said the priest, sounding annoyed.

"That's the house up there, those lights."

The priest could barely make them out. They were—miles away anyway. Good lord, how many wars had it taken to acquire a front lawn this size?

"This is the golf course here. The buffalo tear the hell out of it. If it was me, I'd stick them somewheres else, but he likes looking at them from his window, so they just go on replacing the divots. You ever seen a buffalo divot? Tell you something else about buffalo," he said with a confidential air. "They're *major* defecators. We got someone on staff, that's all he does."

They drove over a stone bridge. The priest saw swans and Canada geese in the moonlight.

"When I was a kid growing up they called it 'Extreme Unction.' You remember that? I guess that was before your time."

The priest didn't like the allusion to his youth. He said a bit stiffly, "It's called the 'Sacrament of the Anointing of the Sick' now."

"That's nicer. Takes the sting out, doesn't it? 'Extreme Unction' always sounded so severe, you know? Like 'Unction with Extreme Prejudice.'" He chuckled.

The young priest thought it was a little funny, but he wasn't in the mood to laugh. "Is Mr. Becker a practicing Catholic?"

"Sure."

Sure? "I mean—"

He pointed. "That's the chapel over there." The priest made out an ecclesiastical silhouette surrounded by poplars on top of a hillock. "That's where everyone's buried. Underneath, in the crypts." He pronounced it *crips*. "They've got this plumbing system, I guess you could call it that, to get rid of the methane. Apparently you can actually get explosions. You imagine, you're laying a wreath on Aunt Martha's crip and baboom!"

The car crunched to a stop in front of the large Georgian mansion covered in ivy, not a moment too soon as far as the priest was concerned. He reached for the door handle. He felt a hand on his shoulder. He turned toward the melted face.

"Before you go in, Padre, there's something I should tell you."

What now?

"He's a little doped up."

The priest nodded. "Thank God for the drugs."

"Yeah," the man chuckled, "thank God for the drugs. Look, Padre, he's likely to tell you this story. Don't take it too seriously, if you see what I'm saying."

"No," said the priest. "I don't." What a strange man.

"It's this story he's made up for himself, to get through a bad part of his life."

16

"Story?"

"So you know, okay? He lost his granddaughter couple of years ago. She was like a daughter. I mean, he raised her from when she was a kid. The buffalo were a birthday present to her when she was five, so you can appreciate how he felt about her, right? How many kids when they're five get a herd of buffalo? Anyway, she died, and it hit him real hard."

"I'm sorry. Was it ... leukemia, or ... ?"

"It was an overdose of cocaine."

"Oh Lord. I'm sorry."

"Yeah. One of those things. Nice kid, good-looking. Extremely good-looking, in fact. She was going to be an actress. Actually, she was already an actress but she was just getting started. She had this part in a play. Then"—he shrugged— "end of career. It was an accident. But they're *all* accidents."

"That's terrible."

"Yeah."

"We need to do more than we're doing. While I was in the seminary I did some fieldwork in a hospital where—"

"She was all he had left, I mean"—he gestured toward the mansion— "aside from all this. He was an orphan. Worked his way up from zip. He had a son and he died, a wife and she died, so the granddaughter became, like, his life, and then she died, and when that happened, he went a little—he made up this fantasy for himself about how he... anyway, if he starts telling you this story about how he killed a bunch of dope dealers, don't believe it. You're not dealing with some major criminal here. He's a very sweet old guy. Just play along. You see what I'm saying?"

"You mean he's deranged?"

"Deranged. That would be a way of putting it. But only in that particular region of his brain. Otherwise he's fine, except for the fact that he probably isn't going to make it through the night."

"Is it cancer?"

"Cancer. Yes, you might say he's got a cancer on his soul. Medically speaking, he's fine. You know the old bit about how people died of a broken heart? That's what he's got."

"I see. That's awful. I—"

"You know, he supports fifty Catholic orphanages, and you should see them. Top of the line. I've stayed in hotel rooms that weren't half as nice as some of these kids have."

The priest felt awful, yet he also had the feeling this man, whose name he didn't even know, was putting the arm on him.

"You are going to forgive him, right?"

What an appalling question. "Mr.—"

"Felix."

"Mr. Felix—"

"No, that's a first name."

"Frankly that's an inappropriate question." Yet the man stared at him in such a way he found himself saying, "But... of course."

"Good. Come on, let's go see the old guy." The priest followed him up the front steps and into the house. A long marble corridor seemed to go on forever, past two flanking rows of battle helmets from the ancient world, from Sumeria, Egypt, Crete, Sparta and Rome, mounted and spotlit on top of alabaster columns. The priest shuddered. The man said matter-of-factly, "Those are real."

At the end of the marble corridor they came to a door and went in.

The room was wainscoted in bleached pine, the walls covered in red morocco. The fire was going, even at this strange hour of the morning. The priest's eyes were drawn to a painting above the mantel of what appeared to be a bum in a top hat, with a raggedy blanket wrapped around his shoulders and a bottle of booze lying on the ground. On another wall he saw a rack of expensive-looking shotguns, blued barrels lambent with firelight, and something incongruous set into the wall behind glass: an old mailbox, a heavy piece of wood with a sheet of corrugated tin folded over like the canopy on a Conestoga wagon. American folk art? But now he turned toward the far side of the room and saw him, propped up on a cloud bank of pillows, gray, with the mummiferous gauntness of approaching death. Still, there was something faintly comical about the eyebrows, bushy and curled at the outer edge like a caricature of a nineteenth century colonel. The old man's eyes were closed. The morbid accessory was there: an IV monitor with a red LED display indicating the dosage of the fluid running onto the thin arm. A woman was sitting on the opposite side holding his hand. The priest could not help notice her good figure and attractive face. She looked up at him and smiled through horn-rimmed glasses in a friendly way. Felix whispered, "Hi, Jeannie." She shook the priest's hand and left.

The man leaned over the bed like an archaeologist afraid of disturbing important dust. He said, "Charley?" The priest was surprised that a servant would call his employer by his first name but everything else was so strange. "I brought you your priest, Charley."

The papery eyelids trembled, opened slowly and the eyes fastened directly on the priest's. They were amazingly alive in contrast to the rest of him, like people standing on the deck of a sinking ship waving to be rescued. They blinked.

"Padre?"

"Yes, my son," said the priest automatically.

"Son?" The voice was a croak, a susurrus of air forced over dried up vocal cords; but there was still authority to it. "How old are you?"

"Twenty-nine," the priest answered before he could protest the role reversal of penitent and absolutionist. Who's asking the questions here?

The eyebrows stirred like great birds in their nests. The old man looked up at Felix, who smiled and shrugged as if to say: In the middle of the night you were expecting an archbishop? He turned back to the priest. "You're ordained, right. You got papers?"

"Yes," said the priest.

The old man nodded. "Felix," he said, "get the padre something to drink."

"No, thank you."

The old man raised his hand with difficulty to shake the priest's. "I'm Charley Becker. Thank you for coming to see me on such short notice." He held on to the priest's hand. He grinned. "I have gold in my veins."

"Yes, my son."

The old man stared. "I do. If you put some of my blood on a slide, you'll see gold. It's true."

Gold in your veins. They all want to take it with them. The priest felt sorry for the man, even if he was an arms dealer. He opened his sin satchel and removed the accoutrements of his trade: the silver box—an ordination gift from his aunt—containing the cotton balls moistened with the holy oils, the narrow purple stole, which he hung around his neck. Felix patted the old man's arm and said he would wait outside.

"Stick around," said the old man. He said to the priest, "Felix knows it all." Then he grinned. "Don't you, Felix?"

"That's right," said Felix. He caught the priest's eye and winked. "I'll just be over there."

The priest made the sign of the cross. "Bless me, Father," said the old man. "It's been a while since my last confession. I killed a man."

"Yes, my son," said the priest with flawless compassion.

"A very fine man."

"Yes."

"I killed him with my own hand, this hand right here."

The priest had closed his eyes and was nodding the way he did inside the confessional, lubricating the release of words with drops of "Yes."

"He was like a son to me, you see."

"Yes."

"The others deserved to die, but not Felix."

Felix? Felix was twenty feet away. Of course, he doesn't know what he's saying. He asked, perhaps a bit too brightly, "What others, my son?"

"Oh, must have been forty, fifty by the time we were through. Never did count 'em all up."

"I see."

The old man looked up quizzically. "You do?"

"Yes." The priest nodded encouragingly.

"You're being awful understanding about this, Padre."

"Are you sorry for killing these other people?"

"I am not."

"I see." In the seminary he'd read a psychological study suggesting that in some extreme cases the priest should feign opprobrium in order to freight the absolution with the desired gravity. Nothing too heavy, mind. "That's very serious," he said, as if to suggest he might need to consult with a bishop.

"I killed them close up, with my own forty-five," said the old man. "Close enough to get wet. Wet work, that's what they call it. It's an actual term."

The priest nodded. "If you are not sorry, then do you have the intention of not committing these sins again?"

The old man regarded him strangely. "I think we're all right on that score, Padre."

The priest whispered the closing words of the ritual. He asked the Lord to lift him up and give him strength. When it was over, Charley said to the man with the melted face, "See the padre gets something for his trouble," then he closed his eyes, perhaps to start in on his three Hail Marys and three Our Fathers. These young priests, they gave such light penances.

I

1

"Mr. Robertson to see you," said Miss Farrell.

"Send him in," said Charley Becker. He had hired Robertson away from Northrop six months ago. He was a balding jock in his mid-forties who rose at 4 a.m. every day to strap on blood-pressure monitors and LED pedometers to run seven miles. He strode in, beaming, hand extended, bursting. "CB!" he said.

Charley nodded. "I've been looking over the log to N forty-nine ninety."

"N forty-nine ninety... forty-nine ninety."

"Those are the tail numbers of the G-4 you've been living in the last six months."

"Right. Hell of a machine. The comparables just can't touch it, in terms of ceiling. I can't stand fighting it out with ATC for a decent vector. You have to plead with those bastards, it's so shoulder-to-shoulder up there."

"I see you took it to Chicago and back four times last week."

"We're *burning* on the PEMCO deal."

"Uh-huh. Well, only thing I smell burning is paper money, mine. Let me acquaint you with some figures. Costs $4,700 and change to keep that bird aloft per hour. Round trip Dulles-Chicago, that's two hours, that's $9,400, not counting down-time. Times four, that's $37,600. Figuring in downtime, comes to $50,000. Divided by four, that's $11,500 per trip."

"Right. As I say, we're real close—" But Charley was already punching buttons and a voice fresh as bathroom deodorizer was coming in over the speaker box: "Thank you for calling American Airlines, Susan speaking, how may I help you?"

"Good morning, Susan. Got a fellow here needs to get to Chicago."

"Would that be first class or coach?"

"Well, now. He does like his luxury. But let's say coach. I'm sure he's got frequent-flier miles he can upgrade with."

"Round trip would be... let's see if I can get this computer to tell me... $670. Actually, it goes as low as $218."

"Two-eighteen, you say? Now, Susan, he's a bit touchy what altitude he flies. One thing he hates is going shoulder to shoulder with a lot of other aircraft. I was wondering if you could fix it so his plane will be above all those others."

"Uh—"

"Oh, and he's particular about what vector he's assigned by Air Traffic Control."

"Actually, we don't handle that here. You'd probably want to speak with ... if you'll hold I could ask my supervisor."

"No, that's all right. Thank you kindly."

"Thank *you* for calling American."

Robertson left. Miss Farrell's voice came on, sounding surprised. "Natasha's just walked in."

"Well, send her in—"

The door blew open. "You son of a *bitch*!"

"Sugar—" She came straight at him, cheeks ruddy from the October wind, breathing like she'd walked up all ten floors. Snorting, Charley would have said, if it weren't such an unfeminine term, though there was something of the charging bull to her aspect. Her long legs disappeared-finally-into a short black leather

24

miniskirt. The jacket, he imagined, was of indeterminate Middle Eastern origins, with raggedy sheepskin cuffs and irregular bits of mirror stitched in along the sleeves. She looked like a cross between a *Vogue* model and an Afghan mujahed. She looked gorgeous. She planted her hands knuckle down on Charley's desk, a bad sign, and glowered at him with the full-moon eyes. It was her spring-loaded position; she was cocked and ready to fire. Charley felt his back flattening against the chair.

"You look a little pale, honey. You getting enough exercise?"

"Don't patronize me."

"A fine hello." He was trying to buy time while his brain raced to decipher the cause of the storm.

"You're a damn liar, Charley."

More input. Klaxons rang inside his skull, red lights flashed, neurons strapped on flak jackets and ran down corridors shouting and shutting watertight bulkheads against the norepinephrine that was already up to their knees. Aoogah aoogah, dive dive. Something seriously wrong here. More input, damnit! "Uh," he managed lamely, "how do you mean, lie?" She was giving him the microwave stare now, rearranging his molecules, cooking him from the inside out. Don't say a thing, it'll be taken down and used against you. She had a round face, she looked like the ladies painted by whatsisname, the one he could never pronounce. Anger ... Inger ... Ingres. Those nineteenth-century French ladies with skin soft as butter and their chins resting on a crooked finger, the picture of domesticity—you could almost smell the *coq au vin* in the oven—except that the eyes always seemed to be undressing the painter. What angst Ingres must have gone through in those quiet parlors—

"You have the nerve to put me under surveillance."

"I don't know what you're talking about."

"Like you didn't know what I was talking about when someone bought the building I rent in. My own rent-controlled apartment and suddenly there are cameras all over the place and round-the-clock Arnold Schwarzenegger doormen."

"Aw, we been through all that, sug."

But clearly they were going to go through it all again. "Doormen," she muttered, "in a five-story walk-up."

"I told you, the real estate division buys a lot of buildings. It's, it's a small world."

"Bullshit."

"You know I don't like it when you speak like that. They don't inform me about every little ... rathole they're going to buy."

"Rathole. That's my home."

"Nonsense."

"What about that show I was auditioning for that suddenly you become a major backer of?"

"Coincidence."

"You're just like Nixon. You look straight into the camera and lie."

"I don't see the shame in supporting the arts."

"I was humiliated. Then you start having Felix hire people to spy on me."

"That's a terrible thing to say. I am not spying on you."

"Your righteous indignation needs a tune-up, Charley."

"Now look here, girl, you want to go live in a neighborhood looks like Bey-root"—his accent tended to deepen in periods of stress—"I don't see the harm in providing a little peace of mind."

"Your peace of mind, you mean."

"Have you seen the rape statistics for that neighborhood? 'Cause

I have." He pressed a button. "Jeannie, bring the rape statistics for Natasha's new"—he said it sarcastically— "neighborhood."

They glared at each other. He said, "If you won't take my money, I've got a perfectly good apartment there that I can't hardly use anyway 'cause of my tax situation. I told you a hundred times you're welcome to it."

"Sutton Place? Are you serious?"

"The hell's wrong with Sutton Place? Not enough violent crime for you? Okay, I'll have Felix truck in some muggers. How many you want?"

"God," she said. "You just don't get it, do you?" It wasn't a surrender exactly, but she went over and sat on the edge of a sofa and lit a cigarette, staring out across Roosevelt Island toward the Mall and the Capitol.

Charley watched her. It disturbed him that she smoked. He'd offered her a significant sum of money when she was thirteen if she wouldn't smoke until she was twenty-one, which she dismissed at the time as an "obvious bribe." Well, this wasn't hardly the time to get on her about smoking. He tried, "Where'd they screw up this time?"

"They were good. I'll give them that."

"Not that good."

She laughed. "He used women this time. As if you didn't know."

"That so?" he said disingenuously.

"Uh-huh." She blew a thin stream of smoke toward the Lincoln Memorial. A 727 flew past with its wheels down for landing at National. "They're kind of butch. Where does Felix find these people anyway?"

"Oh I don't know. Around, I guess."

"Do you pay them the same as men?"

27

"I'm sure of it." She stared. "I'll check on it."

"They followed me down here on the shuttle." She looked at her watch. "What time do you have?"

"Past noon. Twelve-oh-six. How about some lunch?"

"They're a little slow. Either that or Tim was a little late."

"How's that?"

"Friend of mine is calling Building Security at noon to say there are two armed women outside the building waiting to kill you."

"Sweet Jesus, girl." Charley grabbed the phone. "Security, this is Charley Becker—"

"They're both sort of dark, so my friend is saying they're Libyan. I thought that would cut the reaction time, but"—she looked at her watch— "I'm not too impressed, frankly."

"—you took a call a few minutes ago, it's false alarm—"

"Aren't the Libyans pissed off at you for not selling them something? High explosives, chemical weapons—"

The door banged open. Three of Felix's people pushed through, pistols drawn, followed by Miss Farrell.

"You all right, sir?"

"Fine."

"We found two women outside the building, they're armed. They claim—"

"It's all right, just, it's fine, let them go."

They left. Charley said, "That was a damn fool thing. Someone could have got hurt."

"That's right," she said, a study in imperturbability. "Maybe now it won't happen again." She slung her bag over her shoulder and stubbed out the cigarette.

"Leaving?"

"Gotta get back."

"Stay over, honey. We'll chopper out to the farm and have dinner. I'll fly you back to New York on the G-4. If Robertson isn't using it."

She kissed him on the top of his head. "Got a rehearsal."

"You got a show?" He brightened. "Why didn't you say? That's just fine!"

"Yeah." She grinned.

"Well, that's just, that's great. What is it?"

"Oh no."

"I'm not going to do anything, I promise."

"I'll save you and Felix tickets for the opening."

"Oh, come on, Tasha, tell me. All right, just tell me what it's about."

She said, "It's a very contemporary piece."

"Contemporary," he said suspiciously. "Contemporary about what?"

She considered. "It's about redemption."

"Redemption. It's religious?"

"No." She laughed. "Not exactly."

"This isn't one of those deals where you don't wear clothes. Now Tasha—"

"No. It's an adaptation of Jimmy Podesta's book."

"Who?"

"Gotta run. No more bullshit, okay?" She kissed him again, threw in a hug.

"The way you talk. Your grandmother would die."

"'I should sin to think but nobly of my grandmother.'"

"How's that?"

"*The Tempest*. Shakespeare."

"The outdoors one." Miranda's speech ends: "Good wombs

have borne bad sons." The night he came to see it, she left the line out, earning herself a note from the director.

"I'll see you, okay?"

The moment she was gone Charley was on the phone. "Felix? Those women you got, they're no good. ... Well, I don't care who recommended them. We need to try something different. Meantime get someone over to the twelve-thirty shuttle."

2

It was one of those spaces on the lower Lower West Side, maybe a hundred seats and cold enough so that most people kept their coats on. Charley and Felix sat in their front-row seats, Charley staring glumly at the Xeroxed sheet of paper that served as the program, Felix adjusting the squelch on his radio.

"'Wired,'" said Charley. "What's that mean?"

"Drugs," said Felix.

"She said it was about redemption. She didn't mention drugs."

"Maybe it's about giving up drugs." Charley grunted. Felix massaged his disability, the torn cruciate ligaments in his right knee. One month away from his gold shield and he steps into a pothole chasing a perp down a dark street. He did a casual scan of the audience behind them.

There was a paragraph of bio on Tasha on the sheet. Nothing about the Lycée or the Virginia prep school with a name like expensive dessert wine. He'd been going to her plays since she was, what, five? He wasn't sure about the arc from the Virgin Mary in the school Christmas pageant to Alison in *The Young and the Wired*, but he'd given her standing ovations at all of them, except the outdoors Shakespeare one where she played the daughter of the sorcerer: eighteen, blossomed, floating out onto the grass, barefoot, her long hair laced with jasmine and baby's breath, in a body stocking glimmery with what looked like ground diamond dust in the spotlights. He had to close his eyes, finally, it was too much, he started to feel like the hunchback, Caliban. She noticed that he didn't stand at the end. It was days before he could look her straight in the eye, and when he did... The lights were coming up. There she was, saying,

"I don't *believe* this shit!" He felt Charley tensing next to him. She and another actor were down on all fours on a shag carpet, desperate over having just dropped an "eighth" into it.

"Eighth of what?" Charley hissed at Felix.

"Cocaine," Felix whispered. Charley sat in his seat for the next two hours with his cigar clamped between his teeth like the pin of a hand grenade.

Backstage after it was over, he refused to shake Jimmy Podesta's hand. It might have developed into a scene but for the arrival of a photographer from *The TriBeCa Times*. They went back to the apartment, Charley, Tasha and the director, a young hotshot out of Carnegie-Mellon named Tim Tamarino.

Charley studied the young man. He was presentable, intelligent and articulate, though Charley wondered about the eyes; they were a tad soulful for his taste.

"Maybe your difficulty with the piece," Tim was explaining, "is that you're taking it too literally. For instance, when Alison goes into rehab, it's not just a drying-out place for cocaine addicts. There's a recontexturalizing going on. By rehab we mean that Alison is *rein-hab*iting herself."

"You want some more meat?"

"Charley," Tasha sighed.

They had coffee afterward in the indoor patio with the columns from the Alhambra and the large mosaic pool. Charley tossed croutons to Confucius, the old carp, a gift of the Chinese government. He said, "I'm like the Arabs. I love water because I grew up in dry country." Confucius shoved croutons about non-commitally in the water. Tasha sat on the edge and dangled her fingers in the water. "I'm from Texas."

"So Tasha said."

"I was raised by nuns. Mexicans. They came over the Rio Grande when—"

"Pops," said Tasha, "Not with the How-I-started-from-scratch. It's kind of late."

"Well, I—"

"I'd be fascinated," said Tim.

"Some other time maybe," said Charley, reinserting his cigar.

Tasha came over and put her arms around him from behind.

"This is a very beautiful home, Mr. Becker," said Tim.

"Oh, this isn't home. Virginia is home. I can only spend so many days a year in New York or the IRS—"

Tasha kissed him on the top of his head. "Maybe you could tell Tim your life story *and* your IRS war stories next time."

Tim looked at his watch and said, "I better be off."

"Drop me?" she said.

"Sure."

"Don't you want to spend the night here?" said Charley. "We got your bed made up."

Charley had antennae like the National Security Agency and they picked up the microburst transmission that passed between Tasha and Tim.

"I want to go over some notes with Tim while they're fresh."

"Notes?"

"On the performance." She kissed him. "Thanks for coming, Pops."

"Pleasure," said Charley.

"How you lie." She smiled. Tim shook his hand, a good firm shake, the kind Charley liked.

"You'll let me know if you decide to sublet," he smiled.

"All right." Charley laughed. "I will."

On the way to the door he said, "I told her she could live here, it's hers anyway, but she likes it down there in Bey-root."

"Why don't you feed yourself to Confucius," she said.

"He'd choke, most likely."

"I don't doubt he would," she said, sounding so like her grandmother.

Natasha was ten months old when on one otherwise beautiful spring evening her father—Charley's only child—drove the Mercedes into an oncoming car, killing himself, the waitress he had just picked up and the four occupants of the oncoming car. The Maryland state police lab fixed his blood/alcohol content at 0.43. At the service in the private chapel, the priest clung manfully to the theme: "It is not for *us* to judge Charley Junior." After the ceremony Charley locked himself in his study with a bottle of bourbon and his checkbook and sat down to write out the final payoffs incidental to his son's short life.

Charley junior's wife did not attend the funeral owing to a headache. Charley thought of that as he wrote out zeros for the families of the waitress and the people in the other car. She was a coldhearted stunner from hunt country—long on breeding and short on cash—who'd married Charley Junior for his daddy's money, pure and simple. She moved with the baby to New York a few days after the funeral without bothering to inform Charley and his wife. Charley flew into a rage.

"Charley," said Margaret, "you'll do yourself no good if you turn the baby's mother against you."

He had no leverage. He'd given Charley Junior a large sum when he reached twenty-one—unwise, unwise—and now she had that. He went up to New York and saw her and did what he did well, he made a deal with her: she'd receive large monthly trustee fees in return for—letting Charley have the baby on weekends.

One weekend she arrived with bruises. Charley grilled the Mexican nanny. The nanny said she fell. She arrived with bruises another weekend and this time Charley put the nanny through a grilling that wouldn't have been out of place in Nuremberg. In tears the old woman told him: the mother was never there, and when she was she was drunk and when she was drunk she hit the child. Charley called Tasha's mother and told her he was keeping the child.

The FBI showed up at the farm two hours later and it was an ugly scene, the baby screaming and clutching at Charley, Margaret in tears, the Mexican nanny in tears, the FBI—mindful that they were dealing with a friend of the President's—straining to settle the matter without recourse to handcuffs.

A few weeks later the phone rang in the middle of the night, the Mexican nanny. Come quickly, she said. He made it in less than two hours, remarkable, given the distance, the hour and the FAA violations involved. He got past the doorman and pounded on the door. He and the mother screamed at each other through the door until the nanny let him in the service entrance. The baby was bleeding from swollen lips. He picked her up and started for the door. The police, summoned by the doorman, arrested him in the lobby and she charged him with kidnapping. Charley decided he would do his case more good by refusing bail while his lawyers negotiated with his daughter-in-law's lawyers. She dropped the charges. On his release, Charley went to the Yellow Pages and looked under "Investigators—Private" and the first entry he came to was A Security (followed by AA Security and AAA Security—they were hopscotching each other backwards to get the first listing) and the man who answered was Felix Velez, recently forced off the New York police force on a Disability. They met at a coffee shop around the corner.

The next day Tasha's mother was sitting in the Palm Court of the Plaza Hotel having drinks with a friend when she noticed that everyone was staring at her. She turned and there was Felix, holding a sign above her. It said: "Baby beater." After a dozen incidents—at the theater, on the sidewalk, during (and this was truly embarrassing) a runway show presenting Givenchy's fall line—she called Charley and said all right, let's talk.

3

She forced herself to read the paragraph one more time.

Rox Van Ander and Susie Schwartz are especially fine as a pair of postmodern Brenda Fraziers whose biggest problem in life seems to be where their next gram of cocaine is coming from. The third member of the trio, Natasha Becker, is another matter. Half the time she seems faintly embarrassed by her lines' the other half she spends playing emotional catchup. You're left wondering if she isn't a member of the technical crew who had wandered down off the catwalk to give acting a try. It's not that she phoned in her part. She faxed it.

She'd gone out early to buy the paper, opened it at the newsstand and burst into tears in front of the Pakistani vendor, who figured someone must have died. She came back and undressed and poured about a half pint of high-viscosity sandalwood bath gel into the tub and stayed there submerged in an amniotic sac of hot suds for nearly two hours. She wrapped herself in the oversize terry and was sitting in the kitchen with her knees drawn up protectively against her chest, hair slicked back, sipping cambric tea.

The stuff about the catwalk should have done it, but no, he had to go back for another bon mot, the tweedy, hyphenated little dwarf. She fantasized him in old age, alone and miserable, all his friends driven away by bons mots, poor, living in an SRO hotel with no medical insurance and itching all over from a chronic skin condition for which there was no—

Tranquilo. Forget it. Forgive your enemies, like Pops says: makes them madder than hell. Next time she ran into E. Fremont-Carter she'd smile like a lady, tell him how much she enjoyed his work and then knee him right in the balls the way Felix taught her.

It dawned on her she hadn't read past the paragraph. He had good things to say about Tim's direction, a few obligatory jabs at Podesta. Nothing more about her fax instrument, thank God, no need to waste mots on a corpse, right? What a disaster. At least there was no show tonight. So what shall we do tonight, Tash? Suicide? Nah. Two things of Stouffer's macaroni and cheese and a quart of A & W root beer and get into bed with P. J. O'Rourke, or his new book, anyway. So why hadn't Tim called?

She jogged all the way down to the Battery and back, better than twice her usual daily distance. Tim still hadn't phoned when she got back. Felix called from Virginia. He'd just heard about it. He said he was coming up to New York and locate this E. Fremont-Carter and tear him a new asshole, and the way he said it she knew he would. He got her laughing. Ten minutes later her grandfather called, alerted by Felix. He wanted her to come down today, now, this minute, he'd have the chopper pick her up at the East River heliport. She'd be there in time for supper. Pops. What a piece of work. His solution to everything was—send in the helicopters; America in Vietnam. She cried, not because of what the tweedy dwarf had written, but because she wanted nothing more than to get into a helicopter and fly to the farm and be taken care of, but it would be giving in. "I can't, Pops," she said. "Got to get back on the horse." Her grandfather said he was proud of her and not to pay any mind to the press, they never got it right. She said she'd call tomorrow. She put down the phone, feeling better, and rang Tim.

He said he'd been out to brunch with the new head of Williamstown, who was talking to him about being the Boris Sagal Fellow this summer. "That's great," she said. "That's fantastic." He said it wasn't real money, but Williamstown was Williamstown. He went on about it until there was a pause in the conversation the size of the skating rink at Rockefeller Center and she said, "You want to talk about the weather now?" That got a little laugh out of him and he said, "Why don't I come over." There was something weird in his voice. "Yeah," she said, "why don't you."

She de-cocooned out of the terry and put on white stretch pants like thick leotards and a loose black cashmere sweater and her grandmother's pearls, brushed the shine back into her hair and Visine'd the red out of her eyes. She suspected some puffiness remained. So Tim would know she'd been crying. Hell with it. What was he expecting after a review like that—the Ivory soap girl?

There was no buzzer to let people into the building, so the drill was to call from the corner phone booth—assuming the crackheads hadn't jacked it—and she'd toss down the keys. She'd moved into this apartment in a huff and a hurry after finding out her grandfather had bought the last one—and there were certain drawbacks, such as the no-buzzer situation, the radiator situation and the fire-escape situation, since presumably fire escapes weren't supposed to quiver when you put potted plants on them. But she liked the idea of tossing keys down onto the street. It was a very ethnic thing to do, tossing your keys down to a lover in the street. Hard to imagine that on a Streetcar named Sutton Place.

Muffee!

Stanley! What are you doing in that revolting T-shirt?

She waited and waited and when the phone finally rang she was... indisposed. She had the answering machine set to kick in after two rings. She could hear Tim saying, "Natasha? Hello? I'm here. Are you there? Natasha?"—puzzlement turning to impatience turning to click. Oh God. Not the best time for this to happen. He hung up just before she picked up. She went to the window and yelled. She was about to run out after him when it rang again, a reprieve. She tossed the keys. It was four floors down and the key chain was heavy, since it had to hold all the keys necessary to open a New York apartment. Tim did a cool matador's side-step and let them smash onto the pavement. Tim, so cool. He let himself in, came up the stairs and walked in. He gave her a kiss, but it was perfunctory, somehow.

She asked if he wanted something to drink. The way he said no was all business. He had his leather briefcase with him. Snap, snap. He took out the paper, prefolded to the review, and laid it on the coffee table. Wonderful. You want me to recite it from memory? Then he reached into his pocket and took out a small vial full of white powder, which he set on the table next to the review.

"What," she said, "is that?" though she knew exactly what it was.

"This," he said, "is your authenticity."

It had come up a few times during rehearsals, always to one side so as not to embarrass her in front of Rox and Susie, who, to judge from their authenticity, had hoovered half the Peruvian gross national product up their nostrils. Their authenticity was so for-real it wouldn't get past a dope-sniffing dog.

"Tim," she pleaded. He picked up the review and read the paragraph out loud, as though he agreed with it. Her eyes welled.

"It's complicated for me," she said. She hadn't told him about her alcoholic father or her alcoholic mother. She started to, once, but it sounded stupid and self-pitying. Why not just say she'd tried it once and was allergic. Everyone understood allergies; allergies are so much easier to justify than abstinence.

He read the paragraph out loud again. "Timmy," she said. "Please."

"Natasha, if the role called for you to play the piano, you'd take piano lessons. You don't have to become Alicia de Larrocha, but you'd want to know where your fingers went."

"Uh-huh, and to do *Whose Life Is It Anyway?* you'd want me to go sever my spinal cord?"

"That's reductionist. We're talking about locating a precise emotion. As it stands, you're improvising." He held up the review. "And it shows."

39

"Will you stop waving that thing."

"Actor's choice, Natasha. That's what it's about."

"Funny," she said. "I thought it was about whether or not I do snort cocaine."

"Louis Malle once told me, he said, 'You put an extra next to an actor and nine times out of ten the actor ends up looking like an actor and the extra looks like the real thing. Why?' You know how Louis talks—"

"No, Tim. I haven't met Louis Malle."

"You'd like him. And I think he'd like you." Tim did Louis Malle's accent: "'Because the actor is an *actor*. He isn't *real*.'"

"Great. So I should aspire to be as good as an extra, is this the moral?"

"I'm not into morals, Natasha." Tim stood up and went to the window. It was just for effect. "I spoke with Bernie and Karen this morning."

"Yes," she said, trying to sound casual, but he'd gotten her attention.

"I think I made it all right."

"Just tell me, Tim."

"They're not happy."

"They were happy Thursday night."

"Time flies. What's happened is they had a call from the Schumpelmann Organization."

"Oh," said Tasha. The show might move uptown? Tim was giving her this look: And you may not be coming.

"Thanks, Tim."

"Don't shoot the messenger." He sat down beside her and stroked her hair. "I just want it to work for you. I think we can get to where Bernie and Karen will be happy again. It's not over till the fat lady sings." The fat lady was Tim's code for the *New York Times* theater critic. "If we get to where we need to be before she sings I think we're all going to be happy, me, you, Bernie and Karen."

Actor's choice: her life had suddenly boiled down to making Bernie and Karen happy by snorting cocaine. In its own shabby way it was like Noel Coward having to sleep with a rich woman to get backing. What will you do, Noel? Hold my nose and think of England. So how do you hold your nose and snort coke? "All right," she said heavily.

"Do you have a mirror or something?"

Tim chopped it up into three-inch-long lines, perfect replicas of the lines of milk powder they used onstage. He rolled up a fiftydollar bill, the same they used in the play, a preview-night gift from Bernie and Karen—maybe they'll have it bronzed if the show goes uptown—and handed it to her. Her fingers were shaking.

"It's all right," he said.

"Will you do it with me?"

"I don't do cocaine."

"Jesus, Timmy. I'm nervous."

"You'll be fine. And don't sneeze. This cost a hundred and a quarter."

"Where did you get it?"

"One of the ushers."

"Which one?"

"Whichever. I'm not sure I even know his name."

She stared at the cocaine. "Is it—"

"It's good," he said, "the best. Authenticity, right?"

She did one line, then another. It did not burn, which Tim said was a sign of good cocaine. Her gums went numb until she could tap her front teeth and they felt like pieces of tile. She felt enormous energy and confidence and segued right into her coke soliloquies, Tim nodding, making notes, even smiling here and there, something he never, ever did during rehearsals. She felt happy, as happy as she could ever remember. It was like freeze-dried happiness crystals, just add nose and boom. After a while it didn't even feel chemical. No question about it, Tim was right, authenticity was everything, she couldn't wait to get back up onstage—too bad no show tonight, she was ready, instrument tight as catgut—and mix it up with old Rox and Susie. Tim was chopping up more lines. She did the "coke whore" bit where she pretends to be fascinated, enthralled, *mesmerized* by the guy doling out the coke. She went into an ad-lib rift about how much she admired Tim's work and how she'd been following his career for so long. It was so authentic it actually seemed to annoy him.

Then came a point where no matter how long the lines were they didn't seem to work as well and suddenly the room began to feel very warm. She went to open the window and Tim said, "Are you kidding? It's freezing in here. Don't you have heat?" He went over and started inspecting the radiator the way men do when they pretend to have mechanical knowledge, getting down on his knees and saying in that male way: No wonder, there's no thromboggle-toggle on this thing and I haven't got my tools with me. She would have been amused by this and maybe even incorporated it into the soliloquy she was doing, except she wasn't feeling well, she was feeling hot and it was getting hard to breathe. She felt her forehead. It was like ice. Her hand, she noticed, was shaking almost violently. Was this—was this normal? "Tim?"

The way he looked at her scared her. "Tim?"

"You okay? Tasha?"

She was on the floor now, looking up at the ceiling, which the super had been promising to have painted for the last five months—yeah, right. Someone was piling cinder blocks on her chest, making it very hard to breathe.

"Timmy?" It hurt to speak. Her throat was like a kiln. Tim was holding her forehead and her hand.

"Pops?" she said. "Felix?"

He pulled up her sweater and put his ear to the round of her bosom and listened. There was no sound, only the pounding in his own chest.

Fuck fuck fuck. Shit shit shit. Fuck fuck fuck.

He put his hand to her throat the way he'd seen in the Vietnam movies. Nothing, just his own pulse. His hand was shaking now. Jesus, what was this, transference?

Still on his knees beside her, he thought: Dial 911. He went for the phone and he had the phone in his hand when he thought: Hold on, hold on a second. What is the point of dialing 911 now? There was no emergency. She was dead. Sweet Jesus, this couldn't be happening. Please. Rewind the tape. We're going to shoot this scene over. Rewind, goddamnit, I am not happy with this scene.

The clock on the bookshelf said ten after six. Just move the big hand back five minutes, that's all. Five minutes. Okay, ready? Okay, let's take it from the middle of page 17: "She needs to go on a lowsemen diet." There's no "rewind" on the machine, only "play."

You're panicking. Stop it. Think. Breathe. In, out-slow, in, out-slow. Okay. Call 911. All right. All right. All right. I'm going to. Just a moment here. What do I say? Do I say: There's been a little problem with cocaine here and... Jesus, this is not a "little problem" here, this is a major fucking disaster. The mirror, the coke, the razor, Bernie and Karen's fifty. Great. Wonderful. Is this your cocaine? No, Officer. Well, whose is it? You have the right to remain silent, you have the right to an attorney... What the hell happened? Is this what happened to the Kennedy kid, to that black basketball player? No. Those two were doing, like, massive quantities. There's still half a gram left here. Jesus, Ramírez, what kind of coke is this? So good you drop dead? You Puerto Rican piece of shit, Ramírez. Well, you're in it same as me, pal, up to your fucking—

Stop. Breathe from the diaphragm. Okay, flush the coke down the toilet. Wait a minute. They'll do an autopsy, they'll find the coke one way or the other. They'll find the coke and then I'm dead too. Might as well be. Probably end up envying her for Chrissake.

Look, make a choice. Call 911 or get out of here. It's not like you're going free. My God, this is going to be with you for the rest of your life. The rest of your life. Jesus, it's like Frank Capra in reverse, *It's a Horrible Life*. Rikers Island. Great. If you're *lucky* you'll get for a roommate the guy who killed John Lennon, or Joel Steinberg. Joel can keep me up all night explaining to me how he didn't really kill Lisa. It was really Hedda. Great, fucking great, Tasha. Is that what you want? Me and Joel fucking Steinberg in the same cell. Me and, and, and Mark David Chapman in the same cell? Mark can read to me from *The Catcher in the Rye*, tell me which of Lennon's songs he liked best, "Day in the Life" or "Imagine." Can you see me in there, Tasha? Doing Chekhov at Rikers Island with Black Muslims? *The Three Sisters*? Can you see it? After the show, instead of a cast party they sodomize the director. Maybe I'll get AIDS and they'll let me out early on humanitarian grounds. Tasha, for Christ's sake, get UP, please get up off the floor.

He was in the bathroom now, splashing water on his face. His heart was beating. He put his hand over his chest to try to slow it down.

He found a handkerchief in her bedroom and used it to wipe his fingerprints off the glass vial and the mirror. He wiped every surface he thought he might have touched. The fifty—better take that too. Knowing fucking Bernie, he wrote down the serial number.

Let's see. The review. The page was folded over to show the review. It was lying there right next to the coke. Move it a bit closer to the coke? Or is that too obvious? Yes, that's too obvious. Leave something for the audience to put together on its own. The review is fine where it is. Wait, is a cop going to notice something like a review? Should the paragraph be circled in red or yellow-highlighted? No, that's too much. But it needs something else.

He held the vial with the handkerchief and knelt and put Tasha's still-warm thumb and index finger on it—was she right-handed? yes, she was right-handed—and pressed them there. Then he held the vial up to the light and saw what looked like a print.

Okay, let's get this scene on its feet. Let's block the scene. The cops walk in the door, the first thing they see is the body. Then they see the coke on the table. Are they going to see the review? They'll come back to the review. The first cop leans over you and the second cop goes to the coke and puts his finger in it and tastes it and, like, nods. *Good shit*. Thanks to you, you rat bastard, Ramírez. Okay, then he sees the review, and he picks it up and reads it. And the second cop says: *So why weren't all the locks on the door locked—*

Keys. Good, the door needs to be locked from the *outside* so it looks like she locked it from the *inside*.

They were in the bowl next to the door. He put his ear against the door to listen. Did ears leave prints? No, Jesus, ears do not leave prints, you're being paranoid.

Using the handkerchief as a glove, he opened the door, let himself out and shut it. There were three dead-bolt locks to contend with. Jesus. That's right, he remembered her telling him that she lived in a three-lock neighborhood. The dead bolts were incredibly noisy. He was sure someone was going to see him before he got them locked. Boy they were noisy, so noisy he didn't hear her moan on the other side of the steel door.

4

Charley and Felix sat together in the back of the limousine, sinuses suffused with gun oil. They'd been cleaning shotguns when the call came from a Detective Mullen of the Sixth Precinct and they used what rags they had on hand.

Felix saw the crowd of reporters and TV people outside the main entrance to the bright blue brick-and-glass building on the corner of Thirtieth and First Avenue. He told the chauffeur to drive straight through the intersection to the side entrance on Thirtieth.

The reporters saw the limousine pulling up and closed in. Charley got out and was pinned against the car. The housekeeper had put a pair of woman's sunglasses on him, left behind by a houseguest, as he left, the Jackie 0 paparazzi-proof type, big and round, the kind that make you look like a stylish insect. Felix managed to get between him and the press, but he couldn't clear a path to the door that said:

46

UNDERTAKERS AND POLICE OFFICERS

PRINT YOUR NAMES ON ARRIVALS AND DEPARTURES CLEARLY

THANK YOU

They shouted at Charley and jabbed at him with their boom mikes, then there was a voice, familiar, practiced, New York–weary and seen-it-all-before: "All right, let's give them some air, let's move back, folks, that's it." Detective Mullen.

He got them inside and Charley found himself standing in a black marble lobby while Felix and the detective spoke to a black man behind a black desk. The outside of the building was done in a bright, almost gay, blue ceramic brick; the inside was all business. An inscription ran across the wall in raised steel letters.

TACEANT COLLOQUIA, EFFUGIAT RISUS. HIC LOCUS EST UBI MORS GAUDET SUCCURRERE VITAE.

What did that mean? All he recognized was HIC. Scripture? How was anyone supposed to know? Suddenly he was shouting at the old black man behind the desk and the man, with an air of no offense taken, was handing him a smudgy Xerox. "Let conversation cease, let laughter flee. This is the place where death delights to help the living." But what did *that* mean?

A man in a white jacket with script stitching that said Dr. Thomas E. Bratter was introducing himself in a kindly, confidential tone of voice. Charley and Felix followed him down a half flight of stairs and the smell shoved through the gun oil. They'd tried to disguise it, but when nature asserts its claims there is basically no arguing with it. Death would never be lemon fresh or minty green, no matter what they sprayed it with. Steps, yes, I see them, said Charley.

The meat lockers were arranged two high along a large gleaming metal cube in the center of the tiled room. Autopsies were in progress behind glass doors on the outer wall. As they passed Charley heard bored voices saying, "The pericardial cavity contains twenty cc's of fibrinous yellow fluid. The pericardial surfaces are smooth and glistening." Another door opened: "... the septum is in the midline and the nares are patent. The ears are unremarkable and the external auditory canals are patent. The teeth are in poor repair."

They came to compartment number three. Charley and Felix saw their distorted reflections in the brushed steel, like faces at an amusement park. The typed card on number three announced: BECKER, NATASHA P. The needle on the temperature gauge pointed to thirty-six Fahrenheit.

Metal sounds: the door opening, ball bearings turning, click. He saw her foot. Her toe was tagged. A sheet covered the rest of her and he remembered when she was seven and cut up one of her grandmother's Pratesi sheets to make a Halloween ghost.

The sheet came back. Her skin was bluish and her mouth was open. Don't look at me, she said, I'm a mess. He touched his hand to her cheek and started at the coldness. Charley junior had still been warm when he reached the hospital.

Then they were in a brightly lit office with the sun streaming in, coffee was being offered and declined. Dr. Bratter was being very courteous, and such a busy man too. Charley had read an article on him in the *Times* not two weeks ago about some personality thing between him and the mayor

"How old was she, Mr. Becker?" —apparently the mayor thought he ... what? Sorry. Twenty-two. "Is there a history of coronary disease in your family?"

"No, my wife died of cancer and my son—we die of other things."

"Did your granddaughter use controlled substances?"

"No, her daddy and mother had, they were, they had drinking problems and she—she smoked cigarettes, that was her vice."

The ME looked over at the detective and the detective said that they had found a small container of cocaine at the scene. It was being analyzed. Charley shook his head and said that wouldn't have been hers. Dr. Bratter said—he put it this way—that "a white granular substance was visually observed in her nasal cavities."

A door opened and someone came in with a clear plastic bag. Charley saw white pants like thick leotards, a black cashmere sweater, pearls, panties. The ME was saying he understood how "difficult" this was and that he would try to expedite "things." What things? The autopsy. No, Charley said, I'm taking her with me now, I will not leave her in that place. The detective was explaining that it was necessary under law in these circumstances and then Charley was on the floor and they were loosening his tie and Felix was saying it's going to be all right, boss, it's going to be fine.

Another embarrassing funeral in the private chapel, another sermon on the theme: "It is not for us to judge." "How awful for poor Charley," whispered a friend of the family. He looked so slumped up there all alone in the first pew. The casket came in, covered with a spray of Arabian jasmine sent by the nuns. Felix in sunglasses walked in front as chief pallbearer. Tim, who had broken down and told Charley that they were lovers, walked beside it. You could see what pain he was going through. Bernie and Karen sent a nice wreath on behalf of the cast and crew. The organist played a Bach air as the winter light streamed brilliantly through the Chagall window and Charley's Labrador retriever, Spook, wandered in during the eulogy, wagging his tail, and walked up to Charley and began licking at his hand. It was the saddest thing. Everyone said afterward that the dog coming in was the saddest thing.

But the Chagall window was transcendently beautiful that day, everyone agreed about that too.

Charley had brought the chapel over stone by stone from Italy—after the fashion of self-made Americans desiring some instant background. Charley had been collecting Chagall's work since the late forties and went to him to make a stained-glass window behind the altar, a Crucifixion scene. Chagall told him that only a "vulgar, rich American would ask a Jew to make him a Crucifixion," to which Charley said he wanted someone with experience at crucifying saviors. He hired an astronomer to calculate exactly what day of the year the sun would be brightest through the window so they could dedicate it in its fullest glory; the astronomer mentioned in passing that if the chapel were angled fourteen degrees more to the south the window would receive 45 percent more light. Chagall demanded that the chapel be rotated on its axis. Charley, who had been paying the artist's staggering—and, for that matter, unitemized—bills without a peep, put his foot down and said no, which put Chagall into a work-stoppage funk that lasted almost a month, until Charley said he was going to hire Julian Schnabel to finish the damn thing if he didn't get back to work.

Finally it was completed and Charley bribed the Archbishop of Washington to come and consecrate it (by making a large donation to the renovation fund for St. Matthew's Cathedral). The veil came down precisely at 1028 hours on June 22, and it was a sight to take your breath away. Jesus was suspended in midair, his face a mask of peace and triumph. The Virgin Mary and disciple John were standing together. The centurion whose servant Jesus had healed a few days earlier as a favor was sitting on the ground with his face in his hands. The colors were—the whole thing seemed to move, they were so vibrant. It was Einstein's bent light that shot through it with hallucinatory energy. And the blood, good heavens, the blood. Chagall had used huge, uncut Burmese rubies for the blood that fell from Jesus' wounds. It dripped into a red river that ran across the bottom of the tableau, no calm, Stygian affair but a wild, roaring rush of whitecaps, the kind that shoots through narrow canyons. The banks were lined with calla lilies with snakes for pistils. Underneath the river was the inscription

HIC EST ENIM CALIX SANGUINIS MEI

which means in Latin: "For this is the Cup of My Blood," the words Jesus is said to have spoken to his disciples at the Last Supper. Right above the HIC was a man with bushy eyebrows and X's for eyes, dipping a beer mug in the river: Charley, drunk on the blood of the lamb. "How 'bout that?" he said, actually flattered, counter to Chagall's intention.

The medical examiner made the call himself; that was decent of him. Charley was embarrassed over the episode in his office and apologized. Dr. Bratter said that was hardly necessary.

"It was a fresh myocardial infarction precipitated by a spasm of the coronary arteries," he said, reading from the report, which made it somewhat easier. "She died of a heart attack, Mr. Becker." He explained about vasoconstriction of the coronary vessels, something like that brought about by a lifetime of gorging on butter, or a thrombosis. Oxygen can't get through to the heart muscle, and it dies. The hard part: "As to the cause of the spasm," he said, "we determined it was due to a prolonged intranasal inhalation of high potency cocaine, consistent with that analyzed by the police." Time of death was fixed at between eight o'clock and twelve midnight the night before she was found.

Tim was wonderful in the days following, calling Charley often to ask how he was doing, to chat, reminisce, to see if there was anything he could do. Charley was touched by his attentions and saddened to think that here was a young man he wouldn't have minded having as a son-in-law.

Tim phoned one day to say he had just spent over an hour with Detective Mullen going over—again—the messages he'd left on Tasha's answering machine. He called back the next day, sounding harried. Mullen had wanted to go over them again. "It was a little surreal, frankly," he said. "He actually asked me about my 'whereabouts' the night it happened. He actually used the word 'whereabouts.'" Charley said not to take offense, he was just a policeman doing his job.

"The worst part is thinking: Here I was calling her and leaving these pissed-off messages on her machine and she was there dead the whole time."

"You couldn't have known," said Charley.

"I might have known. I should have known. She was so serious about the Work. When that asshole's review came out that morning, I should have known."

"You think that's what it was, the review?"

"Sure it was. The paper was open to the review right there on the table next to the cocaine. That's where they found it. It's obvious, isn't it?"

Tim didn't call again after that, but he did send a thoughtful note saying how busy things were now that the show was moving uptown. He enclosed Jimmy Podesta's tribute to Natasha in *The TriBeCa Times* and said that E. Fremont-Carter was reportedly pretty shaken up by the whole thing. He said Podesta was going to dedicate the opening-night show to Natasha.

Charley was not pushy with Detective Mullen. He knew how people hate it when the rich start throwing their weight around. The presence of Felix—a former colleague of Mullen—provided a note of professional collegiality.

"We don't have any 'suspects,' Mr. Becker. It's not that kind of situation."

"What kind would you say it is?"

"It would appear to be a self-inflicted situation."

"Mr. Tamarino," said Charley, "you questioned him."

"Twice."

"When you question someone, do you reveal information to them about evidence?"

"Of course not."

"Of course. Could we hear those telephone messages?" There were five of them. Detective Mullen played them for Charley and

Felix. In the first he said, "Tasha? Where are you? Natasha, hello, I'm here. Are you there, Natasha?" There was a two-hour gap between the first message and the second, and an average of half an hour between that and the third, fourth and fifth, all of them variations on the same theme: "Where the hell are you? You didn't show at the museum, how come?"

"The background sound in the first message," said Felix, "that's not a museum."

"I asked him about that," said Detective Mullen. "He changed it slightly. First time, he said he was calling from inside the museum, second time I asked, he said he used the pay phone outside on the street."

"So he changed his story."

"Not significantly," said Mullen. "Anyway, his whereabouts are accounted for. He was with a guy named Emiliano Ramírez, works as an usher at the theater, from five o'clock to seven-thirty at the Spring Street Bar and Grill and after that they went to a club downtown called Gulag. They were there from approximately seven fortyfive until two a.m. The ME says she died between eight and twelve, so there we are. I can't say much for Mr. Tamarino's taste in clubs, but he was there, apparently."

"How do you mean?"

"How do I mean? The band at Gulag was called Tipper Gore and one individual I spoke with identified himself as Phlegm."

"What about the keys?"

"I can't account for the keys, Mr. Becker."

"But the door was locked and you couldn't find her keys."

"Correct. Also, there were no prints on either doorknob, which is unusual, but not conclusive. It's winter and people wear gloves."

"Murderers wear gloves."

"Yes, they do. But what motive did you have in mind? She seems to have been a very well-liked person from what I can gather."

"All right, but the keys. The building superintendent didn't let her in. Where are the keys?"

"I don't know where the keys are, Mr. Becker."

"What about the thing you said you inhale cocaine through? The straw. There was no straw."

"No. But a lot of times they roll up a dollar bill and snort it through that. Sometimes they use a hundred-dollar bill. It depends on the socioeconomics, if you follow. I had the bills in her wallet tested for trace amounts."

"And?"

"Two of them tested positive for cocaine. But that doesn't mean anything, necessarily. These days, seventy-five percent of all the bills in circulation that they test, test positively for cocaine. In Orange County, California, recently they tested twenty-four bills for cocaine and twenty-four tested positive."

"So it means the bills in her wallet weren't necessarily the ones used?"

"That's correct."

"So the keys and the straw, that's two suspicious pieces of evidence."

"No, sir. That's two missing pieces, not evidence. Look, Mr. Becker, I appreciate what you're going through. A lot of families go through exactly what you are. I've put more into this case than, frankly, I ordinarily would've, out of respect for who you are and all, and because Mr. Velez used to be on the force. But I want to be honest with you. The evidence does not support a continuing investigation. But—but—I'm not dropping it, I'm going to stay on it to the extent I can and as long as I can. I'll keep Mr. Velez fully advised. I'm afraid that's really all I can do. As I say, I appreciate what you're going through."

5

The District Attorney for the County of New York rubbed his eyes from lack of sleep. A U.S. senator from New York had been indicted the day before and he'd been asked to go on *Nightline*. The show started late due to the play-offs, then Koppel went over and by the time he got home to Pelham Manor it was two in the morning. Then he couldn't get to sleep because the stupid ass production assistant must have given him regular coffee instead of decaf and finally at four he popped a Valium only to be awoken at five by the baby screaming.

The Assistant District Attorney opened the door and walked in tentatively. He was still in his twenties, just out of Yale, or Harvard?

"Sit down, Ed." The ADA sat. It was only his second time in the holy of holies.

"What do we have?"

"The police think she may have been given the cocaine by the boyfriend, Timothy Tamarino. He's the director of the play she was in. But it's very soft. He—"

"You want some coffee? I've got to have some coffee. Helen, bring me and Ed two extremely large black coffees. How do you take it?"

"Black is fine," he said, though he took cream and sugar.

"Go on," said the DA, speed-reading the file: the police 61, the phone company report, the unanimous statements from Tasha's friends attesting to her drug-free lifestyle.

"It all hangs on the first message on the answering machine. Mullen, the detective in charge, questioned him on two separate occasions. On the first, Tamarino says he placed the call from the lobby of the Museum of Modern Art. But in the background you can hear a boom box Dopplering past—"

"What?"

"A large portable tape cassette player—"

"Ghetto blaster."

"Right—going past, playing a U-2 song, I believe"—he checked his notes— "right, 'Running to Stand Still.' The point is the museum doesn't allow people inside with boom boxes. Mullen confronted Tamarino with this the second time he interviewed him. That was probably a mistake. Tamarino said now that he remembered, he made the call from a pay phone outside."

"Goddamn right it was a mistake. Still, it's not much."

"No, it isn't. Mullen says the thumb and forefinger prints on the cocaine vial were so clean that they looked planted. Plus the door was locked and they can't find the keys."

"That's something."

The ADA nodded. "But the ME put the time of death at between eight p.m. and midnight and Tamarino was with someone at a club from seven-thirty to well after midnight."

"Gulag?" said the DA, reading. "For Christ sake. Where does it end? Discos named after Auschwitz? Dachau? Bergen-Belsen? Sometimes you just want to pull the handle and flush. So that's it?"

"Yes. As far as the Sixth Precinct Detective Squad is concerned."

"What do you think?"

"I think it's ... very thin."

"Thin? It's cellophane. It's Saran Wrap."

"But I think it was Tamarino's cocaine. And I don't think keys walked out of there by themselves."

The DA sighed. "Missing keys. Not enough here for 220.3 and even less for a 125.15."

The ADA scrolled up the numbers on his brain screen: sale of a controlled substance, B felony; second-degree manslaughter, C felony. "Mullen said, off the record, that he'd be willing to arrest him and shake his tree to see what falls off, but I didn't think you wanted to go that route."

The DA stared into middle space. "You don't remember the Kennedy case, do you? David Kennedy. Couple of years ago, '85, '86?"

"April 25, 1984. The Palm Beach police charged two bellhops at the Brazilian Court Hotel with selling cocaine and conspiracy to sell cocaine. Six months later they both copped a *nolo* to selling and the conspiracy charge was dropped. Eighteen months' probation and expungement."

The DA nodded. "Good, Ed. That's good preparation."

"Thank you, sir. Sir? My name is Bill, actually? Bill Allard?"

"Jesus Christ. I didn't sleep. I'm sorry. Jesus. Of course you're Bill."

"By the way, I thought you handled that question very well."

"Question?"

"On *Nightline*, about whether you're interested in the AG job?"

"Oh, right. Okay, so the Kennedy case ... what?"

"It was a very unpopular prosecution. Here are the editorials." He put a manila folder on the DA's desk. The DA looked at them blearily. "You want to gist them for me?"

" 'Prosecutorial zeal' is all over them. There's not a lot of support out there for rich white kids who OD on cocaine. And they had much more to go on in the Kennedy case than this one. They had witnesses who told the grand jury they heard one of the bellhops bragging about how he sold cocaine to a Kennedy. Even with that it was a no-win."

"You know who I feel sorry for in all this?"

The ADA shook his head.

"Ethel. What that woman's been through. Well, look, we're not going to let that influence us, but Jesus Christ, Mullen has to make his own decisions, damnit. What does he think this office is? This really, this really pisses me off."

"Yes, sir."

"You tell Mullen to make his own fucking decisions. If he's got a case, *bring* us a case. If he doesn't have a case, don't bring us a case. And while you're at it, tell him I do not appreciate the way this thing has been handled. Tell him I'm going to speak to Brown about this—personally."

"Yes, sir."

Helen said, "It's Morley Safer, from *60 Minutes*."

"All right. We all set on this, Ed? ... Morley?"

6

Charley sat by the light of the fire, Spook beside him, staring at the mailbox in the display case on the wall surrounded by all the leather-bound books.

The orphanage was started by Mexican nuns who fled over the border into Texas during the anticlerical hysteria of the revolution when three of their order were raped and crucified on saguaro cacti. They bought an abandoned farm on the outskirts of McAllen.

They found him in the makeshift mailbox one cold winter morning, badly dehydrated and the color of plum, swaddled in a week-old comics section of *The Star*. They named him Karl Becker after the local fishmonger. All the children were named after local merchants. Sister Rosa Encarnación had hit on the scheme. Herr Becker would show up every Saturday afternoon in his truck with whatever he hadn't been able to sell that week, cases of reeking skate and shark, sometimes a discolored eel or two. They changed his legal name to Charley when America entered the Great War in 1917, but the nuns went on calling him Carlos.

Old Raul looked up and saw Carlos bleeding from his nose and both ears and a tooth was gone, the second this week.

"Aiy, Carlito." He took the boy in and washed his face and plugged his nose and let him swish some homemade mescal around inside his mouth, which left a pleasing numbness on the boy's sore gums. He let him watch him prepare that night's dinner, some horsemeat donated by a rancher with two orphans named after him. Raul tasted the horse and chopped up another handful of the slender green serrano peppers he used liberally to disguise the rottenness of the meat. He held one perfect specimen up for Carlos to admire. Carlos reached for it. "*Con cuidado*," Raul urged. "I knew a man who went blind because he rubbed his eyes after holding a pepper." Raul told glorious lies. He had a scar on his belly from where he'd been knifed; he told Carlos that was where General Pershing had shot him while pursuing Pancho Villa after Villa's (and Raul's) historic attack on the town of Columbus, New Mexico. "Black Jack" Pershing had become the hero of the war with Germany, so Carlos was extremely impressed to know someone who had been shot by him. Raul said the bullet—made of silver—had been intended for Villa but that Raul had thrown himself in its path. Villa had not wanted to leave him there, wounded, but Raul insisted. Raul expertly sliced the pepper into thin strips and then cut those crosswise so that no piece was larger than the head of a matchstick. "The serrano is like Christ," he said, stirring the pepper into the horsemeat stew. "It takes all the sins of the world unto itself. That is why it is so full of fire." Carlos took a furtive pull on the bottle of mescal. Raul saw it but didn't say anything.

Bryce, Lockmuller and Gómez came for him again that night, stuffing a gag in his mouth and carrying him, squirming, out of the converted barn that served as a dormitory, to one of the shacks. Lockmuller had a length of barbed wire. He looped it loosely around Carlos' neck while the others held him. "You bite me again and I'll strangle you dead." Carlos watched as Lockmuller unbuttoned his trousers. Gómez kicked him from behind. They'd demonstrated what they'd do to him on a polecat if he told the sisters: gouging out its eyes, cutting off its feet, then hanging it by its tail over a fire.

The next morning one of the nuns noticed Carlos wasn't saying his morning prayers along with the others. At first they thought it was willful and punished him for it, but as the weeks went by without the boy speaking, they began to wonder. They took him to the doctor who had five boys named after him. He poked about Carlos' mouth and couldn't find anything and suggested withholding food and water from him to see if that would get him to talk. Sister Imaculata announced to the other sisters her conviction that Carlito's muteness was the work of the Dark One. The priest who said Masses on Sunday in the old barn was a bent old man and kinder than most, but at the age where not enough oxygen was getting through to his brain. He came principally for Raul's mescal.

Carlos recognized the smell on Padre's breath as he peered into his face, trying to see the Devil through the two small windows on the boy's soul. He hung a couple of rosaries around Carlito's neck and splashed him with holy water until he was sopping.

"Ego te expulso!" he shouted. Grappling with the Dark One required strengthening himself with Raul's mescal. Carlos calmly watched, dripping wet with holy water, as the old priest invoked the Lord to drive out the evil inside him. The Devil was too much for him, however, and after one session the old man passed out on the floor. When he awoke he told of a dream he'd had in which the Blessed Virgin appeared to him and told him that she had taken away the boy's speech as a sign of Her Favor. Sister Imaculata wondered about this, having smelled his breath, but she knew herself that the ways of God are not to be fathomed, and a priest, even drunk, is a priest, and so kept her suspicions to herself.

A year went by and one night Carlos awoke from a bad dream to see three silhouettes moving out the door: Bryce, Lockmuller and Gómez. He followed them to the tractor shed. He crept up to the door and peered in and saw the three of them sitting around an oil lamp with magazine and newspaper pictures spread around. He saw they were pictures of Amelia Earhart, who'd just flown across the Atlantic Ocean, wherever that was. They had their trousers off and were dipping their hands into a can of axle grease and rubbing them on what the nuns called the *lugar del diablo*, the Devil's playground, if you will. Carlos watched. The nuns preached hard against this particular form of sin, saying it was like driving nails into the hands of Christ. It explained why they hadn't been dragging him off in the middle of the night the last few weeks.

Around midnight the following evening the entire orphanage was awoken by screams of intense pain. No one had ever heard such screams, even the nuns, who had witnessed some terrible things in their time. There was a moon out and there they could see Bryce, Lockmuller and Gómez in the yard with no pants, holding their groins in a way that left little doubt as to the location of their agony, which seemed to increase with every minute. They jumped into the well, but this seemed to have no effect. By now the sisters had habited themselves and were trying to get from the wretched three some clue as to the cause of their pain, but they could give no coherent explanation. They just screamed and ran around in circles until the doctor came. He gave them injections that made them pass out. When they came to, he questioned them. He went to the tractor shed and examined the axle grease, found small bits of serrano pepper mixed up in it. He suspected the nuns. The sisters locked up Bryce, Lockmuller and Gómez in the root cellar for a couple of days. They emerged blinking like salamanders and scratching at chigger bites. They ran off a few days later and never returned. Shortly afterward, Carlos' powers of speech returned, an event the nuns celebrated by holding a candlelit prayer vigil on the top of a small hill nearby, where they planted a small wooden cross made by old Raul.

Four years passed and the Depression was on and there was not much to eat, mostly rotten produce wriggly with weevils and tortillas so thin the sunlight shone through them. One night while they were sipping mescal to take the edge off the hunger, Raul started to tell Carlos about a still someone had over in Pharr and what money they were making selling bootleg liquor. Raul had a small still for his mescal; it only produced a bottle every two days. Raul made a sketch on a piece of cardboard.

Next day Carlos organized the boys into teams. He and the first team stole the twenty feet of copper tubing from Ambrose's hardware; the second took a hundred pounds of corn from the troughs of Diefenbocker's hog farm. They set it up in an abandoned chicken shed a quarter mile down the road. The first few batches proofed out at somewhere over the lethal limit, occasioning one case of temporary blindness. Raul fine-tuned the proportions, sending the boys off to steal various ingredients—vanilla, ipecac, molasses, sugar—until it got so it went down without taking the esophagus with it. Raul knew a man named Geronimo, in Donna who said he'd take all he could get and sell it to the truckers on the Harlingen run. Carlos negotiated Geronimo's price up by half and within a month they were bringing in fifty dollars a week, a fortune. Carlos and Raul kept ten for themselves, and gave the rest to the nuns in the form of anonymous weekly donations of chickens, rice, chocolate bars and comics. The nuns held another candlelit vigil on the hill and planted another small cross of thanksgiving. Then Geronimo got arrested for stealing tires.

This was not Geronimo's first arrest and this time the Hidalgo County sheriff said he was going to put him away forever. Geronimo used his only bargaining chip and—nursing a grudge over Carlos' knocking his price up so—told about Carlos and the still, leaving out that he was a boy over at the Mexican nuns' orphanage outside of town. Thinking that it might enhance his situation, he embroidered some, telling the sheriff that this Carlos had got a little carried away and killed a man; he laid it on thicker than barbecue sauce. By the time he was finished the sheriff was passing out shotguns and calling in extra deputies and giving the order, as they lay in wait in a ditch by the chicken shed, to fire at the first sign of trouble. Then the sheriff barked, "Put your hands up in the air or we'll shoot!" A figure darted out of the shack and started to run, the moon caught his tin belt buckle and one of the deputies thought it was a gun and opened fire and soon they were all shooting and by the time it was over nineyear-old Irving Mayer—named for the town haberdasher—was on the ground with his legs and back full of buckshot. Charley took some pellets from the same blast in his thigh, but kept going, disappearing into the high grass in the darkness.

The bishop up in Corpus handled it cleverly, bringing the reporter with him to Irving's hospital bed and apostrophizing in his heavy brogue: *What kind of a monster does this to hungry orphan children?*—leaving aside for a moment the Eighteenth Amendment. It went all the way up to the governor's office in Austin. The sheriff had to resign and ended up as a six-dollar-a-week guard at the state penitentiary, the only consolation being that was where Geronimo was putting in his time.

Two nights after the shooting, Raul was on his knees in front of his little shrine to the Virgin, begging her for the fiftieth time that day to keep him from being arrested, when he heard the door creak open and saw Carlos, filthy, limping and one leg covered in dried blood.

He poured moonshine over his leg and removed what pellets he could. He kept the boy hidden there with him for a week until he had his strength back.

"I'll go tonight," said Carlos. "You want to come with me?" Raul shook his head and pointed to his eyes, opalescent with cataracts. He packed some food for him and they stood outside and embraced. "Wait," said Raul. He went back into the shack and emerged with a rosary that he said Pancho Villa had once personally spat on and pressed it into Carlos' palm.

Carlos had gone half a mile when he turned back. There was a row of sycamores along the road outside the orphanage, and he kept in their shadows until he reached the mailbox. He had often dreamed about his mother, very clearly. He could hear her weeping as she carried him to it, hear her tears falling on the newspaper she'd wrapped around him. In the dream he tried to hold on to her as she put him inside the mailbox; then he was inside the mailbox, suffocating and trying to get out. He always woke up at this point, crying for his mother. Once one of the nuns—a young one—took him back to her bed with him and caressed him, even his *lugar del diablo*, which gave him wonderful sensations of warmth and happiness. Unfortunately, the nun went away not long afterward.

He pried the mailbox off its oak post and, cradling it in his arms, ran along the dirt road to the barking of dogs. It was five miles to the railroad tracks and by the time he reached them his wounds were running. The tracks ran north, to Alice and Corpus Christi. He knelt by the rails and dug a hole and buried the mailbox, marking the spot with a cairn of stones. He said a prayer over it, swearing an oath to come back and get it someday, then stretched out by the mound of stones and fell asleep. The sky was just turning blue over the Gulf when the whistle woke him. It was a fast train and it nearly killed him climbing on.

Charley stood. Spook's head jerked upright as it always did when he thought there might be a walk in the offing. His eyes watched Charley as he went to the phone by his bed. The one word he recognized— "Felix"—did not signify a walk. He put his head back on the warm carpet and went back to sleep.

66

7

They were sitting in the front of the black sedan, trying to keep awake by drinking strong, hot Cuban coffee out of the thermos the cook had packed for their duck-hunting trip in the Chesapeake. Everyone thought it was a good idea for the two of them to get away. Tasha's death had been so hard. A little shivering in a duck blind off the Eastern Shore would be just the thing, no telephones, no staff, only the two of them, passing the flask in the pre-dawn chill waiting for a flight of mallards.

They were in Alphabet Town, a herniated bulge of lower Manhattan jutting out into the East River, where the avenues are named after letters.

Charley was no good at waiting—most self-made rich people aren't; Felix was. His eyes never strayed from the top floor of number 316.

Charley checked his watch for the one hundredth time. Just after 3:30 a.m. Better not drink any more coffee. He was jittery enough and he was tired of pissing in the alley. He stared at the boat in the vacant lot next to number 316. What was a boat doing on East Eighth Street between Avenues B and C?

Her lines reminded him some of the first boat he got work on out of Port Aransas after running away from the orphanage. She was eighteen, maybe twenty feet, and riding a wave of smashed-up chunks of white porcelain from old toilets and urinals, heaved out the building, probably, that used to occupy the lot—afloat on a sea of crappers. There was a ratty old heavy black armchair with springs and foam stuffing coming out sitting on her foredeck. Charley wondered who sat in it on hot summer nights, drinking wine and dreaming of black marlin. She had a name. It was spray-painted large on her hull: NOAH'S 8TH STREET YAGHT. Everything in this damn city was either misspelled or in Latin. He imagined God, fed up, with the enormity of the city's sins, loosing forty days and nights of acid rain and *Noah's 8th Street Yaght* rising up higher and higher, even higher than the World Trade Center, and coming to rest in the suburbs, atop Mount Kisco, the dove returning to Noah with a letter from the zoning commission saying his ark was in violation of local codes.

His eyes strayed to the car in front of them, a red Chevy, abandoned, up on blocks, the windows smashed in, glass all over, seats stripped. It had Connecticut plates and there was a bumper sticker proclaiming, somewhat risibly in the present context, I BRAKE FOR WHALES. Whales were not a major concern in Alphabet Town. Here the mottoes tended more to: CRACK KILLS. LA LUCHA CONTINUA. OUR CHILDREN ARE DYING. A sidewalk Siqueiros had been busy painting heroic murals of veiny forearms impaled by hypodermic needles, eyes exploding from pent-up crack smoke. Someone had copied Edvard Munch's "The Cry" in a blackened doorway littered with vials and dried vomit. In Alphabet Town art was not for witty aperçus in rooms full of Chardonnay; it tried to keep you alive. But what, Charley wondered, did it mean: YOUR DICK IS IN YOUR HAND WAKE UP 1933?

Felix stirred in the passenger seat beside him, and now even Felix checked his watch. 3:56. Charley knew nothing was going to happen tonight—in his soul, he knew it, and knowing it made him hungry.

"You want a sandwich?" Felix said he'd have a roast beef if there was one left. He said he was tired of eating cucumber sandwiches. The chef was English. Charley found one that looked like roast beef and gave it to him. The thin sandwich was tiny in Felix's hand, all out of scale.

"How come"—Felix chewed— "he always cuts off the crusts? I never understood that."

" 'Cause he's English. The English are more civilized than us. Margaret was always saying that."

"Why is cutting off the crusts civilized?"

Charley considered. "They feed the crusts to the pigeons so the pigeons don't have to eat garbage. The English eat a lot of pigeons, see."

"That doesn't sound civilized to me. I wouldn't eat pigeon."

"Hell, I don't know. What'd you used to talk about when you did stakeouts?"

"Getting laid. The Mets. How come the English cut the crusts off their sandwiches. That was a big topic of conversation."

Voices crackled over the police scanner. "Ten-sixteen, holding one. New York, one-five-six, Oscar Peter Bravo." Felix said they were checking a license plate. "Ten-ten, pick up aided case, Twelph and Avenue D. Send a bus."

"Bus," said Charley. "What's that?"

"Ambulance."

"Aided case?"

"Someone needing assistance, alive or dead." The thought took form simultaneously between them: the blue skin, the open jaw.

Felix said, "We used to play this game. The boundary between the Ninth Precinct, where I was, and the Thirteenth is along Fourteenth Street, right down the median strip. Some guys from the Thirteenth would find a body on their side of the line. These bodies, they could be real unpleasant, so they'd haul it across the street and put it on our sidewalk and call it in as one of ours. We'd get there, and you could always tell if it had been moved, so we'd haul it back across the line and call it in and say: No, uh-uh, it's one of yours. And they'd come and haul it back and say: No, it's yours. Sometimes this went on for hours, back and forth, these poor stiffs getting dragged back and forth, back and forth."

"That's a terrible story," said Charley.

"Yeah, but now you're not thinking of her anymore." Felix sat up. "Here we go."

Charley said into the radio, "Uncle Bob, Uncle Sam." They were using NYPD radio codes: "uncle" for undercover.

"Uncle Bob."

"Stepping out."

"Roger."

Two men came out of number 316, walked down the stoop and turned east on Eighth Street, toward Avenue C. One of them was Ramírez. "Shit," said Felix.

"Who's that?"

"I don't know," said Felix. "Better let him go."

"No," said Charley. "I'm not sitting here another night." He said into the radio, "Uncle Bob. Go." Felix opened the door.

A blue van was parked in front of the abandoned Chevy. The side door slammed open and two men of considerable size jumped out, one with a Remington pump, the other a nickel-plated .357. They were wearing blue windbreakers painted with large yellow letters: DEA.

Ramírez and the other man turned and ran the other way but found themselves looking at Felix, also in a DEA jacket, pointing a Smith & Wesson Model 59.

"Federal agents," he said. "You're under arrest." The two DEA men took them from behind and spread-eagled them over the remains of the Chevy that once braked for whales.

"Toss 'em," said Felix. The DEA men frisked them. They pulled a Tando knife out of Ramírez's boot and a packet of tinfoil out of the front pocket of his jeans. Inside were two dozen tiny plastic Ziploc bags of crack.

"Hey, man," Ramírez said, "these aren't my pants." Amazing, the things they would say.

One of the DEA guys laughed. "Those aren't your *pants*?"

"No, man, swear to God."

"He says they aren't his pants."

Felix said, "Are you Emiliano Ramírez?"

"No."

"But those are Emiliano's pants. You're in violation of USC 841-a-1. You have the right to remain silent, anything you say can and will be used against you in a court of law you have the right to a lawyer if you cannot afford a lawyer one will be appointed for you do you understand these rights? *Comprende sus derechos?*"

"Yeah yeah, man. Look, these aren't my fuckin' pants, man. I was up there, I put on the wrong pants."

"You put on the wrong pants?" Felix stared. "I'm going to have to talk to your valet, then." He turned to the other man. "What's your name, my man?"

"Ramón."

"What's your problem, Ramón?"

"I got no problem with you, man."

"I think you do. You been hanging out with my man Emiliano. I think you got a serious problem."

"No, man, no problem. I ain't hanging out with him."

Ramírez said, "These are *his* pants, man. He loaned me his pants."

71

"Hey, *fuck* you, man!"

"Friendship," said DEA. "It's a beautiful thing."

"Okay," said Felix, patting Emiliano's shoulder, "this one into the choo-choo. We're going down to the federal lockup, Emiliano. I hope whoever's pants those are put a toothbrush in them." One of the DEA men handcuffed Ramírez and put him inside the van.

Felix said, "Okay, Ramón." Ramón lifted himself off the hood. His hands were shaking. "I don't want to see you again, Ramón. Ever, do you understand?"

"No problem, man."

"If I ever see you again, I'm going to be unhappy."

"No problem."

"Go."

Ramón started walking west, toward Avenue B. Felix got in the car and pulled out into the street. "I think my man Ramón made a ca-ca in his pants."

He looked in the rearview for the van. It hadn't pulled out yet. Felix stopped. "What's going on?" They couldn't see.

Ramón had reached the corner by the church when the bullet hit him, a good shot at that distance with a pistol. He fell forward onto his face, blood spurting out of the tiny hole in the center of the back of his skull.

The van pulled out into the street and caught up. They had the light and got on the FDR northbound at Twenty-third Street.

8

It was going on midnight. He was at the corner of University Place and Thirteenth, about to cross, when he heard his name being called. He turned and saw the limousine at the curb. At first he thought it was Bernie's, then he saw Felix in the driver's seat.

"Charley?" He peered into the open window, saw the glow of a cigar.

"Well, don't just stand there," said Charley in a friendly way. "Get in."

"Actually, I'm on my way to a meeting."

"A meeting? At this hour?"

"Yeah."

"Well, get in anyway. I'm cheaper than any cab."

"I don't want to take you out of your way."

"Out of my way?" Charley laughed. "I got no meeting to go to. Come on, it's cold."

"You sure?" Tim got in. The glass partition was down. He said, "How are you, Felix." Felix did not return the greeting, which struck Tim as a little rude, frankly. Tim never liked Felix, the way he looked at him.

"Been trying to reach you," said Charley.

"I know. I'm sorry. It's been crazy. You heard about the show?"

"I did. I think it's great."

"I should have called."

"Don't apologize for being a success. I'm just happy I ran into you like this. What a coincidence, huh? In a city this size."

"Yeah. So, you ... doing all right?"

"Fine. You?"

Tim sighed. "I'm doing all right. Industry is the enemy of melancholy."

"I like that. Is that Shakespeare?"

"Just a saying. It means—"

"I think I grasp it. I like it. I think I'll put that in our little

73

newspaper. My company has a little in-house newspaper. Sayings of Chairman Charley sort of thing. I like to put inspirational things in it. I'll put that in. Don't you like that, Felix?"

Felix didn't answer. Charley whispered to Tim, "Don't mind him. Cuban, you know. Moody. I think it's all that sugar in the blood."

The streets were going by the wrong way. "Actually, I'm going uptown," said Tim.

"No problem," said Charley. "What time's your meeting?"

"Well, now. I mean, it's my meeting. It starts when I get there."

Charley chuckled. "It's good when they become your meetings. I remember when it got to the point they were my meetings. You know how I made my first serious money? Landing craft. I was coming home from the war—I'd been in the infantry—I was coming home from the war, getting on a ship, and I saw all these landing craft, miles of landing craft, sitting there with nothing left to invade, and I said to myself: I bet those could be had for a *song*. All I had to do was come up with the song. Now, Margaret's daddy, he was a terrible drunk, that's the only reason he would have let her marry someone like myself, first mate on a charter fishing boat. I never told you about how I married Margaret, did I?"

They were going into the tunnel. "Brooklyn?" said Tim.

"You know, when I first saw Brooklyn, there was ships fighting with each other trying to get space at the piers. Now look at it. Unions. Look back there," he said, toward Manhattan. "That's where Herman Melville first sailed from. You know what he wrote? He wrote something beautiful and true: 'Our souls are like those orphans whose mothers die in bearing them; the secret to our paternity lies in their graves, and we must there to learn it.' I didn't know it until someone explained it to me, but did you know *Moby Dick* isn't about whales."

"No."

"It's about orphans. I'm an orphan. That's why my family was so important to me."

"Charley, where are we going?" They were driving through an abandoned area of waterfront, into a warehouse on a pier. Tim saw an RV parked in a far corner. They pulled up alongside of it.

Felix opened the door for Charley. Charley got out. Tim stayed inside. "Come on," said Charley, "got someone I want you to meet."

"That's okay."

"Well, I can't introduce you if you stay inside the car."

"I can't."

"You can't? What do you mean?"

"I have agoraphobia."

"What?"

"Fear of spaces."

"Felix," said Charley, "we got anything in the first aid for agoraphobia?" Felix stuck his head in the door; Tim got out. What he saw inside the van gave him a bad start. Ramírez was sitting scrunched on a settee between two large men. One of the men was reading *Architectural Digest*, the other *House & Garden*. He saw another, similar-looking man by the kitchen area taking apart a coffee-making machine. He looked up at Tim in a way that was frightening for its apparent lack of interest.

Charley said, "I believe you know Mr. Ramírez there. That's Mr. McNamara on his left and Mr. Bundy on his right. And over there is Mr. Rostow. You making coffee, Mr. Rostow?"

"I'm trying to make cappuccino, but these instructions are in Italian."

"Plain coffee would be fine. Sit down, son," he said to Tim. "Mr.

Ramírez has made certain allegations. He's said you called him around four-thirty on the day my granddaughter was killed in a state of some excitement and threatened to give his name to the police as the supplier of a certain gram of cocaine unless he met with you immediately."

"That's completely—"

"Hold on, hold on, I want to hear your side of it, but hear me out. He says you told him to meet you at this bar on Spring Street and made him stay with you until seven-thirty, when you both went to this place, Gulag, until after two."

"That's absurd. That wasn't it at all."

"Okay. The floor's all yours."

"I think I know why he's saying this, though. Yeah, it makes sense. He's probably the one who gave Tasha the coke."

Ramírez exploded. "You lying piece of shit. He's lying."

"I don't like that language, Emiliano."

Tim whispered, "Charley, what's going on here? This guy's a *coke* dealer."

"I know. We been watching him."

"Well?"

"That's why I'm curious why you'd be spending time with him. Successful person like yourself."

Tim sighed with relief. "Jesus, is that it? It was research."

"Research?" said Charley.

"You know the character in the play, José? The dealer? We want to change his part a little. One of the stage people told me about this guy here, works as an usher sometimes at the theater, only so he can sell coke. That interested me, so I decided to interview him and see what I could find out about the dope business. That's why we went to that place, Gulag."

"I see."

"He's fucking lying!" Ramírez shouted. Bundy swatted him on the head with *Architectural Digest*.

But Ramírez went on. "He called me on my beeper and told me she's dead, man, she fucking died and I'm gonna tell the cops it was you if you don't do like I say."

"Charley, please—"

"It's all right, son. I know it couldn't have been you anyhow. The medical examiner said she died between eight and midnight, and you were in that club with him then."

"Right."

"And you left her place at four-thirty."

"Right."

Charley grabbed a fistful of his shirt and pushed him against the wall. The Winnebago shook. "You son of a bitch."

"Charley, you've got me confused. I wasn't at her place." Charley reached under his arm and drew his old Army Colt .45 and put it to Tim's forehead. He said, "Talk."

"She called me. She was upset about the review. She said she'd bought cocaine from this usher at the theater. She said she was going to do the whole gram until she had the role authenticated. I pleaded with her not to do it. I told her it was dangerous. She said she didn't care. Christ, Charley, you know how she was. I rushed over, called her from the phone booth, that was the first message I got on the machine. She let me in. By the time I got there she was already flying. She'd done like half the gram. She was gone. Then she just keeled, dead."

"Why didn't you call for help?"

"She was dead, Charley. There was no heartbeat. I gave her CPR. She was dead."

"You should have called for help."

"She was *dead*. Either your heart is beating or it's not beating. Hers wasn't beating. I panicked, okay? I'd just heard the show might be moving uptown, my first real break, and, and I panicked, okay? I'm guilty of panicking. But that's all. The medical examiner doesn't know what he's talking about. She was dead at four-twenty or four twenty-five. By the couch."

Charley threw open the door and went outside. He put his head against the metal side of the RV and pressed it there. Felix went to him. Charley moaned, "They found her in the bathroom. He left her to die."

Felix started up the steps. Charley stopped him.

Five minutes passed before the door opened and Charley reentered the RV. Tim was sweaty and pale. Charley said somberly, "I will not drag her good name through the papers. It's done. You'll have to live the rest of your life with this and I pray to God it drives you screaming off a cliff someday. Now get out."

"Charley, I feel badly—"

"GET OUT."

Tim closed the door behind him and breathed in the cold night air, still trembly. Felix said, "I'm supposed to take you back. Get in."

"I'll walk, that's all right."

Felix stared. "You wouldn't last two minutes in this neighborhood. Get in." Tim climbed in back, Felix in the front. He started the car. The glass partition slid up. Tim was grateful for that. He heard a hissing coming from beneath the seat. It seemed a little too loud for heat. He looked. Two streams of white smoke. He reached for the door handle; it was locked. It was a chemical smell, like, actually it was—Jesus—wonderful. He felt great. He'd never felt this great. It was so incredibly great, like a great opening night, only more ... great.

Charley and Ramírez spoke in Spanish. "Who gave you the cocaine you sold to Tim?" Ramírez had not quite grasped the essence of his situation and was now demanding his lawyer and phone call. Finally Charley said to Ramírez that he could discuss the matter either with him or with the two men bookending him.

Ramírez said, "If I give you his name, he will kill me."

"No." Charley shook his head convincingly. "I promise you that will not happen. And I will pay for the information."

"How much?"

"Five thousand dollars."

The prospect of money seemed to relax Ramírez. "Fifty," he said.

Charley considered. "No."

"Forty-five."

"Ten."

"Forty."

Charley said, "Ten. And my offer is good for ten seconds. After that"—he nodded in the direction of McNamara— "our negotiation will proceed to another phase."

Ramírez gave a name and address in Hunts Point. Charley pointed to the crucifix around his neck.

"Are you Catholic, Emiliano?"

"*Sí sí. Muy católico.*"

"Hold the cross in your hand." Puzzled, Ramírez held the crucifix.

79

"Repeat after me: I swear by the Holy Cross of Jesus and by His Holy Mother, the Virgin, that what I've just said is true, and if it is not true, then may I spend eternity in hell and may my grand-mother, mother, aunts and sisters spend eternity in hell."

"No problem, man." That wasn't quite the right answer. Charley was disappointed in Emiliano. He cocked his .45. Ramírez produced a different name and address, and a phone number. Charley dialed the number on the cellular telephone and handed it to Ramírez, the .45 aimed at his head. "Prove it," he said. Ramírez called Uguarte and said he needed more "oranges." Amazing, the codes they used—like someone listening in wouldn't know what "oranges" was.

Charley said, "Who do you want to get the money?" There were some awkward moments as Ramírez figured it out. He began to cry and that didn't help. He said to send the money to his mother, Rosa, and gave her address. Charley cocked his .45 and urged him to be a man. At which point Ramírez began blubbering. "*Por el amor de Dios, un cura. Por el amor de Dios, un cura.*" Charley lowered the gun. Felix caught the stricken look.

"What's the problem?" he whispered.

"He's asking for a priest."

"Yeah. So?"

"Well, I can't shoot a man who's asking for a priest."

"Why?"

"You know *why*."

Rostow came over. "What's the problem?"

Felix said, "He wants a priest."

"Uh-huh. So?"

"So."

Rostow shrugged. "It's always like this. When you want a priest, there's never one around."

"You Catholic, Rostow?" said Charley testily.

"Presbyterian."

"Then I wouldn't *expect* you to understand."

Rostow looked at Felix. Felix drew Charley off to one side. "I don't get it. You're saying you want to take him to a church, *then* shoot him?"

"No," said Charley. "I'm not sure that's feasible."

"Okay."

"My bill's going to be high enough as it is, Felix. I don't want that on my tab."

"Okay," Felix said, shrugging. "I'll shoot him."

"No. We got a Yellow Pages on board?"

"What?" said Felix.

"A Yellow Pages, a telephone book, damnit. Hell with it." Charley punched 411. "Operator, give me the name of a Catholic church, please. Any church. I don't have a particular church. Look, it doesn't matter. Oh, for cryin' out loud. St. Mary's Church. *Any* St. Mary's. First St. Mary's you got. ... Fine. Yes. ... *Thank* you. Christ in heaven, where do they get operators like that, in the Soviet Union?" He dialed.

"Excuse me," Rostow was whispering to Felix, "but what the hell is going on here?"

"He's calling a priest," said Felix.

"Hello?" said Charley. "I'm sorry, I know it's late, but I need to talk to a priest. ... You are? Good. All right now, Padre, now listen up. Got a man here gonna die—he's slipping fast—and he wants to say his piece to a priest ... No, there's no time, believe me, he's almost gone as it is. ... No, this is not a joke, on my heart, this is very serious."

Charley stabbed at the "hold" button and pointed the pistol at

81

Ramírez and said, "Okay, Emiliano, I got your priest on the line. You say one word not directly related to your immortal soul and you'll be in hell before he can give you forgiveness and you'll spend all eternity there wondering why you were so damn stupid."

Ramírez's confession went on for a full ten minutes. Even Rostow, McNamara and Bundy were impressed. Charley felt indecent holding the gun to old Ramírez's head like that while he unpacked his sorry soul, but there wasn't much he could do about that.

Tim was discovered on the floor of his apartment next to a crack pipe and several rocks of the same, dead of an acute heart attack. They found massive traces of it in his lungs and blood, enough to kill several people. Everyone was stunned. This obsession with authenticity was getting out of hand. Who was next, the set designer? Theater people were calling the play *MacWired*, because it was starting to look as jinx-ridden as *Macbeth*. Bernie and Karen were horrified, though the publicity was frankly having a tremendous effect on sales. Jimmy Podesta wrote a piece for the *Times* Op-Ed. Charley sent a nice floral arrangement to the funeral, along with his regrets that he couldn't attend. He remained in seclusion on his island in the Chesapeake, but he did issue a statement through his company spokesman saying it was a tragedy such young and talented lives were being taken while the government refused to get serious about the problem.

9

Senior Agent Frank Diatri (that's Dee-atri), holding his yogurt and bran, stepped off the elevator of the nineteenth floor of 555 West Fifty-seventh Street in New York City, Divisional Office of the Drug Enforcement Administration, and right away everyone made a fuss.

"Frankie! How ya doin?"

"Great," said Diatri.

"Yeah?" said Gubanovich unconvincingly. "You look great."

How the hell were you supposed to look, like you just got back from a Carnival Cruise? Alice and Marge came up and started kissing him. "Oh, jeez, Frankie, we were so worried," Alice said. "Didja get the card?"

"Do you want some coffee, Frankie?"

"I'm not supposed to drink coffee."

"Oh, Frankie, I'm sorry! What am I saying?"

"Marge, it's okay. I'm fine. It's these doctors. They don't want you to do anything."

Marge said, "My aunt had the same thing."

Diatri stared. "Your aunt got shot?"

"No. But they hadda take some of her intestine out." She whispered, "Do you have to wear a bag?"

"No, Marge. Listen, I gotta go eat this yogurt. If I don't eat yogurt every two hours, I die."

"Aw, Frankie, you're sure a—here, you get another kiss."

"I'm going to have to get shot more often," said Diatri. He must have been stopped twenty times on the way to his desk, everyone wanting to know the particulars. It was a little embarrassing, to tell the truth. He hoped Marge hadn't been going around telling everyone he had to wear a bag. His desk wasn't too bad, except for a Styrofoam coffee cup by his phone that looked like a bacteriological experiment, with gray fur growing out of it. But there were flowers—white carnations—with a note saying: "From NADDIS with love." Aw. He recognized Phyllis' handwriting. He was always asking Phyllis to run his Narcotics And Dangerous Drugs Information System searches on the computer. Phyllis used to have a crush on him, but now she was dating a guy in Asset Seizure. Should have—probably just as well. But that was nice of Phyllis. People are always so nice after you get shot; except for Suzie. Suzie actually seemed a little put out when he got back after getting wounded the second time, like she would have rather had the monthly VA checks instead. Turning on Cronkite every night during dinner. Sweetheart, I just got back, can we not watch the war on TV every night, please?—

"Frankie!"

"Gene, hey."

"You look good."

"That's what everyone is saying."

"Listen, Frankie, what happened with Kincaid was a fuckin' disgrace. Five to fifteen for illegal possession of weapons. I mean, they should've nailed the fuck's ears to the wall with a Hilti gun."

"Hilti gun?"

"Nail driver. What the hell is that?" he said, pointing at the Styrofoam cup.

"It's just an experiment I'm doing."

"It's disgusting, Frank."

The Special Agent in Charge called him down to his office. "You look great, Frank."

Diatri gave his stomach a loud whack. "Never better." The SAC winced. "I was just going over your medical. You were leaking pretty bad there."

"Two quarts," said Diatri.

"You know what the worst part of being shot is these days?"

Not this again. "How's Ellen, Jim?"

"Same-same. The blood. The blood is what scares me. I mean, I'm sure you got good blood."

"Yeah," said Diatri. "They test it."

"Me, I'd make them run it through fucking chlorine first. Then charcoal. You know what I'd like to set up? Our own blood bank. You know, I sent a memo to the AA about it."

"Good idea, Jim. And what did the AA say?"

"I haven't heard back yet. You know how it is down there."

"Oh yeah," said Diatri.

"So, what are we going to do with you?"

This was a very strange question, he thought, the kind you'd put to a summer intern, not a Senior Agent who'd twice passed up a promotion to Group Supervisor and five extra grand a year just so he could stay on the street. Diatri told people he did it to keep the five grand from going to his two exes. "Your medical says you're fit, but I thought we might, you know, ease back in."

"We?" said Diatri. "You sound like the nurses." He gave his stomach another demo whack. The SAC winced. "Frank, will you stop hitting yourself?"

"What does it say?"

"It says you're okay—"

"Okay, then. What do you got for me?"

The SAC handed Diatri a sheet. It was court order for a wiretap. Diatri said, "A T-Three? Are you serious?"

"I got Title Threes up to my crotch, Frank. I could really use you."

85

Diatri stared. He twisted the ring on his wedding finger. It was a leftover from a UC job a couple of years ago where he had to look like a pimp. He bought all this stuff at one of those community-conscious boutiques on Times Square that sell Ninja swords, bull-whips, blowguns, choke wires and kukri knives. It looked like a Sicilian version of a West Point class ring, with a tiny photo of the young Frank Sinatra underneath a hunk of cheap blue glass. People gave him grief about it. Diatri continued to stare.

"Okay," said the SAC. He handed Diatri a folder. "We got a call from the Ninth Precinct."

"The Fighting Ninth," said Diatri, untensing.

"They found a body on one of their sidewalks yesterday. A Ramón Antonio Luis, local crack dealer. Twenty-two caliber in the back of the head. Puerto Rican kid works at an all-night gypsy cab place on the block told them he saw some people wearing our raid jackets. It's all in the 6i," he said, handing Diatri the police report.

"We have anything going down there?"

"No. We had two groups out that night, one in Brooklyn, one in the Bronx."

"Is Internal Security working this?"

"They're ... no. We gonna work this ourselves, then if it turns out there's something, Internal Security can get involved."

"I see this is a real red-hot case."

"Look, Frank—"

"Luis' biggest prior was for," Diatri read, "two ounces. *Ounces,* Jack? You want me to work someone who does ounces?"

"Someone maybe wearing our raid jackets popped the guy. It could be an important case."

"Yeah."

"Hey, if you'd rather work the T-Threes ..."

Diatri got up. "No no. I'm honored. I mean, we can't have scumbags going around popping each other wearing our raid jackets."

"Personally," said the SAC, "I think the kid probably needs glasses. Frank, I'm sorry about Kincaid. If it's any consolation, they went fucking berserk in Washington over it. The administrator went to Bennett and requested a meeting in the White House."

"Uh-huh," said Diatri.

"The White House doesn't want to piss off the State Supreme Court, so they ended up not having a meeting."

"Uh-huh."

"Jesus, Frank, don't be so fuckin' nonchalant. I'm telling you the Administrator himself took it all the way to the fuckin' White House."

"I'm grateful, Jim. Truly."

"Don't let it eat you up."

"Hah. Hey, I've only got so much intestine left, right?"

"Right. That's it." Diatri started out the door. "Listen," the SAC said, "take your time on it. Ease into it. Remember what happened to Shamalbach."

Diatri sat at his desk munching lactose tablets and read over the 61 on the shooting of Ramón Antonio Luis, male, Hispanic, five eight, 145, mid-thirties, fourteen priors, mostly assaults, B and A, possession, possession with intent, possession with intent, possession with ... babum babum babum. Nothing interesting here at all except the caliber of the bullet that had interrupted such a promising career. Twenty-two long rifle, the "Devastator," same that Hinckley used on Reagan, the roach motel of small-arms ammunition: bullet goes in, can't go out, breaks up into little pieces. Generally, dopers wanted a lot of bang for their bucks: 9mms,

87

.357s, .380 ACPs, 7.65s, .44s, .45s. Some were using the new 10mms. In this market, a .22 was unusual. The mob used to use .22s because they went in fast and clean and ricocheted around inside the skull, pureeing the old cauliflower.

Diatri couldn't remember his NADDIS access code. It disturbed him. It was like forgetting your Social Security number. "Sylvia, give me Gubanovich's access code, would you?" Sylvia looked good. What was that she was wearing, seamed stockings? Who'd have thought those would come back. There was nothing in NADDIS on Ramón Antonio Luis. A million and a half files in the data base, and nothing on him. Two ounces was just nothing to get excited over these days; certainly Diatri wasn't excited. His Sig Sauer 9mm felt a little tight against his stomach.

The Puerto Rican kid at the AMANECER CAR SERVICE ABIERTO 24 HORAS on East Eighth Street reacted the way people usually reacted when they saw Frank Diatri flash his badge. Diatri could inspire nervousness even without showing ID. He was strongly built, just under six feet, genetically pre-tanned, with liquid brown eyes that glommed on to yours and didn't let go until you'd accounted for yourself. Despite the permanently disappointed look, he smiled easily and people were usually grateful for that; the Puerto Rican kid was. Diatri spoke Spanish with him. The kid said he was sure the jackets said D-E-A. Diatri had him step out onto the sidewalk. He pointed to an ad in a bus shelter on Avenue C and asked him to read what it said.

"A-t l-a-s-t S-t-r-e-e-p t-a-l-k-s."

"*Veinte/veinte,*" Diatri grinned.

He stood on the sidewalk by the Church of Santa Brigida where

Ramón Antonio Luis had died. The blood had congealed into a threefoot-wide brown patch. Diatri thought of lying in his own pool of blood and the elevator door closing and the elevator going up and the door opening and the woman seeing him and screaming and running back to her apartment—Thank you, ma'am—and the elevator door going down to another floor and a little girl seeing him and screaming and running away. He was going to die in the elevator going up and down, up and down, with the doors opening and people screaming.

Detective Korn showed him the photographs from the scene. "A real fucking tragedy," he said.

Diatri looked at the close-up of the back of Luis' head. "Powder burns?"

"Not a speck," said Korn admiringly. "And a twenty-two pistol. Look at that shot. Right in the ten ring."

"Marksman, huh?"

"This," said Korn, "was a samaritan."

"I'm getting a sense here," said Diatri, "that you didn't like Ramón."

"He sold crack."

"I know, but look at him here. And in front of a church. Someone could slip."

"You know what you do with that? Throw a little sand on it. Look," said Korn, "just between you and I, if you guys had something going on and something happened—it's not a problem for me."

Diatri laughed. "Aw no, you don't mean that."

Korn looked at him. "No," he said. "Course not. I got a seventy-nine-year-old woman in Peter Cooper this morning someone beat to death with a steam iron after they raped her. Also I got a three-year-old kid whose father squashed his head in between the radiator bars because he was crying." He sighed. "They get such terrible deaths, these kids. Luis here, on my scale of one to ten, he doesn't even show up."

10

"How many?" asked Miss Farrell.

"Two," said Charley, scanning the clipboard she always met him with at the elevator.

Two ducks over five days? Miss Farrell was not herself an aficionada of blood sports, but still it seemed an inglorious bag. It surprised her that Mr. Becker would be hunting at all, the season being closed. He looked tired, she thought, though certainly better than he looked at the funeral. Usually he came from the island with more color in his cheeks.

She was just bringing coffee a few minutes later when she heard him shout, "God*damnit*!" He had *The New York Times* spread in front of him. He often swore when reading it, especially Mr. Safire's columns, but as she set the coffee down she noticed the paper was open to pages 2 and 3 of the Metropolitan section, not the editorial pages.

"Get me Felix," he said, not lifting his eyes from the paper. She studied her own copy of the *Times* while waiting for the call to go through. She found no clue to the old man's explosion. Felix came on. It was not a good connection. He said he was on the New Jersey Turnpike. She put him through. She couldn't resist listening to the conversation.

"You read the paper this morning?" said Charley.

90

"The paper? No."

"They with you?"

"No. Is there a problem?"

"You bet there's a problem. There's a very significant problem. Where are they?"

"At the dock."

"I'm coming back to the island. I'll see you there tonight. Out."

She used the excuse of bringing in an updated list of people who'd sent condolence letters. He'd tossed the paper to the side, but he'd torn a piece from the bottom of page B3. Back at her own desk, she compared the missing piece with her copy. All she found was a small story, a filler item:

MAN SHOT TO DEATH
IN EAST VILLAGE

A man with a history of narcotics violations was found shot to death early yesterday morning on East 8th Street shortly before dawn.

Police say Ramon Antonio Luis, 34, of no known address, was killed by a single gunshot to the back of the head. A spokesman for the Ninth Precinct Detective Squad described the killing as "clearly drug-related," but added, "We're pursuing this as we would any murder, vigorously."

It couldn't have been that. Then she noticed next to the story was the runover from the story on page Bi, about the opening of Felix Rohatyn's new restaurant. Must have been that. Perhaps Mr. Becker was upset at not being invited.

There was a fog on Chesapeake Bay and it was just as well since it matched his mood. Charley walked up and down the wood plank pier, grinding an unlit Upmann into a chewy wet stub. Spook, having given up on being thrown something to retrieve, had jumped in anyway and swam alongside, keeping pace with his master. Charley reached the end of the pier and turned around, Spook following. Back and forth, back and forth, boots clumping on wood, Labrador grunts in icy water.

Charley was trying to decide which one of them had done it. Rostow, he'd bet. Rostow had been "allowed to retire" from DEA after shooting the bodyguard of a Peruvian *narco*. Self-defense, yes, but they're so touchy down there about our people killing their people. It's not legal, strictly speaking. Only a sudden infusion of U.S. aid, which the State Department wrangled out of DEA's appropriations, got him out. They found him doing security for a manufacturer of high-speed dental drilling equipment in Wilkes-Barre, Pennsylvania.

McNamara and Bundy he found through his friend the colonel, who ran the Army's SERE school at Fort Bragg. Survival Evasion Resistance Escape. Charley had given four hundred POWs a week at the Greenbriar Hotel after they got back from Vietnam, and he and the colonel had stayed in touch over the years. Charley had come down to visit the school, and was impressed. The colonel could take men scared to death of snakes and after they spent thirty days in that school of his, every water moccasin in his swamp would have four, five, sometimes six hungry troopers following after it trying to get to it first. The instructors were impressive, most of them having served with the Special Forces in Vietnam— as the colonel had before his five and a half years at the Hanoi Hilton—a number of them recruited by CIA into the Special Operations Groups. "Some of my executives are getting a little flabby," Charley explained. "I have in mind a program that would combine exercise, diet and survival. We have offices overseas, and you saw what Ross Perot had to go through to get his boys out of Teheran after that maniac took over. I'm thinking of calling it 'Upward Bound.' I mean, show me a man who'd chase down a water moc for his dinner and I'll show you one *hell* of a motivated manager." The colonel was only too happy to oblige him with the names of some of his former instructors. Charley interviewed dozens of them. Word spread through the company that the old man was setting up some kind of horrible fitness program. Miss Farrell got a call from the VP for sales asking if it was true all the divisional heads were being sent to some swamp in Louisiana to eat snakes. She hadn't heard anything about that, she said, but the gentlemen Mr. Becker was interviewing certainly appeared to be the kind for whom a diet of reptiles would pose no problem. "Jesus," muttered the VP.

Charley settled on McNamara and Bundy. Big Mac described himself as a hands-on kind of guy who had gotten very wet in Vietnam but who had drawn the line at eating Vietcong liver. "Something the folks in Psy Ops thought up," he explained to Charley. "The Vietcong, they believe that you have to be whole to enter heaven, so the idea was to take out the liver and bite a chunk out of it and leave it on the ground beside the body." He shrugged. "You want to know the honest truth, I was just never partial to liver in the first place." Bundy was a weapons specialist from Georgia, a sniper. His dossier was full of "CITATION CLASSIFIED"s and he would not say what they had been for, other than to point at each and say, "Thousand meters, seven hundred meters in a crosswind, twelve hundred meters."

A few days after Charley had made his selection, Felix, posing as

93

an FBI agent, paid McNamara, Bundy and Rostow separate visits, asking them if they'd been approached by a Mr. Charles Becker in connection with certain criminal services. They each denied it and reported the contact to Charley. It was something Charley prided himself on, being able to get the measure of a man right.

He heard the rumble of the engines through the fog and then saw the running lights, red and green, heading straight for the pier. Spook started swimming out to it. Charley told him to come back, stop being foolish, you can't fetch a whole boat.

Felix was at the wheel, looking ragged from not having slept in two nights, carrying a limp body up a four-story walk-up and then driving the other from Manhattan to Cambridge, Maryland. Ramírez was in a crate marked "Frozen Turkeys—Perishable." Spook came running down the pier, wet, and started barking at the crate as though it contained a year's supply of Purina Dog Chow. McNamara and Bundy, being the two largest, did most of the carrying as the procession moved by flashlight down the pier and along the shore and up the path that cut through the honey locust to the clearing of heather and moss where Charley, over Felix's strange objections, had decided he was going to put his garden. Sure enough, he started in as soon as they'd set the box down, none too gently.

"Boss," he said, "I wish we wouldn't put them here."

"Felix, we been over that."

"She had a special feeling about this place."

Charley said, "You remember that walrus tusk?" It was one summer he took *Conquistador* up to New England. They were in Nantucket and she found a walrus tusk in a shop; it had a hole drilled through the tip and a leather thong looped through it. She had the sweet arrogance of youth; was appalled to find a walrus tusk for sale in a store. She asked the owner what the hole and thong were for, and he said they'd used the tusk to club baby seals to death and the thong was just so they could hang the club on a nail in the wall after they were done killing the baby seals. That did it. She made Charley buy the thing—$500 worth of walrus molar— and scoured the town until she found a scrimshander to scratch "Save the Seals" all over it, and while he was at it, "No Nukes," and "Arms are for loving," and other slogans that made Charley groan to pay for.

"Yeah," said Felix. "So?"

"She said it was to get the 'negative energy' out of it. That's just what we're doing here. Getting the negative energy out."

"No no," said Felix. "you're putting negative energy *in*. This is a special place and you're filling it up with drug dealers."

"Think of them as fertilizer," said Charley. "I'm thinking of planting—it's too shady for roses. Maybe some ferns and wildflow- ers. Those meadow anemones she liked. Maybe some wild columbine. That's hardy. Lady slipper, blue lobelia." Felix was look- ing more and more like a basset hound, but it was something he could not explain, there was just no way he could explain it.

McNamara and Bundy dug and said they hadn't done any dig- ging since the early seventies and wanted to know if there was Ben- Gay, because they were going to need it tomorrow. Charley kept looking over at Rostow, but he wasn't going to say anything yet. Spook kept barking at the crate. When the hole was deep enough they opened it up and tossed Ramírez in and shoveled it over. They all stood around for a moment wondering if Charley was going to call a priest on the cordless and ask him to say a few words.

Back in the cabin Charley waited until they'd settled in with beers by the fire. He took the *New York Times* clipping out of his pocket and put it on the coffee table. The men stared at it. Charley said, "All right, who did it?"

It was obvious. A CIA polygrapher had told Charley once you could usually tell if a man was lying if he looked up and wiggled his eyes.

"Rostow," said Charley. Rostow picked up the clipping and read it and put it down.

"A little collateral damage is inevitable," he said. The others nodded. So they were all in on it. Well, goddamnit.

"Collateral damage?" said Charley. "Hold on just a moment here. He was walking away and, and you shot the sumbitch!"

Rostow said, "Mac and Bundy and I agreed that a no-witness policy made sense." McNamara and Bundy nodded.

"Agreed? Who the hell are you, the board of trustees?" Bundy started flipping through *Colonial Homes*, Mac looking over his shoulder. During the Ramírez planning session the two of them had gotten into an argument over whether kilims went with Saltillo tiles. It occurred to him that he—rather, the late Mr. Luis—was the victim of the incentive package he'd put together. In addition to the million dollars—and the medical, the stock options—they'd each receive a CPI-adjusted yearly bonus of $100,000 for the rest of their lives, as long as the operation remained secret. It was meant to encourage mutual enforcing. If one of them said anything, the other two were likely to look him up and express their unhappiness over the loss of their retirement package.

"Well, damnit," said Charley, it being about all he could say.

Rostow said, "There wasn't time to get him a priest, but I did him in front of the church there. You must get some credit for dying in front of a church, right?"

"Right," said Mac helpfully, looking up from *Colonial Homes*.

11

"Book me five suites at the Biltmore Hotel in Coral Gables," said Charley, charging out of the elevator from the rooftop chopper pad at his old velocity. He was still in his hunting clothes, tracking dust from dried mud. These hunting trips were certainly restorative, she thought; he no longer looked the broken man he was at the funeral. "For tonight," he said, peeling off his jacket and tossing it onto the sofa. He left a trail of clothes on the way to the shower, an old habit from his days on the shrimp boats along the Gulf coast. Margaret used to give him hell for it. Miss Farrell picked up his jacket. There was something on the sleeve.

"Tonight," she said absently, studying the stain. Charley took quick showers. He was on his way to his desk in the oversize terry bathrobe when Miss Farrell's assistant's voice said on the boom box in a worried tone, "Sir, there are two men here from the FBI to see you."

Miss Farrell looked at the jacket she was holding and folded it to her breast. There was a back way out of Charley's office; she headed for it. On her way out she heard Charley say, "Send 'em in. And can we have some coffee, please?"

They were in there twenty minutes. Miss Farrell couldn't concentrate. When the door finally opened, she looked up, stricken. She heard Charley say, "And the politician says to the Devil, 'What's the catch?'" The FBI men laughed. Charley followed them out. He shook their hands and said, "I'm sorry to cause you all this trouble."

"What was that about?" she asked.

"Oh," said Charley, "I strayed a little too close to Andrews on the way back from the island. Air Force Two was on final and, well, it's nothing, really, just ... You know," he said, chuckling, "I used to let Tasha handle the controls sometimes and the same thing happened, we just kissed the inside of the Restricted Airspace and all hell broke loose. They scrambled an F-4, buzzed us, nearly knocked us down. Damn near wet my pants. Course, she thought it was the greatest thing ever happened. Tell Chuck to have Forty-nine ninety fueled for Miami with a five o'clock wheels-up. Now what do I have for today?"

"What's going on in Miami?" Miss Farrell asked.

"Office been swept this month?" They'd found a listening device in the sofa a few years ago after a visit by a man representing Futaki DSM Corporation. Charley left it there so he could feed it disinformation about Becker Industries' progress with SmartPlastics, until Futaki was convinced BI was a year behind schedule.

"Yes," said Miss Farrell.

Charley whispered, "Eastern Airlines."

Miss Farrell arched her eyebrows in appreciation, though on reflection she wondered why on earth Charley would want to acquire such a headache at this, well, stage in his life. "Do you want me down there with you?"

"I would very much," he sighed, "but Lorenzo is just paranoid about leaks. What's left of it, it's his company, so I have to play by his rules."

"Who's going?"

"Me and Felix. Plus some people from M and A." Mergers and Acquisitions.

She could feel his eyes following her as she walked out. He said, "Jeannie?"

"Yes, Charley?"

"Are you seeing anyone? I don't mean to pry. I just—"

"No."

"Well," he said, pleased, "perhaps when I get back you'd care to come out to the farm. As a guest, I mean."

She sent the clothes to be cleaned. The jacket she took home and soaked in lighter fluid and burned.

Felix, Rostow, McNamara and Bundy were waiting for him on the tarmac at Opa-Locka when the G-4 whined to a full stop Charley stepped out into the warm Miami night and reflected that Miami was one of few places where there was nothing unusual about a private jet being met by four large men with armpit bulges. He rode in front with Felix, another habit that drove Margaret nuts.

"How's it look?"

"It looks like it's not going to be easy," said Felix.

"Well, we're working our way up the food chain," said Charley. "The fish are getting bigger. What about the hotel?"

"It's nice. Which's good, because I have a feeling we're going to be here for a long time."

The Biltmore was a grand affair, built in the twenties at the height of the Florida land boom and subsequently vexed by the worst hurricane in the state's history and the stock market crash. Since then it had served a variety of inglorious functions, such as military housing, until finally the city of Coral Gables bought it—

rather than watch it slide further into desuetude—pouring fifty million into it to restore it to its quondam jazz Age splendor. Architecturally it was a tad difficult to pin down, and right away McNamara and Bundy fell to arguing over what was Mediterranean versus Moorish, Spanish Revival or Beaux Arts or Gothic Renaissance. Listening to them while he checked in, Charley was certain of one thing, anyway: no one would mistake them for a couple of hired killers.

He had sandwiches and coffee sent up to the Everglades Suite. "All right," he said, "what's the plan?" No one spoke up. "What's the matter?" said Charley. The sandwiches were on a platter. Mac reached for an olive and held it up to his eye and peered through the hole.

"Don't," said Bundy. "Don't do that."

Chin's beeper had gone off during the interrogation and right away it was clear he was more terrified by the prospect of not returning his boss's phone call than by these men who had plucked him somewhat roughly off the street, and in a way the reason had to do with olives.

The late Antonio Chin's boss was Jesús Celaya Barazo, the purpose of their stay in Coral Gables. For years he had been importing a thousand kilos of cocaine—one metric ton—each week from the Reynaldo Cabrera family of Medellín. Then, suddenly, Barazo announced he had found a new supplier and would no longer accept shipments from Cabrera. Since the loss to Cabrera's organization amounted to about $15 million a week—as well as his invaluable contacts in the Bahamian Defense Force—he sent three of his people to Miami to persuade Barazo to continue to buy his product. Two days later Cabrera received a parcel delivered by Federal Express, packed in dry ice—for a small additional charge.

The box contained six eyeballs, each run through with one of those miniature plastic swords used to enliven canapés. Cabrera was himself no stranger to these kinds of interoffice memoranda; his own business protocol included slicing a man's throat open to his sternum and pulling his tongue out through it, the so-called "Colombian necktie," throwing men alive into pits full of tusked wild pigs and sundry other entertaining ways of inculcating in employees a sense of company loyalty. Nonetheless, Cabrera elected to cut his losses and seek alternate wholesale arrangements in the Sunshine State.

Barazo lived inside a walled compound in South Miami, at the corner of Southwest Sixty-fourth Street and Seventy-fifth Avenue. Not for him the glamour of a Key Biscayne or Coral Gables address, and just as well, since there were two federal warrants on him outstanding, which together could put him back in Danbury. Charley was somewhat surprised, if grateful, that a man with such legal difficulties should be living here under everyone's nose, but as they say, capital goes where it's well treated. Chin said the ground behind the wall was mined and beyond that were a half dozen Rottweiler dogs Barazo kept half starved so they'd stay mean. He fed them the remains of whatever animals he sacrificed to his Santería deities. And they say ours is a faithless age.

"I borrowed a gas company uniform and showed up at his gate," said Rostow. "This golf cart comes humming up with two guys with MACs. They pointed them at me. They said they didn't want the meter read."

"He's spooked," said Felix. "Ramírez, Uguarte, Sandoval, Chin. His people are disappearing. He probably thinks it's Cabrera finally getting some payback. He's not going to come out and play."

"Then we'll just have to go in there and get him," said Charley.

"In what, a tank?"

"We could blow him to DEA," said Rostow. "Apparently even Miami-Dade doesn't know he's here. The house is in someone else's name."

"What the hell good would that do us?"

"He might make bail. We could make our move while he's on his way back to the house."

"What if he doesn't make bail?"

"Then he's out of circulation. Having him whacked on the inside, hell, that's easy. And cheap."

"Then what? The trail goes cold. Come on now, boys, we can do better. I know it's tough, but you've been doing a fine job and I know we can do this."

Bundy said, "There's a tree line across the street from him, casuarinas, some are pretty tall."

"Go on."

"He has a pool. Chin said that's where he gets his exercise. I could get up there with a .308 and shoot him in the nuts while he was doing the backstroke, then we could get him in the hospital while he was having them sewn back on."

Charley thought about it. He nodded. "That's a possibility. But what if you missed? You might hit an artery or something. He might bleed to death."

Bundy looked at Charley. "Sir," he said quietly, "I do not 'miss.'"

"I'm sure you wouldn't, son, but it's, I don't know, it's messy."

Rostow spoke up. "Why don't we let him chill out for a while. Six months, whatever, let him get his confidence back. We could make it look like Chin just ran off on him, so he wouldn't think it was Cabrera."

102

"Six months?" Charley snorted. "That's not how I do business."

"I know. We Arc Light him," said McNamara.

"We what?"

"B-52s. That stuff you were telling us about they use on the space shuttle? HMQ?"

"X, HMX."

"Why don't we chopper over him at night and drop some on him."

"I'm not sure we're quite there yet, Mac," said Charley. "Boys, I think we're losing sight of something here. Barazo isn't the end of the chain. We got a whole other *continent* to deal with after we get done with him. Let's keep that in mind, all right?"

Felix said, "There's something we might as well look at now."

"Well?"

"This is a guy who puts toothpicks through people's eyeballs. Once we get him, how are you going to make him talk?"

"Damnit, McNamara, will you put down that magazine? You can design your damn dream house on your own dime." It was frustrating. "Felix," he said, "put on that tape of Chin. Now let's listen close, everyone. There's got to be a way. There's always a *way*."

12

"Whaddya got?"

"A cold," said Diatri. "I still got this cold, it won't go away."

"Yeah? That's too bad. On the Raid Jacket case, you got anything?"

"That's what I'm saying. This cold. That's what I got on the Raid Jacket case. I got it standing in the rain. You ever been out to

Potter's Field? It's out on Hart Island. Let me tell you, this is a sad place. All those bodies that no one wants. And these City yo-yos they got doing the burying. They don't exactly lower you in. They just tossed this guy in. I mean, I thought the box was going to split open."

"Tossed who in, Frank?"

"Luis, Jim. The guy in the Raid Jacket case. That 'hot' case you gave me?"

"Right, right."

Diatri blew his nose. "Two weeks I've been sucking on zinc tablets. I thought maybe someone would show up at the guy's funeral. No one. So the guy's a scumbag, but scumbags have family—friends, even. You'd think someone would have showed up at his funeral. You want to know the truth, Jim, it was almost sad. I mean, if no one shows up to watch them bury you, it's like you never existed, right?"

"How are you doing otherwise? Your stomach?"

"My stomach is fine, Jim."

"Don't start hitting yourself, Frank. I just asked. Oh, by the way, Mr. Kelly called from DC. He asked about you."

"No kidding? So often when a man moves up in the world, he forgets the little people. Not Mr. Kelly."

"Take care of the cold, okay?"

The SAC walked off, leaving Diatri to blow his nose and sift through the personal effects of Ramón Antonio Luis spread out on his desk. The evidence clerk at the Ninth Precinct had mistakenly sent them to the FBI laboratory and it had taken two weeks to get them back, Detective Korn finally handing them over in a plastic bag held at arm's length as if it contained a live bubonic rat. A pack of Marlboros, a gold chain with the Virgin of Guadalupe, a

Porsche key ring with a single key Technical Services said belonged to a Master's brand padlock, $1,200. Robbery was certainly out.

"I'm going out, Alice," he said.

"Okay, Frankie. Don't get shot."

Diatri stopped. "What did you say?"

Alice went on typing. "I said don't get shot."

"Well, what the hell kind of thing is that to say? Jesus, Alice."

"What's the matter with saying that? You're always getting shot. I just said, 'Don't get shot.'"

"Couldn't you just say, 'Be careful,' or, or 'Have a nice day' or something? 'Don't get shot'? Jesus."

Diatri stood on the sidewalk on East Eighth where Luis had died. The brown blood puddle was now just barely visible. He tapped the key ring against his palm. The last address the PD had for Luis was "Unknown."

They found him face down, headed west, the bullet came from behind, so we know he was walking west. Okay, clean hit, middle of the night, probably silenced since no one heard a shot, professional, possibly, though why pay a pro to pop a lower-echelon scumbag? Still, looks like a professional hit, so ... a professional would be waiting for him, and where would he know to wait for him? Diatri looked down the block. NOAH'S 8TH STREET YAGHT? What was a boat doing here? Never mind the boat. The nearest building was number 316. A sign over the door said:

THIS LAND IS OURS. PROPERTY OF THE
LOWER EAST SIDE JOINT PLANNING COUNCIL.

The door was open. Even through his cold he could smell the urine. It was a broken-down building, but underneath the accumulation of crud he saw the remnant of a parquet floor that in its day had been lovingly waxed and buffed. Families had lived in this building and raised children and filled vases with cut flowers and cooked meals and sung around the piano at night—crunch, a crack vial broke under his foot.

He tried the doors on every floor. No one home. He found the padlock on the eighth floor. Master's brand.

He unlocked it and, very slowly, pushed the door open, about an inch, until he saw the wire. He got down on his knees and with his nail clippers snipped it. He pushed the door open the rest of the way.

The wire ran from the door through an eye hook to the trigger of a sawed-off twelve-gauge held in a bench vise and aimed at the knees of whoever walked in the door. He broke the gun and examined the load. Number nine shot. Skeet load. Good spread.

The room was dark, not much light getting through the windows, which he guessed had last been cleaned when Kennedy was President. There were candles all over the place. Empty packs of Marlboros, Doritos, Oreos—the kind with extra filling. Bottles of Dos Equis Mexican beer. A Spanish-language glossy magazine open to a spread on Prince Andrew. There was a steel trunk by the sofa doing duty as a coffee table. Two pharmaceutically brown bottles on top, procaine and mannitol, dental anesthetic and baby laxative. He found the cocaine inside the trunk, about an ounce, not much, but it had the rocky texture and micaceous glint of the good stuff. People who didn't know better mistook numbness for a sign of purity; the baby laxative just added bulk—and made people have to go to the bathroom a lot. They could stretch the ounce by a third, anyway, and retail it for four thousand, more than enough, in this world, to justify shooting off someone's legs.

Diatri was looking through the rest of the apartment when he heard the creak of feet coming up the stairs. He drew his Sig Sauer and crouched behind the door.

"Emi?" he heard. It was a woman's voice, an old woman's, and scared. "Emi?" She pushed open the door and walked in.

"Hello, ma'am—aggh!" The woman shrieked and sprayed him full in the face from a hand canister.

"Ow!" Diatri shouted. "Shit! Ow! Shit!"

"Back!" she yelled. "Or I do again!"

"No! Federal agent! *Policía!* Ow!" He groped for his ID, waving it at her.

"Oo," said the woman. "Sorry. I think you are mogger."

Diatri stumbled toward a chair, moaning, holding his face.

"You okay, meester?"

"No, I'm not! Jesus. Get water, something."

"You wait, I get." She came back with a damp rag that looked like Egyptian mummy wrappings. Diatri took off his shirt and gave her his undershirt and wet it from a bottle of club soda.

"You gon to arres me?"

"Yes. Assaulting a federal officer with chemicals. Jesus. What's your name? What are you doing here?"

"I look for my son."

Diatri said, in a softer tone of voice, "Is your son's name Ramón?"

"No."

"What's your son's name?"

"I go now."

"No, ma'am. What's your son's name?"

107

"Emiliano Ramírez. He stay here sometimes. He missing for more than two weeks. I come here for two weeks to see, but I don have key. He take me to church every Sunday but he don come. I go to Missing Persons burro. Please don arres me, mister. My sister dying of cancer. You know cancer? If you arres me, she no have no one to—"

"Okay, okay. Look, let's—Jesus, that hurts—what is that?"

"Mes."

"Mace? Where'd you get—never mind. This is your son's place? Well, your son is in a lot of trouble, Mrs. Ramírez. No, not right in the eye, just, just let me have the bottle, thank you. You see what that is on the table there? That's cocaine, Mrs. Ramírez."

"He don have cocaine."

"You just told me he stays here."

"No."

"Yes, you did, Mrs. Ramírez. You just told me."

"His friend stay here. This not his place." She looked around. "Too dirty."

"Ramón Antonio Luis, do you know him?"

"No. Yes. That his cocaine. Luis is bad person, not like my Emi."

"What does your son do, Mrs. Ramírez?"

"He work."

"What kind of work?"

"He work in a theater. He's good boy. Never no trouble with police. Okay I go? My sister have to have inyection."

"Uh-uh. I'm afraid we're going to have to go talk to some people, Mrs. Ramírez."

The old woman began to cry and suddenly Diatri was telling her it was okay and letting her wipe her nose on a corner of his undershirt.

***

Diatri hadn't been inside a parish rectory in over twenty-five years. A lot had changed in the Church since then—Vatican II, a Polish Pope—but it was all depressingly familiar: the housekeeper with a hacking cough and wearing slippers because of her bunions, heavy furniture, heavy drapes, carpets that needed more than a Hoover and a warped print of a fifteenth-century Madonna who looked like she'd rather be in Philadelphia. The room in which she left him smelled of stale cigarettes, family problems and funeral arrangements.

The priest who walked in was in his mid-to late forties, athletically built, with a wide, friendly face and eyes that augered through their thick lenses at Diatri, putting him instantly on the defensive.

"Father Rebeta?"

"Yes." He had a strong grip. "Detective Diatri?"

"Special Agent, with DEA."

"Ah"—the priest nodded— "drugs. Sit, please."

"Padre, I understand—"

"You were in the military."

"Uh, yes."

The priest smiled. "Italians don't say 'Padre,' but they do in the military. Where were you stationed?"

"Overseas. You found Mrs. Ramírez through—"

"Where overseas?"

"I was in I Corps, along the DMZ."

"Sure. Khe Sanh? Con Thien? Camp Carroll? The Rockpile?"

Diatri started twisting Old Blue Eyes around his pinky. The priest's eyes went to the ring. Diatri put his hands on his lap, out of

109

view. "If you don't mind, I'd like to ask you how you and Rosa Ramírez found each other."

"No, of course." Father Rebeta told him about the strange phone call he'd received in the middle of the night. Diatri noted it took place the night after Luis was shot on East Eighth Street. The priest said that at first he was convinced it was a sick joke someone was playing, until he heard the man say, "Okay, Emiliano, I have your priest on the phone."

The priest said, "And the confession I heard, that could not have been a joke. I went to the police and told them. They told me it must have been a joke. The only thing I could think of was to go to Missing Persons and see if anyone had reported a missing Emiliano. They said they didn't give out that information but I made a pest of myself and sometimes"—he tapped his Roman collar— "this is good for something, and eventually they let me see their list. There were eight missing Emilianos. I was able to narrow it down to five on the basis of the date of the call, and after going to see the five people who'd reported missing Emilianos I came to the conclusion it was Mrs. Ramírez's son, Emiliano."

"And you reported this back to the police?"

"Yes."

"And—"

"And they couldn't have cared less. I got a lecture about their case load."

"What convinced you it was Mrs. Ramírez's son?"

"Intuition—and the time frame, I suppose," said the priest. Diatri caught it, a slight upward flicker of eyeball.

"This other voice," said Diatri, "it called you Padre, like I did?"

"Yes."

"Tell me about his voice."

110

"Deliberate, intelligent, commanding. Accustomed to being obeyed. Rather calm. His syntax was revealing."

"His what?"

"Choice of words."

"What about his choice of words?"

"He said, 'Got a man here gonna die.' He didn't say, 'I'm going to kill a man.' There's a difference, isn't there? Look at the way that first sentence is constructed. As though the man's death is an action independent of his own agency. As the saying goes, hypocrisy is the homage that vice pays to virtue."

"Seems to me you're hanging a lot on this syntax."

"Everything hangs on grammar, Frank. Everything. The soul reveals itself through language. Do you remember when Nixon started using 'we'? Everyone said he was being pompous, using the royal 'we,' but that wasn't it at all. It was the two Nixons talking, his superego splitting away from his self. He was talking, without real-izing it himself, about the two Nixons."

"One was plenty. We're getting a little off the track here, Padre."

"Not really. Not really. I've spent almost twenty years of Saturdays sitting in a black box listening to people spill out their souls through words. I have an appreciation for the words they choose. Like a blind man, I suppose."

"I get to see their faces when they confess," Diatri said. "That way I can tell when they're pulling my chain."

"Oh,"—Father Rebeta smiled back— "I can tell too."

"So what about the voice?"

"It was Southern, actually more Southwestern. Sharper, some twang to it. Texas maybe, Arizona, New Mexico. Someone from the Deep South would say, 'Got a man here gonah dah.' He said, 'gunna die.' It's a tighter diction, less elasticity, it snaps back faster.

111

Also, his use of 'Padre' would be consistent with that. Unless, of course, we're talking about a military man, like yourself. But we're ignoring the more important aspect of it, aren't we?"

"If you say so." Must be a Jesuit.

"Why would a man who was about to whack another man in cold blood go to the trouble and risk of calling a priest in the middle of the night to hear his confession?"

Diatri said, "Because he's a Catholic himself."

"Yes, exactly."

"But if he's about to kill this guy, why does he care about giving him confession?"

"You tell me."

"No," said Diatri, "you tell me."

"It's obvious, isn't it? Because he's compassionate."

"He's about to kill the guy and he's compassionate?"

"Think it through."

"Are you a Jesuit by any chance?"

"I was, yes. But I'm diocesan now, as you can see."

"Uh-huh. Well, you're doing fine, so why don't *you* think it through."

"Okay." The priest smiled. "A Catholic would almost certainly know that sacraments cannot be administered over the telephone. The Church has changed a great deal, despite our current Pope, but she has not yet reached the point of Reach Out and Forgive."

"So?"

"So, the man who placed the call, knowing it didn't count, was doing it anyway, presumably to make the man he was about to ... whack ... feel better."

"Okay. Go on."

"On the other hand, though the confession was not, strictly

speaking, valid, the very fact of the man's desiring confession would constitute volition—the desire for forgiveness. And as you no doubt recall, desire is nine-tenths of the law."

Diatri smiled. "So he's looking eight to ten centuries in Purgatory instead of a million consecutive life sentences in the Hot House?"

"We don't speak of 'Hell' the way we used to, Frank. We speak of Separateness."

"What did he tell you during this confession?"

"You know I can't tell you that, Frank."

"Why not? You said it wasn't a valid confession."

"No, but given the man's volition, I would treat it as such nonetheless. But nice try."

"That's very disappointing, Padre."

"I can tell you that his life had not been a paradigm of sanctifying grace."

"Well, that really narrows it down for me, especially in New York City. So many paradigms of sanctifying grace walking around."

"I am trying to help."

"Let's recap. You think you got a telephone call from a Southwestern Catholic compassionate guy who was about to kill a Hispanic scumbag named Emiliano. Does that about do it?"

"I'm certain he didn't mean for me to hear him say the man's name. I heard a phone tone just before that. I think he meant to put me on hold and pressed the wrong button. He said other things, but I couldn't hear."

Diatri leaned back in his chair and stared at the priest for a moment's effect. "Why don't you just tell me what it is you and Mrs. Ramírez are holding back."

They stared at each other for a good half minute. Finally the priest said, "On one condition."

"This is a federal investigation, Padre. No conditions."

"In that case, I can't really say."

"All right. I'll consider it."

"Consider it?"

"Favorably."

"In that case. Two days after I got the phone call, Rosa received an envelope through her mail slot containing ten thousand dollars. Five hundred used twenty-dollar bills."

"Funny how she neglected to mention that little detail to me. Does she still have the envelope?"

"No. I asked. She burned it. But there were no markings."

"That's really too bad. What about the money?"

"Spent. She bought a new television—"

"Great. Little Emiliano missing and she's the Queen of K Mart."

"—for her sister, who's dying of pancreatic cancer. That's one of the worst kind. The rest she's using on getting her into a private hospice out in Flushing."

Diatri stood up. "Thank you, Padre."

"Frank, may I ask you something?"

Frank. "Yes."

"Do all priests make you nervous, or is it just me?"

"You don't make me nervous."

"Then why have you been doing that with your ring the whole time? By the way, is that Sinatra?"

"It's, I gave up smoking. It's something to do with my hands."

"No it isn't." The priest smiled.

At the door, Diatri said, "If they got word there was going to be a major battle, they would fly in two things. Frozen steaks and priests. We could always tell when the shit was going to hit when we saw the frozen steaks and the priests. I haven't had a steak since January 1968. And I used to love steaks." Diatri shook his hand. "Thank you for your time, Padre."

13

"You want to cut?" said Felix.

Charley grunted no and said he wasn't going to play another hand if it was going to be another goddamn game with eighteen goddamn wild cards. He was half crazy from the waiting. Two weeks in the Everglades Suite—to hell with the vaulted ceilings and the great view—had him pacing like a stuck lion. A cage is a cage, even if it is Spanish Revival. Two weeks of waiting on a scared-stiff doper to come out and play. Two weeks of waiting, of playing poker, an eternity to a man like Charley. He was so bored he said he was thinking of buying Eastern Airlines just to have something to do.

"Why can't you just deal straight poker?"

"Because it's dealer's choice and I'm winning. I'm up $z6,400. Nines, threes and sixes wild. Four, you get an extra card, cost you half the pot. Arrange 'em and roll 'em."

"That's whorehouse poker," said Charley. "And I'm not going to play it."

"All right," said Felix. "Then pay up."

"Just deal."

They rolled over their cards one by one and bet. Felix said, "Six kings." Charley shook his head the way he might at a tax increase.

Felix pulled his chips over and methodically stacked them into the neat piles that annoyed Charley, who let out a cloud of disapproving cigar smoke and went and stood on the balcony. The lights of Key Biscayne glittered across the water.

"What about a tunnel?" Charley said. "We rent the house across the street and go in under the wall, under that minefield he's got. Minefields, in downtown Miami. What's this country come to, Felix? We go up into his bedroom and catch him with his pants down. Use some of that stun gas."

Felix finished stacking his chips. "Let's give it another week, boss."

"No, I'm sick of waiting. You tell Rostow and the boys we're going to meet right here tomorrow morning, ten a.m. We're going to meet right here and we're going to discuss a tunnel."

He knew better than to argue. It might pass of its own accord, like a low-pressure zone. He checked his watch and said, "I better go." He strapped on his pistol and gathered up his now worn medical journals, resisting the weariness that attached itself to the task so as to not encourage Charley's tunnel scheme. He opened the refrigerator and removed the small saltshaker with the hinged lid. He shook the grains to make sure they were loose, checked the holes in the shaker to see they were clear and slid it into the pocket of his jacket. "Maybe tonight'll be the night," he said. Charley was still staring off toward Key Biscayne with his back to him.

"Ten a.m.," said Charley.

They'd chosen the hotel for its proximity to Neon Leon's restaurant on Southwest Seventy-third Street between Southwest Fifty-eighth Avenue and Fifty-eighth Place. Felix reached the Winn-Dixie—

"The Beef People"—parking lot across the street ten minutes after leaving the Biltmore. He shut off the engine and checked his watch; it was two minutes to eight. At eight he saw Rostow emerge from Neon Leon's and walk toward him. He got in, shut the door, and let out a disconsolate belch. "Got any Pepto?" Felix nodded at the glove compartment. Rostow opened it. There were three new bottles of Pepto-Bismol. Rostow opened a bottle and took a long slug. He licked his lips pink.

"How's the squid tonight?"

"Sucks," said Rostow. He sat with the bottle of Pepto open between his legs. "I've been thinking—"

"So's the boss."

"—about Mac's idea. The incendiary. The problem is getting our own fire truck. We're getting hung up on the truck. It doesn't have to be a truck. Why does it have to be a truck? Why can't it just be an ambulance?"

"He's called a meeting tomorrow at ten. He wants to dig a tunnel."

"A tunnel." Rostow took another swig of pink. "I don't know if Bundy is going to go for any more digging. He says burying Chin put his back out. Says he's having lumbar problems. But I can't eat much more of this shit."

Felix crossed Southwest Seventy-third Street and walked into Neon Leon's. There was a Lucite copy of the Venus de Milo in the lobby, lit from beneath so that her stumps and severed neck glowed brightly. Felix wondered if this was intentional.

The maître d' gave him a bright smile. "Dr. Allende! Like a clock!" He led Felix to his regular table, reserved for him every night the last two weeks, a well-lit corner booth where he could read his medical journals. Felix sat and, again resisting the temptation to sigh, spread his magazines out before him: *New England Journal of Medicine*, *Journal of the American Medical Association*, *Gastroenterological Review*, *The Lancet*. Tonight he'd wrapped *JAMA*'s cover around the new *Sports Illustrated* so that he wouldn't have to spend another night pretending to read about renal dysfunction.

His regular waiter, Ignacio, appeared. They spoke in Spanish.

"You're late tonight," Ignacio reproved him with mock severity. "Four minutes."

Felix made a clack-clack gesture with his hand. "Medical conferences give doctors an excuse to talk too much."

Ignacio nodded knowingly. "How long is the conference?"

Felix gave a world-weary shrug. "Until we find a cure for cancer. What's good tonight?"

"Nothing," said Ignacio.

"Okay, I'll take the nothing and some fresh fish, grilled, no butter, no sauce. And coffee."

"*A sus órdenes*," said Ignacio with his customary flourish.

As always, Felix asked if the squid was fresh—just to make sure it was on the menu—and, as always, ordered something else. *Calamares en su tinta*, squid in its own ink. A bowl of *calamares en su tinta* was a dinner out of Jules Verne: rubbery white tentacles rising out of a creamy, purple lagoon. What a strange obsession. Chin said that Barazo had developed a taste for it, even before seeing it for the first time, after someone told him it was the favorite dish of Juan Carlos de Borbón, King of Spain. (It isn't.) Barazo scattered hundred dollar tips at Neon Leon's like autumn leaves; they were only too happy to have it, fresh, on the menu every night, over the objections of the chef.

Felix opened his *New England Journal of Medicine* and scanned an article about a surgical procedure developed by doctors in Belfast, Northern Ireland, to repair kneecaps shattered by IRA bullets. The article interested him more than most, being familiar himself with the geography of knees owing to his own torn cruciate ligaments, but he was soon lost in the technicalities of the protocols and thumbing listlessly through learned articles on hyperthyroidism, shingles, and sundry -ectomies and -omas. Finally he switched to his concealed *Sports Illustrated* and read with fascination an article about a Mexican priest who supported his orphanage by wrestling professionally under the name Fray Tormenta—Brother Storm. Every Saturday Fray Tormenta would hitchhike into Mexico City from the town of Xometla and earn fifty dollars for getting into the ring and being brutalized by gigantic Aztecs with names like El Insolente and Torquemada. Felix learned that in Mexico wrestling is not faked; ears get bitten off, limbs broken, genitals. ... At dawn Fray Tormenta would return to the orphanage, usually unconscious in the back of a pickup truck, in time to say morning Mass for his orphans. Felix's eyes were burning by the end of the article. He was tearing it out to show to Charley when his beeper went off.

They did regular beeper checks, so he walked to the phone with no particular urgency. He dialed and reached Bundy in half a ring. Bundy's voice was urgent. He said, "He's moving. Two cars. The Package and a girl up front, three goombahs following. They just turned right on Sixty-second Avenue. He's heading your way."

Felix hung up and walked back to his table. He sat down and noticed that his hands were trembling. Ignacio appeared.

"Your fish, Doctor. Aren't you well?"

"Fine."

"You've been working too hard. That's no good. Who's going to take care of us when the doctors get sick, eh?"

Felix poked at his fish. It was pointless putting any in his mouth, since it had gone completely dry. Barazo was headed for the restaurant, would walk in any moment, a man who beat up teenage girls, cut off the heads of animals to propitiate Afro-Caribbean gods, put plastic cocktail swords into people's eyes. Felix explained to himself that it was entirely rational to be scared of a man like this, but this didn't help.

Jesús Celaya Barazo made a Miami entrance a few minutes later. First to enter was one of the bodyguards, two hundred and fifty pounds or so of Ray-Banned malevolence, followed by another of similar aspect, followed by the Package and his woman. She was dark and beautiful in the conventional way, but it was the dress that demanded attention, if it could be called that. Generically it seemed more of a wet suit, though one designed to attract, rather than repel, sharks: shocking white, with a neckline that plunged itself below the navel, clearly designated by means of a conspicuous opal. The lower half of her outfit consisted of rubber hot pants and the stays of a garter belt that stretched taut a pair of black nylons studded with rhinestones. Her five-inch heels made her taller than Barazo, and forced her to walk somewhat like a circus clown on stilts. The third goombah followed behind, meting out mind-your-own-business stares to those male diners unable to concentrate on their food. The rubber left little to the imagination, and Barazo's face showed his pleasure at the libidinous fission triggered by his woman's colliding nuclei.

He was himself a heavyset man somewhere on the dark side of forty with a short ponytail and, somewhat oddly, the mustache now permanently associated with Hitler rather than with Oliver Hardy. The rest of his face was concealed under a three-day beard and oversized red sunglasses. It was a face not open to the general public.

The maitre d' created deferential bow waves as he led the party to the corner banquette that Chin had told them was reserved only for him, much the way Dilly's in New York always keeps a table for Sinatra, even if he's singing in Australia that night. Two bodyguards took up positions on either side of the booth, hands thrust into shoulder bags that Felix recognized as the rig used by the Secret Service to deemphasize their Uzi submachine guns. The third kept by the door, scowling at anyone who entered.

Champagne arrived at the table. Felix watched over the top of *JAMA*, heart beating loudly in his ears, trying to keep his hands from rustling the pages. The girl sidled up against Barazo. From his own table, he could see beneath Barazo's table and what he saw alarmed him. Fear seized him. A man who has his female companion administer manual labor under the table while he contemplates a dish that would make most stouthearted men gag is no man to be trifled with. Felix wanted to get out of there, right now; he reached for his wallet to pay. They could dig a tunnel or drop a hydrogen bomb on him, but this was not going to work. My God, look at him. She's ... Ignacio, quickly, the check. She's finished. A finger bowl? With flower petals in it. Now she was licking the fingers ostentatiously. Classy.

Felix opened his wallet to get money and there she was, looking up at him from her high school graduation picture, taken a few days before that night in the clearing on the island. He stared. He took it out of the sleeve and turned it over and read what she'd written there, ironic words, given what had happened a few days later: "To my best friend in the world, love, T." Felix turned it over and put it back in the sleeve and when he put the wallet away his hands were no longer trembling and his heart was quiet in his ears. When he looked back at Barazo's table he saw the maitre d' nodding with a smile that could have lubed the chassis of a half dozen stretch limos; and pressed the timer on his watch. During two weeks of ordering, he and Rostow had devised a squid algorithm. The *calamares* should arrive on Barazo's table in six minutes.

Felix waited three minutes and got up and started walking as if he were going to the pay phone. When he passed the counter on which the cooks set the dishes to be picked up by the waiters, he stopped. He peered over the counter. The kitchen was a sweat hive of activity. One of the cooks stood nearby, hunched over, clobbering the claws of stone crabs with a wooden mallet.

"*Hola,*" said Felix. The cook looked up and nodded politely. Felix said in Spanish, "The food is good here, really good."

"*Gracias.*"

Felix reached inside his pocket and flipped open the lid of the saltshaker. "I've eaten here every night for two weeks and each dish is better than the one before."

The cook smiled again, this time more easily. He said, "You must be getting pretty sick of it, then."

"*Al contrario.*" Felix beamed. "I only hope I can eat my way through everything before I leave town."

"Have you tried the grouper? It's good. We poach it in a scallop broth with cilantro. It's nice."

"You know, what I really want to try is the *calamares en su tinta.* I bet that's really good."

The cook shrugged. "Well, if you like that sort of thing."

"You know, I'd like to try it, but I'm a little, you know, I didn't eat my first raw oyster till a few years ago. What's it look like?"

"Someone's just ordered some." He shouted, "*Oye, Milton,*

122

dame los calamares." He set the dish on the counter in front of Felix. "Here," he said. "It's peasant food."

Felix leaned over to smell, the shaker ready inside his hand. "Um," he managed. "*Sabroso.*" The cook turned back to his half-hammered crabs.

A moment later a hand whisked the dish off the countertop.

"So," said the cook, looking up. "Are you going to order *calamares?*"

"I think I'll go for the grouper, thanks." Felix smiled.

"Good choice," winked the cook.

Felix returned to his table almost weightless with relief. He sat down and picked up his coffee cup and when he saw Barazo's table he nearly spilled it. There was nothing in front of Barazo.

Felix searched the other tables with his eyes and saw it. The bowl of *calamares* was in front of a middle-aged woman who was viewing it with some uncertainty. Oh my God, he thought, oh no.

In the next instant the maître d' appeared at the table and grabbed the dish without so much as a beg-your-pardon and began berating a waiter loudly in the mother tongue. *Idiota! Son los calamares del Señor Barazo!*

The squid were set, with apologies befitting nobility, before Barazo, who began greedily to eat. He forked a tentacle and offered it to his girl, who made a face. Felix was sure that Barazo would have slugged her for that if they'd been alone. If they made it home tonight, probably he would. From this he deduced she was a new girl. Barazo ate without interruption. Felix remembered the old fisherman in Hemingway's story urging the great marlin to eat the bonito at the end of his line. When Barazo began to wipe the bowl with his bread, Felix got up and went to the phone. "Yellow Cab? I'm at Neon Leon's. Please send a taxi to pick me up." He went back to the table.

It happened suddenly. One minute Barazo was leaning back, smoking a cigarette, and the next he was bringing up squid with ballistic velocity, as if a poltergeist had performed the Heimlich maneuver on him. Truly, it was not a pretty sight.

Felix quickly made his way to the table, demanding in a loud voice, "What did this man have to eat?" The maître d' had gone white. Waiters were rushing with towels, a new tablecloth, an empty salad bowl. The bodyguards, helpless in the face of having no one obvious to shoot, nevertheless directed their professional energies on the waiter with the salad bowl, punching him in the chest and sending him sprawling. The girl, whose person had received a copious share of Barazo's gastric ejecta, was screeching hysterically for towels. Barazo himself was pitched forward over the table making noises like a distressed sea lion.

"I'm a doctor," Felix shouted. "What did this man eat?"

"Squid," murmured the maître d' almost inaudibly, "in its ink."

"SQUID? IN ITS INK?" Felix shouted back. "Exactly as I suspected. This man has food poisoning." The guard moved in on the maître d'.

"No," he gasped miserably. "It's not possible. We use only the freshest ..."

Felix was scribbling furiously on a notepad. He tore off the page and handed it to one of the bodyguards. "Call this number immediately. Tell them to send an ambulance. Tell them Dr. Allende is here at the scene." He turned to the maître d'. "And a fortunate thing too!" The bodyguard roughly shoved his way through to the phone.

Felix located a dry area of Barazo's wrist, put his finger on it while looking at his watch and counted to ten. "Hm!" he said, shaking his head. "Hm."

The door burst open a remarkably efficient three minutes later as two heavyset men from the Emergency Medical Service rushed in with a collapsible gurney. Wincing only slightly, at the sight, they took Barazo's vital signs. Felix, somewhat caught up in the moment, kept barking orders at them; McNamara finally said, "We can *handle* it, Doctor, thanks."

They strapped Barazo onto the gurney and wheeled him out, bodyguards following. At the door Felix shouted back at the maître d', "You better save the rest of those squid for the health inspectors!"

Bundy and McNamara pushed the collapsed gurney into the back of the ambulance. Bundy got in the driver's seat, Mac into the back. Felix climbed in. Then the bodyguard started in. Mac held up a hand. "Sorry, it's against reg—"

The bodyguard shoved him back brusquely, and when Mac renewed his complaint, pulled out a MAC 10 machine pistol and pointed it at him. "Drive," he said.

"All right," said Mac, "but that thing better be registered, because I'm going to report this when we get to the hospital, and there are always police at the Emergency entrance."

The prospect did not faze the bodyguard in the least: "Move it."

Bundy pulled out into the street with the siren going. Through the rear windows, Felix saw the other two bodyguards get into their car and pull out behind them. He was looking for Charley and Rostow's car when the bodyguard said, "Where we going?"

"Mercy," said Felix, putting a stethoscope to Barazo's chest.

"How come not South Miami? It's right there, four blocks."

Felix yelled, "Look at him—he's been infected with a, a staphylococcal enterotoxin." This much was true, a scruple (1.296 grams) easily filched from a microbiology lab in Stony Brook, New York.

Felix said angrily, "Can't you see that he needs to be destaph, destaphylococcalized? They don't have the facilities for that at South Miami."

The bodyguard stared suspiciously. Felix shouted, "Do you want him to die?"

"Okay, but fast."

Bundy was doing seventy on the South Dixie Highway, northbound, siren screaming. Mac caught Felix's eye: move back, give me a clear shot. As Felix did, Bundy swerved to avoid hitting a car. Felix fell toward the bodyguard, who felt the bulge under Felix's arm. He reacted instantly. He dove into Felix like a linebacker, breaking three of his ribs and shoving him back into Mac.

His first shot went through the forward bulkhead, missing Bundy by a few inches. The second went into Mac's thigh. Felix grabbed the man's arm. The third shot went through the ambulance's rear window, shattering it. "Shoot him," Mac grunted. "Will you please shoot him?" Mac was pinned against the forward bulkhead by Felix. Felix, occupied by the intense pain in his chest and the bodyguard's 9mm, had no hand available at the moment to reach his own weapon. A second later Barazo's chase car slammed into the back of the ambulance. Felix heard another rib crack.

When he opened his eyes he saw the bodyguard's face, livid with rage, pressed up against his own, mouth open. He could see the fillings. He is trying to bite off my nose. Mac had reached around Felix and managed to get ahold of both the man's hands. Felix couldn't reach his gun, but flailing with his left he felt something come into his grip. It was the sphygmomanometer. He got it around the twenty-one-inch neck and Velcroed it shut. The bulb was hanging down the bodyguard's back. He had to reach to get it in his hand, putting his nose in dangerous proximity to the snapping teeth. He butted the man's nose hard with his forehead, causing himself extreme pain. Bulb in hand, he began to pump.

The blood-pressure cuff began to inflate. The bodyguard, realizing what was happening, struggled, but Mac held him tightly. Felix pumped and pumped and the bodyguard's face went red, then purplish. He made a sound like the person in the next stall in the public men's room usually makes. Finally he went limp. Felix and Mac pitched forward on top of him. Felix saw the pressure meter on the blood-pressure cuff: 300 over … nothing.

Mac tied a tourniquet above the two holes in his thigh. "Look at that," he said, pointing to his jeans. "I bought those new last week." Felix held his stomach and groaned.

Up front, they heard Bundy shouting into his radio, "Crossing Southwest Seventeenth Avenue."

"Where the fuck are they?" Mac said.

The plan called for Charley and Rostow to cut off any chase vehicle. "They pulled in front of them and the fuckers just kept on going. Drove right through them. They had to jack the wheel clear."

"Great," said Mac, staring at his seeping leg wound. "Can you move?" he said to Felix. Felix nodded. "Take this." He handed Felix a length of surgical tubing. "Unlatch those doors, tie this to them loose, so it'll give."

Mac said to Barazo, "Excuse me, but I need this," and undid his straps and pitched him roughly onto the floor. Barazo moaned. "Okay," said Mac, "let's get this one onto it." The bodyguard was heavy. The ambulance kept swerving and being slammed from behind by the chase car.

"All right," Mac panted once they'd gotten the inert immensity onto the gurney and strapped him in. The blood-pressure cuff was still around his neck, the bulb dangling behind. "Let them get right behind you," Mac was saying to Bundy. "Then when you hear 'three,' floor it, hit it *hard*. You ready?" he said to Felix. Felix, holding his rib cage, nodded.

Same principle as launching a bobsled, essentially. When Bundy hit the accelerator, Mac and Felix shoved. The gurney hit the doors, the doors blew open and the gurney with its two hundred and fifty pounds of meat took off. It went through the windshield of the car behind. The car veered off the road into a stand of palmettos thoughtfully planted to welcome people to Key Biscayne, and burst into flames.

Charley sent Rostow off with Mac to take him to Fort Lauderdale and let him out at a secluded part of the beach. Rostow would call the police and report a shooting. The police would arrive to find yet another mugging victim. Bundy took Felix to Mercy Hospital. Alone, he turned his attention to Barazo, tied securely to a chair that was bolted to the cement floor in the basement of the safe house. He sat and smoked a cigar until the staphylococcus had worked its way through Barazo's GI tract. He gave him some Coca-Cola to settle his stomach, and then turned on the tape recorder and began.

He explained what it was he wanted. Barazo told him to go fuck himself. Many times. Charley was a believer in letting a man get things out of his system first, so he let Barazo go on until he was exhausted. Then, with a you-give-me-no-other-choice expression, Charley put on surgical gloves and surgical mask and eye protectors and went to a corner of the semi-darkened room and wheeled out a stand from which intravenous bags are hung. He attached the tubing to the needle with nearly faultless verisimilitude, rolled up Barazo's sleeve—Barazo struggling—wet a cotton ball with alcohol and rubbed the inside of his arm, located a vein, nodded with satisfaction and gently inserted the long needle. (He'd done this for Margaret in her final illness, so he was adept.) This done, he produced a cooler, one of the playfully designed red-and-white jobs one associates with sun-drenched days at the beach. He flipped back the lid in full view of Barazo and removed a plastic bag full of red liquid. The label read:

DANGER: CONTAMINATED BLOOD
HIV-POSITIVE

Charley watched Barazo's eyes closely, and it was amazing what he saw in them: a clear readiness to die. Give the man that, his ruthlessness contained contempt even for his own life. "You know, Jesús," he said, appearing to adjust the bag one last time before opening the stopcock and letting the blood (Karo syrup and food coloring) seep into his veins, "while you're dying, you know what people are going to be saying about you, don't you? They're going to say, '01' Haysoos making himself out to be such a tough guy and the whole time he turns out to be a *maricón*. How about that?'"

14

"Sorry about this," Diatri said to his Whole Crispy Fish Hunan Style, chopsticking through thick, crackled skin to steamy white flesh. The fish stared back with a Churchillian pout, lower jaw a-jut, eyes sullen with plum glaze.

Diatri said sympathetically, "Hey, it could have been worse. You could have been a lobster. You get dunked live in boiling water, then people wearing bibs with your picture on them fight over your claws. At least this is more dignified."

He considered: one dead scumbag on East Eighth, his missing roommate Ramírez, Ramírez's mother with ten grand through her mail slot, a smart-ass priest who thinks he heard Ramírez's confession over the phone in the middle of the night.

"Let me try something out on you," he said to the fish. "Ramírez and Luis get into an argument, Luis storms out, Ramírez follows him and pops him on the sidewalk, freaks out and splits and on his way out of town shoves ten grand through his mama's door to tide her over."

The sea bass frowned. "Why didn't he call her? Why did he leave the coke behind? What about the $1,200 they found on Luis? What about the raid jackets?"

"Maybe he wants his mother to think he's dead in case Luis' friends came looking for him. Maybe he didn't want to carry an ounce of blow on him after whacking someone. Maybe he freaked after whacking Luis and didn't think to take his money. As to the raid jackets, you noticed Detective Korn's attitude problem." Diatri whispered to the fish, "Did it occur to you that maybe the Ninth Precinct has some vigilante thing going?"

"That's crazy," said the fish.

"Yeah?" Diatri dabbed away the plum sauce from his lips. "You're so smart, how come you're on the menu?"

"You finish?" Diatri jumped. These Chinese waiters, the way they creep up on you.

130

"Yeah."

"Or you wan talk more with fish?"

"No, that's—I'll take some tea and the check."

"What fish say?"

"He said you use too much MSG." It was nine o'clock. It was time to go see Victor.

Diatri drove north on Third Avenue, toothpick in place and humming "You Gotta Turn the Lights Down Low If You Want to Boogie Real Slow." Dropping in on Victor like this always put him in a pleasant mood. Victor was a dope lawyer who had made one mistake a few years ago.

Victor was on retainer for the Ochoa family of Medellín. A teenage nephew of Jorge Luis Ochoa, son of Don Fabio Ochoa, founder of the illustrious dynasty, was caught coming through U.S. Customs at Kennedy Airport with a pet boa constrictor stuffed with twenty condoms full of cocaine inside it. His uncle called Victor.

A few days later, the Bogotá police, acting on an anonymous tip (from Don Fabio), arrested an Eastern Airlines baggage handler. They turned up trace amounts of cocaine, an empty box of El Gigante brand condoms—the same kind—and a National Geographic book on boa constrictors with the nephew's flight number written on the back. The baggage handler confessed that he had planted the cocaine in the nephew's boa while it was being loaded into the plane; his accomplice at Kennedy was supposed to snatch the snake at the other end, but had screwed up. The Bogotá magistrate handling the case forwarded the information to the U.S. Justice Department. The U.S. District Attorney decided to prosecute nonetheless, but Victor had his ducks all lined up and presented an impassioned Fourth Amendment-based defense to the jury: how would *you* like it if Big Brother took your dog Skippy away from you and sliced him up just to see if he'd eaten anything illegal? The nephew was acquitted. A few months later the Bogotá baggage handler quietly escaped from prison and retired on an annuity provided by Don Fabio.

Victor submitted a bill for two million dollars. The Ochoas paid well, but even they thought this was on the high side. Uncle Jorge transferred a million laundered U.S. dollars to Victor's Cayman Islands account. Victor, who had an ego problem, was outraged and decided to get even. He'd gone up against Diatri in court a few times. He called him and said he had something for him. He said to meet him at the new Central Park zoo, by the snakes. Victor thought that was a nice touch. At the meeting, he gave Diatri the name of Ochoa's New England distributor and the time and place the next shipment would arrive in Bridgeport, Connecticut. It was a good tip, producing arrests and a 500-kilo seizure. (In those days, 50o kilos was a good haul.) A few days after the arrest, Diatri sent Victor a tape recording of their conversation at the snake house. Victor called up Diatri, hysterical, trying to make himself into Jesus and Diatri into Judas, an analogy Diatri rejected. "What do you want from me?" Victor cried. "What? What? *What?*"

"I want lunch," said Diatri.

"Lunch?"

"At that Four Seasons restaurant, the one where Kissinger and Cronkite and those people are always eating. I've always wanted to eat there."

Victor showed up, sleepless and pale. When they were seated,

Diatri said, "How come we couldn't get a table closer to the fountain? I'm going to need binoculars to see Kissinger from here."

Victor said, "There's a hundred grand in the briefcase."

Diatri said, "Victor, if you ever offer me money again, I'm going to send that tape to Don Fabio and he's going to cut off more than your retainer. Forty bucks for *sole meunière*? No wonder I've never eaten here before."

Diatri had learned over the years that showing up unexpectedly in the middle of one of Victor's dinner parties forced Victor to come to the point more efficiently.

The maid answered the door. "He have guests," she said.

"Tell him Mr. Frank is here, would you, please? From Manhattan Cablevision."

Victor appeared in the foyer clutching his napkin like a security blanket. "Are you crazy?" he hissed. "You know who I have in there? John Gotti, Jr."

"No kidding," said Diatri. "The one who punched out that woman? Classy guy. Is that carbonara? I love carbonara."

"Call me tomorrow at the office, Frank."

"Do you know a Ramón Antonio Luis or Emiliano Ramírez?"

"No. Look, he's got his people downstairs in the lobby."

"Is that who they were? I thought they were furniture movers wearing suits. That smells good. It's important to use the Italian parsley. My first wife was always using regular parsley and it's an entirely different taste. You know what I do? I add a little sour cream, but not too much."

"Look, I don't know those people."

"They're scumbags. Naturally I thought of you."

"What do you want me to say, Frank?"

"So what's junior like? Chip off the old cellblock? Get it?"

"Jesus Christ, Frank."

"They're Alphabet Town scumbags. Ramírez disappeared and someone popped Luis in the back of the head. Twenty-two caliber."

"Shit happens."

"Manuel Uguarte from South Jamaica? You wouldn't know him? Carlos Sandoval, Flushing Meadow? They both disappeared recently. I thought, all these disappearances, maybe they're related."

"People disappear, Frank. I don't know—"

"Okay," said Diatri, pushing past Victor, "but I can only stay for a few minutes. I already ate."

"I don't know about any Ramírez or Luis. I've heard of Uguarte and Sandoval, okay? Uguarte buys from Sandoval, Sandoval takes deliveries from another guy who just disappeared. Antonio Chin."

"Chin. I don't know the gentleman."

"Twenty-Mule Team Tony—he runs the mules for Jesús Barazo out of Miami."

"Barazo? Barazo is in Honduras."

"No, he isn't in Honduras. He's in South fucking Miami."

"I'm shocked, Victor. Shocked. He's got two federal warrants out on him."

"Yeah, and he's making assholes out of you people, okay? I gotta get back inside."

"Tell junior you're talking to Henry Kissinger. What do you mean these people are missing? How do you mean, missing?"

"Jesus Christ. Missing. Like the kids on the milk cartons."

"What else?"

"What do you mean, what else?"

"Victor."

"Barazo used to handle for Medellin. A lot. Then he cut some arrangement with someone else."

"Who?"

"No one knows. Barazo knows and no one asks Barazo, he's fucking—"

"Is he the guy who—"

"Yeah. So maybe Medellín is settling up. I don't know. That's all I know. On my mother's grave, that's all I know."

"Victor, your mother lives in Delray Beach."

"It's a figure of speech, okay, Frank?"

The next morning Diatri was on his way to the SAC's office when Golina from Intel said, "Hey, Frank, you hear about Barazo?"

Miami was in the middle of one of its periodic renaissances and three blackened corpses on the Rickenbacker Causeway was not the image the Chamber of Commerce was pushing this winter. Diatri had to keep ducking to avoid getting stabbed in the eye by pointing fingers. In addition to the two federal warrants, Florida itself had three state warrants out on Jesús Celaya Barazo, and here he'd been living right under everyone's nose at 7411 Southwest Sixty-fourth Street. The Metro Dade PD was pointing its finger at DEA, DEA was pointing at Metro Dade, and IRS—he was paying *taxes*, for crying out loud!—IRS was pointing right back at DEA; the Mayor's office was pointing fists at everyone and the C of C was ripping out its hair. Minefields, in downtown Miami? Goat heads in the garbage? Victor was right. Barazo had managed to make everybody look like an asshole. And where was he? His dental records didn't match the uppers or lowers of the blackened goombahs in the car. Victor said he bet Barazo was in Medellín. Revenge is a canapé best served cold, right?

The staff of Neon Leon's had all disappeared—vanished, apparently terrified Barazo's people would assume they were in on the hit. The owner had hung a CLOSED DUE TO DEATH IN FAMILY sign outside like a wreath of wolfbane. The police questioned the owner, who had not been there that night; he didn't know anything. Diatri had been parked in a van across from the man's home for two days when he saw a Gran Marquis pull up and two men get out. They did not look like Jehovah's Witnesses. One went to the front door, the other around back. Diatri got out and went to the back. He listened at the door, unholstered his Sig Sauer and went in. The sound was a woman sobbing, a man being struck in the face with open palms.

Diatri crept along a corridor toward the noise. He saw a swinging door and went in, keeping low, and found himself in the kitchen. At the far end was another kitchen door, which lead to the dining room. The voices were in Spanish. The woman's sobs were in Spanish. The man was saying he didn't know anything. He kept saying his squid was fresh every day.

Diatri searched for the spice cabinet and found what he was looking for, a half gallon of extra-virgin—what else, in a good Latino home?—olive oil. He emptied it onto the floor by the forward swinging door. He found an eighteen-inch cast-iron frying pan, good for paella, he imagined as he held it, cocked, in his hand.

He couldn't remember the Spanish word for fire. It was ridiculous. He spoke fluent Spanish. But the word refused to budge. That particular synapse was a damp wick. Finally he just said,

"Fire!" He tried to make himself sound like a frightened female cook.

The man came through the door. He hit the oil and went backward. Diatri brought the frying pan down on his face, probably harder than absolutely necessary. *"Qué pasa?"* said the other. He came through the door gun first. Diatri brought the frying pan side down on his wrist and broke it, then broke his nose on the upswing. The EMS technicians made jokes about the olive oil. The owner was beaten up pretty badly. Diatri went to the hospital with him and stayed with him and when he was released the man insisted on taking him to Neon Leon's and making him a paella. By the time Diatri left, with the address of Ignacio the waiter's cousin down by Homestead Air Force Base, the owner was overcome with gratitude and emotion and told him the dish would forever after be listed on the menu as "Paella Diatri." Diatri was genuinely touched. No family, two divorces, no children; getting into the car, he reflected that "Paella Diatri" was about all he was likely to leave to posterity. By then his stomach was starting to cramp up on him, and he was getting the cold sweat that always preceded these bouts. He stopped at a medical-supply store on the way to Ignacio's cousin's to pick up saline and an IV-rig.

They assigned him a young agent from Intel named Liestraker. Liestraker stood up when Diatri walked in, trying not to reveal the pain, and extended his hand and said how it was an honor. "Thank you," said Diatri. "You got any Rolaids?"

Liestraker grinned. "You ate Cuban?"

"Uh-huh. I want you to go to your AUSA and get a grand jury subpoena and check the registers of all the hotels in the Greater

137

Miami area for a male possibly of Cuban origin posing as a Dr. Allende, mid-forties, five-ten, hundred ninety pounds, heavy athletic build, brown eyes, close-cropped haircut, no distinguishing physical characteristics, checking in December 7 or 8 and checking out December 22. Start with hotels close to the restaurant and work out, but cover *all* of them."

Liestraker said, "Cuban origin, no distinguishing marks? In Miami? Are you kidding?"

"No," said Diatri.

"Why hotels?"

"He wasn't from here, so he had to stay somewhere."

"How do we know he wasn't from here?"

"His Spanish accent was wrong, New York maybe. Also, he asked a waiter directions a couple of times."

"*All* the hotels?" These new guys.

"I've got to go ... back to the motel. Call me."

Diatri was just inserting the butterfly needle into the antecubital vein when the phone rang. It was Liestraker. "Do you know how *many* hotels there are in the Greater Miami area?"

"No," said Diatri, reaching over and pulling the tubing around his upper arm with his teeth like a parrot. "Ha muny?"

"Four hundred and sixty-seven."

"Then you better get started." Diatri started the glucose drip. The first bottle would empty into him in an hour; the second always took longer. "Something else," he said. "Call round all the RC churches. See if anyone fielded any strange calls the night of December 21."

"Strange?" said Liestraker. "Strange how? Sightings of the Virgin Mary?"

Diatri had already hung up. He set the drip regulator and lay

138

back and let the rattle of the old air conditioning lull him to sleep. He dreamed he was underneath a waterfall floating on his back in a pool of cool blue water and standing at the top of the waterfall was Paulina Porizkova, smiling and beautiful, tossing a huge, huge Alka-Seltzer tablet to him that floated down toward him in Super Slo-Mo.

15

He felt badly for Felix, he truly did. Hunched over the gunwale, making sounds like a dying seal. *Rrroaaaa*. Having his ribs wrapped up tight as an Egyptian mummy, that couldn't help.

Charley dipped the washcloth into the ice water at the bottom of the cooler and put it on the back of Felix's sunburning neck. "You want a cracker? That might help." Charley's suggestion was followed by a basso profundo *rrrruuuuua*. Charley patted his back. "That's it. Let it out. Don't fight it." Take a cracker the size of the Ritz to soak up what was ailing Felix. Should have put on that scopolamine patch. Felix could be stubborn. Didn't want drugs, wanted a clear head.

The Gulf Stream was rocking the boat in the cleavage of its D-cup bosomy swells. It was hot, the sun beat down on the chum slick. Charley reached over the side and cut the line holding the perforated white bucket of mashed grunt and watched it descend. The water was so clear out here beyond the hundred-fathom curve. Small fish followed the bucket, pecking at the loosened chunks of greasy meat, darting and retreating with the glee of looters. Charley followed it down to where the water turned cobalt and the bucket became a speck on its way to becoming a free lunch for great marlins. Suddenly it was many years ago and he could hear Margaret's voice.

"Daddy has a nervous stomach," she was saying.

"Ain't nuthin' unusual about that," said Charley, coiling a line.

Margaret smiled at him. "Isn't."

"Huh?"

"Not *huh*, Charles. And it's *isn't*," Margaret whispered, though her daddy couldn't have heard over the sound of his overboard retching. "You're not trying, Charles."

"Maggie—"

"Margaret."

"Why don't we get him inside. He's gonna sunstroke himself out here."

"*Going* to *get* sunstroke. Daddy," she said, "I want you to come inside now and lie down. Charles, you take that arm now." The captain stayed aloof at his controls on the cabin top while the first mate helped the daughter of the drunk who'd chartered his deep-sea fishing boat get her father down below out of the scorching sun. The man had prepaid in full, so it was no skin off his ass; it was just a mystery why a man who drank like that would come down from Houston to Rockport to go deep-sea fishing when he couldn't hardly stand. It was his genes that would kill Charley junior, his grandson, on that road in Bethesda thirty years later. It's all genes, Charley thought. You can run from that double helix, but you can't hide. ...

Rrrruh. Charley wrung out the washcloth and put it on Felix's neck. "You know," he said, "it makes you appreciate all the more what your people went through leaving Cuba in those leaky boats getting away from Castro."

Felix appeared to derive no consolation from this. Charley said, "We oughta head back into Cat Cay."

"No," Felix said, and spat. "I'm okay."

"Well, I'm getting sick watching you. I'm taking her in." He climbed up onto the tuna tower and started the engines and throttled up to 2,100 and pointed her north-northwest. He said into the radio, "Papa Dog One to Bird Dog."

"Bird Dog."

"I got a sick sea dog out here I'm taking into the flat and level. You okay on supplies for tonight?"

"We got a severe mosquito situation here, Papa Dog."

"Well, I'm sorry about that but you boys are capable of handling that." Mac and Bundy had gotten a tad soft since Vietnam, considering Bundy had told him about a time in the Delta when he'd spent three entire days in his ghillie suit crawling across a hundred-meter rice paddy teeming with leeches, pinned down by snipers, so thirsty and hungry he started eating the leeches after the second day. Now he was griping about mosquitoes. "Roger that, Bird Dog. I'll bring some more of that bug juice with me." They used something called Skin So Soft, by the ding-dong Avon Calling folks, a bath oil that repelled bugs. Mercenaries smearing themselves with ladies' bath oil. Charley looked over at his radar screen and there it was, a green phosphorus dot at ten o'clock, bearing 110 and moving fast.

"Stand by, Bird Dog, we got a possible heading your direction." Charley put his binoculars on the horizon and waited. He saw her, bouncing off the Gulf Stream's crests like a giant flying fish. The speed these things were capable of took your breath away—or could give you a spine problem. Men with gold chains would turn up at the boat shows with briefcases full of hundred-dollar bills— twenty pounds of hundreds to a million; that was how they counted their money, they *weighed* it—to buy the latest hot boat. U.S.

Customs had some hot boats, but these—these boats were pure speed. Charley clocked her on the radar. Eighty-five miles an hour. "You up to this?" he shouted down at Felix. Felix chambered a round into the shotgun he had Velcroed under the gunwale for quick release. He looked up at Charley as if to say that dying could only be an improvement. A minute later they saw the plane.

It was a twin-engine Piper Aztec, coming out of the southwest, less than a hundred feet off the water to avoid Miami Center. Fat Albert, the Customs aerostat over Cudjoe Key, might have picked it up, but unless they had a chaser on station, the plane would be on its way back to Panama with a bellyful of fuel and cash before they were clear of Cape Florida. The plane veered toward them. Charley and Felix scrambled to switch places, Charley in the fighting chair, Felix at the controls in the tuna tower. The plane swooped over them. Charley waved. It circled back toward them and for a moment Charley thought it might open up on them. Barazo said it was fitted with a fifty-cal, but that was probably bluster. If dopers started turning their planes into fighters, that was *all* the excuse the military would need to go after them with F-14s. Charley waved again. The plane flew past toward the beach on the west shore of Andros, where German U-boats used to put in. Charley saw him lining up for his final approach. "Papa Dog, you see him?"

"Roger."

"Going in."

Charley watched the plane with collegial interest. Setting down on a fifteen-degree-inclined sand beach was nice work. Most of these pilots were American boys, vets and crop dusters, Charley thought with a somewhat conflicted admixture of sorrow and patriotism. Look at him, he's got dry tanks, he's got to set her down on sand in a ten-knot crosswind with the possibility of the beach turning into a hot LZ if the Bahamian Defense Force decided Barazo's monthly retainer wasn't enough and leave himself enough room to touch-and go if bullets start zipping through his windows; then there's the problem of where do you go, with maybe five minutes' fuel? He was going in. Charley found himself saying, "Tad more starboard rudder, windward wheel down first. Good. Real nice."

Course, at these prices you were always going to find a pilot willing to take the risks. According to Barazo, Sánchez paid his pilots $2,000 per kilo. Five hundred kilos per load—a million dollars, for seven hours' flying. Fancy, Charley thought, switching places again with Felix, steering an erratic course toward the beach, a million dollars for seven hours' work. What did it work out to? Figure round trip, since the pilot had to haul Barazo's payment for the cocaine back to Sánchez on Isola Verde. Fourteen into a million ... Lord in heaven, $71,428 an hour. About what Mike Milken was making.

"How you doing, Bird Dog? Bird Dog?"

Bird Dog panted. "He put down too far north. He's two clicks north of our position. Repeat—"

"I heard you. Get on the hump, son."

Felix said, "There's three of them in the boat." The Black Max had nosed up onto the beach right beside the Piper. They were refueling.

"Try to keep out of sight," said Charley. "They aren't going to fuss with an old man. But you *look* like a cop." Felix was pouring a beer over his shirt. Authenticity. You have to inhabit the role. They were a few hundred yards off the sand beach now, the water turning from turquoise to white. Stunning beach; it deserved better than this. Charley revved his engines into the red and throttled back, smoke and water churning. He went aground just a few feet offshore. The Hatteras lurched, Charley fell off his chair with a loud "Damn!"

He stumbled to his feet all wobbly. They were pointing their weapons at him, Ingrams and Uzis. Must have an aggregate rate of fire of 3,600 rounds. The pilot was Anglo, the others *Latino*.

Charley staggered and fell down and got up and gave them all a great big grin. "Howdy!" He let out a loud, beery belch. Charley had given thought to his wardrobe: black knee socks, Bermuda shorts, a beer-drenched T-shirt—stunk, in this sun— that announced, from neck to belly:

MY WIFE SAYS I HAVE
A DRINKING PROBLEM.
I AGREE.
MY PROBLEM IS
I DON'T DRINK ENOUGH.

"This here island Biminimi? Bimininom—" Belch.

The pilot said, "Bimini's that way, about a hundred miles."

Charley looked in the indicated direction and sighed. "Damnit, Felix, I *told* you it wunt Binimi. Felix? My friend," he said to the men on the beach, "has imbibed himself, and he was the navigator." Belch. Charley peered. "Is that an *airplane*?"

One of the Latinos waded toward them, weapon first. He peered over the side into the well. Felix was lying on his stomach on a deck cushion, mouth open, arm across his face, snoring.

"Worthless." Charley shook his head. "No offense. Him being Hispanic and all."

144

"Fuck you, man."

"Well, whud I say?"

The pilot took a few steps. "What's the problem, man?"

"I don't know," said Charley. "Musta said something. *Habla oosted espanol?* You *hablo espanol mooey*—"

"Hey, shut the fuck up, man."

"And they says manners are dead," Charley grumbled. "You boys care for a cold beer?"

"Get this fucking boat out of here."

The pilot spoke to one of the other Latinos, who called to the one by the boat, "*Spera, Chavo. Spera.*"

The pilot walked toward Charley's boat. He was in his late thirties, dirty-blond hair, and might've been handsome but for the ugliest scar stitched across his forehead, a real scar, the kind that says: "*Scar.*" It looked like someone had sewn the top of his head back on with twelve-pound-test fishing line. He spoke to Charley in a jus-tween-us-white-boys. He had a Southern accent.

"Mister," he said, "you need to back your boat out of here now. Start your engines. Come on now."

But Charley was looking at the plane, entranced by the plane. "You landed that? Here?"

"I ran out of gas. These guys here were passing by and were kind enough to loan me some high octane. Best you move along now, mister."

"That's some flying, son," said Charley. "Frank Borman would be proud of you."

"Look, mister—"

"I'm going, I'm going. Rush rush rush. Everyone's in a rush. And they say it's better in the Bahamas."

"Papa Dog."

145

"What was that?"

He'd forgotten to turn off the radio. Once again, the human element fails us.

"Whut was whut?"

"Papa Dog, we are still one click from your position. Do you copy?"

The pilot pulled his gun out now. The Latino in the water was wading toward the transom and pulling himself aboard.

Charley was standing in the tuna tower, as exposed as a referee at a tennis match, and surrounded by McEnroes with machine pistols.

"Fuck is going on, mister?" said the pilot.

The other man came over the transom and pulled himself into the boat. Felix stirred, looked up, blinked. "Who are you?" he said, sounding drunk. The man hit him across the face hard with his MAC 10.

"Hey!" Charley shouted. The man aimed his weapon at the tower and fired. There were eight shots to the short burst; only one of them hit Charley, in and out the shin.

"Hold it," the pilot commanded. He waded aboard. Felix groaned. Charley dealt with the pain in his leg. The pilot was pointing his gun at him. Charley said, "What the hell you boys so damn worked up about?"

"Get down off there." The pilot drew back the hammer on his .38. Charley came down the ladder, one excruciating step at a time. He fell down the last two rungs and landed on the deck by the ice cooler. The man with the MAC had Felix by the shirt and was about to smash him in the face again. Charley said, "Don't do that, please."

The man hit Felix again with his gun.

Charley's eyes flashed. "You tell your friend to stop that. Tell him now."

"He wouldn't take orders from Jesus Christ himself. Who was that on the radio?"

"How the hell should I know? Just tell him to stop. If it's money you're after, I got a coupla hundred in my wallet down below and some traveler's checks."

"Hey, man," said the Latino, "I ain't no fucking thief."

"No," said Charley, "course not."

"I'm gonna shoot these fuckers *now*, man."

The pilot said, "Hold on, Chavo, okay? Just hold on."

One of the other men by the Cigarette boat shouted, "Fuck is *happening*, man? Let's get out of here."

"I'm gonna shoot 'em now, man."

"Look, mister," said the pilot, "you wandered into a situation here."

Charley said, "If you're going to kill us, at least don't let me die with a dry mouth."

The pilot seemed unsure, then a flicker of compassion crossed his face. "Okay. Go ahead."

Charley reached for the cooler. "You want one?"

"Uh, yeah. Thanks."

Charley flipped back the cooler lid. "What kind you want?"

"It don't matter."

"I got different kinds."

"It really don't matter, mister. Anything."

"Bud?"

"Bud's fine."

"Miller?"

"Fine."

"I got Colt .45."

"That's nigger beer."

Charley said, "Maybe I'll have the Colt then." He shot the Latino in the arm. Felix ripped the shotgun from its Velcro sling and blew a hole in the man's back the size of a cantaloupe. The pilot turned toward Charley and found himself staring into the barrel of his Army issue Model 1911. "Drop it," said Charley, "or I'll drop you like a dog."

The side of the boat splintered from automatic-weapons fire. Felix, the pilot and Charley hunched low in the well of the fishing boat, Felix firing a few aimless rounds over the side. Charley kept his gun pointed at the pilot's forehead. They heard the motorboat's engines start up, a powerful rumble, five zoo-horsepower outboards firing, churning sand and water, backing off the beach. Felix kilroyed his face over the side; one was at the wheel, the other firing at them. "They're leaving," Felix shouted. "Where the hell *are* they?"

"Humpin'," said Charley, breathing hard. "They're humpin'."

Came a sound like a cannon from the tree line down the beach; made the Uzis and MAC sound like toy guns. A sound with *balls*, 165 grains of copper-jacketed lead leaving the barrel at 3,100 feet per second. It met up with the man's skull. He went over the side.

Rostow, wheezing from their mile-and-a-half with all the equipment, spotted through the binoculars. "One down," he said. Bundy brought back the bolt on the Winchester .300 magnum, placed another round in the receiver and chambered it slowly, gently, so as not to deform the copper jacket against the throat. He sighted through the scope. The driver, spooked by the fact of his companion's exploded cranium, was crouching beneath the dash, trying to back the boat out into deeper water.

Bundy lowered the rifle. "Let me have the fifty."

Rostow unslung the other rifle, a custom piece of gunsmithing. It was a fifty-caliber sniper rifle designed for SEALs and Special Forces by a firm out in Phoenix. It weighed twenty-one pounds, had a twenty-nine-inch barrel, took two to four ounces of pressure on the trigger and was mounted with a lo-power Leupold scope that created intimacy between shooter and target. Ordinarily a gun this size gives a fierce kick, but its designers had affixed a special muzzle brake to the end of the barrel that trapped the volcano of gas that followed the bullet out and deployed it to pull the gun away from the shooter's shoulder. Still, she kicked.

"You might want to use earplugs," said Bundy.

"Just shoot. He's getting away. Jesus *Christ*."

"Told you." Black smoke started to pour from one of the engines. Bundy drew back the fluted bolt, laid another cigar-sized fifty-caliber round and chambered it. He shot out the engines one by one. He took his time. The boat went dead in the water about a thousand yards out.

"More like twelve hundred," said Bundy.

"What now?" said Rostow, looking through the binoculars. The driver still wasn't showing himself. Bundy took a round out of a different box. "I don't like to use these," he said. "They leave kind of a smear in the barrel. But of José out there isn't giving me a hell of a lot of choice in the matter." Bundy sighted and squeezed. At this distance it took almost two seconds for the tracer to hit. The back of the boat was covered with gasoline. It made a fireball against the western sky. The boat sank.

"Hope they like their meat well done," said Bundy, removing his earplugs.

149

16

Almost dawn. The cigarette ember glowed between his sweat-wet fingers. Her sexual energy was, Christ, miraculous. Smoke rose into the blades of the fan, making their obedient revolutions. Outside it was still, except for the occasional shriek of the howler monkeys.

He looked at her in the faint light. She was lying on her stomach with her hands flat against the mattress, face toward him, like Gauguin's kanaka mistress, Tehura, in the "Manao Tupapau," but without the frightened look. He reached and ran his finger along the cleft between her buttocks. Her eyes opened-they were such light sleepers. She ran her tongue over her lips. He shouldn't have touched her. He was dry inside, pumped out. He had to get some sleep. Morning already, Christ.

"I love you," she said. The only words he'd taught her in Spanish. He should probably teach her some more, but there was a purity to such a simple vocabulary; and it was all, really, that he wanted to hear from her.

She put her mouth to his ear and made a pinhole with her lips and inhaled, producing a most—*urrnh*—exquisite sensation, as if she were trying to suck out his brain. She was descended from headhunters. Some of her people still performed the old rituals, trapping the soul inside the head by sewing up the lips, nostrils, and eyes and shrinking it in hot sand and resins. Only a few years ago a French photographer had left Manaus in search of a story and disappeared. Eventually a missionary priest was shown a head with blond hair and Caucasian features. Well, he thought, as Soledad plugged the vacuum she had created inside his ear with the moist tip of her tongue, if this is how they remove the insides, no wonder those puckered, leathery faces all have that serene look.

She went back to sleep. He couldn't. He lit another cigarette. He wanted to have her painted. But after the manner of Gauguin's "Manao"? Or Goya? The later Goya, after he'd gone mad from licking his brushes covered with lead-based paints. A parody of Goya might be just right. As "La Maja Desnuda," the naked countess that so inflamed Madrid society.

Or—he drew on his cigarette—after Manet's "Olympia"? Soledad lying on a divan wearing nothing but a black choker. Ideal! He was seized by a brilliant inspiration—where do these ideas come from? He would have the artist do the servant woman hovering at the foot of the divan in a photographic likeness of, hm ... Ursulina de Gomayumbre, dowager duchess of Lima society, descended from practically everyone, one of Mama's oldest friends. He'd have copies made and display them in the window of the gallery on the Paseo. Ha! The old bag would drop dead of embarrassment. Or make her husband confiscate it. Better make copies. Better, make lithographs. If the point is merely to *épater les bourgeois*, a painting will do, but for revolution, it's lithographs you want.

He fell asleep. When he opened his eyes an hour later the room was warm already, flooding with light. There was a knocking on the door. Virgilio's voice, muted, urgent. "Niño."

"What?"

"It's Miami. The lawyer."

He got out of bed with the sheet wrapped around his waist like a sarong. He combed his thick black hair back with his hands, lit a cigarette and coughed. Ought to switch to filters. He went into his study, picked up the phone and gave the code so the lawyer would know it was he.

The lawyer made it sound as though he hadn't slept since the incident. In fact, all he knew was what he'd gotten from the Miami *Herald*. "Medellín," he said.

The news filtered through to the left side of his brain, which was not yet entirely open for business today. "I'm listening," he said.

"The police and the DEA are saying it's a turf battle."

"What do you hear?"

"Almost nothing. No one seems to know. Or no one's taking credit for it. But Chin, the one who does transportation, he disappeared a few days before Barazo."

"What do you mean, disappeared?"

"Just like that—disappeared. You want my opinion, I think Chin sold his information to our friends in Medellín and left the country."

"I'm not paying you for your *opinion*. I want to know what happened."

"I'm working on it, Niño. I haven't been to bed in two days."

He hung up and summoned Virgilio. Virgilio appeared, as if out of air. It was his virtue. "Have you heard from Sánchez?"

"He called from Isola Verde at four this morning."

"From Panama?"

"His pilot had just radioed him. He broke a strut landing on the beach at Andros. The Cubans had to bring him a part from Nassau."

"I don't like that."

"Neither did Sánchez. But what could he do?"

"Ariella should have changed the rendezvous point. As a matter of course, he should have changed the rendezvous."

"*Sí*, Niño. I think he was trying to show continuity."

"He showed stupidity, Virgilio. I knew Barazo, Virgilio. I worked with him. And let me tell you, Ariella is no Barazo."

"*Sí*, Niño."

"He's not strong enough to take over from Barazo. We're going to have to look for someone else. All right, when is the plane due into Panama?"

"This morning."

"What *time* this morning, Virgilio?"

"Ten."

"Then Sánchez should be here by"—he looked at his watch—"four o'clock."

"He said there's a front off the coast of Ecuador. That's why he was so pissed about the strut."

"Bring some coffee. I leave in—Christ—an hour. Strong, Virgilio. I didn't get much sleep last night."

Virgilio grinned. "*Sí*, Niño."

He stepped into the shower and turned the two chromed handles. Cool water blasted out from sixteen nozzles, creating a Heraclitean vortex. He had flown two men over from Munich to install it. It felt so delicious. Sometimes he just let himself get lost in there with his thoughts. A little warmer. He soaped his groin. It was tender. Their teeth were filed when they were young; he was seriously considering flying in a dentist to round them off.

Barazo gone. Missing. Presumed ... dead? No, if Cabrera was going to kill him, he'd kill him. Medellín was direct if nothing else. Subtlety was not an arrow in their quiver. If Barazo was missing they had probably taken him back whole to Colombia. But to take Barazo alive you'd need steel nets and tranquilizer darts and Christ knows what else, a shark cage. Barazo was an animal, no beauty of nature. The people you had to deal with in this business—*qué horror*. Barazo was pure id. If Barazo ever bent over a flower it wasn't to smell it but to blow his nose on it.

They'd only met once, in Panama; the interview set up by del Cid. Barazo had the minister in charge of the Bahamian Defense Force on his payroll, an arrangement that went back to the days when he was making marijuana runs in DC-3s. He was a peasant, Barazo, a total crudity, something from underneath a rock—but a snob nonetheless, proud of his Bahamian connection: "I deal only with ministers, nothing below cabinet rank." He boasted of his friendship with Noriega. Doing business with him was one thing, but boasting of being Cara Piña's (Pineapple Face's) friend. My God, please.

"So," Barazo said, "why should I waste my time with you? Cabrera sends me seven hundred and fifty kilos every week."

"Because I can send you a ton. For the same price."

"How?"

"I'm vertically integrated." Barazo probably thought that was something to do with getting an erection. "I do my own farming, refining and transporting. I control every aspect of production. The families in Medellín and Cali want you and everyone else to think they're the only ones who get their hands on ether and acetone. I have access to the finest precursor chemicals in the world, Don Jesús." (It caught in his throat to call him that.) "I'm even thinking of installing a pipeline from Brazil. Well, I'm joking"—Barazo wasn't laughing— "but the point is, I take it from leaf to *pasta sucia* to *pasta lavada* to *pasta básica* to hydrochloride under my own roof. And I pass on my saving," he said, "to the wholesaler. Cabrera charges you twelve thousand U.S. a kilo, correct?"

"Ten," Barazo lied.

He was expecting that. "Then my price is eight, with a quarter again the volume. And a guaranteed purity of ninety-five percent."

"Bullshit."

"Testing for purity is as simple as … finding out if you're pregnant. Either you are or you aren't. If it tests out less than ninetyfive percent, it's yours, no charge."

Barazo nodded.

"With that kind of quality you're going to pass along your savings to your people. Or," he added with a grin, "not." Barazo gave a little grunt. "By my own calculation, you'll be making about three million more a week. Before taxes, that is. Of course, if you're afraid of upsetting Cabrera, I completely understand."

"Cabrera fucks the sheep on his farm." Charming.

Two weeks later, Barazo Federal Expressed the eyeballs with the little matador swords. After that it made sense to tighten security around Yenan: booby traps—which were constantly blowing up monkeys and jaguars—Beni and his SAM-7; and for insurance, a monthly retainer to Garza in Bogotá in case Cabrera found out the identity of Barazo's new supplier. Redundancy, Virgilio; make sure you never run out of options.

So—had Cabrera finally decided after all these years to get his revenge on Barazo? Sánchez will have an insight when he gets here.

"What?"

"Niño, the plane! You'll be late!"

"What?" he shouted over the roar of the shower jets.

"It's eight o'clock, Niño. You've been in there an hour."

Yayo was waiting on the tarmac. Today the motorcade consisted of four cars: the armored Range Rover and three others, two in front, one behind. The lead car emitted from its front fender an electromagnetic pulse that detonated mines. It was developed by the Spaniards after the Basques blew Franco's chief of staff, in his armored car, over the roof of a building. El Niño got into the driver's side of the Range Rover. Yayo squeezed his Incan bulk into the front passenger seat. Flores rode in back and briefed him as they drove through the dismal traffic toward the slum of Las Barriadas.

"Channel 7 for sure, Channel 5 maybe. *El Comercio* says they're sending someone, but they always say that. *La República* is sending Gaetana. Oh, and guess what—¡*Mira!*'s coming."

"¡*Mira!*?"

"You know it's serious when ¡*Mira!* starts showing up, eh?" Flores joked.

Papa wouldn't permit the magazine in the house after it published photos of Franco's mistress, Chu Chu Valpina. "LA VERDADERA 'PASIONARIA'!" But the servants used to read it anyway in the kitchen, hovering over the pictorials of Gina Lollobrigida and Cantinflas and Ordóñez the bullfighter and of course the royals. Royals were the mother's milk of ¡*Mira!* If Princess Anne fell off her horse, ¡*Mira!* treated it like the Second Coming. Once the pastry cook and the gardener got into a shouting fight in the pantry over an item in ¡*Mira!* saying that the Conde de Barcelona—father of the present King of Spain—was having an affair with Jacqueline Kennedy. (JFK was still alive.) Papa heard it and came in and tore the copy into pieces with his huge hands and discharged them both and cuffed him hard on the ear simply for being present. ¡*Mira!* continued to be a thorn in his existence. Just a few months ago he'd caught Soledad with a copy of it. An Indian girl who couldn't read, whose only Spanish was "I love you," staring, fascinated, at photographic spreads of Julio Iglesias and Joan Collins. He'd lost his temper a little, snatching it away and ripping it into pieces—just as Papa had, it only now occurred to him—and yelling at her with words she didn't understand: "Pretty boys! Sluts! Garbage!" He gave her a scare. She started to cry. Suddenly he's down on his hands and knees piecing the wretched thing back together, Julio's face, Joan's left breast ...

"They'll do the Robin Hood angle, you can bet on it," Flores was saying. "Yayo can be Father Tuck."

"Brother Tuck," El Niño corrected. Yayo made no response, Uzi on his lap. El Niño said to Flores, "Try to keep *¡Mira!* away from me."

They were going through a red light. It was one of the virtues of having an armed motorcade. At the far end of the intersection he saw a gamine, seven or eight years old, filthy, hair matted, half naked, holding a stick with a piece of rag attached to it. He braked. The security car behind almost smashed into them. "Shit," said Flores. "Niño, come on, we're late." But he was already out the door, Yayo following with his gun drawn, shouting orders at his men in the lead car to form a cordon. He was a nightmare to protect, like Gorbachev, always jumping out of cars. Someday—

The gamine saw large men with guns converging on her and turned and began to run. He caught her after a few feet. She struggled in his arms. He soothed her. "It's all right, beauty. We're not going to hurt you. I promise."

He held her tightly. The stench was appalling. Her right eye was runny with pus. Some of them this age had syphilis, gonorrhea, AIDS. By ten they were old; by fifteen, according to one estimate, 80 percent of them were dead.

Traffic was backing up behind the stalled motorcade. One of

Yayo's men held up his submachine gun; the honking stopped. In respects, Lima is similar to Los Angeles.

Yayo had his frantic look. He whispered to Flores, "Is he wearing his vest?" Flores rolled his eyes-how should I know? "Please, *patrón*," begged Yayo, "get back in the car. Please."

"What's your name, beauty?" He stroked her matted hair. "Where do you live?" There was no answer to that.

"Flores," he said, holding out his hand. Flores took out a roll and peeled off bills. He handed them to El Niño. El Niño took the whole billfold and put it in the gamine's sticky hand and closed his own over hers. The gamine grinned at him. She reached into her rags and produced a *basuco* cigarette and held it out to him. They made them from *pasta sucia* and tobacco: the high came mostly from the kerosene and hydrochloric acid and other chemicals, not from the coca. He stared at the crudely rolled cigarette in the sticky palm. He took it from her and said, "Thank you, beauty." The girl smiled.

He stood and got back in the car and drove the rest of the way in silence. Flores didn't say anything until they reached the edge of the crowd in Las Barriadas.

Flores' people had built a small stage in front of the building hung with the banner that said CLÍNICA LIBRE, and had set up food and drink stands, had hired musicians, put up lights and posters and loudspeakers. The atmosphere was that of a political rally, an election without candidates. His people were scattered throughout the crowd of five hundred to get the chant going, organizing their roars into iambs, "Ni-ño! Ni-ño!" Soon they were all converging on the stalled motorcade. Then the hot TV lights were on, bathing everything in that lurid glare. Dr. Núñez was on the stage with a microphone, shouting, "Let him through! Please, let him through! He's here! He's come! But we have to let him through!"

Yayo put himself at the head of the phalanx, but even Yayo could not penetrate this. They all wanted to touch him, to tear off a piece of clothing for a talisman. Their arms insinuated between Yayo's men, hands plucking at him. His blood was rushing, it was good, but thank God for Yayo's men, they'd tear you to pieces with their love otherwise. It made him think of when Papa had taken him to the plaza when he was very young to see the god Ordóñez kill bulls. A total disaster. Ordóñez put the sword into the bull, the bull hunched his great shoulder muscles and the sword flew out like a missile, followed by a tremendous gush of blood. He began to cry for the bull as it writhed on the ground while Ordóñez strutted in his suit of lights. Papa, mortified, took him home and made him put on his sister's clothing, made him go to school in a dress for a week; regarded with satisfaction the bruises he returned with every day.

They had to lift him onto the stage over the heads of the crowd. He held up his arms to silence them, but they kept chanting. He shook hands with Dr. Núñez. Dr. Núñez made an *Ecce homo* gesture. Niño took the microphone from him.

"This is *your* clinic now," he said. "And no one will take it from you!"

Something went flying through the air and landed on the stage by his feet. A rosary. He picked it up and, smiling, shook his head. "Listen to me. Science is the answer to our problems. Not"—he waved the rosary— "this. This was brought by the Spaniards." He tossed it back into the crowd. "*This*"—he pointed to the white-washed building behind him— "was brought by me!" The crowd roared.

"He's good," Dr. Núñez said to Flores.

"Yes."

"What does he want? I mean, he's not going to run for office again, is he?"

Flores made a face. "Pah—he's finished with that shit."

"So, why?"

"He wants to help people."

"Sure, but why?"

"He wants to make the government look like assholes."

"Ah," said Dr. Núñez, satisfied. He stepped forward and shouted into his microphone, "¡Viva El Niño!"

"Viva El Niño!" the crowd shouted back.

Rosaries flew through the air.

The reporters were negotiating their way through the crowd in front of the stage. He saw a blonde followed closely by TV lights. Antoniela Catamarca, Channel 7. Good-looking. Christ, a guy was putting his hand up her skirt for a grope. She hit him. The man just grinned. Kids were slicing at her cameraman's belt with razors.

"Yayo." He pointed.

Yayo and his people got her up onto the stage. She was shaken. "That filthy, disgusting *cholo*"—she pointed at the man— "he, he—"

"Don't blame him too much. Beautiful women like you never come to Las Barriadas. That was probably the happiest he will ever be in his life."

"Well, I don't know about that." But she was already adjusting herself in a compact mirror. She held his microphone to his lips; such an obviously phallic act, he thought. How do they manage it?

"This is the sixth so-called free clinic you've established in Lima," she began.

"Wait," said her cameraman. "I'm not getting power. Shit, those little fuckers stole my batteries."

160

The other reporters were on him now. He wondered which was from *¡Mira!* He heard a man's voice say, "Sendero"; he turned away toward another reporter. The man said more loudly, "It's alleged that you're connected with Sendero Luminoso."

He turned toward the man. Robles, from *El Comercio*. He said into his own microphone, "Señor Robles here, from the great newspaper *El Comercio*, which only comes to Las Barriadas to hunt Communists, wants to know if I am connected to the Shining Path? I told him my connection is to you. What do you say?"

"Kill him!"

He turned back to Robles, who had gone pale. He smiled. "There's your answer. Next question?"

La República wanted to know why he wouldn't stand for the municipal elections in November. "I want to help Peru, not make things worse." The reporters laughed.

"What about the foreign debt?"

"It is Peru that is owed, not the other way around. Let the imperialists return all the gold and silver they took from us. *Then* let us look at the balance sheet."

"Brigitte Nielsen, the former wife of Rambo, is in Peru making a film. What is your opinion of her?"

"What?" *¡Mira!* "I—have no opinion on this." Yayo, get this idiot away from me.

"Are you related to Julio Iglesias?"

"No!"

"But you're an Iglesias."

"I have not used that name for years," he said testily. He turned to Dr. Núñez. "Come on, let's see the clinic."

"Of course, Niño."

161

As they went in, reporters following, Flores nudged the doctor and whispered, "Remember, only the really sick ones."

"They're all 'really sick,' Flores." There was an old man gasping with asthma, a boy with a crushed leg needing amputation, several horrible worm cases, dehydrated infants. In one ward they came to a shrieking *basuco* smoker tied hands and feet to the bed because he had scratched the skin on his legs down to the bone. Flores whispered to Núñez, "Christ, Núñez!"

A man coughing up blood from consumptive lungs, a rabies case, drooling, blank-staring stroke victims, a failing kidney, cancers of the bone and throat, AIDS. The reporters had grown quiet. They came to a woman whose husband, Dr. Núñez explained, had gotten drunk on *pisco* and thrown a pot of boiling chicken grease on her.

Núñez whispered to El Niño, "Frankly, *patrón*, it would be better if she died."

El Niño sat in a chair beside her bed and took her hand. She squeezed it. He said into her ear, "I am going to take care of you." She made a croaking noise. He stood and told Núñez that he would make an arrangement to fly her in his own plane to Texas, where there was a famous burn unit.

"Bravo, El Niño!" Flores clapped.

Outside in the hallway, El Niño whispered to Yayo, "Find the husband and return the favor." He was grateful to reach the outside again and hear the crowd.

Better still, to be back inside the cabin of the Falcon, climbing above the Andes. In truth, he hated Lima. It was a squalid remnant of a squalid conquest. The real Peru had always been on the other side of the mountains.

He drank a scotch and felt the tension go out of his neck. He was exhausted. An early dinner, maybe once with Soledad, beautiful, brown Soledad. Soledad was the real Peru. He should have kept her original name, but "Cicurrakka" was, well ... Soledad was a good name, signifying her isolation, with him, between the two cultures.

A faint humming from beneath his feet, a shifting of hydraulic fluids ... sometimes it was triggered by a noise, sometimes by a color, sometimes there was no trigger, just the memory of humming along in that idiotic vehicle, the golf cart, across oppressed lawns, her father talking about some snapping turtle that inhabited the pond between the seventh and eighth holes.

"Fearsome old thing. They tell me he might be forty or even fifty years old. They think he got the groundskeeper's dog a few years ago, can you imagine? Do you have them in Peru, Antonio? Snapping turtles? I imagine you've pretty much got *everything* down there."

He managed to shake it off. When he opened his eyes he saw not the manicured, artificial green of the golf course but the lush eastern slope of the Cordillera Oriental descending into the Huallaga Valley, cradle of the still-New World.

Virgilio was waiting with a pained expression. Virgilio worried all the time, it was another of his virtues.

He listened without comment to what Virgilio had to report. When they got to the house, he lit a cigarette and made Virgilio go through it again, word for word.

"When Sánchez didn't report in, I called the field in Isola Verde. No answer. I mean, the phone didn't even ring. Nothing. Finally Miguel calls me, scared out of his brain, like, like, like—"

"Okay, Virgilio. Go on."

163

"He said the pilot had called in saying there was a problem with the landing gear, and, and, and Sánchez was all pissed off because of the front off Ecuador and—"

"Yes yes."

"So the pilot called in a half hour out, with the proper ID code. Sánchez gets into his plane and gets it warmed up because he wants to leave right away as soon as they've got the money loaded—"

"Yes."

"And the Aztec appears and lands and taxis up next to Sánchez's Aerocommander and suddenly everything's in the shit, there's shooting and, and Nestor and Freddy are dead, and Julio's dead. Miguel said he got off some shots, then Sánchez's plane takes off and things start to blow up."

"What starts to blow up?"

"Everything! Everything! The hangar, the, the work sheds. Sánchez's plane flies over and everything starts to blow up. The next thing Miguel knows is he's lying in a field twenty meters away with his pants on fire and no hair. He's—"

"What about the money?"

"Gone, Niño. It's all burned. They must have dropped into the hangar or something with the bomb, or—I don't know, but Miguel says the whole place is full of burned hundred-dollar bills."

"Where's Miguel right now?"

"Shitting himself in the Balboa safe house. With no hair. I think he's drunk, Niño. He wasn't making any sense when I had my last conversation."

"All right, listen to me carefully. First, get the men assembled. Call Vidal in Tingo and tell him we need more men, twenty at least. Second, tell Beni to get his missiles ready. Three, get Miguel on the phone, I don't care how he is, it's important that I speak to him right away. Four, call Garza in Bogotá, tell him to get his team to Cabrera's place-never mind, I'll speak to Garza myself. Five, seal the place, nothing in, nothing out. Especially nothing out, understand? Do you *understand*, Virgilio?"

"*Sí*, Niño." Virgilio ran to the door and stopped.

She was standing in the doorway, wearing a T-shirt that came down to above her waist. She had on nothing else. She smiled at him.

"Go upstairs." He pointed. "Now!" She gave him a hurt look and ran noiselessly up the stairs.

A few moments later the sirens went off, drowning out the sound of the jungle.

17

The square of projector light whitewashed the wall. McNamara sat by the carousel with his bandaged upper thigh extended, trying to get the mechanism to work.

Felix was on the couch, quiet. Ever since they started planting them here on the island, Felix had been acting morose. Charley could not figure it out. Tried to cheer him up and all he got back was grunts. Look at him, like he's just been force-fed a dead toad. His ribs are still hurting him. Charley's leg throbbed some. It was good the bullet had gone straight through. Probably should have hired a doctor at the outset. Mac and Bundy had some training, but it was starting to get wet—

"I'm going to have to do this manually," said Mac. "The advance mechanism's all screwed up."

The square of harsh light turned into a face, youthful with fine features, mouth open in laughter.

"Antonio Fabiano Iglesias y Cáceres," said Rostow, using a pool cue for a pointer. "Father a wealthy Lima manufacturer and exporter. Deceased. Education: Markam, elementary school in Lima for rich kids run by German nuns; Culver Military Academy, South Bend, Indiana; Williams College, Massachusetts, BA 1970. University of Miami Medical School, dropped out after one year. Worked for father's company 1972; left 1972. Ran for Senate 1973 on platform of nationalizing various industries, canceling foreign debt and banfling bullfighting. Defeated. Left Peru, resided Bogotá, Miami, Honduras, Paris, Zurich. Returned Peru 1979 following death of his father. Turned family residence into mental asylum." Rostow read from his notes: "Caused a stir among neighbors. Residence was in Miraflores district, where the rich people live. City government intervened on zoning grounds. Ran for Senate again." Rostow said, "This is strange—he announced his candidacy in a cemetery."

"Cemetery?" said Charley.

"Yeah," said Rostow, "he gave this speech saying since all the dead people in the cemetery had voted for his opponent the last time, he was going to get their votes this time around."

"Huh," said Charley.

"Lost election, left Lima. Said to be involved with Sendero Luminoso—Shining Path—guerrilla movement in Ayacucho. Moved to various Amazon district towns, Tingo María, Uchiza, Tocache Nuevo, eventually his own compound, Yenan—that's the next slide. Changed name to El Niño."

"The Kid," said Bundy.

"Christ Child," said Felix.

"Correct," said Rostow. "There was this weather phenomenon in the Pacific Ocean in 1982 where these warm currents caused all sorts of problems, floods and droughts. Caused eight billion dollars' worth of damage around the world, and fifteen hundred deaths."

"Don't seem right to name something like that after Baby Jesus," said Charley.

"South American fishermen named it," said Rostow. "It happened right around Christmastime. Next slide."

The square on the wall turned into a large-scale topographical map of northern Peru. "The upper Huallaga Valley," Rostow said, pointing with his cue toward a region northeast of Lima. "Here's Tingo María down here, and up here"—he placed the tip a few inches north of the town— "is his place. He calls it Yenan."

"Yenan? Is that a town?"

"Sánchez says it's named after a place in China. I don't really know what the story is with the name."

"Let's find that out." Charley made a note.

"Right. Okay, here's the deal. You've got your Andes Mountains running north and south like a twenty-thousand-foot wall between Lima and the Huallaga. And to the east of Yenan, you got three thousand miles of Amazon jungle. Between a rock and hard place.

"Now, the Huallaga's where they grow the best leaf in the world. The soil and the altitude are just right for it. Leaves there have an alkaloid content of .79; the stuff down here in the Valle de la Convención is only about .33.

"The government in Lima didn't mess much with the Huallaga until Sendero moved into the valley in '83. I was there from '81 to '84, until I. ... When Sendero moved in to provide protection for the *narcos*, Lima got nervous. Sendero is *bad* fucking news. I mean,

167

they make Iranians seem reasonable. Their hero, historically, is this Indian Tupac Amaru, who the Spaniards tied to horses two hundred years ago and tore apart. They buried the limbs in like four different provinces—the Spaniards were always doing this sort of thing; you can see why the whole place is so fucked up—and suddenly there's these rumors that the limbs are regrowing. The leader is this guy Abímael Guzmán, they call him Presidente Gonzalo, I don't know why, and no one's seen him for like ten years. They're Maoist, basically, but they think the Chinese Commies are soft and forget the Soviets. When I was in Lima the lights would go out about every two hours because Sendero had blown up another pylon. They'll hang dead dogs from lampposts, kill people in ways you don't want to hear about. In Chimbote once they tied a stick of dynamite to a duck—a duck—and blew up a telephone exchange."

"Can't be all bad," said Mac.

"They started providing security for the dopers. It's a great arrangement. They charge a 'revolutionary tax' on every kilo. It works out great for everyone. This whole area here"—he circled the Huallaga— "is a *zona rosa*. The Red Zone. It belongs to them."

"Scandalous," said Charley, exhaling cigar smoke.

"Every now and then the government decides to do a little pecker flexing and they'll drop in some paratroopers for the photo opportunity, but the moment those boys hit the ground they run for the river—*run*—where the patrol boats are prepositioned for the extraction."

"Hm," said Charley.

"Now, what our boy did was, his innovation was to figure a way around Colombia. Traditionally the Peruvians only handle it up to a certain point. They take the leaves and soak them in these pits

168

with kerosene and sulfuric acid, then skim off the residue. That's called *pasta sucia*—dirty paste. Then they wash that, right there in the river, and turn it into *pasta lavada*, washed paste, or *pasta básica de cocaína*, PBC. At that point they fly it into Colombia, where they refine it with ether and acetone, and some other precursor chemicals turn it into cocaine hydrochloride, the powder. This guy figured a way to do that himself and cut out the Colombians, which probably didn't make them happy. Sánchez said he owns his own chemical factories in Brazil."

"Vertical integration," said Charley. "Smart businessman."

"Extremely smart. If he's moving a metric ton into the country every week, then he's probably clearing two hundred million a year."

"Jesus," said Charley. "I don't make two hundred million a year."

"Next slide. Here's a sketch of Yenan, according to what Sánchez told us. Four-thousand-foot airstrip for his jets, barracks, drying sheds, soccer field, soaking pits, main house, aquarium"

"Aquarium?"

"Maybe he likes fresh fish. Communications shed over here, and here," said Rostow, lowering his tone a good octave, "is the radar facility, which is where they keep the Stingers."

"Stingers," Charley grunted.

"He thinks they came from Peshawar, from the muj."

Charley shook his head. "I *told* Casey not to give those people Stingers. I told him it'd be nothing but trouble."

Rostow drew a circle around the compound with his pool cue. "The perimeter's booby-trapped seven ways from Sunday. Sánchez said that's how they get a lot of their fresh meat. Jaguar, tapir, they got these giant rats, apparently called capybaras. He said they're pretty good."

"I never ate jag," said Mac.

"It's like dog, but stringy," said Bundy.

"You never ate jaguar."

"I ate leopard once in Africa."

"When did you eat leopard?"

"In Angola."

"Bullshit."

"Boys," said Charley, "let's save the gastronomy for later, if you don't mind. Go on."

"That's about it. He's got himself a tight little asshole in there. He's got the Andes on one side, a jungle on the other, a security force from hell, Stingers, a mined perimeter. I don't want to sound downbeat, Mr. Becker, but this isn't going to be easy."

"Is that why you all signed on for this job?" Charley pulled himself up out of his chair painfully. "Because it was going to be *easy*? Mac? Bundy, is that why you boys signed on?"

"No, sir," said Bundy. "I signed on for the money."

Charley hobbled over to the projection wall. "Gimme a little more scale," he said. The sketch of Yenan disappeared, replaced by a largescale map of Peru. Charley stared at it, cigar smoke curling upward into the projector light.

He said, "It's been right here the whole time, biting us on the ass."

II

Two months later

18

Charley stood on the bridge of the *Esmeralda* and surveyed with a squint the Amazon port city of Iquitos. A huddle of beggars surveyed him back.

He didn't feel right looking down as he did on them from his gleaming white high-tech perch. The yacht stood out so, here. Her pristine whiteness seemed to rebuke the filth about her. Lord, she seemed to be saying, when's the last time you took a *bath*?

At least, Charley comforted himself, he'd had the presence of mind to change her name from *Conquistador*. Be like steaming into Gdansk on a yacht named *Blitzkrieg*.

The beggars were trying to get his attention. They shouted, "*Capitán! Capitán!*" and polished the air hopefully with rags. Leishmaniasis had eaten away the nose of one man, leaving a hole, a sad and terrible sight. Charley waved back.

Conquistador had been Margaret's idea. She bought it without telling Charley after reading that Ibiz Fahoudi, the international arms dealer, was under financial pressures. She took Charley to Miami without telling him why and presented it to him as another of her faits accomplis. "Damnit, Margaret, it's a whore-house." "I'm going to make it lovely," she said. Yachts bored

Charley; he felt trapped on them. He installed a cantilevered flight deck on the upper deck to allow him to fly his UAVs—unmanned aerial vehicles; model planes. *Conquistador* became a miniature aircraft carrier. Margaret would be below taking the sun on the fantail deck, Charley and Tasha would be on the flight deck reliving the battle of the Coral Sea, scale-model Avengers coming in too low on final and hitting the sides and blowing up, Margaret shouting up at them to stop, giving up, going on with her reading.

"Capitán!"

Charley reached into his pocket. He was an old-fashioned man, had never used a credit card—didn't believe in them—always kept a thick, comforting wad of cash. He peeled off a few bills and was going to crumple them and toss them down to the beggars, then that didn't seem right either.

A security guard looked out of his shed and saw them and came out waving his stick and shouting at them, *"Fuera, fuera! Fuera!"* just like Sister Angustia used to do when the chickens wandered in during Mass. Charley called down to the crewman standing watch at the gangplank to let the beggars aboard. The beggars came scrambling up, turning as they did to give the wharf guard various unmistakable hand signals. The man with no nose was grinning and made a hissing noise through his exposed sinuses.

Charley came down the stairs and there they were, standing improbably in the main salon. He approached them with his customary Chargin' Charley gait. The beggar nearest went into a half crouch, thinking he was going to hit them.

He shook their hands and asked their names.

"Okay," he said in his fluent Spanish, "I want to do some business with you. I want to buy some prayers."

The beggars nodded.

Charley said, "You're all Catholic, right?"

"*Síí*," they said together.

"No Jehovah's Witnesses or any of that?" One took out an old rosary looked like it might have belonged to one of the Apostles. Charley peeled bills off his wad, handing each a hundred dollars. "Okay, I want Hail Marys, a hundred of them."

"*Sí, patrón.*" Another said, "What about some Our Fathers?"

"All right," he said, peeling off another round, "I'll take a hundred of them, too."

The beggar with no nose said, "*Capitán*, how about Acts of Contrition?"

"All right, fifty."

The oldest one, with an abscessed eye like a runny egg, stepped forward and said with gravity, "*Patrón*, we cannot forget Our Lady of Lourdes." The other beggars murmured assent.

"How many you think she needs?"

"*Pues*," said the old man thoughtfully, "it's hard to say. Our Lady of Lourdes said, 'Pray to me.' She didn't say how much to pray, but ..."

"*Sí*," the others said, nodding.

"Prayer bandits," Charley uttered. He handed over the rest of his wad.

"*Patrón?*"

Charley had already started back up the stairs.

"What's your name? So they'll know who the prayers are for."

"They're for Natasha."

They waved their money at the guard on their way out the gate.

Senator Gallardo arrived with his entourage on schedule. Charley was standing at the head of the gangway to receive him, Felix by his side. Felix whispered, "He's got a photographer with him."

Charley, grinning, whispered back, "You ever see a politician who didn't? ... Felipe!"

"Charley!" burst out Senator Gallardo, giving him a manly *abrazo*. It was like old friends. Actually, they'd never met, but they'd spoken on the phone so many times over the previous months it felt like old friends.

The senator gestured at the enormity of it all. "I thought it was the *Titanic*!"

Charley laughed, the senator's entourage laughed, everyone laughed. Charley said, "My yacht is your yacht."

"I accept!" Everyone laughed. Felix introduced himself to the photographer, a woman. "Do you work for the senator?" he said.

"No no. Just sometimes. I'm free-lance."

"Press?"

"Sure."

"Are your pictures for the senator, then?"

"Yes."

"You see, Mr. Becker's a very private man. Just between you and me, he's a little worried about kidnappers."

"Ah."

"You'll only give these photos to the senator for his private use, then?"

"Yes, certainly."

Felix grinned. On those occasions when Felix smiled, light came into him.

The senator introduced the provincial governor, the mayor, the commander of the military district of Loreto, the commissioner of customs, to whom Charley expressed special gratitude for his assistance with the formalities.

"Well," said Charley, "would you like to have a tour?"

What a question!

He took them first to his Rogue's Gallery, a bulkhead aft of the forward lounge on which he'd hung pictures of himself with assorted nabobs and panjandrums.

"There's Kissinger. This one was Chairman of the Joint Chiefs under Carter."

"Human rights," said the senator.

"Right. There's Haig, you remember him. Here's the Emperor of Japan. He was a prince then. With a camera, wouldn't you know. That's the papal nuncio, he's a cardinal now. Prime Minister of Jamaica. This fellow here, now, he got himself beheaded by his chief of staff just a couple of months after this was taken. Terrible thing. Good man, too."

The senator said, "A lesson for us all," occasioning some mirthless laughter.

Charley took them to the bridge and showed them *Esmeralda's* sophisticated navigational system, especially the look-down, shoot-down radar mounted on the bow to detect the huge, hull-piercing logs and tree trunks that barreled down the Amazon's current at torpedo speeds.

On their way back to the main salon, Charley pointed out the table that had once belonged to Queen Victoria. "But that isn't the reason I bought it," he said. "I am reliably informed that Tallulah Bankhead once made love on top of that table."

He showed them the Art Deco gold-glass panels from the old

Normandie, the brooding Vlaminck seascape, the gay Dufy watercolor of the Côte d'Azur, Cocteau's sensuous sailor, John Steuart Curry's ancient graybeard mariner battling the furious storm alone on a sinking, wave-swept deck, the gentle Bierstadt coastal scene, various postrealist Mihanovics, Jean-Louis Bilweis' risible trompe l'oeils of scuba divers and mermaids, Montague Dawson's tearjerking painting of a Victory ship being machine-gunned by a U-boat as the crew jump over the rails into the flaming water, Manet's "Absinthe Drinker" mounted playfully over the bar.

"There's an interesting story behind that," said Charley, tending bar himself, as was his wont. "Manet painted a version of that painting and they damn near ran him out of town for it. You didn't paint drunks back in the 1850s. Just wasn't done. One of his buddies was Baudelaire. Baudelaire didn't much like it either, though he drank a lot of absinthe, I mean Baudelaire *drank*. And took drugs. *And* had syphilis. He had a terrible end but Manet stuck by him. After he died, Manet did another version of the same painting, with Baudelaire's face instead of the rag-and-bone man who was the model for the first. Scotch for you, sir, another scotch for you, Mr. Mayor, scotch for the governor, and that was a scotch and Coke for you, sir? Coming up. I had absinthe once. It's illegal, but they do a little bootlegging in a town in Switzerland near the French border. Can you imagine the Swiss doing anything illegal? Here you go, sir, Dewar's and Coca-Cola. *Salud*."

They drank for a while on the fantail salon and then dinner was announced. On their way to the dining room they noticed the Stele, and they all stopped. It had that effect on you.

"Magnificent," said the senator.

"Ain't it just?" said Charley. An art magazine had once said that

Charles Becker could manage to make Michelangelo's "Pieta" sound like a '57 Chevy.

"Stele" stood about six feet tall, an upright slab of poured ferro-concrete interlaced with thousands of strands of fiber optics, so that its dull, rough-hewn surface was speckled with dots of astral intensity. It was named for the monoliths the ancients used to erect to their fallen warriors, or to make a holy place, or in some cases, probably, just because they felt like it. The fiber-optic strands were all connected to a noiseless electric motor inside its base that played a continuous, kaleidoscopic light show over a twenty-four-hour cycle. Pinpricks of brilliant cobalt blue turned crimson, then melted into oranges, yellows, greens and violets, producing a stained-glass window made by aliens: a dandelion burst of fireworks blazed, shimmering tendrils of light cascading slowly into a moonlit sea. Comets screamed across the universe, smashing into each other, exploding in luminescent chunks that hurtled furiously into the ocean below, sending up waves that climbed up and up and up, becoming a mountain that metamorphosed into a temple. Across the front of the temple appeared letters—Phoenician or Greek, perhaps—scratched out in a fiery ink, hot as molten lava, that seemed to flow from an angry Creator's fountain pen. *Mene mene tekel upharsin. You have been weighed on the scales and found wanting?* Charley led his guests in to dinner.

The commissioner of customs squeezed the arm of the military district commander.

"Did you notice something?" he said.

"What?"

"His guests. They're all men."

"So?"

"Where are the women?"

177

"Back home," laughed the military commander. "Maybe he wants to try the *canuweras*." The *canuweras* are peculiar to Iquitos—Venice of the Amazon—prostitutes who ply their trade in dugout canoes.

"They don't look like businessmen to me. Look at them. They look like bodyguards. And what about these matchbooks? *Conquistador?*"

"Well, ask him. Myself, I'm going to eat."

Charley said, "We're having a very simple supper tonight, I hope you don't mind." Stewards entered with platters, cold pear soup sprinkled with mint leaves, poached guinea hen eggs on fried toast layered with chutney and carpaccio, miniature acorn squash stuffed with cold ratatouille and dusted with Parmesan cheese, green tomatoes in balsamic vinegar topped with a cilantro seviche.

"I'm trying to shuck some weight," Charley said, smiling. Stewards appeared with more platters bearing grapefruit sorbet in Siamese incense vessels adorned with candied violet blossoms. Then more platters, the main course: small filets of Chateaubriand wrapped in bacon, grilled mushrooms in *beurre rouge*, pencil-thin spears of fresh asparagus. Château Lafon-Rochet '66.

Charley spoke excitedly about the trip. He said he'd always dreamed of going up the Amazon, and now that he was in the Indian summer of his life he was finally going to do it. He said how grateful he was to the senator for making it possible.

The senator, overcome by the wine and Charley's companionship, suddenly turned to the military commander and demanded that two Peruvian Navy patrol boats escort the *Esmeralda* on her trip upriver.

Charley placed his hand on the senator's arm. "Felipe," he said, "that's most gracious, most generous, but hardly necessary. And of course, it would be a scandal if our friends in the press"—everyone chuckled— "learned that the vital resources of your fine military were diverted to protecting a silly old gringo off on a pleasure cruise."

"But, Charley," said the senator, "the Huallaga region is ... *bueno, un poco desequilibrado*."

Lovely way of putting it: "a little unbalanced." Just a few weeks ago Sendero had floated twenty decapitated corpses down the Huallaga past a base where DEA men were stationed.

"Why not go up the Marañón River?" he said. "Ecologically speaking, the Marañón is fantastic." Everyone agreed.

"I don't doubt it for a moment," said Charley, signaling for the dessert, "but my heart is set on seeing the 'Eyebrow of the Jungle.' I've read so much about it, you see."

"Well," said the senator, "the 'Eyebrow of the Jungle' is in a situation of lamentable extremity. Since the 1970s, almost a million hectares of the forest has been cut down by the *narcos* for the cultivation of coca."

"Is that a fact?"

"Yes. And now as a result we have erosion problems. For the first time in seven thousand years, eh? When the Inca planted his little coca, he built trenches, with stone walls, with yucca plants interspersed here and there to keep the soil from sliding off the mountain. Now—pah!—you think the *narcos* care about erosion?"

"Deplorable," said Charley.

"And what they flush *into* the soil! The chemicals they use for the refining. In one year, Charley, fifteen million gallons of kerosene. Eight million gallons of sulfuric acid. Two million of acetone, two million of toluene and sixteen *thousand* tons of lime. In one *year*."

"Criminal," said Charley.

"Coca cultivation has become the Attila of tropical agriculture."

"I'm sorry, Felipe, the what?"

"Attila the Hun."

"Ah," said Charley, "dessert. I hope you like ice cream."

It was a map of the Amazon done entirely in ice cream: the jungle floodplain in pistachio; the river, snaking from the Atlantic to the Andes, a geographically precise vein of mocha fudge. The cordilleras rose on vanilla slopes to sorbet summits of blue and boysenberry ices. Candied jaguars, marzipan toucans, caramelized coleoptera, licorice crocs and skulls of spun sugar. (Charley wondered, were the skulls in good taste?) Chef Ralph had contrived an active volcano that spouted wisps of vapor by means of a concealed chip of dry ice.

Charley handed the knife to the senator, saying he would be honored if he would make the first cut.

The senator made several false starts. Finally, with a smile, he put the tip of the blade into Lima—represented by a macaroon star. "Since everyone blames Lima for everything these days." Everyone laughed.

Coffee, brandy and cigars were taken on the helicopter deck. The commissioner of customs lit Charley's cigar.

"I found these in an ashtray," he said, showing Charley the *Conquistador* matches.

Charley puffed, looked at them. "Hm," he said, "how about that. Donald Trump was aboard couple of weeks ago, they must be from his boat." Charley winked, "Wouldn't you *know* he'd call a boat that?"

The *abrazos* at the head of the gangway were copious. Charley sent them all off with a case of the wine. Forty-nine ninety was fueled and ready at the airport to fly the senator back to Lima. The next morning it flew back to the States with the stewards and crew. *Esmeralda* cast off her lines at 0900 and Charley nosed her bow into the current. The beggars waved rosaries at him. He gave them three blasts on the ship's horn.

19

"Hey, Frank—Jesus, what the hell happened?"

It was Taccarelli, from Training. "Nothing, it's fine."

"Nothing? You look like a fucking hard-boiled egg."

"I fell asleep under the tanning machine. It's a little sunburn is all."

"Oh. Hey, uh, how's your sister, Frankie?"

Something about the way he said it. "She's much better, thank you, Al."

Taccarelli gave him a conspiratorial wink. "Gubanovich mentioned."

"Mentioned what, Al?"

"You know. Your stomach problem. Kincaid's bullet acting up?"

"Uh, yeah. It's nothing."

"You okay?"

"I'm much better, Al."

"Is it—"

Diatri sighed. "It's my bowel, Al. My small bowel, if you really want to know." These elevators.

"Gubanovich said you were Intensive Care the whole time."

"You two had a nice mention about all this, I see. Well, I got news for you, Alphonse. There's no such thing as Intensive Care

181

anymore. No one cares. Except one of the cleaning ladies. She gave me a flower. It was dead, but it was nice of her anyway. Other than her, no one really gives a rat's ass. One night the guy next to me dies, right? One minute his heart monitor is going beep ... beep ... beep, then it's going beeeeeeeeeeeeeeep, you know, we-nowcon-clude-our-broadcasting-day? Six minutes. I counted six minutes before they came. I'm yelling for them and I would've got out of bed except for this tube in me the size of a garden hose and I'm a little afraid my plumbing is going to come out with it if I get out of bed. Six minutes. You know what they were doing? They were watching the ball game. The guy was cold by the time they came in. He was a TV dinner. Suddenly they're charging in shouting, 'Stand back, stand back!' like I'm trying to block their way, and they start hitting him with the paddles. The fibrillator paddles. They must have hit him twenty times. They had this poor guy jumping like a frog. I'm telling the fangool with the paddles, 'Hey, he's been dead for a week. Why don't you thaw him out first. Put him in the microwave.'"

"Jesus. What hospital was it?"

"The VA."

"The VA? Oh yeah, right, Gubanovich said."

"Next time, I don't care if the SAC does find out. I'm not going back to the VA."

"I'll see you round, Frank. Take care of yourself, okay?"

"You bet. Hey, Al, listen, Gubanovich wasn't supposed to go shooting his mouth off. I mean, I don't mind *you* knowing, but—"

"Not to worry, Frankie. My hand to God."

Diatri went looking for Gubanovich to kill him. After all that, he goes and tells Taccarelli. Jesus Christ. Now everyone will be coming up and asking, "Yo, Frankie, how's the bowel?"

All that, to keep the SAC from finding out, driving himself to the VA instead of riding in an ambulance to a city hospital, where at least you stood a 50-50 chance, sweat pouring off, shouting out Sinatra songs to keep from passing out from the Red Meteor in his gut. Then when he could finally stand up, staggering with the rolling IV stand and a quarter down a corridor full of Korean War vets, calling the SAC on the pay phone and asking if he could take his back vacation now, effective right away. The SAC saying, "Jesus, Frank, we're up to our tits here. Plus we got the Bennett dog and pony show next week. It's a lousy time." Just then the loudspeaker blasting out, "Dr. Deaver, please report to surgery, Dr. Deaver ..." and the SAC suspicious, saying, "Are you in a *hospital*, Frank?"

Diatri bending over from the Red Meteor, holding on to the IV stand. "Yes, I am, Jim. I'm here ... I'm here looking after my baby sister."

"Jesus, Frank. What's wrong?"

"We're not sure at this point, Jim. But it doesn't look real great. They're going to be doing an exploratory. I just need to be with her right now."

"Of course, Frank. I'm sorry. Why didn't you say? Let us know what you need. Anything."

"Thank you, Jim. That means a lot to me."

Then after they finally release him—looking like hell on toast— it occurs to him to get under the tanning machine to get a little color back so the SAC won't wonder. Falls asleep and wakes up looking like Kid Hiroshima. Terrific. Now on top of all that, Gubanovich is going around telling people.

"Hey, Frank. How's your sister?"

"A lot better, thanks, Juanita."

"I woulda sent a card but I didn't know what hospital."

"I appreciate that."

"You lose weight?"

"Just a few pounds. I've been doing a lot of jogging."

"Take care, Frank."

He felt badly lying to people like Juanita. The phone rang. It was Liestraker, in Miami.

Liestraker ... yeah, right, Liestraker. "So how's it going?" Diatri tore open a packet of chocolate powder and mixed it with the baby formula they had him drinking. Baby formula. He stared glumly at the dirty-looking bubbles.

"Reason it's taken so long," Liestraker was saying, "is there's 467 hotels in the Greater Miami area. We had to get grand jury subpoenas from the AUSA to look at their registers, and the subpoenas kept expiring, and I had to keep going back and ..."

"Uh-huh." Diatri drank. It wasn't so bad.

"Then there's the Catholic churches. There's 118 of them. We didn't need GJSs for those, but just calling all of them, that took time. Also ..."

What was his first name? Mike?

"Michael," Diatri interjected. "Let me explain my situation up here. The sixty days is up on my case, the Raid jacket case I told you about. I had to file a Status Rep with *my* AUSA, and he didn't give me Concurrence to Continue. The reason for that is, I don't have anything. What I do have is an in box that looks like Magilla the Gorilla used it for a toilet. Okay? So what do you got, Mike?"

"I've got five names. Hispanic males, medium height, strong build, mid- to late forties, no distinguishing characteristics, occupying rooms in area hotels between December 7 and December 22."

"Okay. Now, I assume you already ran them through NADDIS."

"Affirmative and negative."

"How's that, Mike?"

"Yeah, I ran them through NADDIS, and no, none of them are in it. They're all NADDIS negative."

"Okay, shoot."

The names on Liestraker's list consisted of a Docal, Bollines, Quintaro, Velez and Ravines, respectively a United States Information Officer, a magazine ad salesman, a food wholesaler, a security consultant and a stockbroker. Liestraker gave him what he had on each. He said, "Ravines was busted in San Diego two days ago."

Diatri sat up. "Yeah?"

"He assaulted a contractor. He had this new roof put on his garage and it fell on his Mercedes and crushed it and he beat the shit out of the guy apparently. He's out on a bond. You want to talk to him?"

"No. Maybe. What about the churches?"

"One got a call about a demonic possession but it turned out to be D.T.'s. Plus the usual stuff. No requests for confessions over the phone."

"Anything on Barazo?"

"*Nada*. His people have been pretty busy killing each other. We heard one group of them killed another group on a hot drop on Andros."

"Okay, Michael. That's good work. I'm gonna mention it to the Administrator if I ever see him."

Diatri stared at the five names on his list. Docal was in Bucharest, Bollines was in Tulsa, Quintaro in Chicago, Velez in Rosslyn, Virginia. He worked for a company named Becker Industries.

He got through to someone in Personnel at Becker and identified himself as a credit checker with Macy's department store. Mr.

Velez had put them down as a reference, just checking. ... Right. Previous employer? ... New York Police Department? Right, that's what it says here.

He dialed the main number again at Becker and asked for Security.

"Yeah," he said, "my name is Mariatri. I'm with the Policemen's Benevolent Association in New York and—"

"I'm sorry, we don't handle charitable contributions. You'll have to talk to Mr. Zahn, in Public Relations. I'd be happy to transfer you—"

"No, it's okay. I'm not calling for money, but I get that all the time. You say you're from the PBA and everyone is happy to transfer you. We're just updating our files here and I see one of our former members, Felix Velez, works there."

"Oh, fine. Yes, that's correct."

"Is he there, by any chance?"

"No."

"Does he have a title or anything?"

The voice was amused. "No, not really."

"See, we're doing a special issue in our magazine, a kind of 'Where Are They Now?' feature, you know, like the ones in *Parade* magazine? I was wondering how we should list him."

"He's in charge of personal security."

"Personal security?"

"For Mr. Becker."

"A bodyguard."

"Security specialist."

"Right." Diatri thought: Just what I'm going to end up as, security specialist. Holding doors open for rich people. If I'm not holding a specimen cup and telling people to go wee-wee in it. "Well,

186

that must be interesting work, especially for someone like Mr. Becker. I guess he travels a lot. As a matter of fact, a friend of mine saw him in Miami a couple months ago."

"That's possible. I'm sorry, what did you say your name was?"

"I guess that about covers it. Listen, thanks."

Diatri dialed the Biltmore Hotel in Coral Gables, where Velez had registered, and asked for the manager.

"Yes, this is George Diatriola, with the Miami *Herald*? Good morning. We're doing this story on where major executives and the like, you know, your basic captains of industry, stay when they're in town and it just came to our attention that Mr. Charles Becker of Becker Industries stayed with you a couple of months ago? ... Uh-huh. What was the nature of his visit? ... He didn't say. Well, a man in his position doesn't really have to say, does he? ... Uhhuh. Eastern? Is that a fact? Well, you win some, lose some, right? I kind of wish someone would come along and take it over. It's a crying shame, to run an airline like that. I kind of miss Frank Borman. I don't know if he was a good manager, but I liked those commercials. Something about an astronaut, I guess. Well, Mr. Becker must think very highly of your hotel down there—here. We oughta do an article on the Biltmore. ... We did? Well, sure we did, but there was some feeling around here that it was a little, I don't know, superficial, so I was thinking that we should do another article. I'd certainly like to feature your name prominently in the article, if that's okay by you. Could you spell it for me? ... I never would have been able to spell that. Is that a German name? ... Swiss. That's a really beautiful country you have there. I like those, what do you call them, the chocolates come in that triangular tube? ... There you go. I used to be able to eat three of those at a sitting. So did you grow up near the Matterhorn? ... I'm sorry? An umlaut over the u.

187

Uh-huh, two dots side by side. I'm not a hundred percent sure we can do umlauts, but I tell you what, I'm going to check personally downstairs with the printers and see what we can do … Thank *you*."

He dialed down to New York City police headquarters and had them fax up a record photograph of Felix Velez. Next he dialed Neon Leon's and got the voice saying, "I'm sorry, the number you have called has been disconnected." It was funny the way she said "disconnected" so upbeat, like it was good news, you were really hoping it would be disconnected.

He called Ignacio's cousin's number and got someone who'd never heard of Ignacio or his cousin. He called the owner, his paella buddy, and spoke to his wife, and tracked him down at a golf and tennis club in Dania.

"What happened to Neon Leon's?" he said.

"Business died after the *Herald* called it a 'hangout of local drug lords.' I never knew that. That *cabrón* of a headwaiter never told me about that pig."

Diatri explained he was trying to reach Ignacio. The owner said 'Ignacio was having some immigration problems and was up in Jacksonville somewhere, or maybe Gainesville.

"What about the maître d'?"

"I don't care where he is. He is a bastard!"

"All right. Could you try to locate Ignacio for me? It's very important.

Just then Marie said, "Frank, Mr. Colaris wants to see you."

"What for?" said Diatri suspiciously.

"Roberta told me it's got something to do with a physical."

"A what?"

"A medical. They want to set one up."

188

"How come?"

"I don't know, Frank. But you have been looking kind of sick."

"That's ridiculous. I'm fine. I'm too busy to have some stupid physical."

"Okay by me, Frank, but I'm not the Agent in Charge."

"Listen, Marie. Tell him I just got a tip from one of my CIs and I had to go out on it."

"Aw, Frank."

"Tell him I got good information on a five-hundred—a thousand-key shipment coming in by Greyhound into Port Authority, but I got to go UC on it real fast. You got that?"

"*Frank.*"

"Marie, I'm not asking you to be the mother of my children, I'm asking you to tell the Agent in Charge that a possible major shipment of, of cocaine is coming in and I'm on it, okay? Okay, for crying out loud?"

"All right, Frank."

Diatri went out the emergency exit, walked down three flights and took the freight elevator the rest of the way.

He had to stall the physical at least until the bruises on his inner arms from the IV needles went away. Probably ought to build up his strength a little too. Jog, or something.

He walked down to the Port Authority building on Forty-second with the thought of scaring up a little action—though a thousand keys was going to be tough on such short notice. After a half hour of sizing up various nervous-looking guys clutching attaché cases a little too tightly, he realized he'd lost interest in the small hauls, the one- and two-kilo busts. He decided to head over to the Public Library on Forty-second and Fifth and just maybe read, look through old issues of *Life* magazine. He got very depressed on the way over. The Red Meteor was doing him in, it was only a matter of time.

He went to the main reading room and instead of getting old *Lifes* looked up Charles Becker in *Who's Who*. There was nothing in *Current Biography*, so for the hell of it he went to the *Readers' Guide to Periodical Literature*.

There wasn't all that much on him. He was listed in a recent *Forbes* magazine roundup as the forty-eighth-richest man in the United States. Not bad. He'd married into a little money and turned that into a fortune. The American Way. Diatri wondered if these rich guys competed among themselves for the rankings. He visualized a rich man's marathon, except all the runners were in the back of chauffeured limousines that had racing numbers on their grilles. He went to the *New York Times* index and ate up hours sifting through that for citations.

He took his call slips to the microfilm desk and then went to the viewers. He flicked on the light, threaded the spindle and cranked the film through the viewfinder. It was warm, but he kept his jacket on since pistols in holsters tended to make people nervous, especially in libraries. He cranked for hours, hundreds and hundreds of yards of current events warping and woofing across the scratched glass lens. Mrs. Charles Becker went to the Metropolitan Ball in 1972. Mrs. Charles Becker died in 1975. Mr. Becker took Telemetrics private. Crank. Mr. Becker sold Zacatecas Petroleum. Crank. What was he looking for? This was ridiculous. If he wanted to eat up time—page B3, Metro section—he should get on a plane to Miami with a good print of the Velez photo and take it to the maître d. He could get healthy in Miami, run on the beach, get some real sun instead of lying under that bastard tanning machine, all that remained of his second marriage. Page B3. Russian exiles finding difficulty adjusting to New Jersey. No kidding. He should check with Eastern Airlines to see if there was anything on Becker trying to take them over. Sanit Commission urges study of eastern Long Island landfill. Conservationists "cool" to idea. Shakespeare in the Park threatened by federal funding cuts. That would be a nice thing to do some night, Shakespeare in the Park. Editor's Note: Felix Rohatyn is not 93 years old, as yesterday's article stated. A feminist group "upset" by the "impression" given in yesterday's story that they advocated breast-feeding children into their early teens. Breast-milk had to be an improvement over the stuff they had him drinking. He wondered what breast milk tasted like. Heiress dead of apparent overdose. Nothing about Charles Becker on B3. That was annoying. You go to the trouble of looking it up and it's not there. He checked the date of the citation. B3, all right. Shakespeare in the Park ... he'd always wanted to see *Man of La Mancha*. Maybe some night—

20

No one seemed to have any file footage of Charles Becker, not ABC, NBC, CBS, CNN, not C-SPAN. Diatri wondered how it was possible for any human being in the latter part of the twentieth century, much less the forty-eighth-richest guy in America, to make it to his age without leaving a piece of himself on video.

He set up his office in a phone booth at the Public Library. After two days he found a field producer with WPIX who seemed to remember that she'd sent a crew to the New York City morgue that day, but they'd decided in the end that Natasha Becker just wasn't a big enough heiress.

"If it'd been Cornelia Guest," she said, "we would have gone with it."

Diatri watched the raw footage. He saw the old man in the Jackie 0 glasses being shoved up against his car by the crowd of shouting reporters. He recognized Felix Velez, trying to clear a path.

The problem was, he didn't say anything, just looked dazed as Velez and another guy, a detective, it looked like, hustled him through the crowd. Diatri felt a little sorry for the guy, watching him. He looked like he was about to go into shock.

He went back to the Public and cranked through microfilm.

He'd wound his way through twenty-seven miles of current events when he came to a 1981 story in the *National Catholic Reporter* saying that Becker had just given five million dollars to Mount St. Mary's College in Maryland.

He called up the college's development office. "Yeah, this is Murray Kempton, with *Newsday*? Listen, we're doing a big story on Charles Becker, the philanthropist? He made a very nice gesture to you, I know, back in '81. I was wondering if maybe you gave him an honorary degree. ... You did? Well, for five million, I'd give him one too. You hand those out at graduation, am I correct? Did he by any chance give a little speech to say thanks? ... Is that right? Did you record it? ... Uh-huh. You know, that's just what my article could use, because, as you know, he's such a private guy. I spent hours with him and would you believe he didn't mention anything about this five mil to me? Now, where exactly are you in Maryland?"

Diatri went straight from La Guardia to the rectory. Father Rebeta answered the door.

"Hello, Padre."

"Hello, Frank." They sat in the room of the joyless Madonna.

"Are you ... well, Frank?"

"Fine."

"You've lost weight."

"Let me play something for you," Diatri said. He had pre-cued the tape to start after Charley Becker was introduced. Father Rebeta listened. He made a steeple with his fingers and rested his nose on it. Diatri clicked it off.

"Ecce homo."

"How's that?" said Diatri.

"Behold the man. What Pilate said to the crowd."

"That's him on the tape?"

"Perhaps that wasn't the most apt allusion, under the circumstances. Congratulations, Frank. How on earth did you find him?"

"You're *sure*?"

The priest thought. "Yes," he said. "Though I don't suppose that would mean much in court, would it? I mean, a good defense attorney would take that apart pretty easily, unless you—"

"One step at a time, Padre. You're *sure* that's the same voice you heard that night?"

"No question. Do you mind if I smoke?"

He pulled an unfiltered cigarette—borrowed from the housekeeper—out of his pocket, wrinkled and bent. He straightened it with loving care so as not to break the skin, making a ritual out of it, as if smoking it was the one thing he had to look forward to other than eternal salvation. "I don't really smoke," he said, lighting up. "So who is he?"

"I don't mean to sound like a jerk, Padre, but that's privileged information." He stood up. "I better get back. Thanks for your help. We'll be in touch as the case develops—"

"Sit down, Frank. For heaven's sake. No one's flying in steaks."

It had been over twenty-five years since a priest had told him to sit down. And what do you know, he sat.

"Well," said Rebeta, "we know he's Catholic." He chuckled. "I suppose that's obvious by now. Texan, no formal education, self-made, rich, a defense contractor with a guilt complex—no, there's more than guilt at work here, some genuine, non-intellectualized religiosity—who's just bought himself an honorary degree from Mount St. Mary's College."

Diatri jumped up. "You Jesuit son of a—the whole fucking time, you knew! Get up! Stand up!"

"Why?"

"Because I'm placing you under arrest for withholding evidence in a federal investigation, and obstruction of justice."

"Oh, sit down, Frank."

"DON'T TELL ME TO SIT DOWN! You have the right to remain silent, you have the right to speak to—"

"Calm down, Frank. Just sit down and calm down. George Bernard Shaw said the most redundant sign in the English language was 'Fresh Fish Sold Here.' If it weren't fresh, you'd smell it; that it's fish, is also obvious from the smell; that it's for sale goes without saying; that it's here is most obvious of all."

"What the hell does a CNN anchorman have to do with this?"

"No, George Bernard—it's all there on the tape. The accent, clearly west of the Mississippi, less elasticity to the vowels, the glottal stops are harder. it's more twang than drawl. So, Texas. As Oscar Wilde would have said, 'My dear, *no one* is from Arizona.' It's obvious he had no formal education himself, from the tone of awe. 'Halls of higher learning,' 'ivory towers of knowledge.' Believe me, no one who ever saw the inside of a university classroom would say that. It would therefore follow that he's self-made. It's clear that he has something to do with the old Military Industrial Complex from the way he hauls out that hoary old chestnut about beating swords into plowshares. Finally, it's unlikely that a school like Mount St. Mary's would be giving out honorary degrees to, well, sword makers if there hadn't been a little quid pro quo. St. Peter's Basilica in Rome was built on indulgences, forgiving sins for cash. Mother Church is eternal, Frank, but thirty-year T bills yield eight percent."

"But how do you know it's Mount St. Mary's?"

"The quaint self-deprecating bit about how giving him the *honoris causa* is the first mistake the school's made since 1808. There aren't that many old Catholic schools in America. Georgetown was founded in 1789—"

"All right, all right," said Diatri, defeated. "But if I find out that you knew about this and you're just yanking my chain I'm going to ... be real disappointed in you, Padre."

"Frank, you've obviously been under a strain lately. If you don't mind my saying, you really don't look at all well. What have you done to your skin?"

"I do mind, as a matter of fact."

"Would you like something to settle your stomach?"

"Let me guess. It's elementary, right?"

"You're *holding* your stomach, Frank." Father Rebeta left and came back with a glass of seltzer water.

"So, who is he?"

"I can't tell you that, Padre."

"You could tell me in confession. To keep it confidential."

"Padre"—Diatri stood up and smiled— "you don't have *time* to listen to my confession." At the door he said, "When this is over, I'll buy you dinner some night if you want."

"I like steak."

"Okay." Diatri laughed. "Steak."

21

"Where the *fuck* have you been, Diatri? What do you *mean* going off like that? No one goes UC in this office without authorization! I almost put out an Agent Missing on you!"

"Will you calm down, please, Jim?"

"Don't tell me to calm down, Diatri! I'm your fucking superior!"

"I said 'please.'"

"You're suspended pending medical evaluation."

"What?"

"You heard me."

"What are you talking about, medical evaluation?"

"Look at you, Frank. You disappear for two weeks, you come back twenty-five pounds lighter with weird burns all over you."

"What's wrong with losing some weight? You're the one always posting bulletins about eating right and walking up stairs instead of taking the elevator."

"What about those burns?"

"I fell asleep in one of those tanning machines. What's the big deal?"

"Roll up your sleeves."

"What?"

"Roll up your sleeves."

"Are you okay? Am I hearing this? Roll up my sleeves? All right. Here."

"What's that there?"

"A bruise, obviously."

"A bruise from what?"

"From donating blood. Now you've got something against the Red Cross?"

"Let me see the other arm."

"Jesus Christ."

"Let me see the other arm. What's that?"

"A bruise."

"From giving blood?"

"No. As a matter of fact, that's from something else."

"What something else?"

"I fainted at the blood place and they had to give me some glucose. I'm a little embarrassed about the fainting. You're being very hostile, Jim."

"Frank, you've been acting strange. Someone saw marks on your arms in the locker room. You don't look good. You disappear for two weeks. What do you want me to say?"

"Well, frankly it's been a bit of a strain, what with my sister's disease. A little support and understanding would be nice."

"Yeah, well about your sister, Frank. I checked. You don't *have* a sister. You got no next of kin."

"She's more like an adopted sister, really."

"You're going to the doctor, Frank, or I call in IS."

"Internal Security? I don't believe this. You want to check my urine, is that it? Here."

"What are you doing? That's my coffee mug. Frank!"

22

"Mr. Becker's office."

"Good morning. Is Mr. Becker there?"

"No, he's not. May I ask who's calling?"

"This is Father More, from Mount St. Mary's College, in Maryland?"

"Good morning, Father."

"Good morning, my child. I was just calling to tell him that the Little Sisters of Mercy, with whom we have this affiliation, are making a special novena for him."

"Well, I'm sure he'll be pleased to hear that, Father."

"He's not in, then?"

"No, I'm sorry, he isn't."

"Are you, like, expecting him?"

"No, he's on his boat."

"His boat. Bless him, his boat. I remember him talking about his boat when he came to pick up his honorary degree here. So is he on the Riviera?"

"He's on the Amazon River, in Peru. Hello?"

"The Amazon. Well, God … bless him, the Amazon."

"He will be checking in. I'll tell him about the novena. I'm sure he'll be very pleased."

23

"Frank, I never thought it was dope. I never thought it was dope."

"Uh-huh. That's why you had me roll up my sleeves. Because you didn't think it was dope."

"Someone said they saw bruises! What am I supposed to think?"

"You're supposed to extend a little benefit of the doubt. After seventeen years, I would expect just a little benefit of doubt."

"Frank, why didn't you say something?"

"It's no big deal."

"You go hiding out in some fucking VA hospital so we won't find out you're sick from Kincaid's bullet. Giving yourself intravenous glucose treatments because you can't eat anything. No big deal?"

"A little stomach upset—"

The SAC read from the report on his desk. " 'Evidence of a radioopaque object, probably a bullet, lodged in the right paraspinal muscles at the level of the tenth thoracic vertebra.'" Stomach upset!

" 'Radio-opaque object, probably a bullet.' Shows you what they don't know. I told them before they took the pictures. I said, 'I got 125 grains of semi-jacketed hollow-point still in me, so don't worry when that shows up on the X ray.' I told them all about it, how they decided to leave it in 'cause it was a little close to the spine. And look how they put it in the report. Like they just found King Tut. 'Probably a bullet.' What else could it be? Someone's key chain I accidentally swallowed with my eggplant parmigiana?"

"Frank, we all knew about the bullet. But—look what it says— 'evidence of recent scarring in peritoneal cavity due to leakage of pancreatic and gastric juices.' You're leaking, Frank."

"You know what that means? Gas. That's all that means."

"'Multiple adhesions involving the small bowel with recurrent small bowel obstruction.'"

"Adhesions—"

"'Prognosis unfavorable.'"

"These people couldn't find an adhesion in, in a box of BandAids, I'm telling you. You remember they ran Sheppard out on a heart murmur three years ago? Sheppard ran thirty-eighth in the New York City marathon last year."

"I'm sorry, Frank."

"What are you saying, Jim?"

"I can't overrule the doctors, Frank. You've had a brilliant career. I spoke to the Administrator this morning and he told me he's going to be calling you later. I know some guys would kill for a Disability. You're forty-six years old, Frank. You got your whole life in front of you."

"Oh, terrific."

"I wish you wouldn't blame me for this, Frank. If it was me—"

"I broke the Raid Jacket case, Jim."

"The Raid Jacket case? The Raid Jacket case is dead. You didn't get a Concurrence from the AUSA."

"I broke the Raid Jacket case, Jim."

"You did?"

"We're talking conspiracy to impersonate federal officers, conspiracy to commit murder, conspiracy to kidnap. We're talking conspiracy to violate the Neutrality Act. We're talking eight murders, probably more, and an ongoing violation of the Neutrality Act with conspiracy to murder. We're talking about a leading U.S. citizen with close ties to the U.S. government."

"Jesus. Who?"

"Would have made a beautiful case."

"What do you mean?"

"I'm out. You just said."

"Make sense, Frank."

200

"You got your whole life in front of you, Jim. I'm sure another case just like this will come up and jump you up to Deputy Administrator. Take care of yourself."

24

"Two months and even Eden starts to look like a prison, Virgilio. I'm restless too. But we can't have this."

"With respect, Niño, putting his arm in the piranha tank, it doesn't make anyone happier."

"Fifteen seconds. A couple of bites. In Saudi Arabia, Virgilio, they would have cut the arm off."

"I still don't think that makes them any happier."

"He stabbed Paco in the arm. It was a just punishment. Solomonic, in fact. Fifteen seconds, a few nibbles—"

"Nibbles?"

"Bites, then. The point remains. I'm not going to apologize for maintaining order. That's three incidents this week. Something had to be done or else we'll all start reverting here."

"Reverting?"

"To what's out there, Virgilio. To what we listen to every night in the trees. Our great-great-great-grand-fathers."

"Niño, we need to get some women in here. Or the men are going to start fucking *us*."

"No. We can't afford that now. It's a war, Virgilio. Just because they haven't made their move yet, it's still a war."

"Someone saw Ramón Lados with a cherimoya, in the drying shed."

"There's no rule about not eating in the sheds."

"He wasn't eating it, Niño, he was screwing it. Two days before that someone saw Lobi out behind the lab, with a mango."

Jesus. He'd ordered a mango for breakfast that morning. "All right. If you think it's so important, all right. Tell Eladio you want some *pakis* for tonight."

"I ... why don't we just get some from Madariaga, in Tingo, like we usually do."

"Because Eladio is closer, and more secure than Tingo."

Virgilio had that pained, Gromyko look again.

"What is it, Virgilio?"

"The men say they want girls from Tingo."

"Why?" I'm not going to make it easy for you, Virgilio. There, he's averting his eyes. So the men don't want Indian girls. Don't want *chunchas*, eh? Don't want clean, tight, sweet-smelling Jivaro girls who know how to make a man's cock dance like a python? No, the men want diseased mestiza whores from Tingo with bloody underpants, three-day-old makeup and sour mouths from cheap pisco. Say it.

"It's ..."

Oh, Christ, go on, put him out of his misery. Who wants a good liar for a number two?

"Okay, Virgilio."

"*Thank* you, Niño."

"But two girls only. Fly them in yourself, personally, and out, personally. Take Zamora with you and don't tell that bucket of pus Madariaga that you're coming or it'll be all over Tingo."

"Sure. You know, I could fit four in the Cessna."

"Virgilio—"

"So the men don't have to share so much. For morale, Niño."

"Four, then."

He watched Virgilio bound off the veranda like a schoolboy on his way to the barracks to give the men the good news that they'd all have the clap by this time tomorrow. He followed him with his eyes until he disappeared into the barracks. He realized he was grinding his back teeth.

So you're going to take it personally? Of course not. Then why are you doing that with your teeth? I'm not. Be honest: you're pissed off. Sure, why shouldn't I be? It's insulting. They should ... What? Shouldn't be racist? The whole *country's* racist. It's the most racist country in the world, Peru. That's what I'm trying to change. If a criollo like myself can take as his lover a Jivaro girl, others will follow. I'm trying to set an example. An example? Is that what it is? It wouldn't have anything to do with the quality of the fucking? All right, the sex is fantastic. Forget it, Tony. It can't happen here. Remember what Max Hernández wrote: "One-quarter of Peruvians are whites who are unhappy that Pizarro didn't kill all the Indians. Onequarter are whites who feel guilty about what Pizarro did to the Indians. One-quarter are Indians ashamed of not putting up a fight against the invaders. And one-quarter are Indians who would like to kill all the others."

Your own men, the mestizos, they're caught in the middle. Their hatreds are vertical—they hate up and down. You're not going to change all that just by taking a jungle girl for a mistress. Concentrate on your own enemy.

He wanted to make love, right away. She wasn't in the bedroom. He called, "Soledad?" She wasn't there. The phone rang, Mirko.

"We just got a fax from Garza in Medellín. One of his people got into a problem with one of Cabrera's people."

"What kind of a problem?"

"A shooting problem."

"Christ. I told Garza, no contact. What happened?"

"Garza's man thought Cabrera's man knew he was being followed, so Garza's man shot him."

"Idiot."

"A shooting, in Medellín, it's no big thing. They shot two judges there just last week. Who's going to miss a *sicario*?"

"Cabrera! That's who. Jesus. Look, tell Garza, ask Garza if there's some way of making it look like an unofficial DAS job. A police revenge shooting for the judges. Something."

"Good idea, Niño. I'll get on it."

"Mirko, don't use the fax. And tell Garza he shouldn't be using the fax for these kinds of communication."

"He used that code of his."

"Garza's code could be deciphered by a goat. A stupid goat. Use the scrambler. I paid a fucking fortune for it and no one uses it."

"It makes your voice sound like a *maricón*'s, Niño."

"*Mirko.*"

"Okay, Niño."

Things were falling apart; the center was not holding. The men are demanding whores; Garza's people have fired a shot that might turn out to be like Princip's at Sarajevo; and Mirko won't use essential security equipment because he thinks it makes him sound homosexual.

He called out, "Soledad!" Where the hell was she? He needed urgently to make love.

He found her in the solarium, sitting cross-legged on the rattan sofa. She was wearing an aikido outfit. It was loose above the belt and showed the soft brown valley between her breasts, thank God, as he approached, swelling.

Her coloring books were next to her. She looked up, surprised, reached for one of the books, put it over her lap.

"I love you," she said.

He knelt. She embraced him, took two fistfuls of hair and pulled him to her. There was something diversionary in this.

"What have you got there?"

She caught his tongue in midsentence with her teeth.

"Kthhhhh."

He tugged. She held. He pulled. She held. He pulled. Her teeth clicked hard as he got free. He tasted stickiness, salt, blood.

"Why do you bite me?"

"I love you."

"I love you. What are you hiding?"

"I love you."

"Show me."

"I love you."

"What are you doing with this? I told you. This is bad."

"I love you."

He was tempted to roll it up and give her a good swat with it.

"This"—he waved it in front of her angrily— "no!" He flung it across the room, pulled open her aikido suit and took her, roughly, joylessly, in truth, cruelly. He left her lying on her stomach on a bed of crumpled coloring books, looking back at him—there it was again, this time with the eyes open—the look of Gauguin's kanaka, Tehura. *"The night is loud with demons, evil spirits and spirits of the dead ... perhaps she took me, with my anguished face, for one of those legendary demons or specters, the Tupapaus, with pale lips and phosphorescent eyes, who fill the sleepless nights of her people."*

"I love you," he said. She turned away. He picked the troublesome object off the floor and continued out the door.

25

It lay on his desk, still rolled up from being clenched in his fist, as if it were afraid to unfurl in his presence.

What garbage. But what did *she* see in it?—she who had never been beyond the mountains, to whom even relatively primitive Yenan was a metropolis. What was the fascination, for her, in Julio Iglesias, the transvestite Lupe Maldonado or ex-King Simeon of Bulgaria?

¡Mira! hadn't changed much since Papa banished it from the pantry. Except now bosoms were permitted. Indeed, bosoms had been making up for decades of strict *catolicismo*. They bounced and jiggled on almost every page. Advertisements in the back promised larger ones, but you had to go pick them up at clinics in Buenos Aires. Morgan Fairchild, Joan Collins—Macchu Chu Chu—Oprah Winfrey, Ann-Margret, Jane Fonda, Maria Shriver, Carmen Cremosa—ah, after the bosoms come the serious journalism. SORAYA KHASHOGGI: ADNAN ES INOCENTE. King Juan Carlos and Queen Sophia Enjoy a Vacation in the Balearic Islands with Their In-Laws, Ex-King Constantine of Greece and Queen Anne Marie of Denmark. Oho. His Majesty water-skis. His Majesty falls. His Majesty gets up again. His Majesty enjoys a lunch of grilled sardines and octopus and afterward he will take a nap, as is his custom. Their Majesties are "concerned" about skin cancer. Aha. They use a sun block on their skin. Amazing. Stop the press-es. The King and Queen are humans, like us. Just like we do. Her

Majesty prefers it from a "tube instead of a jar." She is "rumored" not to like the "very greasy kind." Fascinating. And you would have thought just the opposite. An interview with Dolores Fontana, the astrologer. She says that Principe Felipe of Spain is secretly conducting a love affair with Duchess Fergie of York. It's *his* child Fergie is pregnant with. The English Queen "knows" about this and there is a plot in Buckingham Palace to say the child died at birth and to send it back secretly to Spain. The Pope knows about it. He's threatening to break diplomatic relations with England. Jupiter is aligning with Mercury, causing some problems for Virgo, and Capricorn is taking a shit on Aries. ZSA ZSA GABOR, JUZGADA POR ABOFETEAR A UN POLICÍA. Ah, more bosoms. Good. We haven't had tits for at least four pages. Mother Teresa. A Turkish girl with no arms has had a vision of Mother Teresa, and Mother Teresa wants her to build a pedestrian overpass on the outskirts of Munich where she lost her arms after a car hit her. Senator Gallardo Visits with the American *Billonario* Charles Becker in Iquitos. He Is Flown from Lima in Becker's Private jet to the Private Yacht and Back Again. Honestly, Gallardo, your country is falling apart and you're spreading your legs for a gringo with a big boat. Look at the two of you together. The *billonario* looks like he's screwed a few proles in his day too. Well, you two must have had a lot to talk about. How many people you've screwed between you? ... Christ, "The Absinthe Drinker"!

"There's something about it. A boat like that, here. It's too out of context."

"He's a rich bastard," said Virgilio, looking through the magnifying glass. "Like Jota Erre."

"Who?"

"On *Dallas*."

"Dallas?"

"A program. It's ... the men watch it sometimes."

"Gringo TV? They're watching gringo television, here, in Yenan?"

"Just sometimes. They're a little bored with the Chinese and Cuban films. They've seen them all a hundred times."

"Virgilio."

"I'll take care of it. Did you notice something in all the pictures?"

"What?"

"No girls."

"Maybe they're going to pick up girls in Tingo, Virgilio."

"They don't look rich. They look more like bodyguards to me. Especially this one. Bundy. And this one. He looks like he's been through the shit, eh?"

The ascots tied around the necks were wrong, somehow, like silk scarves on pit bulls. The names in the captions, Bundy, McNamara, Rostow, sounded familiar, and also wrong.

He put the magnifying glass over the Manet once again. He knew the original was in the Ny Carlsberg Glypotek, in Copenhagen. The Bibliothèque Nationale in Paris had an engraving. It was unlikely this was a fake. Rich bastards like this didn't usually go for fakes. He's got Dufys and Picassos in there, a Vlaminck, a Gainsborough, obviously real. So this—my God, it had to be authentic. There was something different about it, but the photo was too grainy to tell. He needed to call Bendinck, in Brussels.

"Niño." Virgilio was pointing at one of the guests. "Look at the way this one is turning away from the camera. He doesn't want his picture taken. I know him."

"Rostow." Something about these names.

"Three years ago, in Tingo, you remember, a DEA guy shot and killed one of Pepi Campo's people?"

"The gringos had to buy him back for a lot of money. It was a big diplomatic mess."

"That's him. That's the one. His name was ... it wasn't Rostow. There was a picture of him in *La República*. I remember. That's him."

"Call Yayo in Lima. Tell him to send a fax of it, right away. Immediately, Virgilio."

Bendinck called back and said that Manet's "Absinthe Drinker" was still in the Ny Carlsberg Glypotek. Rupert was his usual gleeful self. "Were you thinking of making a shopping trip?" he asked.

"I can't get away right now. Business."

"Pity. I know the Glypotek very well. I'd love to show it to you."

"Do you know it as well as the Kunsthalle in Mannheim?"

Bendinck laughed. "So, were you thinking of an oil or a sketch?"

"It's hard to tell. It's a black-and-white photograph."

"Does the face look like Baudelaire?"

"I can't tell. To be honest, Rupert, I don't remember what Baudelaire looked like."

"The first was done in 1859. The Salon rejected it—"

"I know—"

"He painted another oil version of it after Baudelaire died, in 1867. Baudelaire scoffed at the first one, which must have hurt,

209

since it was a kind of homage to him. Collardet, the bum in the painting, is right out of one of Baudelaire's poems. I forget which, the one that ends: "He ends up bloodying his head and stumbling on the cobblestones like the young poets who spend all their days erring and searching for rhymes." Baudelaire finally went crazy from syphilis, absinthe, laudanum and everything else and some nuns kicked him out of their hospice because he kept swearing from the pain. There's Christian charity for you, eh? In the end, Manet was his best friend. He was there at the funeral, and there weren't many, believe me. It's Baudelaire's face in the second oil. Are you interested?"

"As I say, business is busy."

"Yes, it's in the news."

"What is?"

"Your business. Anyway, it wouldn't be nearly as complicated as Mannheim. It's in a private collection in the U.S. I'm sure the owner can be persuaded to sell."

"Let me think about it."

"Of course. I'll be out of town for a few weeks."

"Where are you off to?"

"Florence. I have a client who's crazy for Quattrocento."

The fax from Yayo wasn't the best quality but the face in the two photographs was the same. He stared from one to the other as he listened to the lawyer in Miami.

"He left DEA after that. Then he went to work for G. Gordon Liddy. You remember him? The Watergate guy. He had a firm down here called Hurricane Force, sort of a private commando team that was supposed to rescue kidnapped executives overseas.

That folded, and he went to do security for Marcos, in Hawaii. After that—"

"Yes, good, but where is he *now*, Rubén?"

"I spoke to his ex-wife, the most recent one. He's got four. She told me he's a mercenary and he kills people and doesn't report the income."

"She told you that? Why?"

"She hates him. He owes her alimony. In fact, she asked me to help her find him."

"Who did you say you were?"

"The IRS. They always cooperate when you say you're the IRS."

"Good thinking. What about Becker?"

The lawyer went through what he had, mostly from *Who's Who* and the business publications.

"... 1981, formed buyback partnership with 3M Corporation and bought back all public shares of Zacatecas Petroleum, turned around and sold company to T. Boone Pickens for $1.2 billion ... 1982, received Knight of Maltahood, or Knighthood of Malta, in recognition of services to—"

"Ya ya, okay, he's rich, he steals from the poor, gives a little back and gets a medal from the Pope. What else?"

"There's not very much on him. He keeps himself inconspicuous. This is all from business magazines. He ... was in the papers last year."

"Yes?"

"There was ... an incident involving a granddaughter."

"What incident?"

"She, well, it's—"

"Rubén, this scrambler costs forty dollars a minute."

"She had a little ... OD."

211

"Of ..."

"Yes, but obviously it's her own fault. You don't blame General Motors if you drive a little too fast and go off the cliff, right?"

The howlers and the capuchins were screeching at each other in the canopy beyond the perimeter. Beyond them the toucans complained and somewhere beyond that he heard the death commotion between a jaguar and a peccary.

Soledad lay naked on the bed, asleep with her thumb in her mouth. He looked from her to the slatted windows and imagined the noises had shapes that came through the window and surrounded her like Fuseli's nightmare creatures. He found himself wishing, for the first time since he had been here, for the reassurance of a city sound, a passing bus, a car horn, a truck, the shout of a cigarette vendor.

He turned to the picture of the gringo on his yacht. His yacht was registered with Lloyd's as *Conquistador*. Well, it showed he wasn't deaf to the nuances. But *Esmeralda* was a little clumsy. The conquistadors came also for emeralds.

Well, *billonario*, do I hand you over to Espinosa? They'll promote him to general, and that's good for me, too.

But does Espinosa deserve you? Espinosa, who wouldn't know a Manet from a Monet, or for that matter, a Manet from a Mapplethorpe.

And you're not the type to put your hands in the air and give up, obviously, since you've come all this way. We don't want bullet holes in "The Absinthe Drinker."

But why bring your Manet on a trip like this, billonario? I can understand the Dufy, the Vlaminck, the Cocteau. But the Baudelaire

212

"Absinthe Drinker"? You don't go into battle with Manets—it's irresponsible!

A light touch is needed. Eladio is needed. Eladio, who can walk across a floor of wet paint and not leave a track. Eladio, who floats on the air of his own beliefs.

"Eladio," he said. "I have dreamed a great white canoe and a *kurinku pataa*, a *pistaco* who comes for the grease of your people to make fuel for his rockets."

26

"Obviously I wasn't going to bring it up this morning in front of everyone."

"I appreciate that, Dick."

"It didn't seem like something for the whole cabinet."

"God no. Who's in the loop on this?"

"It's a tight loop, John. A very tight loop. DEA, obviously, me."

"Well, let's keep it tight until, until we can ..."

"Get a handle around it. Right."

"As of right now, it doesn't feel, I don't think we need to take it down the hall to him."

"We may not be there yet."

"I don't think we are there yet, Dick."

"Anyway, Bill confirms that he's on this river, the—"

"Bill is in the loop?"

"Well, it's Bill's satellite."

"The NSA has satellites. I would have thought as far as keeping a tight loop goes, that NSA would be better."

"Maybe. Maybe. It's just that Bill's satellites have been

monitoring the compliance on the deforestation thing down there and it was on station and, anyway, they're Bill's pictures. Amazing resolution, by the way. You can actually read the lettering on the—"

"Okay. So *where* does it stand?"

"They're several miles west of the village of Shucushuyacu."

"That doesn't mean anything to me, Dick."

"It just means he's well on his way, basically."

"Where?"

"We don't know that."

"Well, why, why can't we just call him up on the phone, he's got to have a phone, and, and say, 'Look here, we know all about this and get your ass back here on the QT.'"

"There's an open-line problem. Our friends would be listening in."

"Well, we don't have to spell it out. Call him and say, 'This is the AG calling and turn your butt around, buster.'"

"Right. So your thinking is that I should make the call?"

"Well, it is your department, Dick. I mean, DEA *is* under your roof."

"Sure, but there might be a, a legal thing, a problem there."

"What kind of problem?"

"If I were to call him and say, 'Get back,' it might be construable as an offer, and I'm hardly in a position, oath-of-office-wise, to do that. There's another dimension. We've been kicking Peruvian butt for, for, for *years* over the extradition thing. Finally we're getting some cooperation and then bango, the top law enforcement officer goes and, and in direct contravention of the convention notifies the, the perpetrator and doesn't tell GOP—"

"GOP?"

214

"Government of Peru. I mean, it wouldn't be very bilateral of us, would it?"

"You're saying I should place the call?"

"Not necessarily. But I am saying we need to think through the who-makes-the-call situation."

"All right."

"There is the argument that it would carry more weight coming from you."

"Dick, I'm right down the hall from him, if you see what I'm saying."

"A hundred percent. Basically you're saying you're not sure you want to be in the tent on this."

"Well, I'm already *in* the tent, Dick. You've already *put* me in the tent."

"Right, well, I thought you'd want to be."

"But the essence of the thing is, is the deniability thing, as far as he is concerned."

"Absolutely."

"So I don't know if it makes sense for me to make the call."

"Well, I think that's, that's a feasible position. We can always fine-tune down the line. As the thing tracks."

"Why couldn't your man call? The one who brought this to you. Say, 'Look here, this is DEA, turn your butt around and, and, and get back here so, so ...' "

"So we can arrest you the moment you set foot on U.S. waters."

"I see your point."

"And we'd still have the open-line problem, John. You can't keep a satellite conversation private. Hell, some, some, some, some kid ham operator in Detroit was listening in while Reagan was on Air Force One giving Cap the go-ahead on Grenada."

"Why couldn't he just talk in generalities? People do it all the time, when they don't want ... Husbands and wives do it. *I* do it."

"Sure, but if some specifics get in ... I'm not even sure the whole fact of talking to him wouldn't open us up to misprision. You might want to run that by Boyden."

"Jesus. This is ..."

"Anyway, you see my point."

"I don't like this, Dick."

"I don't like it either, John."

"It's like, I don't know what it's like, a combination tar baby and can of worms."

"Right. It resonates that way for me, too."

"You know he was a contributor?"

"I didn't know that."

"Yeah. He was a delegate from Virginia."

"There's something else."

"What?"

"His company holds a contract with NASA."

"Oh hell."

"They make something for the shuttle."

"God. You know how he feels about the shuttle."

"Yes, I do."

"The shuttle is, it's, it's an American symbol. He'd feel awful if—he'd feel *betrayed*."

"I think we all would, more or less."

"Yeah, but for him it would be personal."

"It's not an easy call, John. I'm certainly glad it's not my call."

"Frankly, Dick, I see this more as your buck than my buck. At least from an administrative point of view."

"Sure, it's just, it impacts on up the chain, as you say. There's

216

always, we might let nature take its course, though that might open us up to misprision. Again, I'd want to run that through Boyden."

"Look, never mind Boyden. You're saying, suppose the decision was to say, in effect, to hell with it, it's a Peruvian problem, let them handle it?"

"Right."

"Well, that's, that's certainly an option."

"Trouble is, parsing it out, ultimately it still ends up being our problem."

"How?"

"Well, he's going to be caught, I think we can take that for granted—"

"Wait a minute, I'm not sure I'd take that for granted. I mean, if he's done all this that you say he's done, I'd say he's, he's very, he's certainly capable, in a, a horrible sort of way."

"Sure, but, I mean' he's not in Kansas anymore, John."

"He killed people in Kansas?"

"No no, that's, I mean, where he is is a bad place. Even their military doesn't go in there if they can help it. Or if they do it's just for a quick in-and-out photo op, so they can say, 'We're on top of this.' This river he's on, they just floated twenty decapitated bodies down this river past a military base where we have a few people, just to let us know they knew we were there. It's a very bad place, the Huallaga. It's one of the worst places there is."

"I'm aware of that. I read the newspapers."

"Right. Sorry, didn't mean to, it's just, I don't see how he can't get stopped, by someone, whether it's the authorities or the other side, the Senderos or the dopers. And it'll get out. My God. Symbolwise, we're talking Disaster City. The Latinos are unbelievably sticky about this sort of thing."

"This sort of thing? This sort of thing has happened before?"

"Not per se—"

"I've certainly never heard of this sort of thing happening before, unless you want to go back to the 1850s, the filibusters, whatsisname, the one who became President of Nicaragua. Walker."

"Right, Walker. It's just, historically, there's a heck of a lot of bad blood under the bridge, and you know, you just know, someone down there is going to stand up and say, 'This is a CIA thing, a JUNG thing, this thing was approved all the way, all the way on up.'"

"It is certainly not an approved thing. It's an outrageous thing, a, a, a, a *vile* thing."

"Right."

"And frankly it's, it's incredible, that he would get this—to this extent up the river without being caught."

"We did catch him. One of our men caught him, John."

"Well, he didn't *catch* him. He's, he's tooting his merry way up the Amazon. I don't see how he *caught* him, Dick. If he *caught* him, he, he'd be behind bars, consulting with Alan Dershowitz."

"Right, sure, I meant he caught him in the sense that—"

"I don't see that, Dick. I just don't see that. Here you say this guy started killing people in New York City last *year*."

"He's rich, he's got resources, he's—"

"He's a lunatic, Dick. The man is, is a cross between Ross Perot and, and, and Charles Manson."

"John, with all due respect, and believe me we're grateful, the appropriations support we've been getting from your shop is absolutely magnificent. I just don't think we ought to work ourselves into a shoot-the-messenger mode."

"All right, all right. Okay. Look, we better get a working group on this. But we better get some input from various, I guess we need more input then what we have now."

"Right. Can always use more input. Absolutely."

"But I want a tight loop."

"Absolutely. Tight."

"We want Bill, then? Well, we might as well have Bill in. I mean, he's already in the damn loop."

"We're bound to want his satellite again at some point."

"What about State? Do we want them?"

"My problem with that would be, they always viewfinder from the host country POV. They're just going to take the Peruvian angle and run with it. Or leak. Jim is, well, Jim is doing a superb, superb job, but, well, let's face it, John, Jim leaks."

"Uh-hum. There's another Jim problem. Jim and him are, you know."

"Right. The buddy thing."

"Right. If we loop in Jim, the first thing he's going to do is pick up the phone and—well, okay, Jim's out, for the time being. Anyway, this is just the option-formation stage."

"Fine, good. You probably want to get Ray in the tent."

"Ray—?"

"AsSecDef for SOLIC."

"Can you reconstitute that for me, Dick?"

"Assistant Secretary of Defense for Special Operations and Low-Intensity Conflict?"

"Right. Is SOLIC part of JUNC?"

"I think JUNC is part of SOLIC."

"Oh."

"The Joint Unified Narcotics Command sits on SOLIC, is how I think it works. I'd have to look at the org chart."

"So, well, do we loop in JUNC, or—"

"I'd say, I'd say maybe not at this point. I see this more as a SOLIC thing at this point."

"I'm getting lost here, Dick."

"Right."

27

Beebeeb beebeeb beebeeb.

Charley awoke with a snort to find Prescott's *History of the Conquest of Peru* lying heavily on his chest, his .45 stuck inside the pages as a bookmark.

Beebeeb beebeeb beebeeb. Stopped. Charley blinked the sleep fur out of his eyes and opened the book and tried to get the pages into focus. He was only up to Chapter 2, but he already liked what he knew about Pizarro, mostly on account of his being a bastard like himself, the illegitimate son of a colonel of infantry. Charley hoped he would not turn out to be a disappointment.

"According to some, he was deserted by both his parents, and left as a foundling at the door of one of the principal churches of the city. It is even said that he would have perished, had he not been nursed by a sow."

Suckled by a sow, now there's a man who's starting from scratch. Charley read on.

"This is a more discreditable fountain of supply than that assigned to the infant Romulus. The early history of men who have made their names famous by deeds in after-life, like the early history of nations, affords a fruitful field for invention."

It annoyed Charley that Prescott would give you a wonderful

220

detail like that and then snatch it away—sarcastically at that—but he understood that Prescott had been blinded by a food fight while he was a student at Harvard and even then had gone on to write the immense stories of Cortez and Pizarro, so he was willing to cut him some slack. Besides, he wrote so fine, could raise bumps on your arm. And he probably had to hedge his bets in case some historian from Yale showed up with a piece of parchment signed by the owner of the sow saying it was all true and without his sow Pizarro would have starved in infancy and the official language of Peru would now be Japanese.

Beebeeb beebeeb beebeeb. The hell was that? It was coming from the bedside console somewhere. It sounded like one of those traveling alarm clocks, the small black plastic German jobs. But he didn't own one. So what was this noise and where was it coming from? Inside the drawer? Just like Germany to make alarm clocks to wake the world out of a deep, soft sleep. There was nothing in the drawer. It was coming from under the drawer.

Beebeeb beebeeb beebeeb. There it was again.

"Felix," he said into the intercom, "I need you."

Felix couldn't figure it out either. It was definitely coming from inside the console somewhere. Charley wanted to take a crowbar to all that gorgeous bird's-eye maple paneling; then it stopped. Felix said it must be a loose circuit somewhere in the intercom system. Charley went back to Prescott. The thrum of *Esmeralda*'s twin diesels began to work on him as Pizarro and his exhausted men hacked their way and came upon *"an open space, where a small Indian village was planted. The timid inhabitants, on the sudden apparition of the strangers, quitted their huts in dismay; and the famished Spaniards, rushing in, eagerly made themselves masters of their contents. ... The astonished natives made no attempt at resistance. But, gathering more confidence as no violence was offered to their persons, they drew nearer the white men, and inquired, 'Why did they not stay at home and till their own lands, instead of roaming about to rob others who had never harmed them?' "*

Good question, Charley muttered, eyelids getting heavy.

"Whatever may have been their opinion as to the question of right, the Spaniards, no doubt, felt then that it would have been wiser to do so. But the savages wore about their persons gold ornaments of some size, though of clumsy workmanship. This furnished the best reply to their demand."

A large log banged into the *Esmeralda*'s steel hull so hard it jerked the book in Charley's hands.

"From the Indians Pizarro gathered a confirmation of the reports he had so often received of a rich country lying farther south; and there dwelt a mighty monarch whose dominions had been invaded by another still more powerful, the Child of the Sun."

His eyelids couldn't get a grip on his eyes; like trying to walk uphill on ice.

"It may have been the invasion of Quito that was meant, by the valiant Inca Huayna Capac, which took place some years previous to Pizarro's expedition."

Beebeeb.

Charley slept; and dreamed:

Tasha said to him, "I don't *believe* this."

"I'm doing it for you."

"Like hell. I will not be your excuse for mass murder, thank you."

"The way you talk."

"I can talk any way I want. I'm dead. I'm beyond you finally, Pops. I have to say it's almost a relief."

"No, you don't mean that. You don't know what you're saying. You're dead."

"How could you kill Timmy? I'm mortified."

"Yeah, well, I don't suppose *Timmy* is there with you, do I?"

"No one is here. *I'm* not here."

"Where are you calling from anyway?"

"Nowhere. I have to go now."

"Just tell me where. I'll send Felix to pick you up."

"Oh God, that would be great. I'm in—"

"PLEASE INSERT ANOTHER TWENTY-FIVE DEUTSCHEMARKS OR YOUR CALL WILL BE INTERRUPTED."

"Reverse the charges, operator. This is Charley Becker speaking."

"PLEASE INSERT ANOTHER TWENTY-FIVE MILLION DEUTSCHEMARKS OR YOUR CALL WILL BE TERMINATED."

"I'm telling you, I don't have any damn Deutschemarks. Don't you take dollars, for crying out loud?"

"Pops? Please—"

"THANK YOU FOR USING T 'N' T!"

"Tasha!"

He saw guards in watchtowers singing "Reach Out and Touch Someone" through loudspeakers. He woke up.

* * *

"Felix."

"Jesus!" Felix had been sitting on the bow watching with fascination the confusion of the bats. His Uzi, which had been slung from his shoulder, was now aimed at Charley's chest. "Boss, you shouldn't sneak up like that."

223

Charley, in his bathrobe, said, "I wasn't sneaking. It's these slippers. What're you doing up?"

"I couldn't sleep. Rostow put real coffee in the urn. I'm watching the bats. Bundy says they're confused by the ship's radar. He says they're getting the radar beams mixed up in their own, that's why they're doing that, flying so close."

"ECM."

"What's ECM?"

"Electronic countermeasures. Jamming. Look at that. I never saw such a thing before. Whoa."

"You better sit down. They're all over."

"I've never seen a bat that size. And I've seen bats."

"I have a theory about that bat," said Felix. "I think he thinks the helicopter is an insect and he's trying to get it to fly so he can swallow it all in one bite. I don't really like it here, boss, you want to know the truth."

"I had a dream."

"I was reading the Cousteau book. You know the catfish in this river get up to seven feet long?"

"Catfish don't bite you."

"But what about the crocodile that eats seven-foot-long catfish?"

"It was about Tasha. She was upset with me."

"Sounds like her."

"She was upset about this."

"That's just your superego speaking."

"I don't think I got all that big an ego."

"Superego is the conscience. Freud started calling it that, so now all the shrinks do. Was she upset about burying them in her clearing on the island?"

"She didn't mention that. What is it with the bodies on the island? I don't see the problem."

"Forget it. She mention me?"

"Yeah, she said hi. Damnit, Felix, it was uncanny, it was like when she used to call home from Madeira."

"They got eels in this river."

"Eels?"

"Electric eels. Put out a hundred volts, enough to kill a man. Some people on Cousteau's expedition were attacked by iguanas."

"Now that's just nonsense. Iguanas don't attack."

"These iguanas do."

"I don't believe it."

"It's in the book. The men were in a canoe and the iguanas jumped down on them from the trees above. They tore apart their shirts with their claws."

"Well, I'm sure it was an aberration. I been around plenty of iguanas in my life and none of them ever attacked me."

"They've got a snake—"

"You ought to read something else, Felix. Look, they got snakes everywhere, practically. Hell, we used to *eat* snakes at the orphanage all the time. Rat snakes, long-nose, patch-nose, king, diamondback rattlers, all kinds of snakes. Used to go out and look for them on the Harlingen road. I've said *grace* over road-kill snakes."

"Yeah, well, these would say grace over *you*."

"I got no brief against God's creatures. There's a beauty in all of them, you just have to look."

"There's this one called a candiru. It's a catfish, technically. If you can find the beauty in this fish, it's all yours. It's the size of a toothpick, okay? And it swims up your *dick*."

"I don't believe a word of it."

225

"It's in the book. The natives believe it can swim up your dick *while* you're taking a piss."

"That is the most—look, I got all sorts of admiration for Cousteau, but you got to remember, he's French."

"What does that have to do with it?"

"Well, they're always exaggerating. Look at that revolution they had."

"Once it gets up into you, it throws out these little spines, like fishhooks. The pain is incredible. You can only get them removed by surgery. And where are you going to find a doctor out here?"

"It was so real. It was *her*, Felix."

"Rats the size of pigs."

"I was trying to get her to stay on the line, only ..."

"Pink dolphins. Those are beautiful. They were the only things in this book I wanted to look at. But even them—the natives say that they screw human women and make them pregnant. It's in the book. I think I heard one the other night when we were anchored. Like a long sigh. *Unnnnhh*. That's why the natives think they have souls, because of the sigh. You know why I think they sigh? Because they have to live in the same water with all those other things."

"There was this recording kept telling me to put Deutschemarks in the phone or I'd be disconnected. Deutschemarks. Maybe your buddy Freud could figure that out. It was like it was ... Ma Hell speaking. Felix."

"What, boss?"

"You don't think, she can't be. I been over it a hundred times. It was a mistake. I cannot believe that God would send her to Hell for a, for a little mistake."

226

"She's not in Hell, boss. You want to know the truth, I think *we're* the ones in Hell."

"It is kind of gloomy at that. Reminds me a little of the Belgian Congo. I ever tell you about the place I saw there where all the parrots go to die?"

"No."

"You never seen such a place. Terrible smell."

"I'm going inside."

"Look out! Sweet Merciful Jesus, will you look at the size of him. Got a wingspread on him like a B-52."

28

"I really don't see how we're getting around the No Foreign Troops thing, Ray."

"'Troops' really means brigade strength. We're just talking about a unit here."

"A unit of troops."

"Well, strictly, legalistically speaking, sure."

"Well, strictly legalistically is, is sure as heck how the Peruvians are going to be speaking if this thing blows up in our faces."

"John has something there, Ray."

"Look, it walks like a duck, flies like a duck, smells like a duck. It's a *duck*. Let's just all face that. There's no way this thing is, is not a duck."

"It's quacking for me too, Ray."

"Okay, but I'm saying our chances of doing this are in the high eighties, low nineties."

"I'd like to believe that Ray, but, but we just, we just don't really have the track record to, to justify that."

"What about Panama? We managed Panama okay, didn't we?"

"Well, Ray, that wasn't exactly low-intensity. We had twenty-four thousand men involved in, in the Panama thing."

"And women."

"Yeah, all right. The point is, this is more of an Iranian-type thing, not a Panama thing. And you saw what happened there."

"We're not saying that happened on your watch, Ray."

"No, of course."

"In all respect, I disagree. I don't think we are talking about an Iranian-type thing. And if we should discuss the ten percent area where something goes, where the balls aren't breaking our way, then it can be finessed. We could hardly have finessed the Iranian thing."

"Finesse how?"

"Well, as a communications breakdown. You know, SOLIC assumed JUNC had cleared it with GOP, JUNC assumed SOLIC had cleared it with GOP."

"I don't like it, Ray. And I don't think *he's* going to like it either."

"Have you ever seen SEALs work, John?"

"Well, no. Obviously not."

"Let me tell you something about SEAL Team Six. These boys are, you should see them. Sometime just come down to Little Creek and see them."

"I'm a little busy here, Ray."

"Something like this, for them, it's, it's a cakewalk. They could do this in their sleep. It's a straightforward helicopter insertion upriver of the yacht. Our boys float till the boat comes by, they glom on to the hull with these little limpet mines, bang, Mr. Becker's yacht suddenly has serious leak problems. Becker and his people have to abandon ship, end of mission. Our boys just keep on floating downstream to their extraction point. I'll tell you what, I'll look into, see if we can't put together an all-Hispanic team so they'll really blend. It's just not that complicated. We're talking about an in-and-out thing."

"I still don't like it."

"Okay. Then what about cutting GOP in?"

"No no no no. I don't think we're there yet. Bill, do you have people on the inside of GOP?"

"That's kind of sensitve, John."

"Bill, we're all Top Secret/Throne-cleared here."

"That's not Throne level."

"Well, what is it, then?"

"The classification is classified."

"Let's try to work together here, Bill. We're all on the same team."

"It's a question of compartmentalizing—"

"Damnit, Bill."

"We have assets within GOP, yes. That's all I can say, really."

"That's very helpful, Bill. Are they reliable?"

"Well, yes. That's why they're assets."

"Yes, but I'm new at all this, I wasn't dealing with this when I was governor, I mean, but it seems to me, especially with this Noriega thing going on, that all our 'assets' are, are having it both ways, collecting two paychecks. I'm just asking if they can be trusted, is all."

"Down there it's usually a pay-as-you-go. With something like this we'd probably be in a bonus situation."

"Wonderful. Do we have any friends, Bill?"

"How do you mean?"

"Does anyone like us, or, or work for us just on the merits? Or is it all just money?"

"Oh. It's all just money."

29

Esmeralda's anchor chain was taut, links squeaking from the strain of keeping 460 tons of yacht from being swept off in the Huallaga's swift rush. Farther out in the middle of the river, giant logs tore past. Charley had put her nose right against the riverbank, in still water; even so, a wake was burbling out behind her transom.

They sat around the table on which Tallulah Bankhead had allegedly once done the woolly deed. Its fine inlaid surface was covered by a padded tablecloth to protect it from the various metallic objects that were making their rounds: M-26 grenades, radios, collapsiblestock Cars M-16 rifles, CD players and speakers. Bundy was demonstrating grenade etiquette to the new people.

Charley turned on the video and pressed "play."

On came the Becker Industries corporate logo, the eagle holding the globe, which Tasha said looked like a bird trying to dribble a basketball, followed by footage of the space shuttle hurtling through the upper atmosphere. A few seconds later, there were two loud explosions and the solid-fuel rocket boosters separated from the orbiter and began their slow-motion tumble back to Mother Earth.

The voice-over began: "Originally developed for NASA by Becker Industries, High Mass Explosive, or HMX, represents the state of the art in plastic explosives. Here on earth, HMX has literally hundreds of uses. Lightweight, malleable and detonated exclusively by means of an eighty-five percent nitroglycerin power primer controlled by a two-stage safety microchip—also made by Becker Industries—HMX is the first choice of a growing number of government and civilian agencies. With an explosive power of three million pounds per square inch and a flash velocity of twenty-six thousand feet per minute—nearly twenty times the muzzle velocity of a .38 caliber bullet—it's clear why the professionals turn to HMX."

"This wasn't made for ... us?" asked Bundy.

"No," said Charley. "Our sales people use it when they make their rounds. Fire departments, mostly. Police Emergency Services. It's good for when you need to get through a wall in a hurry. Plus some government agencies. Delta Force uses it."

"Oh, okay," said McNamara. "Play-Doh."

"How's that?"

"That's what Delta calls it, Play-Doh."

"You get more bang for your buck than with C-4," said Charley. "A lot more. Your basic C-4 just doesn't compare with this stuff. We package it for Delta special, to look like one of those family-size toothpaste pump dispensers. We add peppermint and candy-cane colors so it'll get past the dogs."

The screen showed technicians putting a stick of it inside an old armored car. "Watch this," said Charley. "That's a twelve-hundred-grain stick, less than a quarter pound. Watch."

"Jesus."

"I'm standing one hundred yards away when they did that. I took Natasha along. She was just a little girl at the time. Anyway, one of my earplugs was in wrong. Didn't hear right for a week after that. *Hell* of a sound."

Charley pressed "stop." He passed the V-shaped stick down the table. Bundy and McNamara were at ease with it; the others handled it as if it would go off if they breathed on it wrong.

"Not gonna bite you. You can put it in the oven, hit it, light a match to it, stick it up your ass and fart, it will not go off without the nitro chip. Okay now, you all met Hot Stick here. They don't call him that for nothing. He's won the Scale Masters Championship three times. That's the World Series of UAV flying, so listen up. Hot Stick, talk to us."

"Yes, sir. First I want to say that me and my crew are proud to be part of the team."

Bundy and McNamara looked at each other dubiously.

"If I could, I'd like to take the opportunity to give the boys a little background on UAVs."

"All right, but we got a full agenda."

"Roger dodger. These aircraft go by different names. UAV, for unmanned aerial vehicle, RPV, for remotely piloted vehicle, or just RC, for remote-controlled. People who don't know better call them 'model airplanes.'

"Now, the UAV, as we know it, originated during World War II when the Army needed to train antiaircraft gunners. Up to then they'd been towing targets, banners or drogues, behind airplanes and letting the ack-acks bang away at them. The trouble was, they tended to lose pilots' so they started to think in terms of self-propelled vehicles. I know Mr. Becker here is familiar with Project Aphrodite. That was sort of our answer to Hitler's doodlebugs, the V-1 and V-2 rockets. The Navy would take B-17s and B-24s that were coming up on the end of their service lives, rig them so they were remotecapable, pack them full of high explosives. The pilot and copilot would get them off the ground and up over the English Channel and then bail out. They put a sort of TV camera

232

on it so a third pilot, flying alongside, could guide the bomber to its target. That's how young Joe Kennedy was killed. The bomber he was flying blew up on him over the Channel."

"I think we're all set on the history, thank you, Hot Stick."

"Roger. Real briefly then, the technology has come quite a ways since then. In the fifties RPVs were basically just your stick-and-stringer balsa-wood units that took hours and hours to build. Now we make the bodies out of preformed fiberglass or foam core. Then in 1972 J. J. Scozzufavva and Bob Violett developed the first duct-edfan jet engine and turned the UAV world upside down. Now we had twenty-three thousand rpms' speeds of up to a hundred fifty miles an hour. From the ground, you cannot tell the difference between these aircraft and the real thing."

"*Horse*shit," said McNamara.

"Except perhaps in the field of sound. A ducted-fan two-stroker will give you scale speed, but it won't give you scale sound. That's where those CD players you boys will be planting around the target perimeter will come in."

Bundy said to McNamara, "*Boys?*"

"As the UAVs approach, they'll transmit a signal to the boom boxes and activate the CD sound track. Mr. Dolby here has figured out a way to give us perfect stereo. Right, Dolby?"

"Uh huh."

"As they approach the perimeter, the signal will trigger the boom boxes on the near side, then as they fly by, the signal will activate the boom boxes on the other side of the perimeter."

Dolby said, "The problem I'm having, I mean, are we limited to these small jobs here? I mean, they'll do it, but they're only hun-dredwatt. I was telling Hot Stick earlier, I could rig us up some fourhundred-watt, eighteen-inch subwoofers with tuned ports and really push some air, you know what I'm saying? Make these dudes think we're the Monsters of Rock. But we'd need more juice. We could get it out of that portable generator you got down in engine room."

McNamara said, "I'm not humping a sixty-millimeter mortar, eighteen-inch speakers and a damn generator into the jungle."

Dolby shrugged. "Too bad, man. Be a totally awesome sound."

"I think the hundred-watt speakers will do fine," said Charley. "Hot Stick?"

"The important thing will be for Mac to time his mortar bombardments to my flybys. Think you can handle that?"

Mac looked at Bundy. Bundy shrugged, as if it would be too much effort. Hot Stick proceeded, unfazed.

"I'm pleased to say our attack profile will include one of the first true turbine UAVs, built by Mr. Brian Seegers himself. Brian doesn't know about this particular application of his technology, but I'm certain that if he did, he would be proud to be taking part in the war on drugs."

Charley stirred. "This isn't the war on drugs, son. This is my war."

"Yes, sir. As you know, true turbines won't give you scale speed, only about a hundred miles an hour. But they will give you scale *sound*."

"I'm counting on it."

"I can deliver a hundred and ten decibels at a hundred feet. But the main advantage of the true turbine, for our purposes, isn't sound, but heat. Ordinarily these engines run so cool you can put your hand to the exhaust. Since we're not worried about reusability, I'm using a low-temperature grease in the shielded bearings and choking up on the ram air inlet, plus running a mix of thirty-five percent nitromethane into the fuel spray manifold. She's going to run hot."

"Hot enough to draw a heat-seeking missile?"

"I guarantee it. I'm pretty sure, anyway."

"Good, 'cause you're gonna be up there in the chopper with me. You don't think adding thirty-five percent nitro is a little on the combustible side?"

"No problem."

"Okay, talk to us about the attack profile. We're going in in three waves?"

"Correct. First in will be the A-io Thunderbolt. One-to-seven scale. She's configured right for the turbines, plus the Peruvian Air Force flies Thunderbolts, so it won't look out of place."

"You got her all decaled?"

" 'Fuerza Aérea Peruana,' yes, sir. I thought it'd be better to wait till the last minute, in case we got inspected back in Iquitos."

"Good thinking."

"Thunderbolt's radio designation will be Slow Boy. Now, the second wave will consist of the two F/A-18 Blue Hornets. They're one-to-twelve scale. These are just—I can't say enough about these aircraft. They just never let you down. These will be our real work-horses, with U.S. markings. They'll look like they just blasted off the deck of the *Nimitz*. Their radio designations are Slim Jim One and Slim Jim Two.

"The third and final wave is Fat Albert. We're assembling him right now. Fat Albert is a one-to-seven-scale version of the Grumman A-6E Intruder."

"Aw, shit." said McNamara.

"There a problem?"

"Go on," said Charley.

"We're going with the 6E configuration instead of the 6A on account of the increased payload factor. The Intruder carries two tandem triplets of five-hundred-pound bombs. Ours will be carrying two tandem triplets of six-hundred-grain HMX bombs. We're talking payload here. You boys who took part in the Vietnam conflict—"

"Conflict?"

"Well" we never actually declared war, as I understand. However, you may recall that the North Vietnamese and the Vietcong nicknamed this aircraft quote the Miniature B-52 unquote, and for good reason. I've never seen a one-to-one-scale A-6E in action, but I've read everything there is to—"

"I have," said McNamara. "I saw one wipe out a whole field of infantry once, just like that."

"I bet it was some sight, huh?"

"Yes, it was. First Batt, First Marines. It was some fucking sight."

"Uh huh. Well, shit happens.

Mac stared.

"Usually it was a Forward Air Controller calling up bad coordinates, not the pilot," said Hot Stick.

"Couldn't find enough of the FAC to ask him. Had to ask the pilot himself. Tracked him down up in Seattle afterward. That happens here, going to track you down."

"This probably won't mean anything to you, but I learned how to fly UAVs from Dennis Crooks and Bob Fiorenze."

"And I learned how to remove lungs from Master Sergeant Bob Ruckhauser."

"Boys, boys," said Charley, "we're all on the same team here, let's try to remember."

"Well, what about that accident he had?" said Mac. "You win one of your Scale Masters trophies for wiping out a section of grandstand, Dip Stick?"

"That was a faulty fuel-control unit."

"So?"

"*We few*," Charley murmured' "*we happy few, we band of brothers.*"

"And even then I was able to get her into an easy graveyard spiral. You have any idea how hard that is to do? It wasn't my fault they all stood there with their binoculars like a bunch of sheep."

Charley said, "Now, I'm sure we all got things in our pasts we'd like to change if we had the chance. We can talk about it on the way downriver. What we need to talk about now is ... What's the matter with him? Dolby? Has he been drinking?"

Dolby, sitting down at the end near the passageway into the salon, had pitched forward onto Tallulah's table.

"Damnit, Dolby, this is no time to take a nap."

Bundy saw it first, a sliver of bamboo protruding from the ponytail. The end of the stick was wound with wool dipped in clay for ballast and a tight seal when the dart was propelled with a blast of air through the hollow shaft. The tip, coated with the sweat of a tiny black-and-yellow frog, was embedded a half inch deep in the muscles of Dolby's neck, a short hop to the brain.

30

"I don't *care* if the Army feels left out, Ray. For God's sake."

"It's just, they feel there's an Army dimension to it."

"I don't see what. It's a river, isn't it? A river is water, isn't it? Water is Navy material, isn't it?"

"Sure, but if you look at the broader context—"

"This is exactly what happened with the Grenada thing. Every branch of the service had to have its thumb in the pie."

"From an Army point of view—"

"Same with the Iranian thing."

"We may be apple-and-oranging here."

"What happened to our loop here, Ray? Dick? This loop is getting out of hand. It's not even a loop anymore. It's a, a Beltway. You've got the Navy, the Marines, now you want the Army in on it."

"The Seventh Special Forces Group is on station down there, in Santa Lucía. The feeling is they have a feel for the area. Besides, John, this came from Colin, not me."

"It came from Colin?"

"Well, Colin *is* Army."

"We just keep adding to this, Ray. We just keep adding and adding and adding. You're going to come in here tomorrow and tell me there's a, a *Coast Guard* dimension. Why don't we get the, the Army Corps of Engineers while we're at it. Why don't we have them go down there and build a *dam* so he can't get upstream."

"It's still a tight loop. If it's the loop you're worried about, you know what the Airborne motto is."

"No, I do not."

" 'Land softly, kill quietly.' You don't have to worry about leaks from the Army."

"I'm not worried about leaks. I'm worried we're going to need an aircraft carrier to transport everyone. And then you'll tell me we need submarines to protect it."

"It's just that SOLIC draws on all the services, John, so it's only natural that all the services would want, would want to input the thing. But I'll go back and tell Colin that you're dead set against the Army dimension. I'll just say, 'John says no Army.'"

"No. All right, look, if Colin wants the Army on board, if he really thinks—whatever."

"I think that's a good call."

"But I want it on the record that I think this thing is turning into a nine-hundred-pound gorilla."

"It just looks that way."

"Bill, what about things at your end? Are we nailed down?"

"I didn't think we were there yet."

"We're not, I just want to know if, is it nail-downable if we do get there?"

"We're more at the probing stage. We're trying to find out who knows what. You've got to know where to put the nails."

"I appreciate that, Bill. But when I take this package down the hall, I don't want to have to tell him, 'Everything's set except for Bill's end. He's looking where to put the nails.'"

"No, we're, we're working something inside DINTID."

"DINTID?"

"Dirección de Investigaciones de Narcóticos y Tráfico Ilícito de Drogas. It's within PIP."

"PIP? Never mind."

"Policía de Investigaciones del Perú. *Federales*. Their version of the FBI. Though I don't think Dave would like to hear it put that way."

"Are we saying to them, 'We may need you down the line, stand by'? Is that the particular nail you're trying to figure out where to put?"

"That's close enough."

"Well, okay, but are they in a position to damage-control it if we get into the banana-peel situation?"

"That's the idea. The problem is containing the information. Down there the shit floats uphill, if you follow."

"No, I don't follow, Bill. I just don't want to have to go down the hall and tell him, 'The problem is that down there shit floats uphill.' *He's* not going to know what *I'm* talking about and I'm not going to know what I'm talking about."

"We're talking about corruption."

"Our—this asset is corrupt, is that it?"

"No, but you want to be careful. One individual we were using down there turned out to be drawing five paychecks, three of them from U.S. agencies. Us, DEA and Customs. And two from competing dopers. Counting his PIP paycheck I suppose that makes six."

"Well, that's just wonderful. That's just dandy. I hope whoever this new asset is has a little more, more self-respect."

"The guy with six paychecks had lots of self-respect."

"Entirely unwarranted, if you want my input. All right, are we, is that it, then? Dick?"

"There's something, I don't know if you want to put it on the table now or down the line. But say we get him back."

"That's the whole point, Dick, to get him back to the United States."

"Right, so are we then in a prosecuting situation?"

"You're darn right we are. We're in a very prosecuting situation. The man is a criminal, Dick. He needs to be locked up."

"Right, absolutely. But we still have the symbolism problem, space-shuttle-wise, and the international problem, plus the other problem."

"What other problem, Dick?"

"Well, let's assume he's going to have some pretty good legal representation. You want to talk about nine-hundred-pound gorillas, my God. You can imagine who's going to be on *that* defense team. And the opening statement to the jury is going to be that the U.S. government ought to be a, a co-defendant, because they knew all about it and that's misprision, and obstruction, to say nothing of convention violation and, and well, about fourteen other things."

"We're not there yet, Dick."

"And there's, you know, a lot of people are going to be cheering him on. The Rich Man's Bernhard Goetz. One man's war against drugs and, and we stopped him."

"From irreparably ruining U.S.-Peru relations, you're darn straight."

"I just don't think Joe Six-Pack out there frankly gives a shit about U.S.-Peru relations, John. Maybe the Op-Ed gang, but that's about it. I think Joe is going to be cheering for Charley Becker, you want my frank opinion."

"I'm just saying—"

"I know what you're saying."

"John, I think what Dick is saying—"

"I know what Dick is saying, Bill."

"Actually, I wasn't saying that."

"Saying what?"

"What you were telling Bill I was saying."

"Maybe the thing to do is go the ad hoc route. Let it ripen a little and look at it then."

"We could do that. We could definitely do that."

"I don't have any problem with that."

31

The shotgun pointed at his face was an old hammeraction twelve-gauge, Charley estimated from the width of the muzzle, possibly a sixteen, and covered with as much rust as the twentieth century had been able to provide so far, making it impossible to read the barrel markings and see if he was about to be killed by a Remington or a Savage. He would not have been musing on this but for Mac's quick reflexes. Seconds after Dolby had keeled into his bowl of eternal soup, Mac had pulled his 9mm pistol out and aimed at the Indian closest to him, whose needle-nosed bamboo spear had no doubt been dipped in something similar to whatever was now puddling in Dolby's stilled bloodstream.

Charley didn't allow his eyes to roam too widely around the dining room for fear of seeming rude to the man who was holding the rusty Winchester—or whatever it was—on him, but he thought there must be better than a half dozen of them. For the moment it was unclear who their CEO was. The pressure was definitely building, though, he could feel it in his eardrums, and it was just a matter of time before Hot Stick said or did something that would get them all killed before you could reach three-Mississippi, so he had to do something, only trouble was what?

It was like getting a dog outdoors on a cold winter's day, but Charley coaxed his zygomaticus muscles into a smile and said, "*Hola*," Spanish for hello. A little lame, but all that came to mind under the circumstances, and it had the advantage of utter neutrality. Only someone suckled on witch tit would take offense at that, and the man with the shotgun did not have an unkindly face. Charley had to read it through red achiote juice and purple tattoo stippling, but the eyes seemed to belong to a man he could do bidness with, as they say in Texas.

Think, now. My yacht is your yacht? My name is Charley, what's yours? Into these lucubrations intruded a keen desire to urinate. He did not relish the prospect of appearing incontinent in front of his men, so he said the next word that dog-paddled across the synaptic gulf: "*Bienvenido*." Welcome.

"*Bien ... venido*," he heard Felix repeat. Soon there was a general murmuring of *bienvenidos*, except from Mac and Bundy, who were not the types to indulge in pleasantries, however strategic, with minatory strangers.

The Indians made no response to these imbecilic pleasantries, but neither did they open fire, and this Charley welcomed, even if he doubted they were going to be able to make an all-night mantra out of it.

The Indian's eyes went for a second to Charley's wristwatch, a quick flicker, then back to the crater he was contemplating making in the middle of Charley's skull. A gold Rolex was a small coal in Newcastle aboard a yacht like *Esmeralda*, but it was portable, certainly it was that, and Charley was rehearsing how to get it off his wrist in one easy and unthreatening motion when the Indian dropped his shotgun, just an inch but enough to reveal the objects dangling from the thong of dried capybara gut around his neck. Charley saw teeth which he recognized from the pictures in Cousteau as coming from the *boto*, from the pink dolphin. Between them was a crucifix. It was handmade, two polished twigs of dark wood tied together with human hair-crude, but truer to the genuine article than what swung from so many pierced earlobes these days.

Moving his hand very slowly, Charley pointed at the crucifix, then at his own chest, where he traced the outline with his finger hard enough to leave a little white welt template before the blood flooded back into the exsanguinated capillaries. The faded cross tingled on Charley's sternum. *We share the same God or X marks the spot*, he could take it either way.

Eladio leveled the shotgun at the *pistaco*'s chest and tightened around the trigger. He told himself not to look directly into the eyes so the *pistaco* would not draw his strength out of him. Hunting *pistaco* was like hunting jaguar: you must not look into the eyes and you must not utter its true name or it will become ferocious.

The *pistaco* was pretending to be afraid of the gun. But Eladio knew that the *pistaco* could not be killed by a gun. They had to be crushed until the bones showed and the eyes were pulled out and burned so they could not follow you afterward. Truly, killing a *pistaco* was more difficult than killing a jaguar. He wanted to start killing this one before he made any more *kistian* signs on his skin, but he knew without turning to look that the two large *pistacos*, giants, truly, had been fast with their guns, and if he shot their headman they would kill his son Zácari and some of the others before they themselves could be killed. The large ones had the look of true grease stealers. How many had they cut up into pieces and boiled to get the human oil for their *Challenger* rockets? Already he could feel the *pistaco*'s voice singing inside him. The killing must begin. He stood back so that the shotgun would get both the *pistaco*'s eyes with one shot. True, it would be better first to crush the skull and then remove the eyes, but he saw no other way. The *iwishin* could tell him what to do, but the shaman was old and no longer went out on the hunt. He asked Tsewa, headman of the spider monkeys, who taught his ancestors the blowgun and the hunting songs. Tsewa told him to begin.

"Apu! Apu!" The voice came from the main salon. An Indian came running with a face like he'd seen God and spoke excitedly to the Indian whose finger, Charley was certain, was about an eighth of an ounce of trigger pressure from scattering his brain all over Tallulah's table, increasing its value as an artifact only marginally.

He was pointing in the direction of the salon, saying the same word over and over: *"Tsugki. Tsugki."* Charley saw there was something else in Shotgun's eyes now, the shadow of a doubt. His gun lowered a few inches, a useful barometric indication of how things stood between them. Shotgun looked at Charley and there were no words necessary, it couldn't have been clearer: *I'm going into the next room to check out this tsugki situation my man here is telling me about, and you better pray I like what I see.* Charley did pray, prayed like an EPIRB beacon in a shark-surrounded life raft beaming up SOS bursts at the cold stars above, hoping one of them was a plane.

* * *

They squatted and sat on the salon carpet in front of it. It was going through one of its waterfall cycles, shimmery, iridescent strands of blue light cascading over invisible rocks into a moonlit pool. When a new cycle began, they sighed in unison. Charley said, "Maybe it would be a good idea if you passed around some snacks and soft drinks. Nothing with caffeine."

Felix approached with a cordless phone and an Uzi submachine gun. He had two handguns tucked inside his waistband. Felix was armed. Everyone had undergone a personal defense buildup. Hot Stick had so many bulbous grenades dangling off him he looked like an overdecorated Christmas tree. Charley's .45 was holstered, though with safety off. For the time being things were under control. What Charley feared most was a generator malfunction. Rostow was in the engine room making sure all the needles were in the black; Felix had been on the phone to the vice president for Operations, up in Rosslyn.

He stood beside Charley, keeping his eyes on the Indians. "I've got someone on the line," he said. "Untermeyer found him through the Smithsonian. It's three a.m. his time. I explained it as much as I could. I thought you should speak to him. His name is Tierney. Untermeyer says he's an ethnographer."

"Ethnographer," Charley repeated in the dreamy tone of voice everyone was using, for fear a single hard consonant would spark the charged air inside *Esmeralda*'s salon and turn it into a combustion chamber. "An ethnographer is someone ..."

"He knows about Amazon Indians."

"Okay," said Charley. "Let's see just *what* he knows." He took the phone from Felix and punched the "hold" button and said in his Monday-morning voice, "Sorry to barge into your sleep like this, Mr. Tierney, but I got a little situation here could use some ethnographizing. I don't know what my associate here told you, but it boils down to I got about a dozen extremely hostile Indians here in my living room all making eyes at a piece of moving art I got on board, sculpture with lights in it, and they look like they're hunkered in for the wet season. ... How do I know they're hostile? One of my people's dead with a dart sticking out of him. ... No, they weren't provoked. ... I appreciate that, but the deforestation of

246

the Amazon is not the issue here, Mr. Tierney. I happen to be a life member of the Sierra Club. Anyway, it was about to get worse when one of 'em started shouting, '*Soo-gi*' and the rest of them went running in like they heard Elvis Presley was back from the dead and giving a free concert. ... I really couldn't spell it for you, Mr. Tierney. ... Uh-huh, uh-huh. ... Same linguistic group. You're saying they are the headhunters or they're *related* to the head-hunters?"

"What?" said Felix.

"Related. All right, then. Good. Fine. Great." Charley cupped the phone and said, "They're just related. ... Yeah, I'm here. All right, you know what *soo-gi* means? ... Uh-huh, uh-huh. ... Well, it's about five foot high, looks like a stele, you know, one of those stone deals they used to put on a dead warrior, got a motor in it runs light through fiber optics, does patterns. ... What kind of patterns? Patterns, like, I don't know. Right now it's doin' like a rainbow and they're moanin' and groanin' ... Yeah, I can hold."

Eladio said to his son Zácari, "How do you think it works?"

"Tierney? You there? ... Don't fall asleep on me now, we're almost finished."

Rostow, Mac, Bundy and Hot Stick were standing by with their weapons pointed at the congregation of Aguaruna as casually as it could be done without being rude, trying to provide comfort for Felix, who crouched next to the Stele, perspiring heavily over a sol-dering iron, a converter and a picnic cooler full of two dozen size-D batteries. The batteries were all soldered together in series. He sol-dered a wire from the negative end of the first battery and ran it to the converter, then attached another wire from the positive nipple of the last battery to the converter. The Indians seemed to regard his ministrations as unobtrusive, but the real test was coming.

"Ready," said Felix.

Charley said, "Everybody ready?" He saw Hot Stick reaching for one of his grenades. "No, Hot Stick."

"I've got to pull the hundred and ten plug before I can hook up the DC bank," said Felix.

"How long is that going to take?"

"I don't *know*, boss."

"All right, it's all right."

"I'm not an electrician," said Felix.

"I sure as hell hope you *are*," said Bundy.

"Okay," said Charley, "here we go. Don't shoot me, boys." He waded into their midst and stood in front of the Stele so as to block their view of it and addressed himself to Shotgun, sitting in the front row.

"On behalf of everyone, I'd just like to say what a real pleasure it's been to have you all visit with us ..."

Felix pulled the plug. The Stele went dead. The Indians gasped.

"It was specially nice that you all could take the time to kill all of my crew, except for these gentlemen here ..."

Shotgun was on his feet with an angry look.

"And I think I can speak for them when I say how pleased they are that you decided not to kill them as well ..."

Shotgun aimed his weapon. It was about to end in a mutual massacre, an exchange of double-ought buckshot, .45s and .38s, frog darts and bamboo blades, and before it was over Hot Stick would probably toss in one of his grenades just to make sure no one survived, when all of a sudden a fireworks display lit up the surface of the Stele.

The Indians sighed. And it was good.

They lowered it from davits into their longest dugout canoe.

Shotgun spoke to Charley. "*Kurinku pataa,*" he said. The ethnographer yawned at the other end of the line that *kurinku* was a corruption of the Spanish *gringo. Pataa* meant headman.

The Indians paddled away in the darkness, the Stele upright in the dugout like a weird grandfather clock from another world. A red sun rose on its surface, burst into a fiery dandelion, then fell, streaming in tendrils through the vastness of space, into the black night water of the Huallaga.

32

"No. Absolutely not."

"DEA thought that under the circumstances, since it was their thing—"

"We've got the Navy, the Marines, the Army, now you want DEA. I knew this was going to happen, Dick. Why don't we just get a 747 to fly them all down there?"

"It's his case, John."

"It is not 'his case,' Dick. Not anymore. It's bigger than that now. My God, it's on *my* desk now."

"I realize that. It's just that DEA made a, a deal with Diatri."

"What do you mean?"

"Without bogging you down in the details, it, basically Diatri got a commitment from, from DEA that he would be in on the, that he would be part of the package."

"I don't understand. Commitment. Who are we talking about here, a, a GS-12?"

"Thirteen. He's a Senior Agent. He passed up a promotion to Group Supervisor so he could stay on the beat. DEA says he's good, very good. In fact, you remember the five-ton seizure in Jacksonville?"

"Of course."

"The one *he* went down there for, for the photo op and hand-shake?"

"*Yes.*"

"That was Diatri's bust. Here's the photo of the two of them together. He even signed it for him."

"He signs photos for everyone, Dick. He's, he's that way. It's the noblesse oblige thing."

"Right, it's just—"

"I'm sure he's a fine agent, first-rate, but why the hell does he have to be part of the, the military aspect? Unless he's good with mines, for God's sake."

"As I understand it, they were about to medical him out on a Disability when he broke the case. He wasn't happy about that and apparently used the fact he'd broken the case as a bargaining chip to get them to keep him on."

"What kind of shop are they running over there?"

"A very good shop, John. It's just, the Administrator is very protective of his people. So he made the arrangement with him."

"Then he made one he wasn't able to keep."

"The sense I got is that if Diatri isn't part of the package, he's not going to be happy."

"I'm not *in* the happiness business, Dick."

"This is Sensitive City, here, John. I don't think it's going to do us any good if, if, you know, here we are doing the war on drugs and cashiering our front-line soldiers."

"In a war, if you get wounded, you get sent home. With honor."

"That's not how he sees it, apparently."

"I don't give a hoot how he sees it. I never imagined this job would entail haggling with, with GS-13s. It's not dignified, Dick."

"I hear you. But all they did was tell him he could be in on the package. After that they're, they've got a plan. They're going to stick him in Congressional Relations. Diatri doesn't know that, by the way. They'll tell him that once it's over."

"Congressional Relations? I would have thought, he looks a little rough-hewn for Congressional Relations."

"They like that. The rough-hewn look. It plays well."

"All right, he can go, but that is absolutely it. I don't want anyone else coming in here and saying, 'Oh, my Aunt Martha needs to go.'"

"Fine, right. When are you going to take this down the hall?"

"When he gets back from fishing."

"Good thinking."

"If we get into the banana-peel situation, I'll want you to be point man. Take over, damage-control it."

"Me? I would have thought Ray."

"You and Ray, I mean. I've already explained it to Ray."

"Uh-huh. What's your thinking as far as my, my being out front?"

"I don't want this washing up on his doorstep, Dick. We need to create some, some insulation. For his sake."

"Right."

"And I'm just down the hall from him, so if my doorstep gets wet, so does his, if you follow."

33

Only an hour of light left. Virgilio and Mirko sat dozing in the bucket seats of their respective high-performance boats. Their men lay about the wooden floating dock with their weapons on their stomachs, listening to the same Julio Iglesias tape they had been listening to all day and it was starting to get on his nerves. Eladio and his men should have been back hours ago. The yacht was only ten kilometers downriver from Yenan. Assuming they had made their attack the night before, that would give them more than enough time to be back here.

"Don't you have something else to play? Something classical?"

The man closest to the tape player said respectfully, "*Sí*, Niño," and took out the Julio Iglesias and after a thoughtful rumination over the bag of tapes, made a selection to please his *patrón*. Sinatra's "Strangers in the Night," sung in Spanish by Charo, filled the muggy riverine air.

"Okay, Niño?"

"*Yes*," he said, too preoccupied to manage more than slight annoyance. He had in mind Tárrega's *Recuerdos de la Alhambra* or the *Asturias* of the incomparable Albéniz, who had run away from his home in Spain at the age of nine, stowed away on a boat to Central America and returned home a man of the world at the age of thirteen. He tried to lose himself in the endless permutations of the surface of the water as it tumbled downriver, toward his enemy *billonario*.

He felt it happening: the malarial memory coming back at him again. He was back on that accursed golf course with her father.

"It's not Amanda who wants to break it off, Antonio. She's *terribly* fond of you. She's doing it for me. I know you're from a *very* good family down there, but let's face it, everything's so darn *unstable* down there. I just wouldn't be happy thinking my daughter was going to be caught up in the midst of some political kafuffle. I don't know about you, but I'm dying for a gin and tonic. What say we head in? I must say, you're being awfully *mature* about all this, Antonio."

He wondered, for the sixth or seventh time, if he should have given Eladio a radio. No. Might as well tie a radio to a butterfly.

He had, however, given Eladio a briefing on the dangers of this particular *pistaco*. The *pistaco* mythology went back—as far as anyone could trace—to 1571. It was the Indians' way of explaining the Spanish Conquest. Sendero Luminoso had revived the myth in the 1980s as a way of turning the people against the Army, with tremendous effect. Tales of horror wrought by *pistacos* were retailed every day. Eladio himself had described to him, in nearly journalistic detail, a slaughter of 30,000 Indians by *pistacos*, how they had hacked off all their limbs and thrown them into a giant cooking pot and sold the rendered grease to the North Americans for their machines, especially the rockets that they sent into the sky to impregnate the moon and create monster children who would ride back down to earth on the backs of meteors, ghastly, shrieking creatures who vomited hot lava.

The forest was the cradle of extravagant animism. Eladio's people believed that everything had a soul, often more than one. And yet the legend of the *pistaco*, the troll-thug who kills to obtain human grease, was hardly peculiar to the Amazon. During World War I the British government's propaganda mechanism insinuated into the public imagination stories of the German "Corpse-Rendering Works," where the dead bodies of fine young English soldiers were melted down to grease German artillery pieces; while across the Channel stories were circulated about the British "Tallow Works" of like ghastliness.

He had told Eladio not to touch anything on the boat. Everything was possessed—especially the pictures—by *iwanchin*, the shadow souls who can turn themselves into anything, deer, owl, butterfly, in order to kidnap the children of the Indians.

Kill them quickly, Eladio, and touch nothing. The boat itself must be disposed of according to certain rituals, which I myself will perform.

So—where was Eladio? He tried to close his mind off from disturbing images of a firefight aboard the yacht. He saw "The Absinthe Drinker" shot up with holes, Baudelaire's manic eyes peering out from under the brim of his top hat, bursting into flames, the boat rocked by explosions—

"Esteban!"

"*Sí*, Niño?"

"Turn off that shit! I said *classical*!"

Puzzled, Esteban switched off Charo. The crepuscular sounds of the river reasserted themselves—frog, cricket, beetle, bird—until they were drowned out by an organ version of "Love Is a Many Splendored Thing."

34

Charley stepped out onto *Esmeralda*'s flight deck wearing his flight suit and .45 snugged in its shoulder holster and took a deep breath. He hadn't slept but a few hours since the Indian attack, and for the first time since it had all begun, he felt his age. It was dark out, an hour to sunrise. Hot Stick was leaning over one of the

UAVs—Fat Albert—adding nitromethane to the fuel mixture. Charley's nostrils tingled from the vapors; it woke him up, gave him a little energy charge. The smell was familiar somehow; then he remembered sitting in the back of the limousine with his sinuses full of gun oil, on the way to the morgue with Felix.

He reached inside the chopper for the radio handset. "Where is everyone?"

"Grasshopper Three, in position."

"Grasshopper Four, in position."

"One and Two, where are you?" Charley said. "State your positions, please."

Felix's voice came on. "Mac says we're a hundred yards from our position. I think we're lost. I can't see anything. Over."

Charley said, "Roger that. Stand by. We are preparing to launch." He gave Hot Stick the signal.

Hot Stick had the leaf blower going, funneling air into the turbines of the Thunderbolt to get them spinning. He held up the spark coil in his other hand and said, "Ready." Charley nodded. He touched the spark coil to the engine. A burst of flame appeared from the afterburner. Charley nodded again; Hot Stick hit the lever release on the catapult and the A-10 shot off *Esmeralda*'s cantilevered flight deck.

Hot Stick maneuvered the joysticks on one of the five Futaba transmitters, bringing Slow Boy into a holding pattern above *Esmeralda*. The Futabas were all wired into a Toshiba laptop computer. He switched Slow Boy's controls over to the computer and got ready to launch the two F/A-18s, already positioned in the bow cats. Charley nodded; Hot Stick released the two levers and the Blue Hornets sailed off, climbing effortlessly as if their small size exempted them from gravity's demands, joining Slow Boy.

Charley and Hot Stick lifted Fat Albert out of its cradle and onto the catapult, gingerly, considering. Hot Stick fired its engine and sent it off. They watched the fireball climb and join the three orange specks circling two hundred feet above.

Charley was about to say some words he'd memorized from the St. Crispin's Day speech in *Henry V* when Hot Stick said, "Awesome, huh?" He climbed into the Hughes with his control apparatus and strapped himself in.

Charley crossed himself. Then he went forward to *Esmeralda*'s flagstaff. He hauled it up the halyard: a red-and-white pennant followed by an "S" pennant, then a "Q" pennant and a "1" pennant. They hung there undramatically in the breezeless pre-dawn air. He climbed into the Hughes and closed the door and started the helicopter's engines.

"What's with the flags?" Hot Stick shouted over the roar.

"'I Am Attacking,'" said Charley.

It is tricky taking off from the small deck of a boat in a helicopter, and Charley was a tad rusty at it. You need to create what's called "ground-effect cover"—the cushion of air that holds the craft up. The moment a helicopter moves off over the water, it's like a trapdoor dropping underneath; you have to put your nose down to gain compensating forward speed.

Charley powered up to a hundred percent, moved off over the water and then pushed down on the cyclic stick between his legs, which put the chopper's nose down. He overdid it. Suddenly all he could see was river, coming up at him too fast. He pulled back on the collective, increasing the pitch of the rotor blades, and forcing more air over them, giving the craft lift. The skids dipped into the water. They were water-skiing. Finally the skids came out of the water. He gained speed quickly and climbed to a hundred feet.

"This is Dragonfly," he said into the radio. "I am airborne."

Hot Stick had lost all his color. Charley said to him, "That's the hardest part, taking off."

They were in the boathouse, everyone dozing. Eladio had still not returned.

Popo's voice came over the radio, loud and excited, "Niño, Niño! I have something on the radar. One definite target and something else, I can't tell, it's not clear."

"What's the position, the range?"

"Three kilometers. It's over the river, north of us."

"Where's Beni?"

"Asleep."

"Wake him up. Tell him to get the Stinger ready."

"Sí, Niño. Should I give them a warning?"

"No. It can't be military. Espinosa always gives us notice ahead of time. Tell Beni to fire. Shoot the first thing he sees."

"Sí, Niño."

Felix sweated. He was smeared with camo grease and weighted down by Dolby's Jungle Stereo System and his end of the 60mm mortar and expecting any second to hear the telltale click of a bouncing Betty mine before it made a stranger of everything from his waist down. Twice things had moved underneath his feet. They'd been walking since before midnight. He was profoundly grateful for the presence of Mac, on the other side of the mortar. Somewhere on the far edge of the compound, Rostow and Bundy were moving, alone, to their own positions, Bundy with his sniper rifle.

"There," said Mac, pointing at an area as black, to Felix, as the rest of it. But sure enough, as he focused, he saw the pinprick of electric light through the chiaroscuro of underbrush. "Let's not get too close," said Mac. "I don't want to get my dick blown off. Get that CD player ready. I'll get this set."

Felix said, "Listen—"

"That's them. Hey, sounds all right."

Charley's voice came on. "Dragonfly to Grasshoppers. Slow Boy is heading your way. Let's give him a big Texas welcome."

Mac offered Felix a mortar round. "You want to kiss it?"

"Why would I want to kiss it?"

"For luck."

"No."

Mac kissed it and held it ready. They heard the Thunderbolt whining by above them. Felix switched on the CD player; Dolby's subwoofers started to rumble out a low-frequency sound track of jets taking off the deck of a carrier.

Charley's voice said, "Fire one." Mac dropped the mortar into the tube. It arced over the trees and into the compound. They heard the explosion a few seconds later.

"Good shot," said Charley, watching. It had missed the chemical shed—the objective—by several hundred yards, but it hit another building Charley thought was a barracks but couldn't tell, the light was too dim. "Put the next about three hundred yards east."

"Roger."

Hot Stick had taken Slow Boy off computer and was making slow, come-get-me passes over the compound. Felix and Rostow's subwoofers were booming out their sound tracks (of planes taking off carrier decks) on either side of the compound. Mac's second mortar landed in the middle of the large grass field in front of the white house that Sánchez had told them was his residence. Charley was puzzled by the absence of people below. Where the hell was everyone?

"A little more to the east, about fifty yards."

"Dragonfly," said Rostow. "I got someone with what looks like a hand-held—yeah, it is, it is. It's the Stinger."

"Bring Slow Boy down there, low, *real* low," Charley said.

"Watch this," said Hot Stick, twiddling his joysticks. The Thunderbolt went into a slow, tight circle over the field; it seemed to hover.

"Good," said Charley.

"He's getting ready to fire," said Rostow.

"Bundy," said Charley, "can you see him?"

"Negative," said Bundy, peering through the scope of his Winchester .300 magnum. "I'm watching the house."

"All right, stay on the house, stay with the house." He had to be in the house, where the hell else would he be? He'd come running out of the house right into Bundy's cross hairs and—then they could all go home.

"He's fired, he's fired!" Rostow shouted.

They saw it launch, saw the orange trail roaring up at Slow Boy.

"What are you doing?" Charley shouted at Hot Stick when he saw Slow Boy break out of its tight circle and head off over the jungle.

"Giving him a run for his money," said Hot Stick.

"It's my money. Just let it ... What are you *doing*?"

Slow Boy took off, Stinger in tow. It was an interesting sight, a grown missile chasing a little bitty airplane.

"Look here, Hot Stick, just let the damn missile connect with the plane."

"This is great!" Hot Stick said. "This is fantastic!"

"Never *mind*."

"Vehicles approaching," said Rostow. "Six, seven of them on the river road."

"Hot Stick!"

"Watch." Hot Stick turned Slow Boy around toward where the vehicles were pouring into the compound.

He didn't know what to make of it. It looked like a plane, and there was something following it. Jesus Christ!

"Off the road!" he shouted at Virgilio.

"Tora! Tora! Tora!" shouted Hot Stick, putting Slow Boy into a dive.

Slow Boy and the Stinger punched into the ground fifty yards in front of him. The explosion blew Sancho's Toyota high into the air. The next thing he knew, his windshield had blown out and he and Virgilio were suddenly in the back seat.

"Nice *going*, son."

"Dragonfly, he's getting ready to fire another one. You better move away."

"Bundy, what's the situation with the house?"

"Nothing. No one's home. It's like Son Tay."

"Mac, Felix, start dropping mortar where the river road comes in. There's vehicles."

"Dragonfly, he's fired another missile. Get out of here, Dragonfly."

"Hold on," said Charley. He pushed forward on his stick, dropping the Hughes so hard the shoulder straps dug into their collarbones. Hot Stick's controls flew up out of his hands and banged into the overhead bulkhead, then came down and bounced off his flight helmet.

Charley pulled back on the stick a little late. The chopper hit the ground hard and bounced back up into the air, vibrating like a washing machine on spin cycle. The Stinger shot by the small clearing overhead.

The lower limb of the sun was now over the eastern horizon. The Stinger, seeking heat, turned toward it and set out dutifully to annihilate it, crashing to earth, some miles later, like Icarus, dismally short of its objective.

"You all right?" said Charley, regaining control of the Hughes and bringing it up out of the clearing.

"Shit," said Hot Stick.

"What is it?"

"The computer cable. They're off computer."

"Well, get back on manual."

"I can't fly three at once on manual."

"Never mind the F-18s, then. Concentrate on Fat Albert. We're going for the house."

"My transmitters—"

"Dragonfly, where do you want the next mortar?"

"Dragonfly, what is your situation? Over."

"We're going for the house. Bundy, what do you see?"

"Still nothing."

"Rostow, what about the cars?"

"Looks like two down. There's men all over, twenty or thirty of them."

"All right, stand by, I'm coming up. What about the Stinger man?"

"I'm looking for him. I'm in range now, I'm close enough for a shot if he—there he is, I see him."

"Well, shoot him."

"Fuck, he ducked behind a building."

"Stay on him. I'm coming up, we got a problem with the planes. They're flying on their own."

"Jesus—"

"You boys clear the area around the white house, repeat, clear the area."

"Roger, Dragonfly."

"Bundy, how far are you from the house?"

"About two hundred meters."

"Okay, stay low, you understand? Hot Stick, you got Fat Albert?"

"I can't find him, he's, he's—I don't know where he is."

"Where's the other two?"

"I don't *know* where they are. Brazil, they're in fucking Brazil!"

"Well, let's get them back to Peru. We ain't finished here."

He pulled himself out of the Toyota and ran to where the Stinger made a crater of Sancho and Luti and—it looked like—half a dozen others. He counted three fires around the compound, one in the barracks, an area near—Christ, the chemical shed. He directed Virgilio to take some men and start hosing down the area by the chemicals. He shouted at Mirko to locate Beni and tell him to stop firing Stingers at the *billonario*'s drogues. He turned toward the house, distant across the field, and saw the girl standing on the porch.

"I got it I got it I got," said Hot Stick. "I got Fat Albert."

"Good. We're going in."

"I can't find the others—"

"Never mind the others. Commence arming sequence."

"Primary safeties, off. Secondary safeties, off. She's hot."

"Turning final. Rostow, you let me know you see that guy with the missiles."

"Roger, Dragonfly."

Fat Albert whooshed by them leaving a smoky contrail.

"We're going in. Five hundred meters, four hundred meters—"

"Dragonfly," said Bundy. "There's a girl on the porch."

"What?"

"Repeat, a girl."

"Three hundred meters—"

"Abort."

"What?"

"Abort!"

"But—"

"ABORT!"

He saw the flash. It took a half second for the sound to reach him. He covered his eyes instinctively, and when he looked back he saw it, a perfect, insolent parody of a mushroom cloud, rising leisurely into the morning sky.

35

"Bundy, acknowledge, acknowledge."

"What the hell happened up there?"

"Bundy, this is Dragonfly, acknowledge. Hot Stick!"

"You said abort."

"Not into Bundy!"

"I wasn't *aiming* for him."

"Shut up. Don't say a word. Bundy, speak to me."

"Must have been an aileron."

"Felix, Mac, Rostow, can you see Bundy anywhere? I'm going in to take a look." Charley hovered over the smoking hole in the jungle behind the white house and craned his head out the window. The force of the blast had knocked over trees in a concentric pattern. Everything was on fire. Charley hovered as low as he could, flames licking up at the Hughes. It was dead in there. An armadillo couldn't have survived.

"Aren't we kind of low?" said Hot Stick.

Charley pulled his .45 out of its holster and pointed it at Hot Stick.

"What are you doing?"

"Take it!" Charley shouted at him. Hot Stick took the gun, looking confused. "Now shoot yourself!"

"What?"

"For incompetence!" He brought the helicopter up into cooler air. Below he saw the compound. Men running, vehicles, smoke, confusion. He saw a girl running across the wide field in front of the white house. She was without clothes. He heard a sound beneath his feet, like pebbles kicked up by a car's wheels.

"They're shooting at us, Mr. Becker."

"All right, everyone listen up. Get back to the ship. Get the anchor up and get going. I'll join up with you."

"What are you doing?" said Felix.

"We're going to stay here awhile, look for Bundy."

"We are?"

Charley flew a wide circle along the rim of the compound.

"They're shooting at us, Mr. Becker."

"Course they're *shooting* at us!"

Charley flew off into the jungle. A quarter mile from the compound, he brought the Hughes into a stationary hover. He reached down and picked up a small Orvis bag off the floor and unzipped it, took out a grenade and handed it to Hot Stick.

"You know how to use *these*?"

"Uh—"

"You pull the pin, open the window and drop it out. Can you handle *that*?"

"What are we doing?"

"We're going flying." Charley took out a grenade with his left hand, put the pull pin in his teeth and gave a yank, chipping a crown. He put the chopper's nose down and gathered speed.

"Niño! The helicopter!"

He'd grabbed an AK from the weapons shed and was standing in the middle of the field with Soledad, who was evincing strange calm, under the circumstances, watching with childlike serenity the events around her as if they were taking place in another world. She said to him, "I love you."

The helicopter broke over the edge of the trees. He aimed the

AK and fired off a burst, swinging the barrel with the deftness of a practiced trap and skeet shooter.

The helicopter disappeared over the far side of the compound. As it did he heard two explosions. The Range Rover lay on its side. Just bought it, too.

* * *

Charley eased back on the stick and brought the chopper to another stationary hover over the jungle.

"You all right?" he said.

"No!"

"Good. Here. I'm gonna take her in a little lower this time."

Charley tugged on another pin and eased forward on the stick. Treetops skimmed by underneath.

He slapped in another banana clip and planted his feet and covered the tree line with the barrel of the AK, just as his father had taught him to do when shooting from the number eight position at a low bird.

The chopper came out of the woods. He swung the barrel as he fired. Then saw the tiny specks tumbling out. He stopped firing and threw himself to the ground. The explosions were close this time. When he lifted his head, it was to see the girl's leg in front of him, she peering down at him with that remote stare of curiosity. "I love you."

The inside of the chopper filled with smoke; alarms buzzed on the instrument panel.

"What does that mean?" Hot Stick coughed.

"Means we're on fire."

"Jesus, we're on fire! We're on fire!"

"Here." He tossed Hot Stick another grenade. Charley pulled the pin, pushed down on the stick and began his last charge. *For if he like a madman lived / At least he like a wise one died.* More the reverse in his case, but the line came to him all the same.

He didn't lead it as much this time. He saw an arm reaching out of the starboard window and emptied his clip at it, saw sparks, smoke. He lowered the rifle and in the next instant heard the explosion and looked in the direction of the chemical shed in time to see five thousand gallons of ether and acetone igniting.

Charley felt something sharp in the vicinity of his right leg. The chopper kept wanting to turn in circles and he had to work the controls hard. He'd lost half his rpms in his tail rotor, the oil pressure was down to nothing, loud knocking sounds were coming from the undercarriage and when he looked down to see what it was he noticed his pants leg was torn and wet.

"You okay?" he shouted over at Hot Stick. He couldn't see with all the smoke. He pulled the emergency-door release and instantly the air cleared inside. Hot Stick was slumped forward over his controls, held by his harness, hands limp by his sides. The left side of his helmet was holed where the bullet had exited.

He had almost no control by the time he saw the ship. He set down so hard on the deck that it bounced and the tail spun around and chopped up the antennae and part of the smokestack. Charley was knocked out from the impact. He dreamed it very clearly: saw the chopper drop into the water and sink bathyspherically, bub-bubbubbling down into the silty murk of the Huallaga; then there were dolphins, pink dolphins like the kind you'd expect to meet only in a hangover, making faces at him through the Plexiglas bub-ble. He heard Felix's voice saying, "Boss, boss," but what was Felix doing, swimming with pink dolphins?

36

The fire burned into the afternoon. The heat was so intense the men kept dropping from exhaustion and dehydration. It began to spread toward the number four *pozo*, where an acre of coca leaves lay macerating in kerosene and sulfuric acid. If that caught, the Andes themselves would go up in smoke. He ran to the shed and started up the bulldozer and drove it out, stripping gears as he went, and plowed a shallow trench between the advancing flames and the edge of the combustible pit. The handles were hot by the time the firebreak was complete.

He walked back to the field in front of the house. His beautiful field, which he used for croquet. Scarred, scorched. Soledad was crouched over something in the distance. She was wearing only white panties that emphasized the lack of any other article. He'd told her not to go naked in front of the men. It was not an easy concept to explain to Soledad, especially with his limited com-mand of her language, until one day Eladio had told him of a say-ing among the men of the tribe: "Your eyes have gone bad from staring at the privates of too many women." He'd put it to her that way: don't ruin the eyes of my men, please, I depend on their eyes.

He'd given her a brassiere, a very sexy one with lace; she fashioned it into a slingshot. For a moment he forgot about the fire and watched her. His eyes wandered across the field and fastened on something that resisted recognition. He approached and stared at it.

The markings on the fuselage said NAVY. It had gone in straight, skewering his croquet field with its Pitot tube. He stared.

"Samin," he shouted. "Give me your rifle." He raised Samin's AK and fired a burst into the repellent object, which obliged by exploding into small pieces that scattered themselves, like flaming leaves, over the already harrowed field. The girl, hunched over whatever it was, raised her head only briefly.

The needlelike Pitot tube was still stuck in the grass; the rest had blown up. He stormed over and gave the needle a good kick. It tumbled like a thrown knife and landed some feet away.

"Toy planes," he shouted. "He comes for me with toy *planes*!"

"Soledad!" he shouted. The girl made no answer. "What are you doing?"

Virgilio came running to say that they'd found Beni—or what was left of him. Virgilio thought he'd been shot before the fire did the rest.

"Good," said El Niño. "It saves me from having to shoot him myself."

Virgilio looked at Samin, Samin at Virgilio. Each decided it would be best to be somewhere else, and ran off, declaring a remembered emergency.

El Niño walked to where the girl was. "What are you—"

It was a howler monkey that had been blasted out of the trees by the force of the explosion when the chemical shed ignited. The monkeys had lost their fear of man over the years and clambered in the trees close to the compound to scavenge. Its fur was smoking.

She smiled at him and handed him a piece of torn-off flesh. Such bounty. Food from the sky—already cooked!

He wheeled away and staggered off. He took deep breaths, telling himself that his reaction was irrational, that she was Indian, to her it was just—food; then he leaned over and threw up.

37

Charley came to propped up on a pillow on the settee underneath the Gainsborough.

The pain was in his head, in the center of his forehead. He reached up and felt something sharp protruding. Felix was sitting beside him.

"What is this?" Charley said, fingering the object.

"It's a piece of glass. I'm going to get it out."

Charley tugged. His fingers were wet with blood; they kept slipping. Charley watched the blood course in rivulets down onto his chest and onto the Naugahyde settee. Margaret had chosen the neutral gray color because Tasha was always spilling things. He felt the blood puddle under his elbows. He blinked. A silvery jet of liquid flew through the air over his head. Felix had a hypodermic.

"What is that?"

"Morphine."

"No. Need a clear head." Felix tried to pull the glass out with tweezers. They kept slipping.

"Use pliers," said Charley. "Whiskey. Bring the bottle."

Charley stared up at Augustus John, third Earl of Bristol. He had never studied it from this angle, looking right up the earl's nose.

Felix returned with a pair of needle-nose pliers and a bottle of Jack Daniel's. Charley took a long pull. Felix went to work. The piece of glass was in there. Charley groaned.

"Gimme that needle." He took the hypodermic and squirted the morphine into the whiskey, shook it up and took another long pull.

"I don't think you're supposed to drink it," said Felix.

"They do in England. Ain't that right, Augustus? It's called a Brompton cocktail—heroin and vodka. They give it to terminal folks." Felix went back to work.

"You know ... Gainsborough hated to paint portraits?"

"Yeah," said Felix, getting a grip on the glass shard.

"What he really loved was landscapes. He married a woman with rich tastes and ... he had two girls and they inherited their mama's tastes, so ... he ... had to spend all his time painting pictures of rich folks ... to pay the bills."

"It's stuck, boss."

"Just give it a yank." Charley took another pull off the bottle. His mouth went numb. A pleasant, warm feeling spread through him. He said, "He liked to play the violin and be outside painting cows and blue skies. Instead he spent the whole time indoors with old Augustus here and ladies with long white necks. I bet he ended up hating rich people. I would have."

"I'm going to—hold on."

"You notice how they're all gray, the people he painted? I have a theory about that ... he was saving his colors for the landscapes. Felix!"

"What, boss?"

"I killed Bundy. There was a girl on the porch. What have I done?"

"Just hold on, boss. It's coming."

"She had this tooth wouldn't come out, you remember that?"

"Yeah."

"Tried everything, string to the doorknob, crust of bread ... *oh*."

Felix applied a pressure bandage. When Charley opened his eyes again he saw the pillow she'd embroidered for him that said AGE AND TREACHERY WILL OVERCOME YOUTH AND VIRTUE EVERY TIME, all soaked. He could hear Margaret. She was saying, "Oh, Charley, not my *pillow*."

He had the throttle opened up all the way. He was going dangerously fast. It was night. The river was a *café con leche* blur in the searchlight. Virgilio's and Mirko's boats were a quarter mile behind, struggling to keep up with him as he slalomed past logs and floating islands of *canarana* grass.

"Niño," said Virgilio over the VHF, "please, slow down. It's dangerous."

He could not tell Virgilio the reason for his speed. It had nothing to do with chasing the *billonario*. The truth was that he was trying to get away from the dead monkey. It had taken hold of his brain; he couldn't shake it loose. Even at sixty miles an hour it held on, jeering, chattering, smashing him with fists, pelting him with sapodilla fruit.

Large insects flew into his face, disintegrating, stinging. He felt the jolt as the boat hit the back of a crocodile, heard the whine of the propeller as it raced in air. The boat landed with a thud, engines churning.

Charley stood at *Esmeralda*'s wheel. The current was running eight miles an hour, so he had to maintain at ten miles an hour for steerage. The riverbank was rushing past him at nearly twenty miles an hour. He was kayaking in an ocean liner.

His head was wrapped tightly. The morphine and Jack Daniel's gave him confidence. He could feel everything the ship was doing through his hands on the wheel; the water rushing by under her hull, the cushion between it and the bank, the propellers digging in when he increased speed, logs bouncing off. Most of all he felt the river carrying him to the sea. The sea was 3,500 miles away but the river would carry him. The river that began in a trickle of crystalline water in Lake Mismi, high up in the Andes, swiftly gathering mass and momentum, becoming a great brown snowball, seven million cubic feet by the time it reached the ocean; it could fill Lake Ontario in three hours. A river that could fill Lake Ontario in three hours could easily carry them to—

"Boss," said Felix. They were on the radar screen—three green specks astern, one ahead of the other. They appeared closer with each stardust sweep of the cursor.

His bow light washed her transom with its beam. There she was. He throttled back. Eusebio, next to him, reached beneath the dashboard for the RPG-7 cradled in its box. It was Soviet-made, fired an 85millimeter, 18.7-pound grenade 500 meters. Sendero used them against truck convoys and tanks.

Eusebio shouldered it and aimed.

"Aim for the stern. Low, right above the water."

"*Sí*, Niño."

He imagined it clearly: the explosion, the boat going dead in the water, the *billonario* surrendering; saw the fuel tanks igniting, Baudelaire's eyes blazing at him from underneath Collardet's top hat as the paint melted.

> *O death, old captain, it's time! ...*
> *Pour out your poison to comfort us!*
> *While the fire burns our brain, we yearn*
> *To plunge to the bottom of the abyss,*
> *Heaven or hell, what does it matter?*
> *To the depths o f the Unknown to find the new.*

He shouted at Eusebio, "No!" and knocked his arm upward at the moment of firing. The rocket arced over the boat in a feckless parabola, landing in the jungle and sending aloft a choir of outraged cockatoos screeching into the night.

Eusebio turned to him and said, "Why did you do that?" He was about to tell him when Mac's bullet hit Eusebio in the chest.

* * *

The river narrowed. Charley steered by radar, trying to keep the center in the middle of the green phosphorescent couloir. Felix shouted, "Starboard!"

Charley swung the wheel to the right. As he did, he looked to the left and saw the riverbank, revealed starkly in the bright halogen glow of the searchlight. He saw striations of red clay. It was beautiful.

Esmeralda struck the riverbank. She took it on the chine, a loud, hollow *thunnng*. Charley held on to the wheel, his feet went out from under him. When he pulled himself back up he could no longer see out the window. A large tree had crashed down onto the foredeck. He saw flailing in its branches. An arm emerged, then Mac, swearing. He'd been thrown from the top deck into the tree.

Charley looked at the radar screen. As he did, the windows on the right side of the bridge all shattered into a blizzard of Plexiglas.

The boat, pinned against the riverbank by the current, scraped forward slowly. Charley pushed the throttle to "full ahead." As she moved forward, she made a greasy squeaking noise against the clay bank. Felix appeared in the starboard doorway on his hands and knees. He held the Uzi over the railing and fired blindly. Grenades went off in the water with a *whump* sound, followed by plumes of water. Rostow was in the bows, tossing them. Mac disentangled himself from the tree and jumped back up onto the top deck and fired the M-60 machine gun. Charley kept his hand on the throttle. He became aware of something that did not belong. He could not see in the dark. He removed his hand from the throttle and the feeling came with it.

They followed in the dark. He looked up and saw the Southern Cross, the Magellanic Cloud. The riverbanks blazed with pulsations of fireflies. Virgilio shouted from his boat over the VHF, "Niño, they're shooting!"

Mirko's voice came on: "Niño! Why doesn't Eusebio shoot with the RPG?"

"Eusebio is dead. Keep firing. No grenades, do you hear?"

"But they're—why?"

"Just do it, Virgilio."

"Fire the RPG, Niño. Please!"

"Virgilio, you don't realize what they have on board."

"Gasto is dead, Niño! Davilo is wounded. I think one of my engines is hit. Shoot, please!"

"The boat is full of gold."

The beautiful word hung there, suspended in radio silence between the boats. He regretted it. The lie. To hold out the promise of gold, *here*, where his ancestors had slaughtered Virgilio's and Mirko's—but how else, *what* else would they understand?

"Gold?" said Virgilio.

"He has gold on board?" said Mirko.

"Yes."

"How much?"

"A fortune, Mirko!" he shouted angrily. "More than you can carry. Now move forward! Concentrate your fire on the bridge."

"Okay, Niño."

"Mirko," he said, "you go up the right side. Virgilio, you go up the left. Together now!"

It was moving up his arm. He said, "Felix."

"What?"

"Shine your light on my arm, would you?"

"Jesus," said Felix.

It was clinging to his upper arm, fans flared out, moving back and forth slowly like elephant ears. What was God thinking when he made these creatures? Charley wondered. It opened its mouth wider than a church door. Charley could see all the way down its throat, translucent in Felix's flashlight beam, a green tunnel that seemed to extend all the way down to its tail.

Felix shouted, "Boats moving up, starboard and port."

The radar showed a curve to the left a hundred yards ahead.

Charley said, "Hold your fire on the one coming up on our right. Let him come up. Let me know when's he's abeam."

Felix lay down on the deck and sighted through a hawsehole. "He's passing the stern ... not yet ... not yet ..." Bullets zippered into *Esmeralda*'s right side. "Now!"

"Hold on." Charley swung the wheel to the right.

He saw the yacht begin to swing toward Mirko's boat. He shouted over the radio, "Mirko, reverse your engines! Get out of there!"

The yacht squeezed the speedboat against the riverbank. Two of Mirko's men saw what was about to happen and jumped off the transom. But Mirko had already reversed his throttles and the outboard engines had churned up out of the water. Mirko's men were shredded. In the next instant, the yacht drove the boat into the riverbank in a loud crackling of fiberglass.

He slowed and shone his light at the bank. The remains of the boat had fallen away. The men had been pressed into the clay like figures in a bas-relief frieze. There was Gorrati with his gun, Jimo, upside down. Ay, Mirko. At the moment of death, Mirko had brought his arms up to protect his face. He stared at the tableau. He wished he had a camera, it was so unusual.

The iguana dropped off Charley's shoulder and ran out of the bridge upright on two legs, hopping from one piece of Plexiglas to another like someone escaping across ice floes.

They were firing at the boat on the port side. Charley heard the loud noise above him from Mac's M-60. Rostow ran aft along the deck with his grenade satchel.

Amorphous green splotches appeared on the radar screen. The antennae had been hit. Charley navigated through the hallucinations. There was a Navy base at Juanjui, eighty clicks downriver. At this rate they could make that by morning, if—ifs sprouted along the riverbank all the way to Juanjui. He switched on the radio and was rehearsing what he would say when he heard: "*Esmeralda*, come in, please"—perfect, mannered English. Please?

"This is *Esmeralda*," he said.

"This is Captain Pantoja of the Peruvian Navy. Stop your engines."

"This is Admiral Chester W. Nimitz of the United States Navy. Go to hell."

"Is that you, *billonario*?"

"Yes."

"Welcome to Peru."

"Thank you."

"The rocket-propelled grenade that went over your bow back there, it was a warning shot. It wasn't nice of you to kill the man who fired it."

"Sorry about that."

"The next is going to go up your *culo*. Do you speak Spanish?"

"Enough to understand you."

"I give you one minute."

Charley said, "Felix. That's our boy on the radio. I'll keep him talking. Tell Mac to shoot the one talking into his radio." Felix ran aft.

"You there?"

"Of course."

"What do you want from me?"

278

"What a question, *billonario*. You blow up my home, kill my men. I want to discuss your surrender. Reparations."

"What kind of reparations you have in mind?"

"Your boat."

"This old thing? I don't know, your river's a little narrow. One of your friends tried to pass me back there and you saw what happened."

"Thirty seconds, *billonario*."

His boat hit a small piece of wood. He put down the hand microphone so he could steer with both hands. Virgilio's voice came on the radio.

"Niño, what's happening? What do you want me to—"

He saw the muzzle flash on the stern of the yacht. The sound was loud, like an elephant gun.

* * *

Felix came running. "Mac got him!"

Charley stared. It was over, finally over. He said, "Tell him, that's good shooting."

The archway of ifs stretching to Juanjui fell away. Charley knew: the sun would come up and they would make it.

He heard a shout from the stern. It sounded like "Incoming!" Then something kicked him in the back, hard, like a horse. It lifted him up and threw him forward, through the window.

279

38

He watched with mounting panic as the fire spread. Why should the ship burn so? He had only fired a single RPG.

"*Billonario?*"

Her stern was getting low in the water. She was sinking. What a disaster.

"*Billonario*, answer."

The yacht's bow swung around to face him, like a wounded mastodon raising itself defiantly on its front legs. She was going downriver backward.

He and the other boat followed, keeping their distance in case the *cabrón* sniper who had killed Virgilio was still alive. The fire in her stern continued to rage. The RPG must have hit a fuel tank, but how was that possible? The fuel tanks were under the waterline, and he placed the grenade deftly in the transom.

A half kilometer later her bow went up on a mudbank in the middle of the river. Thank God. She wouldn't sink, at least. But the fire ...

"*Billonario*, are you there?"

"Charley!" said Margaret. "You come down out of there this minute. You're too old to be climbing trees."

"I'm coming, sweetheart, you hold on."

Tasha was crying. She had climbed all the way to the top and was now frozen with fear and unable to come down. Huge bats were circling her. The bats were the result of a secret U.S. Air Force experiment using recombinant DNA engineering to splice bat genes and Stealth technology. There were serious cost overruns, and the bats escaped. Charley shot at them with his pistol, but the bats were able to jam bullets. He kept firing.

"Boss!"

"Felix, watch out!"

"Boss, stop shooting!"

"Huh?" He was in a tree. The pistol was in his hand. He was shooting. He was upside down. Where was Tasha? Felix's face appeared in the branches.

"Bats, Felix!"

"Are you all right, boss?"

"What's happening?"

"She's on fire. Mac and Rostow are dead. It was an RPG. It hit the bar in the fantail. All the liquor caught fire. We have to get off."

Felix pulled Charley out of the tree on the foredeck.

"I had this dream, Felix."

"It's the morphine. Come on."

They crawled aft along the deck and went into the main salon. Charley coughed from the smoke. The emergency sprinkler system was going, everything was wet. The fire had already consumed the fantail and was working its way forward, making the wet carpet and walls hiss and steam. The gold-glass panels from the old ocean liner *Normandie* had shattered. The pieces glowed in the fire like Art Deco embers. Charley and Felix leaned against a bulkhead to catch their breath.

"We have to abandon ship," said Felix.

"See if they're still out there."

Felix went out on deck. He crawled back in and said, "Two boats."

"Are they together, on one side?"

"Yeah, the starboard."

Charley stared into the fire for several moments. He said, "We'll use the inflatable on the foredeck. Toss it over the port side. There's a Navy base downriver. The current'll take us."

They crawled together up the deck on the port side. Felix wrestled the emergency inflatable life raft off its cradle. It would inflate automatically as soon as it hit the water.

"Tie two lines to it," said Charley. "We'll toss it in together and each hold a line. Once it's inflated, we can get in. But don't let go of the line."

Felix tied the two lines and hefted the raft up onto the railing.

"Felix, listen to me. In case something happens, it's all with the lawyers, the lawyers will take care of everything. You understand?"

"No," said Felix.

"You're, I, you're my only family left, Felix. Who else was I going to leave it to?"

"That's crazy."

"It's all been worked out, Felix. It's all with the lawyers."

"We're going together."

"In *case*, is all I'm saying. When you get to the Navy base, contact Gallardo. That was a damn fine supper I gave him. Let him start earning his pay. All right, ready? Now, we got to hold on to that rope *tight*. That's one hell of a current. We'll be in Juanjui by breakfast time. Don't let go, no matter what. On count of three."

Charley gripped his line and seated himself on the railing. Felix sat beside him.

"One, two, three." Felix pushed the raft overboard and jumped in.

The CO_2 canister inflated the raft in seconds. Felix pulled himself aboard. By the time he'd climbed on, he was fifty yards downstream of *Esmeralda*. He could not see Charley waving to him from the deck, hear him call out, "*Vaya con Dios*, my old and good friend."

"*Billonario*, come in."

The fire was eating the boat. There was no more time. Rafi was on his way from Yenan with two more boats. The helicopter would take off at first light, but by then the boat would be a charred hulk, and the Manet ... the Manet. How could the *billonario* have been so arrogant?

Gómez had taken command of Virgilio's boat. He signaled him over.

As it approached, he saw Virgilio's legs protruding from underneath a rubber poncho they had spread over him. They had covered him, not out of respect, but for morale.

He said to Gómez, "Take your men and go aboard and put out the fire."

Gómez looked at the flaming yacht on the mudbank. "But, Niño, what if they're still alive?"

"Then kill them."

"Maybe we should wait until dawn."

"By dawn it will be burned, Gómez!"

"So?"

"Gómez, there is gold on board. Bars of gold. Do you want it all to melt?"

"*Pues* ... no, Niño, but, with respect, it's too dangerous. The sniper may still be alive. Let's wait for the boats and the helicopter."

"Gómez, you are dismissed. Pitu, take the wheel from that coward. Go and put out the fire."

"With respect, Niño, Gómez is right."

"You disgust me, all of you. Put Virgilio's body in my boat. I will not have him carried in a boat of cowards."

They put Virgilio aboard.

"*Billonario*, answer. We have to put out the fire. Neither of us wants the Manet to burn."

"Mohney?" Pitu said to Gómez.

"Manet?" Charley sat on a litter of Plexiglas crumbs in the bridge. The fine rectangular leather case lay opened in front of him, the finely engraved barrel and stock in two pieces on his lap. He fit them together and snapped them gently shut, then opened them and chambered two rounds of twelve-gauge double-ought buck. He could just hear his gunsmith. "Double-ought, sir? In the Purdys?"

"*Billonario*, we can't let the Manet burn."

How in hell did he know about the Manet? The pain in his head worsened. He took a light swig of whiskey and morphine. Manet? Had Gallardo told him? Was he on his payroll? Did everyone in the country work for the sumbitch? He reached for the hand mike.

"This is *Esmeralda*."

"Thank God, *billonario*. Are you all right?"

"Fine. Fine."

"Your ship is burning."

"I noticed."

"I want to help you put it out."

"Thanks, but you been enough help already."

"Is the Manet safe?"

Charley remembered Sánchez saying something during the interrogation about a room he had in the white house with paintings. Where he kept the surface-to-air missiles seemed more important at the time.

He opened the cabinet behind the wheel and rummaged through boxes.

"You and your men come out on deck. We will not shoot. You have my word."

"Son, you're a drug dealer. Your *word* just ain't enough."

"It was you who violated our last cease-fire, *billonario*. You killed a good man."

Charley found what he was looking for.

"Why you so hot for Manet?"

"Because he was the first modern artist with a social conscience. Because he told the bourgeoisie to fuck themselves. Because he was magnificent. What a question, *billonario*."

"What else you like about him?"

He's delaying. While the *cabrón* with the elephant gun prepares to blow my brains out.

He crouched low in his seat. The men in his boat kept slipping in Virgilio's and Eusebio's blood. It was a mess back there, and not good for morale.

He said to them, "I need one brave man." No one spoke up. "Are you all women? Is there not one man aboard with balls between his legs instead of a tampon string?"

"*Pues*, sí, Niño." It was Cacho.

"Bravo, Cacho. Take my pistol. I'll maneuver directly upstream of the yacht. All you have to do is float downstream to it. Get on the mudbank. Then get aboard. Go to the bridge. I'll keep him talking on the radio."

"What then, Niño?"

Cacho was a bit stupid. But this was why he was volunteering.

"Shoot him, Cacho. With the pistol."

"*Bueno.*" Cacho began to strip.

"Cacho?"

"*Sí*, Niño."

"Wound him. Don't kill him."

He went over the side. He turned to the other men. "Aren't you ashamed?"

"But, Niño, we can't swim."

"*Billonario*, are you there?"

The blade of Charley's penknife hovered over the stick of HMX. Charley calculated: if a foot of HMX was enough to blow apart an I beam or leave a thirty-foot-wide-by-twenty-deep crater in the ground, two inches ought to do it. Say, four inches. He cut off the piece and rolled it on the floor to flatten it, then pressed it onto his palm with the heel of his other hand, reminding himself of an old Mexican woman making a tortilla. That done, he took a nitro chip from its box and pressed that into the doughy tortilla.

The detonator was about the size of a pack of Camels, with a stubby, rubberized antenna and six safety switches. With HMX, redundancy in safeties made sense. In the center was a red button shielded by a hinged lid.

"I don't want to fire another RPG, *billonario*. Come out onto the deck with your men."

"My men are all dead." He put the tortilla and det box in a pocket and took a portable hand-unit radio out of its cradle and switched it to Channel 68.

He stood up. The pain shot through his head like a high-velocity bullet. He took one more pull of whiskey and morphine and set off on all fours like an old doggy.

It was a trick Tasha used to pull on the farm when she didn't want to come back to the house. He keyed the "talk" button and put his lips to the microphone and went: "PSSSSSSSSHHHT *Esmeralda* here PSSSSSSHT."

"Come in, *billonario*."

"PSHHHHHHHH breaking up, switching to Channel PSH-HHHHH."

He reached the main salon. The fire had worked its way forward past the settee. The air was acrid from flame-retardant Naugahyde, the carpet felt soaked beneath his hands, and he dog-walked toward the stairs by the shattered *Normandie* gold-glass panels. He looked to his left as he went and saw Augustus John, third Earl of Bristol, melting in sizzling droplets of Gainsborough gray.

He started up the stairs. He felt something sharp and painful in his hands. He raised them and saw they were covered with hundreds of splinters of gold glass from the *Normandie* panels. There was no time to remove them. He continued painfully on up the stairs.

He reached the top. Carpet gave way to teak. He looked down and saw he was leaving bloody palm prints behind him, palm prints flecked with bits of gold. He crawled behind the marble bar and leaned against the wall and gasped.

"*Billonario*, are you there?"

"PSSSHHHHT I can't make PSSSSHHHHT."

It sounded like running water.

"What are you doing?" he said to his men. They were standing up, pissing over the side.

"The radio noise, Niño, it's making us piss."

"Put those back in your pants or I'll shoot them off."

"But, Niño, we don't want to piss on Eusebio and Virgilio ..."

* * *

His palms flowed blood from a hundred small wounds. He dried them as best he could on a towel. He stood and gripped the frame of the Manet with both hands and pulled it off the wall. He sat down and put it on his lap, took out the HMX tortilla and pressed it onto the back of the painting. He stood up and replaced it on the wall and collapsed back onto the deck. The only bottle within reach was Pernod. He took a long swallow.

He set off at a crawl, following his own bloody trail of palm prints.

He was halfway down the stairs when he saw in front of him a pair of wet brown legs. He looked up. Cacho brought the butt of his pistol down on his head.

He sent up Manco first, then climbed aboard himself. He saw immediately that there was no hope of extinguishing the fire. Cacho was standing proudly over the semi-conscious *billonario*, holding two pistols on him, one of them a Colt .4S he did not recognize.

The *billonario* was very pale, even for a gringo. He was bleeding from the head and—what happened to his hands? Look at them. The bushy eyebrows gave him a fierce look, even in this state.

288

He leaned over him and said, "*Billonario*, where is the painting?"

The eyes opened. Blinked and peered.

"Where is the Manet?"

Cacho, seeking to please his *patrón*, kicked the old man in the ribs to prompt him to answer. Niño hit Cacho in the throat with his own pistol, knocking him into a Mihanovic painting of a rowboat. Cacho gagged, clutching his Adam's apple.

"*Billonario*," he said gently, "tell me. Where is the Manet?"

"Upstairs. Over the bar." He seemed almost pleased to get it over with.

He bounded up the stairs and looked about. The teak deck was—there was a strange, bloody trail—hand prints. He followed them to the bar and looked up.

There it was. He stood, unable to move. It was magnificent. Give the *billonario* his due. On a lot of boats like this it would be a Leroy Neiman up there, or some idiotic nautical doggerel about the bar being closed for five minutes a day.

It was the Baudelaire "Absinthe Drinker" and no mistake. Baudelaire's pupils were dilated, looking directly at him, fixing him with the mad, ecstatic eyes of the lotus eater, *absintheur*, laudanum drinker, hashish eater: *"I have cultivated my hysteria with delight and terror. Now I have felt the wind of the wing of madness pass over me."* Manet had caught all!

He took a step toward the blazing, orchidaceous eyes, but found his own drawn to the frame. There was blood on it. Blood was dripping from the painting. Something was sparkling in the blood. Gold?

He turned, ran and dove down the stairs a half second before the explosion.

39

The shaman sat in front of the lifeless stone, murmuring as he mixed his brew of ginger, nightshade, tobacco water and *ayahuasca*. Eladio and Zácari sat watching him at a distance. Inancia's new child cried inside a hut. At the edge of the village the dogs tore at the head of a peccary.

He finished mixing his brew, set the frothy gourd aside and began to blow over the surface of the stone.

Zácari whispered to his father, "That's a lot of *bikut*." He grinned. "He's going to have great visions."

Eladio said, "That is what I fear." Eladio had never told Zácari what took place many years before, when the tribe lived to the north, along the Río Mayo. Eladio was fishing one day in the dugout when he heard the cries of a young girl. He ran to the source of the sound and saw the shaman forcing himself into Ampuya, a young girl of the village he was holding, bent over a log. She was not yet of age. She screamed. The shaman shouted at her to be quiet, that he was driving out an evil *tsentsak*. Eladio knew to be afraid of the shamans, knew that they possessed great powers. He hid in the bush and watched in terror as the shaman brought his club down on the girl's head and broke it open; watched as he continued his work on Ampuya's lifeless body.

He ran back to the canoe and returned to the village. His father had been killed in a battle with the Tikuna. He told his mother what he had seen. She took him into the forest and shook him until his insides loosened, shouting at him that a *pasuk* had entered his body and given him an evil vision. She told him never to tell what he had seen, or the shaman would summon the *wawek tunchi*, the sorcerer.

But Ampuya, who had gone into the forest to gather *warok* berries, never returned. The men of the tribe searched until they found her body, half eaten. That night the shaman drank *bikut* and had visions of what had happened to her. She had been carried off by an *iwanch* and given to wild pigs.

Years later, after Eladio had come of age, another girl disappeared. The search lasted for days. Eladio was the most skilled hunter of the tribe. It was he who found her, buried, who saw on the body the signs. He reburied her and remained by her grave for five days and nights without taking food or water, dreaming of Tsewa, the ancient headman of the spider monkeys, who had taught his people the secrets of the hunt. On the sixth day an *ajutap* appeared to him in the form of a jaguar and spoke to him.

He found what he sought a half day later, sunning itself in a warm spot. The jararaca is very swift, but Eladio was pure from fasting and moved with speed greater than the snake's, catching it with his hand at the base of the skull.

He returned to the village that night and entered the shaman's hut without noise and found the *pinig* bowl from which he drank his *bikut*. He held the snake's mouth to the rim of the bowl and milked forth the waxy yellow venom. He took the snake back into the forest and asked its forgiveness for stealing from it and released it.

The next night the shaman mixed his *bikut* and drank it to have a vision of what had become of the girl, Chipa. He began to gasp and shudder and cry out. The tribe thought he was having a great vision, and would not approach him as he lay writhing on the ground by the fire.

Only Eladio approached. For this he was thought very brave.

He leaned over the shaman's ear and whispered, "It is my *iwanch*

291

that kills you, old man." The shaman died. Eladio became headman of the tribe.

Now he watched the shaman drink from his bowl and shout at the lifeless stone. He signaled Zácari to walk with him down to the river. They sat in the branches of a *wampush* tree, out of reach of crocodiles. Eladio had many wives and sons, but he loved Zácari best because he was the oldest.

"Tell me," he said, "why do you think the life has gone out of the stone?"

Zácari answered all his father's questions with questions, out of respect.

"Because the *tsugki* inside has fled?" He smiled at his father. "Because the *tsugki* feeds on the gold-and-black things the *kurinku pataa* tied to the side of it before he gave it to us?"

Eladio was pleased. "The gold-and-black things are empty."

Zácari leaned over the bough they were sitting on and spat into the water. A piranha dimpled the surface where it landed. "The shaman will tell us a vision."

"Trust only your own visions." Eladio stood. "They have these gold-and-black things at Yenan. I have seen them. Go there and tell El Niño we need some. Tell him the white men were not *pistacos*."

"With respect, Papi, how do you know?"

"*Pistaco* carries a knife, not guns, and a lasso made of human skin. He wears hair on his face. Tell El Niño that we killed most of them out of respect. Tell him to give us gold-and-black things. Take Kipu with you."

"Yes, Papi. What will you do?"

"I will stay here and watch the shaman. His vision may tell him to sacrifice Inancia's baby."

"What will you do if that is his vision?"

"As Tsewa tells me," said Eladio.

40

Diatri watched the oil streak along the window. He leaned forward and shouted at the Marine pilot, "What's with the oil?"

The pilot shouted back, "These planes are pieces of shit."

"How come we're in them?"

"Realism. It's what *they* fly. Reason they got such fuckin' long noses on them is they're always crapping out and the long noses gives you extended glide ratio so you can land on the fuckin' water, if you can find it."

There were three Pilatus Porter seaplanes. The SEALs were in the first. Diatri was in the second with the SOLIC commander and the JUNC leader. The third plane, fifty miles behind, would extract the SEALs after they had planted their mines on the yacht.

"You mean we're going all the way down there and we're not bringing him back with us?" Diatri had said at the mission briefing aboard the Air Force C-141 on the way down. It was a crowded flight for some reason, people from State, DOD, CIA, a Coast Guard medic—what was the Coast Guard doing here?—Marine pilots, Navy SEALs, Army Rangers and the Joint Unified Narcotics Command people.

"That's right," the JUNC leader replied. "Our mission is to disable the boat and get out."

"Whose plan was this?" Diatri asked. "Is this a JUNC plan?"

"That's all I can say, Diatri."

"Yeah, but it just doesn't make sense. The guy's an American citizen. We're just going to blow up his boat and leave him?"

"This is a JUNC op, Diatri. You're here as an observer. Observe."

Diatri leaned over and said to the SOLIC commander, "Am I missing something here?"

The commander said quietly, "I understand there's a political dimension."

The JUNG leader was in front with the pilot. He tapped the satellite surveillance photo on his lap and looked down at the river and shouted over the roar of the Pilatus' loud propeller, "We shoulda seen it already."

They followed the river. Diatri let the others do the surveilling. He was intent on the mountains to the west, huge, incredible mountains all blue and white. One towered over the others. He found it on his map. Huascarán, over 20,000 feet up, so high you had to gulp for your air. He had read somewhere that Hitler killed the King of Bulgaria that way. The King was being difficult. He wouldn't kill Jews; what's more, he told Hitler that if Jews were going to have to wear yellow stars, then *he* was going to start wearing a yellow star. Hitler summoned him to Berlin to make him change his mind, but he wouldn't. Hitler knew the King had a weak heart, so Hitler flew him back to Bulgaria in an unpressurized plane at high altitudes, and the King died a few days later. Diatri told this story to the SOLIC commander. He thought about it and nodded in a professional sort of way as if to say: Yeah, that would do it. He didn't say much, this commander.

The JUNC leader said, "Hey, Diatri, I hear you're going to Congressional Relations after this."

"What?"

"Congratulations."

"Who told you that?"

"You know, on the topo map this valley looks just like a pussy."

"Who told you that?"

"I don't know. Something I heard. We shoulda passed it by now—there it is, up ahead. This is Cowpuncher One Actual, we got it."

Diatri looked down. He wouldn't have recognized it from the photographs. It looked like something abandoned on the Brooklyn waterfront. As they circled, he saw that some of her yacht whiteness remained along the hull. She was half up on a mudbank. There were people aboard her, a dozen or more dugout canoes tied to her. The JUNC leader took pictures with a video camcorder. The natives, seeing the military markings on the planes, began to scatter into their canoes. The JUNC leader laughed and shouted, *"Didi mau len! Didi mau len!"* The Marine pilot asked what it meant. "Vietnamese," said the JUNC leader, "for 'Get the fuck out of here.'"

Zácari and Kipu followed the path of cashew trees through the booby-trapped perimeter and stepped out of the forest into the compound.

They stood for a moment surveying the damage. Smoke rose lazily from many places. The fire had been a great one. Kipu pointed to the burned-out Range Rover and the blackened human legs sticking out from underneath.

They crossed the large field toward the white house and came upon a dead *guariba*. Its flesh had been disturbed, Zácari saw, leaning over to inspect it. Kipu licked his lips and said they should take it back with them.

When they reached the bottom of the stairs leading to the veranda, Zácari heard the sound of his sister crying.

A moment later, El Niño appeared on the porch. He looked very bad. Some of his hair was burned away and there was dried blood from his ears and nose. He stared at them with a fierce look. He held a pistol.

Zácari held up a hand in greeting and said, "My father sends you his respect."

El Niño did not answer.

Zácari said, "He says to tell you that the *kurinku* in the great canoe was not *pistaco*."

El Niño stared as though the fire was still burning within him.

Zácari held out his upturned palm, revealing one of the goldand-black things. "He sends me to ask you for more of these. They are good for the *tsugki* who lives in the stone the *kurinku* gave to us."

El Niño stared at the battery in Zácari's palm. He raised his pistol and shot Zácari in the face.

Kipu threw his spear, but suddenly many shots were being fired and the ground next to him was bursting with dust. He ran toward the edge of the forest. The bullet hit him in the leg before he reached it, but he dove into the bushes before the men running after him could catch him.

The natives had all fled into their canoes. Diatri and the others stood on the half-burned hulk of the *Esmeralda*. One of the SEALs held up a line with some pennants on it. "Commander?"

Diatri and the commander inspected it. "What is it?" Diatri asked.

"This is a code pennant, this is 'S,' this is 'Q,' this is '1.'"

"So?"

"It's the international signal code. It means: 'You should stop or heave to or I will open fire on you.'"

Diatri sighed. "Looks like they didn't listen."

He made his way into the ship. She was partially heeled over on her side, making it like a walk through the fun house at the carnival. The top deck was gone. The main salon had the sour stink of burned leather. They'd stripped almost everything off her; it looked like they'd been working on pulling up the carpet when they ran off. He continued down another flight of stairs to the cabins. The passageway was dark. He turned on his flashlight, holding it away from his body as he'd been trained. On either side of the passageway were framed front pages of newspapers from the day after the *Titanic* sank. Diatri thought that was a strange thing to have on your boat. He made his way aft, to the master cabin.

It was stripped of everything, sheets, blankets, wall sconces, mattress, clothes. Somewhere in the jungle they were wearing cashmere blazers and ascots and whatever else rich people wear. Bermuda shorts? That would be a sight, Diatri thought, natives sitting around the fire arguing over how to make a really dry martini.

They'd torn the radio and intercom system out of the bedside table. Diatri peered into the gaping hole and saw a dead cricket on its back. Diatri reached in and removed him. Big little guy. How had he gotten in there?

He opened the drawer. There was a book inside: *History of the Conquest of Peru*, by William H. Prescott. He flipped through the pages. Mr. Becker—it was funny, but that's how he thought of him, as "Mr. Becker," maybe because he was rich—had underlined a lot. He came to a page that was almost all underlined and read:

"When the sentence was communicated to the Inca, he was greatly overcome by it. 'What have I done, or my children, that I should meet such a fate? And from your hands, too,' said he, addressing Pizarro; 'you, who have shared my treasures, who have received nothing but benefits from my hands!'

"An eyewitness assures us that Pizarro was visibly affected, as he turned away from the Inca.

"When Atahuallpa was bound to the stake, with the fagots that were to kindle his funeral pile lying around him, Father Valverde, holding up the cross, besought him to embrace it and be baptized, promising that, by so doing, the painful death to which he had been sentenced should be commuted for the milder form of the garrote—a mode of punishment by strangulation, used for criminals in Spain.

"The unhappy monarch asked if this were really so, and, on its being confirmed by Pizarro, he consented to abjure his own religion, and receive baptism.

"Atahuallpa expressed a desire that his remains might be transported to Quito, the place of his birth, to be preserved with those of his maternal ancestors. Then turning to Pizarro, as a last request, he implored him to take compassion on his young children, and receive them under his protection. Was there no other one in that dark company who stood grimly around him, to whom he could look for the protection of his offspring? Perhaps he thought there was no other so competent to afford it, and that the wishes so solemnly expressed in that hour might meet with respect even from his Conqueror. Then, recovering his stoical bearing, which for a moment had been shaken, he submitted himself calmly to his fate,—while the Spaniards, gathering around, muttered their credos for the salvation of his soul! Thus by the death of a vile malefactor perished the last of the Incas!"

* * *

Next to the bottom of the paragraph, Mr. Becker had written "Disgraceful!"

Diatri heard a sound. He crept forward along the dark passageway, gun drawn, toward the source of the noise. At the head of the passageway he found the wine cellar. The bottles were gone. He shone his light down. The native looked up at him and smiled. He was smashed. A giant bottle of wine, the kind they name after Abyssinian kings was lying across his chest. It was the biggest bottle of wine Diatri had ever seen. The native sang:

> *"Ay, Pepito, yo te ruego,*
> *Si, si, si, si es que aun me quieres*
> *Como yo to quiero. Ven hacia me,*
> *Pepito de mi corazón ..."*

He carried him, still singing, out onto the deck. The JUNC leader began to interrogate him in Spanish. "Where are the gringos?"

> *"Ay, Pepito, yo te ruego ..."*

Diatri said in Spanish, "You're not going to get anything out of him."

The JUNC leader shook him. "Where are the gringos?"

"Hey," said Diatri. "Easy. He doesn't know anything."

"Stay out of this, Diatri," the JUNG leader shot back. The native stopped singing. He looked confused. They were all wearing Peruvian military uniforms. Why were they speaking English?

Diatri said, "I said, let him alone."

"Fuck off, Diatri. This isn't your business."

299

"You touch him again I'll make it your business."

"Stand down, both of you!" The commander.

Diatri stormed off forward. He went to the bridge.

There was rubble all over, shot-out windows, splinters of wood, pieces of metal, chunks of fiberglass. Everything useful had been stripped by the natives.

He saw a piece of chart sticking out from underneath—it looked like a stone slab. He saw the brackets on the rear bulkhead—it had come off the wall. He tried to lift it. Too heavy. One of the SEALs was standing watch on the bow. Diatri shouted. "Give me a hand with this, would you?"

The SEAL lifted it easily and leaned it against the remains of the cabinet. These SEALs, they were in extremely good shape.

It was an old stone of some kind, with figures engraved into it in a way that made them seem raised. A giant with one eye was hurling large rocks at some people in a sort of rowboat. The rocks were landing near them, lifting the boat up on the waves they created. Diatri stared more closely. Something was wrong with the giant's eye. It was like he was crying. The guy who seemed to be in charge of the rowboat was gesturing at the giant with a kind of *Va fangool!*

Diatri examined the chart that had been underneath. There were other things: a V-shaped stick of plastique, it looked like a box of computer chips, and a small black box with switches and a red button. The SEAL left. The SOLIC commander appeared in the doorway a few moments later, while Diatri was spreading the chart out on the deck.

It was a Defense Hydrographic Agency navigational chart. He saw "Yenan" written in red felt-tip ink over a spot west of the river. The commander peered over his shoulder.

"Yenan?" said Diatri.

"It's a town in China," said the commander. "Shaanxi province. It's where Mao and Zhou Enlai ended the Long March. It's a holy place, like Concord or Lexington. It was their headquarters from '36 to '47. They launched the final phase of the revolution from there."

"So this guy is into Chinese?"

The commander said, "The only real Maoists left are in Peru."

"Sendero."

The commander nodded. He saw the V-shaped stick. "Don't move," he said. He picked it up carefully, then the box of chips and the black box. He examined the stick and said, "It's not armed."

"What is that?"

"HMX. These are nitro-chip primers. Thirty grains of nitroglycerin in silicon. The computer chip inside is coded not to accept any radio signals except one coming from this"—he held out the detonator box.

"This is powerful?"

"Yes," said the commander. "Very powerful. Four million psi."

A shot. They ran out onto the deck. The native was lying dead from a bullet hole in his forehead. The JUNG leader was holstering his sidearm.

"What the fuck happened? What the fuck *happened*?"

"He figured out who we were, thanks to you, Diatri. You spoke English in front of him and he figured out who we were."

Diatri lunged. The SEALs pulled him off.

"You fucking asshole, you killed him!"

"My orders are to leave the area undetected. You killed him, Diatri, not me."

"You fuck!"

"Diatri!" The commander took him by the shoulder and walked

301

him forward. He was a strong man, the commander. He took him back to the bridge.

Diatri hit the chart table with his fist.

"It shouldn't have happened," said the commander.

"Oh, great."

"But it did happen. So what are you going to do about it? You're going to do nothing. When we get back, I will report this ... *crime*. Be assured of that. Now you get yourself organized, mister. Is that understood?" The commander left.

Diatri stayed on the bridge, watching the river run past the ship. Her bow was pointed into the current. It seemed as if she were still moving upriver. He stood there watching the river. *I hear you're going to Congressional Relations ... Congratulations*. Should have known. They were just keeping him happy until this was over.

"We've been ordered back." It was the commander.

"You told them?"

"The mission is scrubbed."

"We didn't find any bodies. They could be at this, this Maotown, alive, for all we know."

"The mission is over, Frank. Get moving."

"Wait a minute. These are—these are citizens. You're going to leave them?"

"*Orders*, Diatri. Do you understand?"

"No. I don't."

"Let's go, Frank."

"Fuck it. You go."

The commander said, "If necessary, I will have you carried back."

Diatri looked at him. "I would not advise you to try that, Commander."

They stared at each other. The commander took a step forward, Diatri put his hand on his pistol. The commander pushed past him and picked up the stick of HMX.

"All right, listen up. You take the primer, you insert the primer in the explosive. The explosive is malleable. These are the safeties, there are six. They must all be switched off or it will not detonate. This is the selector switch. The positions match the numbers on the nitro-chip primers. This is the test light here; if that's lit, you have power. This is the det button."

Diatri nodded. "Okay."

"This is a twelve-hundred-grain stick. The blast radius would be about a hundred meters. Do not be inside it."

"Okay."

"There's an inflatable life raft on deck."

"Yeah, I saw."

The commander started to leave. He said, "You are going to die, you understand that?"

Diatri stared.

"Do you want me to give a message to anyone?"

"Actually, that would be very helpful," said Diatri. He tore off two pieces of the chart and scribbled the same thing on both. "I leave it all to you. Frank." He folded them and on one wrote the name and address of his first ex-wife, and the other's on the second. He handed them to the commander. "Obliged."

The commander nodded. Diatri thought: This should be interesting. He said, "Could you do one other thing for me?"

The commander nodded.

"There's this priest, a Father Rebeta, at St. Mary's on West Thirty-ninth Street, right down by the Hudson River. Could you tell him ... tell him that he should quit smoking."

The commander turned to leave. The seaplanes' propellers were turning. Diatri said, "Just tell him that I said hello. Tell him that."

41

He was in his private cable car eyeball-to-eagle-high over the Alps. She was skiing down a long, steep slope beneath him, her scarf trailing behind her. It was a stunning day, cool sparkling air, bright sun. Flawless. He was having coffee, settling down with *The Wall Street Journal*. He looked down. She waved up at him, he waved back. There was an explosion. The ridge of snow above her began to fall in slow motion. He tried to open the cable-car window to yell at her, to warn her. He pounded on it but it wouldn't open. He was yelling. Margaret looked up from her needlepoint and said, "Hush now, Charley." The wall of snow overtook her. She disappeared. All he saw of her was the scarf. He ran at the cable-car door and put his shoulder into it. It gave and he fell. An eagle flew by with a cigar in its mouth, scowling. He reached for the eagle and missed and went into the snow, bracing for impact, but kept going and broke through into clear blue sky. The snowbank was really a cloud. He fell. He yanked the ripcord. Nothing happened. He looked down at his hand and saw he was holding a watch fob and chain. He fell and fell. He saw the blue planet loom beneath, with hurricanewhorl eyes and typhoon mouth. The mouth bared wide, revealing rows of snowcapped teeth. His feet were starting to catch fire from the heat of reentry. Damnit, Margaret had forgotten to pack his ceramic shoes!

The blue planet turned into a face. The face said, *"Tranquilo, billonario."*

304

He was buried in snow up to his neck. No ... no ... it was a clean sheet that stretched before him, sloping gently upward at his feet.

He heard, "*Otra inyección.*" He felt the cool alcohol rub on the inside of his arm, the prick of the needle, a warm river flow into his arm and chest.

"Thank you," he murmured.

"*A sus órdenes, billonario.*"

"Do you have *The Wall Street Journal*?" Someone laughed. Why was that funny?

Charley reached for the phone to tell Miss Farrell to bring in *The Wall Street Journal.* They felt very heavy for hands.

"Your hands were cut, *billonario*. They were full of gold splinters. You should be happy."

He held them up. Something metallic tugged at his right wrist. It looked like a heavy-gauge fishing leader.

"Rest, *billonario*. We have a busy day tomorrow." The lights went out.

Charley murmured, "Just orange juice and black coffee, thanks."

Kipu's body lay in front of the stone, where he had died from his wound after telling what had happened at Yenan. Kagkui, his mother, held his head and rocked it as she spoke to his spirit. The shaman blew tobacco smoke over the body so that his soul could leave his body without being seen.

Eladio sat at a distance, cross-legged, grinding achiote pods into a wet, red dust with his thumb against the sacred *yuka* stone from the stomach of a panther. He painted himself and went into the forest to sing the *anen* songs and fast while the men rubbed darts on the backs of frogs and dipped arrow tips in the fang milk of the jararaca.

Reynoso knocked, put his head in. "He wants to see you."

El Niño stood. Soledad was curled up fetally on the bed facing away from him, still holding her cheek where he had struck her. She had not moved since it happened. He sat on the edge of the bed and stroked her hair. She stared past him. He said, "They betrayed me, don't you see? They let the *pistacos* kill my men. If I had not killed Zácari, my men would have killed me out of anger. They would have killed you. It was necessary. Tomorrow I will send a gift to your father to make peace."

Soledad stared away. He left. Outside the room, he said to Reynoso, "Watch her."

He went downstairs to the basement room. Arriaga's men were huddled by the door. They stared at him with the usual suspicion, making him feel like an unworthy visitor in his own house. Arriaga required members of his personal bodyguard to prove their loyalty to him by killing with their hands a member of their family. He knocked and went in.

Arriaga's back was to him. He was looking at the painting.

"Goya," he said.

"Manet. 'The Execution of Maximilian.' But you're very observant. It was inspired by Goya's 'Third of May,' in the Prado."

Arriaga turned slowly in the chair to face him. "I have not come to discuss art with you, comrade."

"No, of course."

"You told your men there was gold on board the boat?"

My men. "My purpose was to take the American alive, with the

306

yacht. The propaganda value is ... impossible to estimate. The men were very agitated after the air attack. They only wanted to sink it. I reasoned that if they thought there was gold on board they would take a lighter touch."

Arriaga stared. He had learned not to fill Arriaga's conversational vacuums. Finally Arriaga said, "And?"

"We got him alive. Also one of his men. We spotted him with the helicopter, floating downriver on a life raft."

"And—was there gold?"

"No. As I say, it was a fiction, an incentive. But it worked."

"And what was your incentive in all this, comrade?"

"To present you with a gift beyond imagining, Comandante. A lot of my men died to get it. Shall we spend our time together examining my motives or may I get back to burying my dead?"

"No one is questioning your motives, Niño." Arriaga gave his vinegary smile as he exercised the prerogative of nullifying what he himself had just said. "What do you propose?"

He listened as El Niño explained his plan. "Good," he said. "Very good. I will communicate this to Presidente Gonzalo personally."

The mention of the name had great shock value; in another time and place it would be like uttering the sacred Tetragrammaton, YHWH. Arriaga was known to be one of the few Senderista cadres in direct contact with Abímael Guzmán. Arriaga had never before spoken the name in his presence. It was both a compliment and a way of reminding him of Arriaga's significance.

"My communications equipment is temporarily out of order. But my own phone is at your service, of course."

Arriaga stared coldly. Guzmán had not been seen in over ten years. It was said that Guzmán's whereabouts were unknown—

even to Guzmán. To propose one's own phone to communicate with Sendero's founder and supreme commander was ... a lapse of judgment.

"I will remain here while the plan is executed," said Arriaga.

"Good," El Niño lied.

"Do you have room for my men? This pathetic old man seems to have destroyed most of your infrastructure." It pleased Arriaga to use a word like "infrastructure" instead of "buildings."

"He was lucky. One of their bombs hit the chemical shed. That's what made the fire. My own house is at your disposal, Comandante."

Arriaga stood and stared at "The Execution of Maximilian." "The men in the firing squad, they're dressed up like penguins."

"Well, yes, you could put it that way."

Arriaga turned to him. "I do put it that way, comrade."

Diatri paddled the inflatable Zodiac out of the current, hugging the riverbank, watching with suspicion the logs that floated past him to see if they blinked. The light was fading and he seemed to remember that crocodiles mostly like to eat at night. He paddled until he thought he recognized a small muddy island on the map and put in to shore and set out on foot.

He told himself over and over that the animals, reptiles, birds, monkeys, bats and unspecified things shrieking in his ears were more scared of him than he was of them, though he knew this to be extremely false. Large insects swarmed in and out of his flash-light beam. Eyes the size of bicycle reflectors flashed at him. He kept touching the compass around his neck to make sure it was there. Rivulets of bug juice and sweat ran into his eyes and stung.

He marched in a southwesterly direction for two hours until he smelled smoke. He stopped to get his bearings, blood pounding in his ears. He saw the glow of light off to the south. He took a step forward and felt it, just below his kneecap.

"How do you feel, *billonario*?"

The face came into focus just as it had months ago on the wall of the cabin on the island.

"Now I see you're still alive, worse."

"You were asking for *The Wall Street Journal*. When I heard that, I knew you were going to make it. Here, drink some orange juice. Morphine makes you thirsty."

Charley gulped. It was cold and sweet. It tasted wonderful.

"Why did you do it, *billonario*?"

"Your dope killed someone I loved," said Charley.

"No no," said El Niño dismissively. "Not that. The Manet. The Baudelaire 'Absinthe Drinker.' How could you have done that?"

"You know how Eskimos hunt polar bear? They take a piece of sharp whale bone and bend it inside a chunk of seal fat and freeze it. The bear eats the fat, the bone straightens, the bear chokes."

"Yes," he said with barely controlled anger. "But you can *replace* seal fat."

"You can replace art."

"It's criminal, what you did!"

"Criminal, you say." Charley laughed. "Well, now." If the bone had not pierced through the bear's throat, perhaps he could at least make it stick in his craw. "The painting's a fake."

"No."

"A copy. You don't think I'd float down into your sewer with the real McCoy? That's back home in the vault."

"You're lying. I had a look before you blew it up. That wasn't a copy."

"Well, now, you won't ever really know, will you?"

El Niño walked toward the door. "Tell me, *billonario*. All this effort and expense—just for the granddaughter?"

"My way of dealing with grief."

"I still don't understand. No one forced her to inhale cocaine. You're a Catholic. You believe in the consequences of free will. What's the problem?"

"You are the problem."

"What's your understanding of me, *billonario*?"

"I'm not trying to understand you, son. I'm just trying to kill you."

"But all this effort, you must have done some biographical research."

"I lifted up the rock. You were underneath."

"Do you feel well enough to move? There's something I want to show you."

Charley was on a narrow bed on wheels. El Niño pushed him out into a damp, cement corridor. A man opened a door. It was dark inside, but the air was less humid. Charley heard an electric fan somewhere. He wondered if this was the room where he would die. He wasn't afraid. Was it the morphine? He said a Hail Mary. He'd been sure he was about to die a half dozen times in his life and each time he'd turned to a woman.

"Leave us," he heard El Niño tell his man. Alone in the dark, Charley waited for the fatal bullet or knife thrust. Instead he saw a spotlight brighten gradually on a canvas in front of him.

The Hapsburg emperor stood between his two faithful Mexican generals, Miramón and Mejía. He was wearing a sombrero. The muzzles of the executioners' guns seemed to touch the victims' chests. White smoke poured out. A crowd of spectators peered over the top of the enclosure.

"Do you know what Renoir said when he first saw this? 'A pure Goya, and yet Manet has never been more himself!'"

Charley stared up at the painting. He lost himself in it for a moment. "You rob museums on the side?"

El Niño smiled. "I use a service. A Belgian. He calls himself a 'deaccessionizer.' Rupert Bendinck, do you know him? He has a lot of North American clients."

"No. I pay for mine."

"Oh, believe me, *billonario*, I *paid* for this. What do you think? It's magnificent, eh?"

"It's lit wrong."

"You're very blasé. I'm giving you a private viewing of one of the greatest works of art of the nineteenth century. Alas," he sighed, "no longer open to the public. It was in the Städtische Kunsthalle in Mannheim. Well, anyway, it was wasted on the Germans. Becker, that's German, isn't it? No offense."

"None taken."

"I suppose the Germans wanted it because it's anti-French, or anti-Napoleonic, which to them amounts to the same. You know the story? Louis Napoleon flattered the Austrian Archduke Maximilian into thinking that a nation of Indians and half-castes would accept a Hapsburg for their emperor. Metternich's comment when he heard about the scheme was: 'What a lot of cannon shots it will take to put an emperor in Mexico and what a lot it will take to keep him there.' As soon as your Civil War was over, Secretary

Seward complained to Napoleon about the Monroe Doctrine. It was more than that, actually. He threatened him with war. So much for old friends, eh? So Napoleon, lacking his uncle's determination—lacking everything of his uncle, as a matter of fact—withdrew his troops and left poor Max to face Benito Juárez and the brown hordes, with only his two Quislings there, Miramón and Mejía. Max sent his wife, the lovely Carlota, to persuade the Pope to send his troops to intervene. The Pope declined. It was too much for Carlota. She went mad right there in the Vatican. She was the first woman to spend a night there. Do you think she and the Pope ...? Manet's comment on the entire sordid affair was to paint the execution in the manner of Goya's 'Third of May, 1808,' in which the first—and true—Napoleon's troops are in the process of slaughtering a bunch of Spanish peons—and to dress the Mexican firing squad in French uniforms! Bravo, eh? He tried to distribute a lithograph of it. Napoleon censored it. There's the power of art for you, *billonario*."

"It's still lit wrong," said Charley.

El Niño went on, borne on the current of his passion. "I first saw it as a child. Papa took us to Europe on a Grand Tour. He was worried that his children were turning out insufficiently plutocratic. My sister and I were always hanging out in the kitchen with the servants. In Europe we stayed with Papa's faded noble friends. He thought that would do it, seeing the splendor that was once the Old World. We stayed in these freezing-cold castles that had been in their families since the Bronze Age. You know the kind. They still lived in them but they couldn't afford to heat them. So where did my sister and I spend our time? In the kitchens, with the servants, where it was warm." He grinned. "My father was proud of being descended directly from the Pizarros. Proud of being a

312

Pizarro! My God. When my bad attitude matured into political consciousness, he comforted himself that I was the result of a regressive, Inca gene that one of our ancestors had brought into the bloodline one night rolling around in the mud out by the stables. The truth, really, is that Papa was a greater influence on me than Karl Marx or Mao or Presidente Gonzalo."

"The plan is to bore me to death, is that it?"

"You were an orphan by fate, *billonario*. I'm one by choice. Is your Catholicism a leftover sentimentality from the Mexican nuns, or does it provide you with the father you never had?"

"It provides a place for people like you."

El Niño laughed. "Ah yes. But surely it's still easier for a camel to pass through the eye of a needle than for billionaire defense contractors? Do you think I do this just for money?"

"No. Being godfather to all those crack babies must give you a fine sense of accomplishment."

"The suffering of the innocents runs through history. Look at your own religion. Every male child in Galilee slaughtered by Herod's soldiers to make way for Gentle Jesus. Look at your own country. What about the baby sitting in the ruin of Hiroshima, screaming for its mother? The little Vietnamese girl running down the road after being napalmed by Uncle Sam's F-4 Phantoms? The crack babies are casualties of a war, *billonario*."

"War," said Charley. "What do you know about *war*?"

"I know that I'm winning one against your country."

"I thought your problem was with your daddy."

El Niño smiled. "My problem has matured. My problem is with history. Do you know who Atahuallpa was?"

"Yes."

"Then maybe you'll grasp the concept, Atahuallpa's Revenge.

313

You have to admit, it makes Montezuma's Revenge seem insignificant by comparison. An amoeba that gives you diarrhea is nothing next to an alkaloid that makes people kill themselves and each other for it."

"As I recall, it wasn't the United States that killed Atahuallpa."

"No, but the United States has long since become the conquistador of record in our own hemisphere." He started for the door.

Charley said, "Son, you're obviously educated, intelligent. Do you honestly believe all this bullshit? Or did you just work it out this way on paper to get you through the nights?"

El Niño looked at him, then at "The Execution of Maximilian." "*That* gets me through the nights. If I were what you think I am, then we would be sitting in a house outside Medellín decorated by Liberace, and I would be showing you a nude with big tits by—at best—Botero."

He summoned his man back into the room. They wheeled Charley down the corridor. He felt a needle go into his arm and went under.

12

Diatri pounded on his leg. It had gone to sleep.

The wire that stretched across his shin disappeared into some bushes about ten feet away. It was tight, and that was a problem. Some booby traps were rigged to go off if pressure was relaxed. He reviewed the traps he was familiar with: bouncing Bettys, friction fuses, rat traps, frag wires. He shone his light at the wire again and all he saw was bushes. It was probably a rat trap wired to a shotgun shell, but it was well worth waiting until light to establish that for a fact. He checked his watch for the two hundredth time and saw that a whole three minutes had gone by since he last checked. Two more hours to sunrise. The numbness came humming up his leg. He checked his watch again. The trick—he remembered this from boot camp—was not to lock your leg. His leg wasn't locked. So why was it numb? Maybe some snake had bitten him and the numbness was ... for Christ's sake, Diatri, relax, it's not a snake. Yeah? So what's all that slithering going on down there? Look, if it was a snake, you'd feel it. I don't know, they got, they got some *small* snakes here, these palm vipers. Will you stop with the snakes? It doesn't have to be a snake. It could be a spider. They have some extremely horrible spiders down here. It's not a spider. It's asleep, all right? They have frogs, you know, that are poisonous. Frank, frogs don't bite. Look, the Super Bowl is on back home. Why don't you play Super Bowl? There's the toss, San Francisco will receive. What time is it? Don't look at the watch. The kick is high! What was that? Diatri shone his light. Something skittered away. This was no good. He felt for his nail clippers. No nail clippers. Terrific. Wonderful. Now the leg was starting to itch. Great.

Denver won. Diatri figured that would take longer.

The sky turned a faint blue and the forest awoke in a mad avian chatter. He saw monkeys in the trees above him. One took an interest in him and swung down to a low branch above him.

"Have you got a pair of nail clippers?" Diatri asked the monkey.

The monkey dropped to the ground.

"Shoo!" said Diatri. "Get out of here." The monkey cocked his head and stared, came closer. "No, no, go away!" The monkey stopped two feet away. Weren't they supposed to be scared of human beings? Diatri made a face. He growled. "Arrrrr!" The monkey made a face. Great, Diatri thought.

The monkey reached for the wire. "No!" said Diatri. The monkey withdrew its hand and scowled. "Wire bad," said Diatri. "Wire *bad. Bad* wire! No!"

The monkey walked over to where the wire disappeared into the bushes. "Yo, hey, Bonzo! No!" Great, killed by a monkey. Diatri fished in his pocket, took out a disposable cigarette lighter. The bushes were rustling. He held it underneath the wire and spun the striker wheel. Nothing. Again. Nothing. Again. Nothing. Bonzo had disappeared. Jesus. He put the lighter inside his armpit, which was about the temperature of the sun anyway. He held it clamped there as sweat poured off him. Then he held it under the wire. A tiny blue ball of flame, barely enough to warm a cold mosquito, appeared. Come on, come on. The wire glowed red, then white. Come on. The blue ball of flame died. The wire cooled. Shit!

He looked up. Bonzo handed him the apparatus. It was a rat trap with a hole drilled through for a twelve-gauge shell. A nail was soldered to the bow as a firing pin. It was a live shell. The nail was against the primer. Why hadn't it gone off?

Bonzo made a face and lumbered off into the bushes. Diatri fainted.

"How are you feeling this morning?"

"Fine." His hands hurt badly. He had some blueness underneath the bandage on the wrist.

"Good. I have something to show you."

"It's a little early for art."

El Niño considered. "Similar theme. This you would call a 'performance piece.'" Two men helped Charley up and out of the building.

Charley blinked in the morning sun. They were in the large field in front of the white house. He noted with satisfaction the extent of the damage. The jungle was still smoking off to one side, where the chemical shed had been.

"You're amused?"

"Looks like you had some trouble here."

"Nothing serious. We will be back to full operational capacity in a couple of weeks. But that was good ether you blew up. Expensive."

"How about that." Charley knew he was being led to his execution. He was not afraid, and this fact pleased him.

They came to an open shed at the far end of the field. Charley saw three wooden tubs with hoses running in and out. Men were standing around expectantly. They looked at him and grinned to each other. Charley was aware of one group of men standing to one side, apart, somehow, from the rest. They were not grinning and bantering with the others.

"Good morning, comrades," El Niño said. "This is Mr. Becker, from the United States. He has traveled a long way to be with us this morning. Let us show our appreciation." The men laughed and applauded.

"You see." El Niño grinned. "Typical Latin hospitality."

A group of men appeared, dragging a man covered with a hood. They brought him to the edge of one of the tubs. El Niño gave a signal and they pulled off his hood.

"And this is Mr. Felix Velez, a friend of Mr. Becker's."

He had been severely beaten. One eye was swollen over and closed. He could barely stand. The worst was his hands. The fingers were grotesquely bent.

"Felix!"

Felix's face contorted into a smile. "Boss," he said.

Charley said to El Niño, "All right, you've made your point. I concede. You win."

"That's very accommodating of you, *billonario*."

"Whatever you want. Anything."

"Anything? And from the man who has everything."

"Including me. You can keep me."

"*Billonario*, for someone who's made so much money, you're a terrible negotiator."

"You want the painting?"

"But you destroyed the painting."

"I told you, it was a copy. I can have the real one here by tomorrow. By tonight."

"Delivered by the United States Air Force."

"No, no tricks. My own plane. I'm your collateral. Whatever happens, you keep me."

El Niño whispered, "You see that man over there? Do you know what he thinks of my Manet? He thinks the soldiers look like penguins. He's the number three Sendero cadre. So I told him, 'Yes, they look just like penguins.' What can you do with people like that? I ask you."

"I have a lot of paintings. *Fine* paintings."

"It's tempting."

"Do it, Antonio."

He turned toward Charley. "Antonio is dead," he whispered. "I killed him." He grinned. "I tell you what, we'll put it to the men. We're a democracy here. Comrades, Señor Becker proposes to give us a painting in exchange for his friend there. What do you say?"

Charley shouted, "And gold."

"That's not going to work, *billonario*. My men don't care for gold. They're politically conscious." He said, "When I was a stu-

318

dent in the States, there was this game show on television where you had to choose between the curtain and the box. America's contribution to world culture. So, comrades, do you want the painting, or Señor Velez?"

The men laughed. "Señor Velez!"

El Niño turned to Charley. "*Vox populi, vox dicit.* That's Latin, the real stuff." He nodded.

"The Amazon possesses the richest aquaculture in the world," El Niño said in the tones of a Marineland tour guide. "And among the many species we have, the candiru is one of the most interesting." The men laughed. "Technically a catfish, the candiru is very small, like a toothpick." The men laughed as if they had heard this before. "It has a great fondness for—how shall we call them?—mammalian orifices." Laughter. "And when the candiru finds one that it likes, it swims up it, like a salmon. Once it has arrived at its destination, it puts out little spines to hold itself there. People who have experienced this unique sensation say it is, well, very unpleasant. The pain of a single candiru can drive a man to chop off his penis with a machete." The men roared. "I wonder what the sensation caused by a *hundred* would be."

"No," said Charley. "Please."

"Let's find out." The men heaved Felix into the tank. He came to the surface gasping and tried to hold on to the edge with his mangled hands. A man standing by the tub brought the butt of his rifle down on them. Felix moaned.

"Felix!"

Felix's face began to contort. He gasped. The closed eye opened. He looked at Charley. "Boss."

One of El Niño's men began unwrapping the bandage of Charley's right hand. El Niño pressed a gun into it. It was Charley's own .45. Charley felt the muzzle of a gun at the back of his neck. El

Niño leaned over and whispered, "Put him out of his misery, *billonario*. But I warn you, if you point that gun at anyone but Felix, you will die before you can pull the trigger, and I will keep your Felix alive for a *week*."

Felix saw what was happening. He gasped, "Boss, please."

"No!" Charley shook his head. "No!"

"Please, boss."

El Niño said, "You both have very good manners, I'll give you that. Everything is *please*."

"Stop this!" Charley shouted.

"You have the power to stop it, *billonario*."

"Boss," Felix shouted, "I slept with her."

"It's, it's all right, Felix. It doesn't matter."

"I slept with her, in the clearing, on the island. Please."

"It's all right."

El Niño said, "He slept with—the granddaughter? Oh, that's not good, *billonario*. But you know what they say about finding good help."

Charley aimed the gun at El Niño. The gun in the back of his neck dug in.

"Please ..."

"Do it, *billonario*. Look how he suffers."

Charley pointed the gun at Felix. Felix smiled, nodded. Charley fired.

43

The compound appeared deserted except for one man with an AK in front of the white house that dominated the large open field.

The place reeked of stale smoke. Diatri recognized another smell. He followed it until his eyes started to sting. It took his breath away, literally. The fumes made him gag. There were NO FUMAR signs all over.

He had seen *pozos* before, but none this size. It must be almost a hectare, he thought, two and a half acres of coca leaves macerating in kerosene and sulfuric acid and—something else, maybe ammonia or carbolic acid. Working his way around the perimeter, he found four more pits of nearly equal size. It was impressive; this was refining like they did in New Jersey.

He made his way back to the edge of the compound and put his binoculars on the white house. Where the hell was everyone?

He heard a shot in the distance.

He saw them. It was a procession, twenty or more, walking across the field to the white house. He focused on a man near the front with white hair and a bandage wrapped around his head. They were carrying him. His head was down. They carried him into the white house.

He waited until dark, until the crickets had a good heavy thrum going. He set the selector switch on the det box to the number one position, disarmed the six safeties. He burrowed down and pressed the red button.

Nothing.

"You son of a bitch bastard piece of garbage," he hissed at the det box. He turned the selector to the number two position and pressed the button. This time, the earth moved.

A geyser of fire lifted into the sky from the second pit. Diatri watched, amazed at his own pyrotechnical creation. It was a volcano, Fourth of July and sunspot all at once. It was great.

Suddenly everyone was shouting and running out of the white

house and a building along the field that looked like a barracks. A man appeared on the veranda and began shouting orders. He ran down the steps. Everyone followed in the direction of the pit.

Diatri crept to the back of the white house, then to the front. He peered around the corner and saw the sentry. "Psst, asshole." The sentry swung around and Diatri killed him with a short burst from his Uzi. He went inside. There were stairs. He went up them. He heard a voice coming from the head of the stairs. "Luis?"

"*Sí*," said Diatri.

"What's going on?"

"This," Diatri said, killing him. He opened a door and saw her. She was lying on the bed, looking at him without fear, as if he might be room service with the iced tea and sandwich. There was a bruise on the left side of her face. She had on a man's shirt that came down just below the point of modesty. She had Indian features. She couldn't be more than ... fifteen? A thin steel cable was fastened to a through bolt in the center of the floor; the other end was pressure-swaged around her wrist. Diatri sighed. There was always some bad sexual weirdness behind the doors he had been kicking in for so long, some naked guy with his dick all coated with cocaine and a terrified lockjawed teenager underneath him.

"It's okay," he said. He held the cable to the muzzle of his Uzi and shot it off. He took her by the hand. They ran down the stairs. He opened the door cautiously, looked in both directions.

"Go," he said.

She looked at him.

"Go," he said. "It'll be all right."

She was fast. He had never seen someone run like that. He watched her until she reached the edge of the forest. She turned and looked back at him. She took off the white shirt and let it fall to the ground. Then she disappeared into the jungle and was gone.

Diatri went back inside. He found a door that led downstairs. He went down. There were several heavy steel doors. He opened one, and found the room empty except for a painting of—figured—a firing squad. The second room was full of weapons. The third door was locked.

He cut a salami-thin slice of HMX off one of the sticks on his web gear, inserted a nitro chip and pressed it against the lock. He went into the next room and pressed the red button.

He heard the explosion, but it came from outside. He looked down at the det box. He'd blown another pit by mistake. He set the selector to number six—the number on the corresponding nitro chip—and pressed the button. The explosion was more immediate. The blast knocked him to the floor.

The door was blown completely off its hinges. The air was dense with plaster dust. He coughed his way into the room and saw him.

He was coated with dust. He didn't move. Diatri leaned over the face and blew off the dust.

"Mr. Becker?"

Dead.

Diatri put his finger to the throat. There was a pulse.

"MR. BECKER!"

The eyes opened, but they were lifeless, glazed. "Mr. Becker, I'm Frank Diatri, DEA. I'm pleased to meet you. You're under arrest."

The old man shook his head and closed his eyes. Diatri rolled up his sleeves and saw the marks.

He got him over his shoulder and walked up the stairs. "You ready, sir? We're going to do this quickly. We're going to ..." Diatri thought: What was the plan? There was no way he was going to hump the old guy back through the jungle to the Zodiac. This guy must have boats, though. All dopers have boats, fast boats. "We're going on a boat, Mr. Becker. Hold on now. Here we go."

He was only twenty feet from the forest when he heard "Halt!" He kept going. Bullets hit the ground around him. Diatri stopped.

They circled him. A man stepped forward, breathing hard. He was missing some hair. Everyone was out of breath. He said, "Put him down."

Diatri pointed to the stick of HMX on his web gear and held up the det box. He did a slow 360-degree circle so they could all see.

He said, "You're all under arrest."

El Niño stared. He said, "Gringo, it's been a bad night. Do not INSULT ME!"

They stared at each other. Diatri held the det box to his mouth and said into it loudly, "Charley Bird, this is Delta Baker Actual. Drop a sixty into that pit about a quarter click west of center field. Over." He pressed the button.

Another gonad-shrinking blast went off in the distance, hurling tons of half-macerated coca-leaf goo hundreds of feet into the air. Everyone watched.

"Thank you, Charley Bird," said Diatri into the det box. To El Niño he said, "You want another one?"

"No."

"Okay. Here's what's going to happen. My prisoner and I are going down that path over there. I see anyone following, anyone twitch, I'm going to call in an artillery enfilade that'll bring the fucking mountains down on you. You like snow? I'll give you so much snow you can turn this fucking place into a fucking *ski* resort. You got that?"

El Niño stepped forward. "That's a detonator in your hand, gringo, not a radio. Don't play games. What do you want?"

"Him."

He shook his head. "No."

"I'm taking him back to stand trial."

"We will take care of that, I promise you."

"Not in your courtroom." Diatri turned the detonator switch to the number nine position and placed his thumb over the button.

El Niño said, "Don't be foolish. You're not going to kill yourself for him. He's half dead already."

Why not? Nothing to go back to. It was perfect and painless, instant disintegration, four million psi and into the cosmos in a blaze of quarks and protons. Go on, press it! Take all these shit buckets with you. Look at them. Thirty of them. *Press* it.

Diatri's thumb closed on the button. The old man moved. It was just a small movement, a breath going in and out of his lungs, but against Diatri's shoulder it felt close, like his own breath. A strange thing happened. The old man began to snore. With all this going on. Some of the men laughed. He'd had an uncle who used to do that, drop off right in the middle of everything and snore. He used to let Diatri steal money from his wallet.

44

He crouched on the floor by the through bolt, holding the cable, examining the parted end. At first he thought she must have cut it herself, but his forefinger came away with a smudging of lead.

Claudio stuck his head in. "Niño, it's Espinosa, on the

scrambler." He picked up the phone on his desk. As he did, Arriaga appeared in the doorway.

"Hello, General," El Niño said. "I hope I'm not disturbing you, but I have something for you. I think you'll be very interested. Do you have your chart in front of you? Look at the river between Campanilla and El Valle. About five o'clock from El Valle, you see the mud island in the middle of the channel? You'll find there a large North American yacht, badly damaged, with an important gringo inside. Dead. I think it's best that way. His crew deserted during the fierce battle when you discovered them trying to leave the country with some valuable Inca artifacts on board, including an arm from the idol of Pachácamac. By the way, I'd like them back afterward. ... Yes. Yes. It's going to be a very big scandal. He's a significant gringo. He knows the President ... Yes. Yes. A major embarrassment. You're going to be a hero. Make sure you have on your clean uniform when the TV people arrive ... No, I'm—Angel, I'm just joking. ... All right. Fine, but not until after three o'clock tomorrow afternoon. I need time to prepare. How's Mariela? And Juanito? ... With the Jesuits? Oh, watch out, he'll grow up to be a Communist!" Arriaga scowled. "Well, don't worry, he'll be too busy screwing all the beautiful girls, just like his old man, eh? Hah! *Bueno, un abrazo.* I'll be watching you on television. Don't forget to smile."

Arriaga said, "How much do you pay this *puta*?"

"Not half what I pay you."

Arriaga walked to the desk and leaned over so that his face was close. His breath was unpleasant. He had been eating fried pork. A real *cholo*, Arriaga. "Comrade," he said, "you confuse bribery with revolutionary taxes. You should not."

"Of course." El Niño managed to smile. "It's been a difficult day." Arriaga left.

El Niño crouched again over the parted wire, looked at the still rumpled bed where ... He rubbed the sharp wires against his thumb. Perhaps there was less holding him here than he had thought. His bank accounts in Geneva, Brussels, the Cayman Islands, were all brimming over. There was, really, no need to continue working. Though business was starting to get exciting. He loved the apartment on the Avenue Foch in Paris. The Manet would have to come with him. He couldn't leave that. Bendinck would contrive a way to get it back into the Continent. Rupert loved a challenge. The idol of Pachácamac would be his valedictory gift to his country. It was fitting.

* * *

A single bare bulb hung from a rafter. The walls and roof were corrugated tin, and though it was well after midnight, it was still hot inside and the *cheep-cheep* of cicadas and the grunting of frogs reverberated inside. Diatri kept putting his hand to his groin, where a few hours ago they had placed the jaws of a large set of bolt cutters. At first he had felt guilty. But he hadn't told them anything very useful, only who he was and who he worked for. He'd thrown in his Social Security number for good measure. He didn't know what was going to happen now, but he wished he had pressed the red button. So seldom does life offer such a clear-cut choice. Why didn't he press the damn button? Because Becker started snoring like Uncle Fabrizio?

He'd persuaded one of the two guards outside to bring a bowl of cool water and a rag. He dipped it in the bowl and squeezed it and laid it across the old man's head, which felt very hot. Once in Vietnam he'd—

The old man bolted up and looked at him and shouted, "Felix!"

Diatri jumped. The bowl clattered to the floor.

"No, sir. It's Frank Diatri. DEA."

"I thought you were dead. Felix!" The old guy was gripping him by the shoulder. He was strong. He peered deep into Diatri as if Diatri might be hiding Felix inside him. Finally, with a look of pain, he let go of Diatri and slumped back onto the pallet.

Diatri remembered from the photographs that he bore a resemblance, same build, hair, permanent tan, the old "olive" complexion.

"What happened to Mr. Velez, sir?"

The old man closed his eyes. Diatri looked and saw a tear roll out the corner of one eye, trickle sideways down along the ear and disappear.

There was a commotion at the door, unlocking, a sliding of bolts. El Niño entered, looked at Charley.

"How are we feeling tonight?"

"Fuck you," said Diatri. El Niño hit him in the face with the back of his hand. Diatri jumped up. El Niño put a pistol to his forehead. "Go ahead." Diatri sat down. El Niño said, "That was for letting the girl go." He looked at Charley.

"*Billonario*, are you well?"

Charley opened his eyes. Diatri had never seen such a look pass from one man to another. It seemed to unsettle El Niño, who said with apparent sincerity, "I'd give you some more morphine but they'll be doing an autopsy on you and I don't want ... Well, I can give you some codeine if you want."

"You're a real prince," said Diatri.

El Niño gave a small laugh. "A count, more likely, if you worked it all out. Maybe a baron. But you'd need a team of genealogists and it would probably take them a month to establish it."

"What's the deal?"

"There's no deal. Well, actually, in your case, yes, there is a deal. Now that we know who you are. I assume you follow sports. You're being traded, to Medellín. It's more in the nature of a payment for a mistake one of my ... incompetent associates committed. I just got off the phone with Reynaldo Cabrera. I'm sure you know of him. Certainly he seems to know about you. He's very eager to meet you. He wants you airmailed. You know that ranch he has outside the city, with a lake? He says to drop you in the lake. But not too hard. He has all sorts of things planned for you."

"What about him?"

"Oh," said El Niño, "that's all arranged. It's going to be on television. Ask Reynaldo to let you watch if you still have your eyes." He stood and went to the door. "Tell you what, as a personal favor I will ask Reynaldo to leave in your eyes until after it's been on. He can always amuse himself in the meantime with your other ... parts. Good night."

A pair of eyes watched through the barred window opposite, then disappeared.

45

"Tearing open the door, Pizarro and his party entered. But instead of a hall blazing, as they had fondly imagined, with gold and precious stones, offerings of the worshippers of Pachácamac, they found themselves in a small and obscure apartment, or rather den, from the floor and sides of which steamed up the most offensive odors,—like those of a slaughterhouse. It was the place of sacrifice. A few pieces o f gold and some emeralds were discovered on the ground, and, as their eyes became

accommodated to the darkness, they discerned in the most retired
corner of the room the figure of the deity. It was an uncouth monster,
made of wood, with the head resembling that of a man. This was the
god, through whose lips Satan had breathed for the far-famed oracles
which had deluded his Indian votaries!

"Tearing the idol from its recess, the indignant Spaniards dragged it
into the open air, and there broke it into a hundred fragments."

And here, he thought, laying Prescott on the desk and picking up
the dark brown arm beside it, the fingers angrily splayed in an attitude of *noli me tangere*, was the largest of those ancient fragments,
passed down fourteen generations, father to son, father to son, to
him, who, regrettably, had been forced to steal it rather than allow
Papa to make a present of it to the National Museum so as to curry
favor with the new leftist government so they'd leave his monopo-
lies alone.

He was only seventeen at the time, but he had staged it with
precocious verisimilitude. The newspapers reported the theft.
ROBARON AL BRAZO DEL DEMONIO DE PACHÁCAMAC. For the precious national relic to turn up, years later, on the boat of a North
American art thief was a stroke of, well—he smiled—it would add
a certain historical resonance to the outrage. Espinosa, that pig,
had no conception of what was being handed to him.

He listened to the night sounds outside his window. The crick-
ets sounded like the telephones that would soon be ringing: in the
Presidential Palace, at the U.S. State Department, at the United
Nations.

He crushed his cigarette and stared out the window toward the
hangar. He had given Claudio discreet instructions. The twin-
engine Aztec was ready, with enough fuel for Panama. "Maximilian"

was rolled up inside a fly-fishing-rod tube already packed aboard. He'd be in Paris in twenty-four hours. What time was it there? He picked up the phone and made a reservation at his favorite restaurant, a small Gascon boîte in the Dixième.

Half hour to sunrise. His heart was thumping out extra beats from the coffee and the anticipation. He decided to call Claudio on the radio, just to check everything again.

Claudio didn't answer. That was annoying. Rogelio would be in the new communications room. He called him. Rogelio didn't answer. Intolerable.

He called Gómez on the intercom. Gómez did not respond. He charged to the head of the stairs and was about to shout for Gómez when he thought better of waking Arriaga. He went angrily down the stairs ready to kick Gómez in the balls for falling asleep on sentry duty. He banged through the screen door. No Gómez. Where the hell was Gómez?

He charged across the field, furious, toward the communications shed, rehearsing the speech that would put the fear of God— better, of the idol of Pachácamac!—into Rogelio, after which he would activate the sirens, authentic, vintage English blitz sirens. There was nothing to match them, and to hell with waking up Arriaga.

Rogelio was bent over the console, passed out drunk, the bastard. He aimed his kick at the back of his chair. Rogelio toppled onto the floor. His eyes were wide open. He leaned over him and looked. He didn't see it right away—a tiny ball of wool dipped into clay at the end of a thin sliver of bamboo protruding from the hair at the base of his neck.

He smashed his fist down on the siren, grabbed Rogelio's Uzi and ran out the door.

* * *

Whoooooooooooooo0000000ooooooooooooooo.

Diatri opened his eyes. What was this? World War II? For a split second, the exciting possibility dangled that it had all been an extremely bad dream. But there was the bare bulb above him, and the old man in the cot next to him. Charley was sitting up, eyes open to the widest f-stop, listening to the strange klaxons.

He burst through the barracks door, shouting at them to get up. They were all in their beds, his men, Arriaga's men, face up, mouths tightly shut like mummies, with red lines drawn neatly across their throats.

He ran back toward the white house. He saw something in the bushes around the side, a pair of legs. Gómez's. He didn't stop. He ran up the stairs and into Arriaga's room. Arriaga was leaning against his pillow, pistol in hand, staring dully, the tip of the dart shaft sticking out between his closed lips like a toothpick.

Charley unwound the bandages from his hands. Diatri crouched by the door. Charley nodded and began to shout, "Help, help!" No guards rushed in.

Diatri took several steps back and ran and put his shoulder into the door. It was made of tin and gave easily. He found himself on the ground outside between two dead guards. They each had arrows sticking out of their—Jesus. He grabbed one of their MAC ios and crawled back inside.

"Indians!" he gasped. "We're under attack by Indians!"

332

"Yeah," Charley said. "That can be a problem down here."

"Jesus. Indians."

"There's an airfield. Come on."

He moved slowly, turning continuous 360-degree circles like a tank turret, an Uzi in each arm, grenades dangling from the web gear on his chest.

The light was dim and the air-raid sirens made it impossible to hear movements. He fired bursts into every bush, any quivering leaf or vine. *Chunchos.* Were they playing a game with him?

"Eladio," he called out above the siren roar. "Don't be a coward. Show yourself."

He kept toward the airfield, reaching to the edge of the number three *pozo*, the only one the gringo hadn't destroyed with his superplastique. He heard something in the bushes to his left and opened fire.

"You hit?"

"No," said Charley.

"Where'd it come from?"

"I don't know."

"Keep your head down. Listen."

They heard, "Eladio? Eladio!" Diatri saw the look come into the old man's face. He started to crawl toward the voice. Diatri gripped his leg. Charley snarled, "Leggo my leg."

He was certain of it. There was something in there. He kept firing into the bush.

* * *

Diatri crawled after the old man, bullets cutting through the bush just above their heads, leaves falling around them.

He pulled the pin and tossed the grenade.

It landed next to the old man and just in front of Diatri. Diatri grabbed it and threw it. It bounced off a nearby liana vine and exploded.

The DEA gringo was knocked out, perhaps dead. His face was black and bleeding. The old man was stunned but was still gripping a submachine gun and looking up at him fiercely, trying to get to his knees. He let him get part of the way up before kicking the gun out of his hands. He aimed the Uzi at the old man's chest and was about to pull the trigger when he felt something sting the side of his face, like a wasp. In the next instant his legs went out from under him and he fell.

He could breathe. But he could not move. Eladio's face came into his vision, above him, then the girl's. He tried to speak to the girl, to explain, but he couldn't. He was paralyzed. It was, they used, he tried to remain calm, it was just a tree resin they rubbed on their darts when they hunted monkeys. The drug relaxed their muscles and made them fall to the ground. It would wear off.

Then he was being picked up and carried. Yes, good. Thank

you. He was in the air—no, please, not that—he tried to scream but nothing came.

He looked and saw the *billonario* watching him from the edge of the pit. Please, help. He began to sink. He felt the most terrible burning in his eyes and tried to shut them but he couldn't. He tried to close his mouth, but it came in, rushing over his teeth in a scalding, tidal surge as the idol of Pachácamac gripped him by the throat and dragged him down into suffocating blackness.

Diatri felt something on his face, a woman's hands. They were smearing something on him, something greasy but very good, very soothing, very cool. He heard a voice through the blur. "Frank," it said. "You're going to be all right."

"My ... face, I can't ..."

"You're going to be all right. There's a real pretty nurse here with you. She's fixing you up. I'm going to give you a shot now, Frank."

Nurse? He tried to make the blur settle but it was like looking through moving water. He thought he saw breasts. He wanted to touch them, but then a warm river was flowing into him and he felt very relaxed. He was dimly conscious of being carried, of being placed in a comfortable chair, of hearing strange voices—*kurinku pataa!*—of a door shutting, of engines starting, of gravity forcing him back into his seat, of climbing and climbing, of a voice that kept saying, "It's all right, Frank, you're with me now, I'm taking you home."

46

"So your thinking is—"

"*The* thinking, Dick. This isn't, this is, what I'm trying to say, do you see what I'm trying to say, Dick?"

"I, yeah, I, I—"

"There's no case, after all."

"Well—"

"Well, *what*? DEA's guy has disappeared."

"We think he's dead. I mean, what else would he be?"

"Good. I mean, I didn't mean it that way."

"Of course not."

"He was, I gather he was pretty good."

"Apparently. Yes. Anyway, without him there's really no, I mean, I suppose we could reconstruct the case ... but as you say, the thinking is—"

"The thinking is, there's a heck of a lot else to do. We're in a war here, Dick."

"Absolutely."

"The Noriega trial thing is going to be, well, it's going to be..."

"I understand, John."

"You do?"

"Yes."

"That's good, Dick."

"How do you, how do you want us to handle the boat situation?"

"I thought that might be better coming from Jim's shop. It's more of a State thing."

"Right. Right."

"American citizen goes on, on a vacation and he's attacked by drug people and his people are killed and, and it's, it's a terrible thing."

"Right."

"It's a question of spin, really."

"Yeah, it has to have the right spin."

"Jim's people are good at spinning."

"Oh yeah. I was thinking, actually this could be a win situation for us, war-on-drugs-wise."

"If it was spun right."

"Sure. Absolutely."

"Hell of a thing, Dick."

"*Hell* of a thing, John."

Epilogue

"Frank?"

Diatri's head jerked up out of his sleep. His chair was pulled up next to the old man's bed. The dawn was coming through the French windows, a soft blue light full of the gossip of nuthatches, thrushes and blackbirds, with a screech of cock pheasant. The LED display on the IV stand gleamed brightly. Diatri saw with embarrassment that his hand was resting on top of the old man's. He pulled it away.

"Yes, boss."

"The priest, is he gone?"

"Yeah, he's gone."

"Shut that thing off, would you?"

Diatri reached over and clicked off the IV. "You feeling better?"

"Frank, he gave me absolution."

Diatri shrugged. "Sure. Why not?"

"Well, it wasn't just any confession."

"You want some water or something?"

"The way he was looking at me, it was like he didn't believe me."

"I think I'm going to have some water. It's, with confessions it's basically, as I understand it, it's the intention. That's all that really matters."

"That's right, Frank. I feel better."

"That's good, boss."

Charley stared at the Baudelaire "Absinthe Drinker." "I'm

going to give that to the museum, Frank. I'm awful fond of it, but it's—I'm going to give it to the museum."

"How about some water?" Diatri reached for the pitcher on the nightstand next to the photo of Tasha and Margaret.

"I'd like a whiskey. Let's us both have a whiskey."

Diatri laughed. "Okay." He poured out a couple of brown fingers and gave the glass to Charley. The old man's hand was weak, but he held it himself. He raised the glass. "To Tasha and Felix."

"To Tasha and Felix," said Diatri.

Acknowledgments

My thanks to: my good friend Mike McGowan, NYPD (Ret.); also: Pete Teeley; Admiral Daniel J. Murphy, USN (Ret.); William von Raab, U.S. Customs (Ret.); Dennis Fagan, U.S. Customs; John C. Lawn, DEA (Ret.); Bobby Sheppard, DEA; Larry Golina, DEA; Ronald Ray, USMC (Ret.); Dr. William Hughes; Dr. Robert Ascheim; Lisa Murphy; John Henderson; Scott Setrakian; Geoffrey Norman, USA (Ret.); Ambassador Marshall Brement; John Tierney; Patrick Tierney; Melody Lane; Jon Winokur; Ambassador Donald P. Gregg; Peter Glenville; William Hardy Smith; William F. Buckley, Jr.; and to my wise and patient editor at Knopf, Ashbel Green. None of the above is responsible for any errors.

To my friend Paul Slansky, who was in on the conception, gestation and birth, my special thanks and love.

The yacht described herein is, with some modifications, the *Highlander*, which belonged to Malcolm Stevenson Forbes. I accompanied him up the Amazon a few years ago on a memorable trip. He died a few days before this book was finished. *Vale atque vale*.

I am indebted to Alex Shoumatoff for his brilliant book *The Rivers Amazon*; also to Michael Brown's *Tsewa's Gift*; William H. Prescott's still-dazzling *History of the Conquest of Peru*; Barnaby Conrad III's *Absinthe: History in a Bottle*; Nicholas Shakespeare's article "In Search of Guzmán" in *Granta*.

Above all, love and thanks to my wife, Lucy; and of course to Caitlin and Duck.